Shattered Fate

PF Karlin

PF KARLIN PUBLISHING
SUGAR LAND, TEXAS

ISBN: 978-0-9890247-4-7
Library of Congress Control Number: 2013903909

Shattered Fate

By Karen Pugh…a.k.a. pf karlin
Linda Fagala…a.k.a. pf karlin

Copyright © 2020 by Linda Fagala and Karen Pugh

Photography used in the production of this book:
Copyright © 2020 by Linda Fagala and Karen Pugh.

Song Lyrics: "Forever in My Mind"
Copyright © 2014 by Linda Fagala and Karen Pugh.

Book cover design:
Copyright © 2020 by Karen Pugh.

Published by:

PF Karlin Publishing
Sugar Land, Texas

This is a work of fiction. Characters, places, and events portrayed in this book are either a product of the authors' imagination or used fictitiously, with the exception of certain towns and locations which were used to provide the reader with a sense of locale of the storyline. Any similarity to actual places, events, or persons, living or dead, is coincidental and not intended by the authors.

ISBN: 978-0-9890247-4-7

Library of Congress Control Number: 2013903909
Printed in the United States of America

In memory of a dear friend,
who helped inspire Linda to start writing this novel.

Acknowledgment

Writing can be a solitary path. So, when Linda Fagala approached me about helping her write a story she'd been working on, I jumped at the chance. Together we embark on many late-night writing sessions filled with laughter and some tears. That was several years ago and Linda has since retired, but without her creativity, a keen eye for detail, and crazy editing skills, the author, PF Karlin would've never been born.

Thank you for walking alongside me on this incredible journey.

I'm so proud to call you my friend.

Karen Pugh

Shattered Fate

Book One ~ Kismet Series ~ Second Edition

PF Karlin

CHAPTER 1

THE TOTAL DARKNESS frightened me. I attempted to open my eyes. I tried to turn my head. Lift my arms. Wiggle my toes. But, my body wouldn't respond. I shouted in my mind for it to move, nothing happened.

Oh God! What happened to me?

The blood coursing through my veins pulsed in my ears. My heart raced so fast I thought it might beat its way out of my ribcage. I listened to the sounds around me…rushing footsteps, the low hum of motors, and the steady beeping of machines.

Where am I? A hospital?

In the midst of the noise, I heard muffled voices, indecipherable, like in a crowded restaurant. I strained to hear and made every effort to comprehend the words being said. My mind couldn't recognize the voices, but one stood out, my mother's. Her words were garbled, but I could hear her sobs. I tried to shout out to her. I tried to open my mouth to formulate words. I tried to make any kind of sound to let her know I was here, but nothing came out.

I fought to maintain my awareness, but my brain just wanted to go to sleep. The experience was like drowning, with black rushing water coming over me. The more I tried to swim to the surface, the more the sinking feeling took me deeper and deeper. I was descending into a bottomless cavern. The fog in my mind grew thicker. It won the battle. Exhausted, I gave in to the onrushing oblivion. The darkness took over, silence swept through me, and I let go.

But into what…

And then thoughts and images began to fill my mind.

CHAPTER 2

I'D NEVER BEEN in love. I'd never felt the race of my heart or tingle of my skin from the touch of another person who loved me. I don't understand the affection two people share or the emotional connection. So, at twenty-two years old, I, Belinda Davies, want to experience that tenderness.

A mild breeze brushed my face and the clean morning air teased my nostrils as I quickened my pace toward the booth construction zone.

It was the first Saturday of April and time for the university Spring Carnival. All the student organizations took part by setting up game booths along a barricaded portion of the street that split the campus in half.

Matt, a friend I dated occasionally, was a Theta Kappa, and he along with his brothers would be working on their booth. Matt was nice enough, but I always suspected his only motivation for dating me was to improve his math grade. We met on a blind date and I agreed to tutor him only if he allowed me to ride Beau, his chestnut gelding. So, this fine morning, I decided to go over to see how his project was coming along and hoped to find Beau.

I spotted the horse straining at his tether to reach the grass beyond the canopy of the tree. Matt and several other fraternity brothers were hard at work nearby, apparently taking advantage of the cool morning.

"Hey, how's the booth coming along?" I surveyed the project and pieces of lumber scattered around Matt. Only a few boards had been nailed together, making it difficult to determine the final outcome.

Matt looked up and huffed out a sigh. "We still have a lot to do." He glanced at my jeans and shoes.

I seldom wore tennis shoes, a telltale sign I was interested in only one thing.

"Come for Beau?"

"Why no," I said with a straight face. "How could I've known you rode him here?" He rode Beau around campus every Saturday morning to flirt. "But…can I?"

Matt saw right through me. He half grinned. "Sure, go ahead. Just don't overheat him and make sure you water him before you come back."

"I always do." I wasn't an idiot when it came to Beau. I loved him. From the first time Matt let me ride the horse, I found it exhilarating.

From the recesses of my pocket, I retrieved a few baby carrots. Beau lifted his head. "Hey, Beau. Carrot?" I stroked his neck. The touch of his smooth coat caused my breath to slow and the edge I'd walked around with all week to fade. I mounted up and we headed to my quiet place.

Beau was such an easy animal to ride. He was accustomed to the sounds of humans around him. I trusted him. Whenever I could, I'd hijack Beau and head for the trails behind the school, retreating into my sanctuary amongst the trees. The woods, lush with spring foliage, created an illusion of total isolation.

I craved time alone. In high school, it became a safety net. I never fit in with the other girls. I was shy and lacked self-confidence because of it and my plain appearance. I never developed the natural assets like them and didn't know how to improve mine. So, I wore no makeup and lived in jeans and t-shirts. Comfy clothes. As a result no one ever asked me on a date. I never went to a dance or my prom. I had convinced myself I wasn't like the other girls and chose a sort of self-imposed invisibility. It made my life less complicated.

Beau and I almost made it to the trails when I noticed a tall, good-looking guy waving his arms frantically above his head. *Is he trying to get my attention?* I slowed Beau to a walk and glanced around. No one else was in sight. I poked a finger at myself, mouthing, "Me?" He nodded. A few butterflies took flight in my stomach.

The guy took off in a sprint toward me. "Hey. Wait up!" He stopped mid-way, panting. "Can you ride over here?" He planted his hands on his knees, gasping. "Before I die."

In the past, I would've just kept riding or used my hair as a curtain to hide myself to avoid any situation that made me uncomfortable. But, I wasn't that girl anymore. I was trying to be different and force myself to take more risks. So, I pulled up the reins and turned Beau in his direction.

The closer we trotted, the more I realized the angle of his gaze seemed to be fixated on only one part of me, my bouncing boobs. Riding up to a stranger was nerve-wracking enough, but his ogling my chest definitely added to my innate self-consciousness. I didn't know how to handle all this new-found attention since I'd become curvier this past summer. In high school, when all the other girls had cute figures, I still had the humiliating shape of an adolescent boy, with small breasts and no hips.

My muscles tensed and my chest tightened. I yanked back on the reins to a dead stop. Beau snorted. I couldn't go over and talk to a perfect stranger. About to turn back toward my safe haven, my roommate and bestie, Abby's little voice popped into my head telling me to keep going, to try something new, and to take a chance. So, I sucked in a deep breath and blew it out, then nudged Beau forward. Fortunately, the guy's gaze moved from me to Beau.

"Beautiful horse. Is he yours?" His eyes shifted to my face, briefly slipping down to my chest, then, drifted back up. His strong-looking hands took hold of the bridle, and then the other stroked the animal's neck. Most people never gave Beau a second glance or touched him. This guy seemed different. He exuded an air of confidence which I admired because I had so little. I tended to be attracted to confident people, perhaps hoping some of it would rub off on me.

"No, I wish. He belongs to a guy I know."

"He's a fine specimen." He continued to look the animal over, instinctively combing his fingers through Beau's mane. "You're a pretty good rider. Been doing it long?"

"Thanks. For a while.

He extended his hand. "I'm Garrett Barnett."

"Nice to meet you. I'm Belinda Davies," I lilted, extending mine. He folded his hand around mine and I noticed my first assumption was correct. His grip was strong, yet gentle. He gave me an intense look as I studied his soft brown eyes and decided I'd like to know him better.

He never let up on his grip. A nice technique. It kept all of my attention on him in an effortless, flirty way. "Nice to meet you. So, this guy you know, are you dating?"

"Just occasionally, but it's not serious."

He released my hand and resumed stroking Beau's neck. "Good. How about going out with me tomorrow evening?"

"Hmmm." Placing my hand on my cheek and looking above his head, I pretended I needed to think about all my other plans. "I'll have to check my calendar, but I think I'm free." I tried not to sound too eager.

A wide grin spread across his face. "We'll start with dinner. Do you like Mexican food?"

He sounded confident like he had the whole evening planned and I hadn't even said yes. "Yeah. It's my favorite."

He asked for my phone number and tapped it into his cell phone. "Great, I'll call later this afternoon after you've had time to check your calendar. If you're free, I'll pick you up tomorrow at 5:30. That okay?"

"Sure."

"Now make sure to check that calendar." A crooked smile broke out across his face.

"Gotta go." I turned Beau toward the woods and gave him a slight kick in the ribs. "I'll check the second I get back to my place," I shouted over my shoulder, feeling pretty good because I had forced myself to go over to talk to Garrett Barnett.

In my quiet place on the trails, I let the reins go slack, relinquishing control to Beau. His soothing back and forth gait relaxed my tense muscles. My breathing became slow and easy. I cleared my mind and enjoyed the fresh pine scent and peaceful scenery. After a while, my internal clock told me I'd been gone too long.

"Okay Beau. Let's go get you some water." The pond in front of the administration building was the perfect spot to water him. So, we took off in a canter. We were cutting through a grassy area on campus when a small group of guys started walking across my path just feet in front of me. None of them seemed to be paying any attention to the fact I was about to plow right into the middle of them. I jerked back on the reins. Instead of stopping, the horse shot up on his rear legs, scaring the crap out of me. My heart jumped into my throat as I held on for dear life. Luckily, I didn't fall off and Beau settled down.

Most of the group scatter like cockroaches before they stopped to stare.

Except for one.

His glacier blue eyes sucked me in. They were as stunning as his face. A shiver blew through me. I squirmed in the saddle, everything inside me hummed. I couldn't look away. I don't know if I believe in love at first sight, but, when he smiled, it took my breath away and my heart thundered into overdrive.

"Are you all right?" Even his deep, silky voice tugged at my heartstrings.

I couldn't answer. I just nodded.

"Come on," one of his friends encouraged. He took a few steps to move out of my way then stopped. Our gaze stayed fixed on each other as I rode past. With my back to him, I tucked my chin into my shoulder and peeked back. He winked. A warm sensation invaded my face. I whipped my head forward so he wouldn't notice my flushed cheeks.

Clutching my hand over my chest, an unexplainable excitement—a sensation I'd never felt before, a type of thrill—filled me. With my heart still pounding, I realized I was experiencing something I'd never had with Matt. How could a perfect stranger do this to me?

It was a short ride to the pond where I allowed Beau a long drink. I stared across the water, haunted by a face that belonged to a stranger. Looking back over my shoulder, I hoped to get another glimpse of him, but he and his friends had vanished.

Beau gave a quick jerk of his head. I pulled up on the reins and headed back.

"Hey, Matt. Can I keep riding?"

He gave Beau a quick once-over. "Okay, but not much longer."

"Why? Beau can't help you build this thing."

Matt snorted, "I might wanna ride."

"I've got my phone. Call me." I rode off hoping to find the stranger again. I took a shortcut between two buildings to return to the place where the group had been and, like before, nothing. My stomach did flip flops the more I searched the campus grounds.

His handsome face forced its way into my head until the ringing of my cell brought me back to my senses.

"Yes, Matt." I exhaled. His timing stunk.

"Come on back. I need a break."

"And just why do I need to be there for that?" My lips clenched.

"Just come back and I'll buy you a drink."

As much as I wanted to keep searching, quenching my dry throat won out. "All right. I'll be right there."

The route back led me down the street where all the booth construction was taking place.

Beau rambled by the Delta Lambda Nu or Delt area. I attempted to figure out what they were building. All the frat brothers were bent over when, in the middle of the construction site, one guy stood up. It was Mister Gorgeous. He turned toward me and a slow smile crossed his face. My chest seized. He stood there, watching me ride by. I couldn't stop staring but managed to crack a smile. My heart picked up speed. Beau continued taking his time, and I did nothing to encourage the animal to move faster.

"It's about time you got back." The jerking motion of Matt grabbing the reins startled me and ended my fantasy.

"I got here as soon as I could."

He tethered Beau to a nearby tree. "Let me help you down."

I threw my leg over the saddle horn and slid down. His hands gripped me at my waist, and then he swung me around. I caught a glimpse of Mr. Gorgeous standing near the street watching us. Matt leaned over and gave me a quick kiss. Before I knew it, he lifted me up and tossed me over his shoulder. I just hung there facing his back.

"Put. Me. Down! MAAATT! Put me down." He just popped me on the butt and walked toward the Student Center. From my precarious position, I arched up and noticed Mister Gorgeous still observing us and grinning. Heat flushed over my body. I went limp—like a corpse—and swung from side to side.

♡♡

Jeez, how embarrassing. Even though I sat at the same table, Matt spent most of his time flirting with other girls. I could've left and he would've never even noticed. Sometimes, I wondered why I still hung out with him. Oh, yeah. Beau. At least I got a free soda and had time to daydream about Mr. Gorgeous.

We walked out the double doors and directly in front of us, at one of the sorority booths, stood my stranger. A petite girl with shoulder-length, blonde hair commanded all his attention. They didn't look right for each other. He appeared to be over six feet tall, with a nice physique, and broad shoulders. He looked so handsome, goosebumps skittered over every inch of my body.

The closer we walked toward the pair, the more I had to control my need to stare. I forced myself to watch my feet. Unable to stand it any longer, I snuck a peek only to find him glancing my way. Summoning up enough nerve between shortened breaths, I smiled. He returned the gesture with a quick half grin and the center of my chest erupted into a frenzy. Fortunately, the blonde and Matt never noticed.

Matt wasted no time after we reached his frat project. He grabbed a hammer and a few nails, saying, "I'll catch up with you at the carnival." Then he picked up a piece of lumber and dove back into the work.

"Okay," I called out over the pounding noise. I didn't think he even heard me or noticed I left.

My mystery man and the blonde continued their conversation from down the street. Her back was to me, but I saw him shoot a glance in my direction. I made sure I didn't walk away too fast. Nonchalant was what I was going for, but as soon as I was sure I was out of his view, I took off running to find Abby.

The big oak tree in the front yard of the house, where we rented a room, was our favorite place to get some study time in. As expected, I found her sitting there on a blanket, reading a textbook.

"Abby! Abby!" I ran the last leg, my chest raising and falling rapidly. I plopped down next to her. "I just saw the most gorgeous guy and we flirted. I wish you could've seen him," I sputtered then rolled over onto my back, lacing my fingers behind my head. "Oh yeah, and I met another guy. Garrett. He's kinda cute. I have a date with him tomorrow night."

Abby just stared. A dumbfounded look washed over her face. "How do you do that? I want to know your secrets."

"Secrets? You should know. You're my teacher."

"And your Mom. Forcing you to take that modeling class last summer was a brilliant move. Ms. Perfection." She scrunched her nose.

"I'm not perfect."

"Oh, please. Give me a break." Abby lifted her palm up, toward me. "Look at you with that long, golden-brown hair that frames your face so perfectly." She shifted her position. "Then there's those knock-me-down baby blues. She wagged her finger. And those girls could turn any guy into putty as well."

I sat up and crossed my arms over my chest. "Will you please stop? You know I don't see myself like that."

Abby huffed. "I know. That's why you have me around to remind you."

I ripped out a clump of grass and threw it at her.

"Hey. I'm just being truthful." She brushed the blades off the blanket.

Male voices and laughter came from the yard next door and interrupted our conversation. The two houses were separated by a tall, thick hedge about seven feet high. Both were rentals with one difference—ours had a landlady living in the residence with us. The one next door was just filled with a bunch of guys living on their own. The two houses had very different atmospheres. Ours was quiet and managed, while theirs was loud and with more traffic.

Abby lifted her brows and thumbed toward the bushes. "Let's check it out."

I giggled and followed my roommate's lead.

I crouched to sneak a peek through a sparse area of the hedge. An audible gasp escaped and I slapped my hand over my mouth. The tall stranger stood less than ten feet away. I grabbed Abby's arm. She stooped next to me and I pointed him out. Her mouth dropped open. I whispered, "That's him. Surely, he doesn't live there. Have you ever seen him before?"

Abby murmured, "No. Jeez, we spend way too much time in class and the library."

He stood sideways, so only his profile was in view. I clenched my jaw about to move to a better vantage point. Just then, another guy joined the group. Mister Gorgeous turned to make room and faced the hedge, allowing me to study his facial features. He had a clean-shaven face and nicely set eyes, thick, dark brown hair that spilled over his forehead, and totally kissable lips that made mine tingle. He had a strong jawline, yet his face was gentle with the most compelling smile. Turning, he walked out of sight, making me want to crawl through the hedge.

"WOW! He's hot," Abby whispered and feigned a swoon, touching the back of her hand to her forehead and leaning back. We giggled a bit too loud.

Someone from the other side of the hedge said, "Hey, what was that?"

We darted for the blanket to resume our studying facade. A few minutes later, a guy sauntered up the driveway toward us. Abby and I shrugged at each other.

She mumbled from the side of her mouth when he was a few feet away, "Who the hell is that?"

"Hey, I'm Brian. I live next door. We heard some strange noises coming from the bushes, so I was sent over to check it out."

We offered no explanation.

He pointed. "Weren't you the girl riding the horse on campus today?"

I froze. "Yes. Why?"

He thumbed over his shoulder to the house next door. "One of my frat brothers was just asking about you. No one knew who you were."

"Oh! Really?" I prayed it was the gorgeous one who was so interested.

"What's your name?" He shifted his weight from one foot to the other.

"Belinda and this is Abby." My throat went dry. Keeping my voice monotone, I inquired, "Who wants to know?"

"Robert. I'll have to tell him you live here. So, I guess you didn't see anything over by the bushes?" Abby and I shook our heads, denying everything. "Well, it was nice meeting you. I have to get back. See you around." He turned and I noticed his half-smile. Yep, he knew it was us.

I bit my lower lip waiting for him to get out of earshot, and then I tugged on Abby's arm. "I wonder if it was the really good looking guy asking about me. How can I find out?"

"You could always pry it out of Brian the next time you see him. Just bat those baby blues at him, and he'll tell you anything." Abby poked my shoulder, snapped her book shut inches from my face, and then winked.

"Oh, yeah." I huffed. "I'll probably never see him again. Look how long we've lived here and today was the first time we've ever met anyone from over there," I grumbled.

Abby started walking toward the house. "Let's go get ready for the carnival. Although, I have a feeling you'll be meeting Mister Gorgeous pretty soon."

CHAPTER 3

ABBY AND I attacked the closet, pulling clothes off hangers. But, nothing appealed to me. I'm a blue-jeans type of girl. I liked to wear them and on a student's budget, that's all I could afford. Abby wanted to turn some heads so she suggested I should wear my new jeans and sweater my Mom had just sent, with my three-inch mules.

I held up the jeans and shook my head. Oh great! Mom knew I didn't like low-rise jeans. She must've picked these up by mistake. I yanked the tag off and struggled to wiggle into the skinny jeans. I had to suck in my stomach to get them buttoned. After slipping on the new, deep V-neck sweater, I scowled. It showed too much cleavage. What was Mom thinking?

I studied my reflection in the mirror and tugged at the V to cover my boobs. My navel peeked out. I pulled down on the sweater and my boobs popped out even more, so I pulled up on the neckline to cover up. Then the hem rode up, again. "This sweater is too small and these jeans feel too tight."

"No, they're not. You're still too self-conscious. You look great."

"I'm not used to seeing so much skin." I pulled at the ribbed V and frowned. Wondering what my backside looked like when I squatted, I checked myself in the mirror. "Look. More skin and my bikinis are showing in these butt-crack jeans."

Abby's hand flew up and cupped her mouth, muffling her snicker. "Well don't squat."

"Yeah, right. You're my official picker-upper tonight if I drop something."

"If you don't quick fussing, I'll make you wear my sweater and then your midriff will be busting out as well." Abby giggled.

I rolled my eyes. "That's all I'd need since you're shorter."

"You've changed so much. You're not that awkward kid I met freshman year." Abby got up from the bed and walked across the room toward me in her three-inch mules. "Between my wonderful tutelage and that modeling class, well, just look at you." She swung her hips from side to side. "And I got the added benefit of learning your sassy strut."

Just as she reached me, she stumbled and I caught her. "That is until one of us falls flat on our face in front of a crowd," I said before we laughed. The hair on my arms stood on end, followed by a prickle. What if I fell, again? One face-planter on a practice runway had been enough for me.

My cell phone rang. It was Garrett. "Hey there. Have you checked your calendar yet?"

"Oh, hi. Umm. Hold on for a second." Picking up the nearest textbook, I ruffled through the pages close to the phone. "Nope. It looks like tomorrow evening is clear. Should I pencil you in?"

A snicker came over the line. "Yes, but please use a pen. I'll pick you up at 5:30." He briefly paused. "How late can you stay out?"

"Not too late. I have an early class." I tossed the book back on the bed.

"Okay, that's good."

"Will you be at the carnival tonight?" I paced back and forth in front of the mirror giving the sweater a tug here and there. Nothing helped.

"I'm actually at my parents' right now, but I'll be back early Sunday. See you then."

"Okay. And I did use a pen."

He chuckled. "Tomorrow."

Abby bumped me with her hip to push me out of the way and gave herself another look in the mirror. "Was that Garrett?"

"Yep, I officially have a date." Another bump to Abby's hip pushed her aside.

"Good. You need someone other than Matt to hang around. You ready to go?" A final blow to my hip gave Abbey a full view of herself. She won the mirror war and proceeded to fluff her hair. "I'm as ready as I can get."

"Me too." I started to follow Abby out the bedroom door and then stopped. My old friend, my blue work shirt hung on the hook next to the door. I could use it to cover my waist and the coarse material against my fingertips gave me comfort. I snatched the shirt.

"Oh, no you don't." Abby yanked the shirt from my grasp then shook it wadded up in her hand. "You're not taking this paint-splattered thing."

"But, I could get cold?" I wave my hand over my bare parts.

"No. You're not covering up with this thing, again." She threw it on the bench and pointed. "Out."

Just before I passed her, I grabbed the shirt and darted down the stairs and out the front door. It didn't look that bad. Only a few little spots were on it.

"Belinda!" She stopped on the porch and placed a hand on her cocked hip.

"Too late." I waved my badge of honor over my head, putting just enough distance between me and her, so she couldn't throw it back into the house.

I pulled my sweater up to cover more of my cleavage and then tied the sleeves of my trusty shirt around my waist. With less skin on display, my nerves calmed.

Abbey caught up. "I don't believe you."

"Believe it."

She huffed and we headed straight for the Theta Kappa booth.

Brent and Matt, our dates, were busy with the final set-up. I wanted to walk around and check out each booth, but Abby preferred to hang with Brent. I told her I'd hook up with her on my second go-round so we could play some games and check out the band.

The Theta Kappa booth, a dart game, was near the end of one side of the street. I walked past the last few booths, checking them out, and then crossed over to the other row of booths.

I was halfway down the row when two fraternity brothers, wearing Delt Cops badges, flanked me. The one on my left said, "You're under arrest."

I snickered and played along. "And just how long will I be incarcerated, sir?" I stuck my arms out so plastic handcuffs could be fastened to my wrists.

"For ten minutes or until you make bail."

I didn't want to waste my money on bail, so I accepted my fate and went along. They led me over to the Delt area, removed the cuffs and put me in a jail-like enclosure.

I moved to the front right corner and strained to see Matt. He'd be my most likely person to pull this stunt. Being his typical self, he was surrounded by a group of giddy females, paying no attention to me. "That jerk."

The warmth of a hand touching my forearm excited every cell in my body. A buzzing sensation raced over my skin like an electrical charge. I gasped and shivered and stepped back.

"Sorry, I didn't mean to startle you."

I looked up just as he pulled his hand back through the bars. He flexed his hand, studying it. My heart skipped a beat and then started racing. I froze, speechless. There stood Mister Gorgeous. I could only imagine how stupid I looked with my mouth hanging open.

When he looked back at me, his expression changed to one of concern. "Are you okay?"

I took a deep breath. "Yes, but when you touched me. It uh…oh, never mind." My face burned hot. I bowed my head. How could I tell a stranger his touch was arousing?

"What were you going to say?"

I lifted my chin and stared. His gaze captivated me. I just took in his puzzled expression until I realized he expected an answer. "Uh. Oh, nothing," I stammered.

His mouth slowly turned up into a smile and he poked a finger at me. "You're the girl on the horse this morning. Brian told me you live next door to him. I'm Robert Pennington."

"Hi." I glanced away, and then looked back at him. "I'm Belinda Davies."

Robert leaned against the jail. "I've been here three-and-a-half years and I've never seen you before."

My heart raced. My face grew warmer and warmer. *Shit*. I was blushing again. I took a step back into a dimmer spot. "I could say the same about you."

One of the jailers interrupted, "You're free to go."

Robert met me at the jail exit. He crossed his arms over his broad chest and attempted to rest against the rickety-looking table the frat brothers used to keep the plastic handcuffs and their drinks. It wobbled and he almost fell backward, but caught himself and managed to prevent the table from flipping over. "Boy. That wasn't a good idea." He chuckled. "Stay!" He hovered his hands over the table. "I think the Delts need to splurge and buy a new one of these."

His recovery attempt made me giggle.

He shoved his hands into his jeans back pockets and rocked back on his heels. "The guy you were with earlier today at the Theta Kappa booth, was that your boyfriend?"

"No." I shook my head for more emphasis. "Matt's just a friend."

This guy was so out of my league. A lump formed in my throat, making it difficult to talk. I caught the edge of the sleeve of my security shirt and fiddled with it.

"Would you like to go out sometime? Say, tomorrow evening?"

My breath faltered for a second. "You're asking me out?"

"Yeah." He half grinned.

"Like on a *date*, date?"

He nodded. "Yes," lengthening the word.

I had to get a grip. Mister Gorgeous asked me out. Abby's little voice shouted in my head, "Step out of your comfort zone and take chances." If I accepted, I'd definitely be doing that, but he scared the crap out of me. I opened my mouth to say no, but "okay," popped out. I gulped. What did I just do?

His face lit up. "Good. What time should I pick you up?"

"I'm not su…" I held my breath. My shoulders fell when I exhaled. I had already made a date with Garrett. "I can't tomorrow. I have other plans. Sorry."

He jumped right in with his next question. "What about dinner on Tuesday?"

I mentally scanned the empty pages of my daily planner. "That works for me." Did I just firm up a date with him? My stomach knotted. "Play it cool. Keep it light," Abby's little voice in my head warned me.

"What kind of food do you like?"

"Mexican and Italian."

"Me too. I'll take you to my favorite Mexican restaurant. Is five okay?" He stepped closer.

"Yeah." So, it looked like Mexican two nights this week. Oh, well.

Robert pulled his hands from his pockets and held his phone in one. "Let's exchange numbers. Just in case."

I gave him my number as he tapped his screen. Then mine chirped. He smiled. "Just making sure."

"Did you think I'd give you a fake number?"

That million-dollar smile never left his face. "A guy can't be too sure these days."

I pulled my phone from my back pocket. "Okay. Your turn." I tapped away in my contact list and then hit call.

His phone rang. He answered it.

"Back at cha." I cocked my head as I hung up.

His face lit up just before he burst into a laugh. I loved his laugh as much as his smile.

I started to put my phone in my back pocket, but fumbled and dropped it. I reached for it and so did Robert. Our hands touched. *That same electrical sizzle I'd experience earlier shot up my arm and through my body. What the heck?* I pulled my hand back.

When I straightened, he was flexing his hand then pointed to mine. "Did I hurt you?"

"No." I didn't dare touch my hand. How could I explain a titillating sensation shot through me, igniting every nerve ending? I slipped my phone into my pocket. "I should be getting back to my friends." I shifted from one foot to the other then started to walk away. "Well, I guess I'll see you on Tuesday. Bye."

"See yeah."

I took my time and strolled toward Matt's booth. I looked back. Butterflies erupted in my chest. Robert never moved. He just stood there. I waved. He gave a nod before the crowd closed in around me, and I lost sight of him.

I ran back to the Theta Kappa booth to tell Abby. I pulled her aside so Matt and Brent couldn't overhear. "Abby, I met Mister Gorgeous. Someone put me in the Delt jail, and he talked to me. I have a date with him Tuesday."

She grabbed my arms and we jumped up and down, squealing like junior high girls. "What's his name?"

"Robert Pennington."

Abby tilted her head. "The 'Robert' that was asking about you?"

I shrugged my shoulders. "I hope so."

"Do you think he had you put in jail?" She squeezed my arms.

"I'm sure Matt didn't do it. So, maybe it was him." I rubbed my arm where he had rested his hand. "Something strange happened every time he touched me."

"What? He touched you?" Her brows drew together.

"It wasn't anything weird. He just touched my arm to get my attention." I made my voice low and sexy. "A kind of very pleasant buzz ran through me. I've never experienced anything like that before."

Abby started to speak, but Matt hollered, "What are you two laughing about?"

"Oh, nothing," we answered, grinning at each other.

Arm-in-arm, I waved as we walked past. "See you later."

We made our way around from booth to booth trying out our skills until we came to the Delt jail. Robert wasn't there.

Abby nudged my arm. "I have an idea. Since you're pretty sure Robert had you put in jail, why don't you do the same to him? Payback."

"Huh. Are you sure? I hardly know the guy." *Is she crazy?*

"Be daring. What harm could it do? He probably won't even know you did it. Just go for it. I'd do it." Abby fanned her face. "He's smokin' hot and he's interested in you." She poked my shoulder.

"Oookay." If she'd do it, I guess it's okay to take the risk. I looked around the area for Robert—a knot formed in the pit of my stomach—and spotted him four booths down across the street.

I grabbed the arm of a passing jailer. "See that guy over there." I pointed to Robert. He nodded. "Yeah. Robert?"

"That's right." I dug in my pocket and pulled out a few bills. "How much will it cost me to have him arrested?"

The guy smiled. "I'll do it for nothing."

"But, I can pay." I waved the money in front of him.

"No. No. It's my pleasure." He gave me a quick once over and then grinned. He stepped in closer. "I'll be right back."

"Okay, but don't tell him who did it."

His smile widened. "For you anything." He twirled a pair of handcuffs around his finger, winked, and then left.

Abby elbowed my ribs. "That guy was flirting with you."

"Pft. No, he wasn't. But he was a bit creepy." I shoved the money back in my pocket then grabbed Abby's arm. "Let's get out of here."

"Girl, you need to start realizing guys like what they're seeing. Despite that old shirt tied around your waist."

Abby pointed to the bean bag toss. "Let's see what kind of damage we can do over there." Luckily, it was within close proximity to the jail, so, I could watch Robert's reaction to being arrested.

After letting my last bag fly, I turned around to talk to Abby and noticed Robert's gaze fixed on me. My breathing increased the closer he came, his stride steady, confident, his shoulders broad.

As his jailers led him past, he raised his cuffed hands. A smile spread across his face making his striking pale blue eyes sparkle. I nearly fainted.

From the jail, he peered out and wiggled his forefinger at me to come over. I pointed to myself, and mouthed, "Me?"

He nodded. Aiming that finger at himself and next the jail, he then pointed at me. He was accusing me of putting him in there.

I shook my head and pointed at Abby, putting the blame on her. After all, it was her idea.

Abby swatted my hand, shaking her head. She darted a finger at me.

A big smile spread across his face and he motioned again for me to come over. My chest thumped and I swore my heart skipped a few beats.

Abby grasped my upper arm and rested her head against my arm. "Well, are you going over there?"

"No. I don't think so."

"Are you sure?" She squeezed my arm. "He's too hot to just walk away."

I let out a deep sigh. "I'm sure. Let's go listen to the band."

I tried to turn away, but Abby held me firm. "You're making a big mistake."

"Maybe. I don't think I can be around him right now."

She lifted her head so I could see her. "Why?"

I whispered, "Remember what I mentioned earlier. He does stuff to my insides that you and I need to talk about first."

Abby's mouth curved up. "Oh. Good stuff I hope?"

"Yeah. Maybe. Stuff I'm not ready for." I rubbed the spot where he'd touched me, remembering...sensation.

"Hmm. All right. We'll talk back in our room."

She tugged at my security shirt. "Oh, hell. You still have this old thing to keep you company for now." She giggled and strutted away.

Robert motioned again. I shrugged and waved and followed Abby.

We made a detour to check on our dates, but found girls in sorority t-shirts surrounding their booth, demanding all their attention. Matt didn't even notice me. That was fine because I had other things on my mind.

This school year I realized I was an afterthought for Matt. Up until this past summer he'd only hooked up with me when he needed help with his classes. We had a nice arrangement, he got the help he needed and I got to ride Beau.

But, since running into Mister Gorgeous, I wanted something more. I wanted more of that heart-stopping feeling I got when Robert touched me. I wanted to find out what caused that pleasant sensation to shoot up my arm and to do that I'd have to be around him. I just didn't know if I was ready for someone like him. He had to be experienced and popular with the girls. How could I ever compete with them? Especially the more seasoned ones.

∽

Abby and I stood in front of the band, swaying to the music, until Brent showed up and asked her to dance, leaving me alone. I continued to sway to the rhythm when a hand rested on my arm. Immediately, my body flooded with electrifying sexual awareness, telling me who it was before I heard, "May I have this dance?" I turned around to face Robert and nodded.

His touch took my breath away as he slid his hand down my arm into mine and led me into the crowd. When we stopped, he placed his other hand at my waist. He moved our clasped hands close between us. I hoped he couldn't feel my heart racing and my chest rising with each accelerated breath. I put my arm around his shoulder and slid my hand up the back of his neck into his thick hair. He leaned his head back into it, lowered his eyelids and exhaled before he focused back on me.

We moved as one to the rhythm of the music. With every sway, I felt that strange new sensation creep into my soul. It made my heart soar. When the song ended, neither of us let go.

We just stood there in silence, lost in each other.

The next song had a hot tempo. "I don't know how to dance to this."

He had a seductive look and a mischievous grin. "I do." He squeezed my hand and spun me out. Then he pulled me back into his hard chest. He placed his hand at my waist and with a quick tug, smashed our hips together. Our bodies moved in tandem. Again, he spun me out then pulled me to him, my back to his chest. His warm breath caressed my neck while he ran his hands down the sides of my body. A shudder blew through me. Suddenly, I was back facing him, his hand at my waist holding me close, our other hands clutched between us. With his lips inches from mine, I longed for their taste. He sent heat pulsing through my veins, and, at that moment, I knew I was his.

Rhythmically, we moved together, our bodies instinctively communicating. My pounding heart almost leaped out of my chest. I noticed people staring at us and leaned close to his ear. "We're being watched."

He looked up into the crowd and smiled, mumbling something about being lost in the moment. He started to return his gaze to me, but something or someone caught his attention and he abruptly stopped dancing. Robert led me in the opposite direction he'd been looking. "I thought you said you couldn't dance to this music. You were great."

"I can't. You're a good leader." I gave that feeble excuse not wanting to admit it was like his body had told mine what to do.

Robert scanned the crowd and grumbled, "I have to go. See you Tuesday." He disappeared as fast as he'd arrived, leaving me standing there wondering what the hell just happened. I replayed the dance in my head. He obviously enjoyed it. So, why was he in such a hurry to get away from me?

I needed to talk to Abby and pushed my way through the crowd toward her and Brent. Luckily, Matt was nowhere in sight.

"HOT mama!" Brent then gave a catcall. He looked me up and down with exaggerated, seductive eye movements. His attention made me feel uncomfortable.

With a wide-eyed look, Abby took hold of my shoulders and gave me an excited shake. "Where did you learn to dance like that?"

"I don't. My body just moved with his." I was still trying to figure out what exactly had just happened.

"I thought you two were going to make out, the way you were looking at each other. Steamy! Where did he go?" Abby searched through the crowd as she rubbernecked, attempting to obtain a better view.

"I don't know. He just said he had to leave."

Strong arms wrapped around my waist. "Are you ready to go?"

My heart jumped as I looked over my shoulder at Matt. I didn't want Brent blabbing about my dance with Robert. I didn't owe him an explanation, but I was confused and he was the last person I wanted to talk to about it.

"I guess so." I became acutely aware my interest in this date had disappeared. All my thoughts were on Robert and how he'd made me feel.

I grabbed Matt's hand and walked a safe distance away from Brent. "Abby, I'll see you at home." She waved.

As we left, I saw Robert with the same petite blonde from earlier in the day. I hoped she wasn't his girlfriend. She had her arms crossed in front of her and a frown. He was rubbing her upper arms, doing all the talking.

I wondered if she'd seen our dance moves and now he had a bunch of explaining to do.

CHAPTER 4

SUNDAY MORNING, SUNLIGHT poured through the lace curtains and bounced across my face. I gave up trying to sleep. Robert had haunted my mind all night, causing me to toss and turn.

Abby lay curled in her bed fast asleep. That girl could sleep through an earthquake. She and I had talked for hours after we settled in our beds. Well, more like I talked and she interjected when needed. Robert's effect on me confused me, but with Abby's guidance, I hoped I'd master these new feelings.

I dressed in a knit top and shorts, picked up an apple off the desk, grabbed a blanket, my textbook, and then headed for the big oak tree out front.

No sooner had I started reading when the silence was broken by the familiar sound of hooves on pavement. Matt on Beau galloped toward me. Matt leaped from the saddle, snatched me up in his arms, and planted a smacking kiss on my lips. "Hey, Babe. I need to kill some time."

That impulsive move caused my book to fly into the air. It landed inches from Beau's hooves. I huffed at Matt as I pushed him away. Then I bent over to retrieve my sprawled out book and placed it on the blanket.

I grasped Beau's reins then stroked his nose. "Hey, Beau. Sorry, I don't have any carrots today. How about my apple core?" The animal proceeded to munch on the remainder of my breakfast.

"I suppose you wanna ride Beau?"

"Can I?"

"Sure, take off." He gave me a leg-up into the saddle then walked to the tree and plopped down on my blanket. "I'll just lie here and wait for you. Anything good to read?" He picked up my textbook, frowned, and dropped it beside him.

"Hey, be careful with that." I gave a half-wave as I rode off.

I hadn't ridden very far when through the crisp spring air someone called my name. Over my shoulder, I saw Garrett waving.

Garrett stood about six feet tall with light brown hair which he wore spiked on top, just enough to give him a hint of the "bad boy" look, except he had the sweetest face. His well-muscled body and defined arms were very impressive.

"Are we still on for tonight?" He took hold of the bridle and stroked Beau's neck like he did before.

"Yes, of course." He seemed at ease around Beau. "Have you been around horses much?"

"I've been around a few in my life. I grew up on a ranch." He glanced up. "Is 5:30 still okay?"

I smiled and nodded. "That's fine."

"How about a ride to the Student Center? I'm heading to the Cave."

"Sure, climb on." I pulled my foot from the stirrup and Garrett hoisted himself up. He locked his powerful arms around my waist, then pressed his chest against my back and held me close. His body against mine felt warm and inviting, but it was nowhere near the sensation I'd felt when I was in Robert's arms the night before.

Garrett was a good rider. He moved with the rhythm of Beau's gait. I moved along with them and soon realized I wasn't the one controlling Beau even though I held the reins. Garrett had taken over by using his legs and the horse was responding. I was just along for the ride.

In front of the Student Center, I saw the Delt jail being torn down, but Robert wasn't around.

Garrett dismounted. "See you later." He waved.

"See ya." I watched him leave and knew I had a big problem. The nagging memory of Robert had embedded itself in my mind and insisted on rattling around in my brain. I knew I'd enjoy my date with Garrett, but now there would be three of us attending.

Beau and I took our time getting back to the house. In my neighbor's front yard, I saw Robert and Brian talking. My heart immediately sped up and my stomach churned. From the corner of my eye, I saw him stare. The corners of his mouth slid upward. Mine did the same. I had to control my impulse to linger and possibly make a fool of myself. So, I forced myself to ride past.

Fortunately, my emotional switch turned off when I passed the hedge that shielded Robert from my view. The thrill of seeing him was now overshadowed by Matt, propped against my favorite oak tree. Dozing.

His eyelids lifted as the clomping of hooves came closer. With a lazy stretch followed by a gaping yawn, he said, "Well, I hope I've waited long enough so that they won't need my help tearing down the booth. I guess I'd better go check." He helped me down then mounted Beau and took off.

I turned and studied the hedge, the only thing standing between Robert and me. Squealing tires caused me to whirl toward the street and see Robert drive by. He nodded. Just the sight of him sent my insides into a frenzy.

I gathered everything up and went inside to see if Abby was awake. She was lying across her bed with her nose buried in a textbook. "Where have you been?"

"Outside reading. Matt stopped by on Beau. He was avoiding the booth teardown, so while he napped under the tree, I rode Beau. I also bumped into Garrett and confirmed our date." I threw my stuff on my bed. "And I just saw Robert next door."

Abby's brows rose. "Boy, you had a busy morning." She pointed toward my phone. "You need to check your cell. It rang twice while you were out."

"Oh. I forgot it." Up until this school year, the phone rarely rang. I only used it to stay in touch with Abby or my parents. Now I found the need for it increased as my social life picked up. I still couldn't quite grasp it being a necessity. My inner self liked having quiet time. Not having the phone with me 24-7 assured me I had that control.

I had two calls in less than an hour. Go figure. The first one came from Robert. *Well, shit*!

The second from Garrett. The time indicated he had called before I saw him.

Stroking my fingertips over the phone, I thought about returning Robert's call but didn't want to seem too eager. I just couldn't stop thinking about him. With all the strength I could muster, I ignored the call and tossed the phone on my bed and headed for the closet.

He'd have to wait. I had a date tonight to get ready for, but my decision was killing me.

∞

I sat at the window waiting for Garrett. At 5:30 on the dot, he pulled into the driveway. I bounced down the stairs but waited for the doorbell to ring and then swung open the door. "Hey."

"Y'all set?"

I nodded. With his hand on my back, we walked to his car, a shiny jet black Mustang.

"Nice car."

"You like Mustangs?" He opened the door.

"Yeah, they're one of my favorites. They're horses." I winked and slipped into the seat.

He chuckled.

On our way, the conversation consisted of the usual chit-chat, our majors, and decisions that led to our chosen fields of study. Garrett was very proud of himself since he had just been accepted into grad school. He said he was surprised that he'd never seen me around campus until now.

I explained that my study habits made me somewhat reclusive. There wasn't a need to tell him my lack of a social life, the first two years, was due to my appearance and low self-esteem. Chances are he had seen me, but didn't remember or chose not to.

In the restaurant, he asked what I wanted, then ordered my meal. He was a perfect gentleman.

"Where are you from?" He took a bite of a tortilla chip.

"Sugar Land. It's a small city southwest of Houston. Where are you from?" I sipped my drink.

"Athens…Texas." He finished off the chip. "You know, I have a friend from Sugar Land."

"Oh. Who?" I popped the red sauce covered chip into my mouth.

"Robert Pennington."

A cough exploded and the pepper spice seared the back of my throat when I inhaled. I grabbed my water glass and took a healthy swig.

Garrett leaned in. "Are you okay?"

"Wrong pipe." I patted my upper chest and let out another cough. *Robert Pennington. Oh Crap*!

After one more swallow, I changed the subject to Garrett's family. We continued conversing while we ate, never returning to the subject of Robert, but he remained in my head, teasing me and interfering with my time with Garrett.

"Do you like to play pool?" he asked on our walk toward his car.

"Yes, but I haven't played for a while." His question sparked a fond memory, making me grin to myself.

"You up for a game?"

"Sure. Are we going to the rec room at the Student Center?"

"No, the frat house."

I glanced at him. "Which one?"

"Delt."

A beat of my heart skipped. I stopped dead in my tracks and spat out, "You're a Delt?"

Garrett, a few steps ahead of me, turned, his browed furrowed. "Is there something wrong?"

"I didn't know you're a Delt." Now, I had a real dilemma on my hands, having made dates with two frat brothers who also were friends. "Um, I have a big problem." My heart sank like a stone. *Damn it*!

"What?" He moved to my side.

I hesitated. How was I supposed to tell Garrett I had a date with Robert? It was commonplace for students to have multiple dates with other people in one week. It just wasn't cool to talk about it with your current date.

Garrett reached for my hand. "Tell me?"

I squeezed my eyelids shut and blurted out, "I accepted a date with one of your brothers." I raised my left lid to judge his expression, then the other.

Garrett's mouth twisted. "Oh."

I took Garrett's other hand in mine. "I didn't know, so I'll just cancel. That will take care of it." As we held hands, I didn't feel a buzz or a sizzle or a spark. Absolutely nothing.

But, I did accept Garrett's invitation first and I had to see it through. He hit all the marks on the gentlemen scale. A girl couldn't ask for more, but the news placed a damper on the evening.

We spoke very little on our drive, just spurts of superficial conversation. I could tell Garrett was very curious about the other frat brother, but he didn't bring up the subject.

The Delt house was hopping with frat brothers and their dates. First thing, I scanned for Robert. Thankfully, he wasn't there. Out of the corner of my eye, I saw Garrett watch me check out the room while we headed for the pool table.

"Is he here?"

I gave him a stern look and ignored him by setting up the balls. "Do you want to break?"

Garrett picked up a cue stick, chalked the end, and broke. One ball went into a pocket. He sank three more then missed.

Bending over the table to take a shot, I heard, "Hey, Garrett." I froze at the sound of the familiar voice. With my upper torso hidden behind my date, all Robert could possibly see were my legs and butt.

Garrett pivoted. "How about a game? You two against us."

You two? Who was he with? The petite blonde?

Robert let out a small grunt. "You're on."

"Hey, I'd like you to meet my date, Belinda." Garrett stepped aside. "Belinda, this is Robert and his girlfriend, Lora."

Girlfriend? *Well, crap.*

Taking careful aim, I sank my shot and then stood. "Nice to meet you."

Lora gave me a once over and snooty half-grin.

Robert had a surprised look on his face. I hoped he'd play along and not let Garrett know he'd met me earlier. He let out a barely audible chuckle and extended his hand to me. "Nice to meet you, too."

I looked at his hand then backed up a step and tightened my grip on the cue stick. I still wasn't sure what I'd felt when we danced, and this wasn't the time or place to try to figure it out. By the look on his face, he understood and dropped his hand to his side.

Garrett racked the balls. "Belinda, do you want to break?"

"No, let them start." I wanted to go last so I could assess the skill level of my opponents. Garrett told Robert to break. He sank four. Garrett sank two. Lora failed miserably and sunk nothing.

Now, "showtime." I toed off my espadrilles and shoved them under the table. Then I named the ball, which pocket it would sink in, and followed through. I smiled to myself. Pool had become a real pastime for me during the first two years of college since I had nothing better to do.

I ricocheted another ball off the side and watched it dropped into its designated pocket. Pretty soon a group surrounded the table. The tight circle caused me to question my ability. The one thing Gary, my pool buddy, pounded home—always concentrate on the shot. I pointed at the corner pocket and sank two balls.

The room went silent. The hairs on the back of my neck stood. Everyone was watching me. My heart sputtered. I had made myself the center of attention. *Why?* I filled my lungs then exhaled. *Okay, Gary, I can do this.* I took another shot and the ball sunk into the pocket.

Those first few times I saw Gary playing at the student center, I watched and studied his moves. After he left, I tried to copy him. I'd sink a few balls but not like him. He'd consistently cleared the table. I was missing something.

Gary had figured out I was watching him and scared the crap out of me when he came over to my table. From that day on, he became my teacher and taught me what I missed, the physics of the game.

As I walked around the table to contemplate my next move, the group stepped back. I concentrated so hard on the game I forgot about the crowd around me.

I moved into position and took aim. Two others bit the dust in opposite side pockets, leaving only the eight ball. I called the pocket, took aim and finished the game.

Garrett's mouth gaped like a fish. "How did you do that?"

"A guy I used to hang around with taught me." I planted my cue on the floor in front of me. The crowd clapped. Unfortunately, my dramatic finish drew more attention my way. I wanted to crawl under the table. Instead, I white-knuckled the cue stick and took a deep breath.

"Garrett, you're dating a pool shark." Robert had a sweet grin on his handsome face.

My pulse spiked at Robert's expression until Garrett planted his lips on mine. He pulled me closer and kissed me more exuberantly. My thoughts moved from Robert back to Garrett, long enough for me to enjoy our encounter. The kiss was nice, but nothing else. No spark ignited my senses. "It's getting late. I think it's time to leave." I glanced back at Robert, but he had turned his attention back to Lora.

Garrett asked all sorts of pool questions on the way home. Thank goodness my house wasn't very far away. He walked me to my front door and said, "I had a great time." He kissed me with his warm, firm lips. "I'll call you soon. Good night." He had walked down a few steps off the porch when he hesitated and turned back. "Was he there tonight?"

I just smiled and went in.

Abby swung her head up as I burst through the door. I couldn't wait to tell her about the night and the complications.

"Abby. Garrett and Robert are friends and frat brothers. You know I can't date both of them. I have to break my date with Robert. Shit!" I stomped my foot. "He was the one I wanted to go out with. Why is life so comp…"

My cell phone rang before I could finish my sentence. I fished it out of my bag. It was Robert. I answered, feeling my world about to end.

"Belinda. Hey. A problem has developed. I have to cancel our date."

I wrapped an arm over my belly, suddenly feeling nauseous. "I know. I'm sorry. I didn't know you both were Delts and friends when I accepted."

"When did you meet Garrett?" He sounded somewhat disappointed.

"Saturday morning while riding Beau around campus."

"Garrett's my best friend. I can't date you while he is. Sorry."

"I understand." My heart was breaking. This guy had gotten under my skin, and I couldn't shake off the thought of him. Even if I did continue seeing Garrett, Robert would be right there with us, preoccupying my mind.

"Well, I guess that's it. I'll see you around." After a long pause, he ended with, "Good night."

I sighed, "Good night." I wanted to cry.

Instead, I threw my phone onto the bed. "How can this be happening to me? I go two years without a real date, get a date with two guys on the same day, meet the guy of my dreams, and then dream guy and the other guy are friends and frat brothers to boot." I threw my hands up into the air. "Then, I have to cancel the date with the guy of my dreams because he asked me last. I can't catch a break!" I flung myself onto the mattress and stared at the ceiling.

Abby spoke in a soft voice, almost cautious-sounding, "How'd the date go with Garrett?" She flipped the book closed.

I rolled over, taking a deep breath before continuing to tell her about the night and how my pool lessons paid off during the challenge against Robert and his girlfriend, Lora.

Abby chimed in, "It's probably best this happened because he sounds like a player to me. He's flirting with you when he has a girlfriend." She pulled her knees to her chest. "I kinda feel sorry for her. Would you want that happening to you?"

"No. Of course not." I hadn't considered how his girlfriend would feel if she found out. How selfish of me. "I'd hate the girl who stole him from me. If he were mine." A sigh slipped out. I guess, now, I'll never get the chance to find out what that electric sizzle was when we touched, unless…

I bounced to my knees with a surge of hope. "Maybe he's ready to move on. Maybe they're not that close. He made the first move."

"Well, be careful. I don't want to see you get hurt."

"I will." Abby was wiser than her years and understood things about the male libido I had yet to experience. "I'm going to get ready for bed."

With the flip of the bathroom switch, I entered the bedroom lit by the dim light of the street lamp. Abby was asleep. I crawled into my bed. The light from outside filtered through the lace curtains and cast shapes on the ceiling. I stared up while the day's events flowed through my mind. Sleep came, but it was restless because my heart was breaking over a guy I didn't even know and was already taken.

CHAPTER 5

OVER THE NEXT several days, the talk Abby and I had kept repeating in my head like a scratched record. So to avoid running into Robert, I didn't go to the Cave and I took a different route to my classes. I spent most of the week hiding in the library, studying. I thought out of sight meant out of mind. Didn't work. My mind kept reminding my body what I was missing when we touched. Stupid brain. Stupid hormones. But unfortunately, I'd see him next door on my way home. He'd smile and wink, giving me hope that someday I might be his girlfriend. Not likely. I needed to get over him. Move on. He had a girlfriend and it wasn't me.

Abby and I had a girls' night on Friday. We discussed what I was experiencing, but it didn't help. Robert invaded my dreams lifting my spirits and then slamming me down. How could this guy I hardly knew cause me this much heartache? Luckily, Garrett called and we went out Saturday night. It was nice, but it only made me want to fantasize I was with Robert. So not fair to Garrett. Abby and I talked again on Sunday and I decided I couldn't hide forever. I had to face my problem and get on with my life. I hoped.

∞

After class on Monday, I strolled along my usual route to the library but Matt intercepted and invited me to go along with him to the Cave. The tables there were staked out by fraternities in a self-assigned manner. Matt and I walked to the Theta Kappa section where I sat and he went to buy sodas. Garrett and Robert strutted in. Robert spotted me on his way to the Delt area. I tried to ignore him, but couldn't. I looked up. He had seated himself facing me. Warmth zipped through my veins. My chest tightened. But our gaze was soon broken when Matt returned and sat blocking my view.

He pushed a drink toward me. "How about coming to the fraternity baseball game today at four?" I just nodded since my attention was elsewhere. Matt noticed me peering over his shoulder. He glanced back. "Two Delts are looking over here. One's Pennington. Do you know him?"

"I've met him. The other one is Garrett Barnett." I took a long draw on my straw.

"Stay away from Pennington. He's a player. I've heard he dates a girl until he bags her and then dumps her." Matt smirked and continued on his soapbox. I didn't want to listen to him bad-mouth Robert. So, I zoned him out and let my mind go with thoughts of Mr. Pennington. Just thinking of him sent goosebumps racing over my skin. Stupid body.

Garrett saw me glance toward the Delt table and waved me over. Matt turned and looked over his shoulder, then turned back. "You're not thinking of going over there, are you?"

"I went out with Garrett. The least I should do is say, hi." I raised my cup. "Thanks for the drink. I'll see you at the game."

Matt pointed in my direction. "You be careful around Pennington. Remember, I warned you."

I nodded. "Thanks, but I think I can handle myself around him." I tried to sound confident, fighting with my screaming insides, because I knew Matt might be right. Maybe I was asking for trouble and walking into the lion's den, but I couldn't help myself. My feet just took me closer and closer.

"Hey. Why are you sitting over there?" Garrett offered me a chair between Robert and him. It was difficult being so close to Robert, but I had no choice. I had to try to be cordial to both of them. Robert repositioned himself, accidentally brushing his arm against mine. A pleasant sizzle hit me. I gasped and jerked back, then scooted my chair away to avoid a recurrence.

Garrett noticed my reaction. "Uh. What just happened?"

Robert and I looked at each other but said nothing. Garrett told him to touch my arm. Robert slowly raised his hand and ever so gently slid his fingers over my forearm. I tensed. My girl parts sizzled. His touch was light, smooth, and lingering. A slow buzz skittered up my spine. My breath hitched. Robert straightened and pulled back his hand. He glanced at it, then flexed it.

Garrett's brows rose. "Ooookay."

I just sat there trying not to be obvious. I hoped he'd drop the subject, but I wasn't so lucky. Garrett ran his fingers over my other arm, but nothing happened. He kept looking back and forth at Robert and me. "What's going on?"

In unison, Robert and I said, "Nothing." We looked at each other. He splayed his fingers through his hair, tugging it off his forehead, and then shook his head.

I sighed. "I seem to be extra sensitive to his touch. That's the best way I can describe it." I looked shyly at Robert then back to Garrett.

Geez. I really wanted to find out what this reaction meant.

This conversation was getting way too uncomfortable, and I needed an out. I glanced at my watch. "I have to go to the library." The chair legs screeched across the floor when I stood and picked up my things. "Bye."

Garrett followed. "I'll walk you there." He nodded to Robert. "Catch you later."

We walked outside in silence. Garrett nudged me. "He's the other Delt who asked you out, isn't he?"

I didn't respond, gripping my books just a bit tighter against my chest.

"I heard about a steamy dance between him and a knockout with long, golden-brown hair. That was you, wasn't it?"

I nodded. This situation had me so confused. Garrett was a nice guy. He was a good catch for someone, but I knew that someone wasn't me. I couldn't get my mind off Robert even though he had a girlfriend.

"When did you two meet?"

"The Delt jail. He introduced himself and asked me out."

Garrett draped his arm over my shoulders as we walked. He stopped and turned me toward him. Placing a hand under my chin, he lifted my face to his. "I really like you, but you two seem to have something going on here." He lowered his head and inhaled a deep breath. "I don't want to fall for you and then lose you later. I'm going to back out. I'll tell him to call you." He took a few steps back.

"You sure?" He had just handed me the opportunity of my life. *I think.* I shuffled my right foot. "I just heard something about his reputation."

He gave his head a quick jerk. "What? What did you hear?"

"That he dates a girl until he gets you-know-what and then moves on."

He cocked his head and spat out, "What? Robert's a great guy! He's a chick magnet, but he's only dated three girls since freshman year. He's not a player if that's what you're saying."

My cheeks warmed. "That's what I heard."

"Well, you heard wrong. He only dates one girl at a time. He's been dating Lora since the start of last year."

"And what about Lora?" I needed to hear something that would ease my guilty conscience. I didn't want to be the cause of their breakup.

He shrugged his shoulders. "I don't know, but if he stays true to his dating record, he'll probably end it with her. Besides, from what I can tell, they haven't been getting along lately."

Great. That's just what I needed to hear. Now, I didn't feel so bad about us flirting.

We reached the library and turned to face each other. "Go out with him. Give yourself and him a chance. You'll see I'm right about him."

Juggling my books into one arm, I put my other around Garrett's neck, and hugged him. "I hope he knows what a good friend you are. Thanks." I gave him a short kiss on the cheek. "See you later."

"Keep me posted on your progress."

I turned and frowned. "No. I don't kiss and tell." *Unless your name is Abby.*

∞

The cool dry air of the Texas spring afternoon caressed my face with a scent of freshness as I opened the library door. At this moment my life was good. I paused to take in my surroundings. The sun, setting behind the taller buildings, cast shadows that gave a romantic mystique to the pathways. All over campus, flowering trees bloomed in their splendor and shed petals like snowflakes on passers-by. This was the type of afternoon I wished I could share with someone special, like Robert.

From the steps of the library, I saw Robert and Lora leaving the Student Center. Life took a rapid downturn. I wished I could've been a fly on the wall to hear their conversation. I wondered if he'd break up with her to date me. If he really was a player, like Matt warned me, would he try to date both of us or should I take Garrett's word instead? My walk home took longer than usual. I had a lot on my mind and again, I needed Abby's advice.

Luck evaded me. She wasn't at the house. I'd have to wait to seek my dating guru's wisdom. I tossed my books on my bed and left to meet Matt at the baseball game.

I approached the Theta Kappa side and discovered the game was well on its way. Matt was walking up to bat. We waved at each other and then I saw Robert standing near third base. He was watching me. I looked around and found Lora standing to the left of home plate.

I wondered why he was looking at me when he was with another girl. His actions confused me.

Deep within the dark hole of her lair, "Monster," my alter ego from my high school days, stirred.

Robert was positioned in direct sight of where I stood. During the game, I caught myself ogling him, admiring the fit of his team t-shirt. It hugged his body, accentuating his upper arms and shoulder muscles. I found it very hard to look away.

On several occasions, our eyes met. At one of those times, he let a hard grounder down the third-base line get past him, costing his team a run.

After that Lora became very interested in my side of the field. With a scowl, she started eyeing everyone then stopped abruptly and gave me a dirty look. Her scary glare made the hairs on the back of my neck stand at attention. I tried to avoid looking at Robert after that, but I just couldn't.

The game ended with a very close score—THETA, 7; DELT, 6. After patting a few of his teammates on the back and shaking a few hands, Matt strode in my direction, his chest a bit puffed out. "You feel like grabbing a bite with the team?"

"I'd love to, but I have to study for a test." I nudged his arm. "Congratulations."

"Thanks." He beamed. "Well, if you can't go eat, let me drive you home."

As we walked to his car, I noticed Lora watching me. She wasted no time and threw her arms around Robert's neck, giving him a kiss then glared over his shoulder at me. Something evil about her stare made me uneasy, and also made me no longer feel sorry for her.

∞

I swung the door to my room open to find Abby studying. She lifted her nose out of her book and asked, "Where've you been?"

"I went to Matt's game. And guess who they were playing and who was there with his girlfriend?" I plopped on the corner of her bed.

"Hmmm." She placed a forefinger to her check. "The Delts?' Then she pointed her finger at the ceiling. "And Robert brought Lora? Awkward!"

"Extremely. She noticed Robert glance at our side. Then she started scanning the crowd and stopped at me." I shuddered. "Abby, you wouldn't believe the looks. She's crazy scary."

For the next thirty minutes, I told Abby about earlier in the day when Robert touched me at the Delt table in front of Garrett and what he'd said about Robert's dating record. "He told me to go out with Robert. Can you believe it?"

"I agree with him. There might be something there, and you need to find out what. Besides, it sounds like it could be fun exploring." Abby fluttered her brows up and down.

"Abby!" I squealed. "What about Lora. I may not like her, but I won't cross that line?"

She flipped her hand. "Okay, then let things play out. If Garrett is right, she'll go away. It's not like he pinned her. That would be different." She shook my arm. "Be patient and flirt with him every chance you get. Let him know you're interested and keep him interested without crossing your line." She relaxed back into her pillow. "You're in college, a great looking girl, and you deserve to have some fun before you graduate into adulthood." She turned the page of her book. "You have to learn to lighten up. The experiences you have now will only come around once in a lifetime." A devilish grin spread across her face. "And why not lose it to someone who really does it for you." She tucked her chin into her shoulder and batted her lashes.

"Okay, enough of that! This conversation is over." I headed for the bathroom.

After cleaning up, I crawled onto my comfy mattress and grabbed my textbook. It didn't take long before my lids drifted shut. I tried to refocus but it happened again. "I'm going to sleep." I snapped my book closed and turned off my lamp. "Good night, Abby."

∞

"Belinda, wake-up." Abby shook my shoulder, awakening me from my dream about Robert and me about to...

I swatted at her. "Go away. You're ruining my dream."

"Your cell phone is ringing. It's Robert!"

"What? What time is it?" I croaked, half-awake.

"Robert's calling." Abby handed me the phone. "It's about eleven."

"H-hello," I stuttered.

"Belinda, it's Robert. Come outside."

"Come outside? I'm in bed." Was he serious?

"Get dressed and come outside. Please."

I inhaled then let out a breath. "Okay. Give me a minute."

Abby gave me a strange look. "What's going on?"

"I have no idea." I slipped into my robe and bunny slippers. About to leave, I put my hand to my mouth to check my breath and then stopped in the bathroom for a quick touchup.

On the porch, I pulled the door shut and then scanned the yard. Robert stood next to the big oak tree off to the side of the house. His face brightened when he saw me.

"What's up?" I clutched my robe tightly around me in an attempt to calm my pounding pulse.

"I'd like to try..." He glanced down at my feet. "Are those bunny slippers?" He snickered.

"They are." I stomped my feet and glanced down at them. "What were you saying? You'd like to try what?" A breeze rustled the tree branches and sent a chill through me.

I wrapped my arms tighter around myself. "I'm getting cold and my bunnies are getting wet."

He shifted his weight. "I'd like to try something."

"Try what?" Now, I was more confused than ever. He was so good-looking, and, in the moonlight, he looked even better. His face and demeanor distracted me, making it difficult to concentrate.

"Let me explain. I also…" He lowered his head, obviously having difficulty trying to explain what he came to tell me. Taking a few seconds, and, without looking at me, he started again. "I also feel something. Your touch excites me…I mean…uh…I feel…oh, I don't know." He gave me a quick glance and continued. "I want to kiss you and see what happens." He stood there observing me. "So, are you game?"

I shook my head and opened my mouth, but the words hitched in my throat. So, I nodded. Of course, I wanted to kiss him.

"But don't tell Garrett about this, okay?"

I nodded again. Evidently, Garrett hadn't told him he backed out and it wasn't my place to tell Robert.

He stepped closer. His hands brushed against mine, causing a tingle. I dropped my arms to my side. He slid his hands up my arms over the material of my robe. The prickle stopped. But having him this close sent my insides into a whirlwind. His hands settled at my waist. His clean scent swirled around my nose. I wanted to faint.

He looked down at me, "You're shorter than I remember."

I pointed to my bunnies. "No heels."

"Of course." A half-smile appeared. "Cute slippers, by the way."

"Thanks." I tried to play it cool on the outside, but, inside, I was a nervous wreck. My mind and heart were running a mile a minute.

He bent down and slid one arm around my waist, pulling me close then lifted me off my feet. I wrapped my arms around his neck. With his other hand, he raised my face up to his. I softened and molded to his body. His touch gave me that tingly feeling again, but when his lips touched mine—Oh! My! God! An overwhelming, intense desire consumed me. Strange feelings I'd never experienced before flooded every inch of my body.

He pulled away and stared at me for a brief moment. The air between us sizzled and crackled with sexual awareness. Then he crushed his mouth against mine, deepening the kiss.

An electrifying surge raced up my spine, firing every neuron. I gasped. My back arched. My body stiffened. My hands slid up the back of his neck, my fingers entwining into his thick hair. I couldn't pull his body close enough. My heart pounded. When I wrapped my legs around him, his hands latched on to my thighs and kneaded them.

Robert's breathing became more ragged, and he pushed me up against the tree. He peppered kisses over every inch of my neck, shooting liquid heat through me.

My back arched again. I tightened my grip around his neck and found his willing mouth, then kept him lip-locked while I savored his intoxicating taste.

His lips devoured mine, slanting one way and then the other.

All of a sudden he pushed away until I was no longer in his arms. Feeling a ripping sensation, I braced myself against the tree.

He stumbled back a step and shook his head. "Whoa! That's never happened before." He panted as if he'd just run a race.

I cupped my burning cheeks. "I'm so embarrassed. I can't believe I did that." My chest heaved. "I need to stay away from you." I turned to run, but he seized my arm and pulled me back against his hard chest. Our lips met and the sensations started again with more intensity.

I found myself losing control in the arms of a stranger and struggled not to let that happen. I pushed him away. We stood staring at each other, sucking in air. He appeared puzzled, his brow drawn and his head cocked. I repeated, "I have to stay away from you." I turned and ran into the house, leaving him standing there with no further explanation.

I ran up to my room and rushed over to the window. Pulling the lace curtain aside, I saw him standing in the front yard with his back to the house. A silhouette of broad shoulders, strong arms, and slender hips were backlit by the street lamp. I ran my fingers over my tingling, swollen lips and relived the events that took place just moments ago. He turned and looked up at me. My heart skipped a beat. We stood staring at each other, neither one of us moving. And then he turned and walked to his car, shaking his head.

Abby joined me at the window. She yawned and rubbed her face. "What did he want?"

I watched Robert drive away. Still reeling and stunned, I continued staring out the window. "He kissed me and my body went berserk. I attacked him and I crossed my line."

Her hand cupped my shoulder. "Are you all right?"

In a muted voice I answered, "He kissed me. I didn't want it to end."

Abby's silence told me she wanted more details. Still dazed, I couldn't talk about it right then. My heart pounded from the thought of him and how he looked in the light, watching me from the yard. "I'm tired right now. I'll tell you about it later."

She knew not to press me if I didn't want to talk.

"You promise? You have to tell me everything." Excitement rose in her tone.

"I promise." I tried keeping my voice calm, considering I was in turmoil over a person I barely knew. This was one time I didn't think I could tell her everything. She would get an abbreviated version.

I crawled back into bed and touched my lips, reliving the kiss over and over again in my mind. Every replay caused my heart to race and my breathing to accelerate. The fantasy was short-lived by the chirp of my cell.

Robert:	Talked to Garrett called. Date back on? Tomorrow night?
Me:	NO
Robert:	Why?
Me:	I can't.

Robert: Why? ☹

Before I answered, I had to think if I really wanted to continue to cross that invisible line I drew in my college sand.

Me: Afraid.
Robert: I promise not to take advantage.
Me: No, me.
Robert: ???
Me: My control.
Robert: I promise, I won't do anything. Give me a chance. ☹
Me: Promise?
Robert: YES

I looked over at Abby. Her nose stuck back in a textbook. Maybe she was right. I tapped in my reply.

Me: Ok
Robert: ☺☺☺

I tapped my finger on the phone. After what I'd experience in Robert's arms, I knew I wanted more. Abby was right. I needed to let loose and I wanted to take a one-way trip to the stars.

I faced Abby. "My date with Robert is back on. I'm not going to be able to sleep." I looked back at the phone still clutched tight in my hand. At that moment, it was my only direct link to Robert.

In bed, I kept replaying the kiss in my mind, not wanting to forget the feelings. Every hour on the hour, I peeked at the clock. My alarm buzzed before my eyelids even closed. I turned it off and wondered what today had planned for me. Then, I closed my eyes.

CHAPTER 6

"BELINDA! WAKE UP. You're going to be late for class." Abby shook at my foot.

I yawned. "What time is it?"

"You have twenty minutes."

"Damn. I didn't reset my alarm." I leaped out of bed, dressed, and flew out the door. I took off running to reach my first class. I couldn't be late. I was never late. Almost to the steps, I heard my cell ringing. I dug in my bag and never slowed my pace. That is until I collided into some one's rock-hard chest and bounced back a step.

I looked up just as the edges of Robert's mouth curled up. "Good morning." He slid his phone into his pocket.

My cell stopped ringing. "Oh, hey. I can't stop." I walked backward. "I'm running late for class."

"Meet me outside the Student Center after you're finished."

"Okay." With only a few minutes left, I took the steps two at a time and sat down just as the professor started his lecture.

Class ended twenty minutes early. Thank heavens. I could barely concentrate. The kiss from the night before, Robert's arms around me, and that fabulous electric sizzle kept my mind far too occupied. All I heard come out of the professor's mouth was, "Blah, blah, blah."

I rushed to the Student Center to wait. The morning sun beat down and I quickly felt the wrath of its direct rays. If I waited out here, I'd look worse than I already did from my mad dash this morning. So, I headed to the Cave, intending to come back outside in plenty of time for my meet with Robert.

My stomach gurgled. Breakfast. After a quick stop at the snack bar, I saw Garrett sitting in the Delt section. Latte in hand, I asked if I could join him.

"Sure, you know you're always welcome." He pulled a chair out.

"Thanks."

I barely got settled when he spoke, "I hear your date is back on with Robert."

"Yeah, but I'm still nervous to be around him." I took a few sips of the steaming brew.

"Don't be. Everything will be all right." He put up two fists. "If he doesn't behave, he'll have to answer to me."

One look at Garrett's arms—I gulped down a big swallow—convinced me Robert would be outmatched. A giggle escaped and was all the encouragement he needed. He continued his crazy antics and had me in stitches until I glanced at my watch. *Shit*! I missed my rendezvous. I stood and guzzled the remaining latte. "Garrett, I have to go meet Robert."

With a toss of the cup in the trash, I headed for the door. To my horror, Robert and Lora walked in holding hands. He didn't look like a guy who had any intention of dating only one girl.

My stomach churned and the coffee soured. I had to be nuts. Matt was right. Robert was a player.

I needed to get the hell out of there. To avoid being seen, I skirted around the interior wall. However, my attempted stealthy escape failed. Robert saw me before I slipped out.

Power-walking toward the library I heard, "Belinda, hold up." I stopped when a hand made contact with my arm. A momentary sense of excitement stirred me. I pulled away from his grasp and sighed and turned to gaze into Robert's glacier blue eyes. I took a deep breath. It was hard to control my urge to stroke his face. I just wanted to kiss him, especially when he gazed at my lips, but held back. This guy's touch did strange things to me, but did I really want to be someone's second string? No, not really, but this was college and everyone dated around. I had to get a grip. We hadn't even had our first date. I needed to wait to see what happens.

After a few seconds, his spell over me broke. Robert's stance stiffened ever so slightly. The expression on his face changed. He became more serious. "Belinda, I waited for you."

"My class let out early and I didn't want to stand in the heat, so I went to the Cave. I planned to go back out, but I lost track of the time. I was on my way when I saw you and Lora come in holding hands." I waited to see his reaction.

His face went blank. He hesitated a few seconds. "I'm sorry." He reached for my arms. I stepped back. He stopped. "She just showed up. I came in looking for you and she followed me. Just before we walked into the Cave, she grabbed my hand." He hesitated for a few seconds. "Look, she doesn't make me feel…like you do." He half-grinned and raised one eyebrow.

Aw, man. I wanted to give him a chance, but how was I supposed to fit into this awkward little threesome? Judging from the way Lora leered at me at the game, my life was on the line and I got the message that I needed to stay clear of her boyfriend.

I looked around for her, expecting her to pop up ready to do me in. "Where is she?"

He tucked a hand in his back pocket. "I left her at the Delt table."

The muscles in my neck tensed at the lame explanation.

He shifted his weight from one foot to the other. "Do you really need to go to the library?"

"Yes, this professor loves to give pop quizzes. I don't have much time to study before class." Was he expecting me to walk back into the Cave, at his side, with Lora sitting there? *Nope. Absolutely not happening.* Even for me, a coed with near-zero dating experience, I knew that was a bad idea.

He lowered his head and rocked back on his heels. "Are we still on for five?"

I sighed and hugged my books to my chest. I might be second choice right now, but if I didn't go out with him, nothing would change. I nodded. "Yes."

His face lit up, pearly whites dominating his face. "Okay."

We stood there just looking at each other. Awkward. I backed up a step. "I really need to get some studying done." I turned on my heels and headed to the library, still unnerved by his touch and the possibility he planned on dating both of us at the same time.

Abby was already there studying. I sat in a chair across from her and pulled out my class notes. I couldn't study. Instead, I absentmindedly doodled Robert's name with little hearts all around the margins as I pondered my situation. My roommate whispered, "Are you excited about your date tonight?"

I leaned toward her. "I'm really nervous. Maybe I should cancel."

"Why?"

I could've included Lora in the whole story, but Abby's voice in my head told me I had no hold on him and this was college. Instead, I gave the abbreviated version. "I just saw him outside and when he touched me…I thought I was going to faint! I felt that arousing sensation again. I just wanted to reach up and kiss him. Abby, what is going on with me?"

She hesitated for a second then gave a quick wave of her hands in front of her face. "It's nothing but hormones. Nothing more than physical attraction."

"But there's some kind of connection here." I white-knuckled the edge of the table. "He told me he feels something too."

Of course, in her infinite wisdom, she would remind me to take it slow and keep it light. Maybe I should've told her about the cozy scene I had witnessed. Then she'd understand my need to run. But how could I ignore that zing? Heat rushed up both sides of my head. "No, it's not! Something more is happening here."

One of the library assistants gave out a soft "Shhh," her way of politely requesting I keep my voice down. I got her point and gathered up my books, giving Abby a dirty look.

Just like I thought, Abby whispered, "Keep it light," and without hesitation, she followed me to class.

∞

I finished dressing in my usual outfit, jeans and a blouse, a few minutes before the doorbell chimed at 5:00. At the bedroom door, I reached for my security shirt, but hesitated and studied it. "Not tonight old friend. Abby has advised me to make some changes." A second bell caused me to fly down the stairs and fling open the door.

There stood Mister Gorgeous with his captivating smile. My heart started racing, butterflies attacked my stomach, and words evaded me. I couldn't believe we were going on a date. Was I his new challenge? And where was Lora? At the moment, I didn't care, and the only word that slipped out of my mouth was a meek, "Hi."

"You ready to go?" His hand reached for mine, but I ignored it.

"Yeah." My voice cracked.

We walked down the steps and started across the lawn. I had to make a conscious effort to keep a little distance between us. All I wanted to do was taste his luscious lips again. It was killing me until I saw the royal blue, two-seater, sports car parked in the street. "Nice car." I had seen it from a distance, but never up close. I stopped to admire it. "What is it?"

"BMW Roadster." He stood beside me and gave the car a lingering once over as if it were a beautiful girl.

"Your parents bought you a BMW Roadster?"

"No. Dad decided he wanted a sedan. I always get my parents' old cars." He eyed his possession. "I like driving it, especially with the top down."

Yeah, I bet. Hot guy in a cool car. Chick magnet. "I've never ridden in a convertible with the top down."

His face lit up. "If it's nice after we leave the restaurant, I'll put it down.

"I'd like that."

With the car several yards away, I thought of doing something I knew Abby would approve of. If I had any chance of keeping this guy's interest, I'd have to be willing to come out of my shell. I needed to flirt. *Like I knew how.* But, I was going to try.

I picked up my pace to put some distance between us. Then I proceeded to get my flirt on by sliding my fingertips over the passenger-side front fender and across the door. All the while, I exaggerated my sassy strut. Once my hand reached the edge of the door, I turned to face him. He stood there with a soft half-smile. His gaze left me breathless and dizzy with desire. I fell back against the car.

He came within inches of me and reached for the door handle. I took a whiff. His woodsy scent tantalized my olfactory nerves. I had an incredible urge to kiss him, but fought it off with all my might.

"Excuse me."

I inched my butt down the side so he could open the door.

"Thank you." He swung the door open. I slip into the passenger seat.

The click of Robert's seatbelt sent my anxiety level soaring. I started to rattle on. "I hope I'm dressed okay. I live in jeans. My whole wardrobe consists of jeans and a variety of tops. They're comfortable." Horrified at how I must've sounded, I stopped talking and sucked in a deep breath to calm myself. "I'm sorry. I'm rambling. I do that when I'm nervous."

He cocked his head. "You wear'em well and they're fine for where we're going."

"A Mexican restaurant?"

"No. Change of plans." He put the car in reverse then placed his right arm over the back of my seat to look out the rear window before backing up. That put his face inches from mine. "I thought we'd go to Uvabianca Bistro. Nicer atmosphere. Is that okay with you?"

I almost stopped breathing. Hesitating to look at him, I answered with a slight crack in my voice. "That's...fine."

"So, why are you nervous?"

"Nervous? I'm not nervous." I reached around my waist for my security shirt to fiddle with the cuff, but it wasn't there. Instead, I flattened my damp palms on my thighs to keep from wringing my hands together.

"Okay. If you say so." He straightened back up and put the car in first gear then glanced in my direction. Heat rushed to my cheeks. He might have noticed because he smiled and changed the subject. That took the attention off me. Thank heaven.

"Garrett said you're from Sugar Land. So am I." He repositioned his right elbow on the back of my seat and rested his hand on the headrest. "I go home occasionally on weekends and for holidays."

"What else did Garrett say about me?" Suddenly I became aware of his fingers playing with my hair. It was a gentle touch, I rather enjoyed.

"Nothing personal. Delts have a code. We don't talk about our dates."

"Oh?" I gazed at him.

He laughed. "No really. He told me he enjoyed your company."

"I see." I changed the subject back to where this all started. "My family moved to Sugar Land the summer before I started high school. They wanted to downsize to save money, so they could put me through college. Thankfully, no college debt for me." To avoid saying something stupid, I clamped my mouth shut the remainder of the way.

At the restaurant, he opened my door and offered his hand. I took it. The minimal contact made my insides stir. He chuckled.

My thoughts raced back to our kiss in the moonlight under the oak tree. My knees almost buckled, but I managed to keep upright. No need to embarrass myself in front of him any more than I already had.

Robert requested a quiet booth. The hostess led us to the back of the restaurant where it was more dimly lit. It had a romantic feel.

After we placed our order, we continued our conversation. "I still can't believe you've been on campus all this time and I've never seen you. And now I see you everywhere. Strange." He appeared puzzled as he leaned back against his seat and crossed his arms over his chest.

"Perhaps I haven't seen or heard of you or your reputation because I spend all my time in class or the library. In the past, I rarely ever went to the Student Center. That's probably why you haven't seen me, either."

He leaned forward and rested his elbows on the table. "My reputation? What did you hear?"

My mouth went dry. Did that really come out of my rambling thoughts? Damn Matt for planting that seed.

"Well?" he asked in a firm tone.

I had to answer him. Do I tell the truth or lie? The truth. "I heard you only date a girl until you get you-know-what and then you leave her."

He frowned, tight-lipped and sat up board straight. "That's not true." He focused on my face. "Belinda. Do you think I sleep with every girl I can?"

Afraid to answer, I curled into the back of the booth like a frightened mouse and shrugged, not knowing who to believe. This conversation was tanking every time I opened my mouth.

He took a minute and looked around the restaurant, then rested against the back of the booth and took a deep breath. His voice softened and he fiddled with his napkin. "I'm sorry." His lashes lifted. "It's just I've heard this before and it really pisses me off when I hear that lie all over again. Who told you this?" A muscle flexed in his cheek.

I didn't want to get Matt in trouble, so I opted for a little white lie. "I heard some girls talking in the restroom."

Robert's reaction to my faux-pas showed me a deeper side of him. I saw the hurt in his face.

I unfolded from my mouse-like posture, feeling more relaxed, yet very stupid. I never seemed to get anything right. How could I be so book-smart, yet not have a brain cell that would allow me to carry on an intelligent conversation with someone of the opposite sex? But, this date was different from any of my others. Maybe that's why I was acting like such a total airhead.

Robert laced his fingers together on the table. His hooded eyes locked on mine for several seconds. Then he looked away for a moment before looking back at me. He seemed deep in thought like he was trying to decide whether to say or do something. Leaning up against the table, he spoke in a hushed tone. "Since you brought up this conversation and seem rather nervous about the subject, I'm guessing you're not like other girls on campus and have never..." The movement of his hands caught my attention. The forefinger and thumb on his right hand formed a circle, and on the other, his middle finger darted through the center.

My face blazed with heat. Oh, shoot. I cupped my cheeks and fell back against my seat. Why did I bring up his sex life? It only made him curious about mine. If I admit I've never done it, would he stop dating me, or would I become a challenge, or would he accept it and not push me to make him my first? I couldn't deny what he insinuated since it was plain as day on my traitorous face. Although I could claim the gesture embarrassed me. But I didn't want to lie. So, I gave a slight nod. I wasn't embarrassed at being a virgin. I was proud of saving myself for the one I loved.

A devilish grin crept across his face. "Hmmm. I've never dated one of *those* before."

Oh, God. I can't believe I just admitted I'm a virgin.

He must have detected my fear since worry lines formed between his eyebrows. He slid a hand, palm up, across the table. "Belinda, I'm kidding. You're safe with me. Relax."

I ignored the hand and just gave him a weak smile. I wanted to trust him.

Our food arrived. We ate in silence, but I felt I was ruining the date.

So, keeping focused on my plate, I spoke first. "Another reason you may not have noticed me before is probably because I didn't look like this my first two years. I changed last summer. I kinda came out of my cocoon. I developed." *Well damn, not again with the stupid confessions.* I briefly lowered and shook my head then glanced up to see his expression.

He stopped eating and watched me. His teeth blazed across his face. "It's hard to believe that you haven't always been this beautiful."

Wow. He thinks I'm beautiful. "You can ask my roommate, Abby. We became best friends my freshman year."

His brows slightly pulled together. "Do you believe in fate?"

I tilted my head and shrugged. "I don't know. Why?"

"Maybe fate kept us apart until now because neither one of us was ready two years ago." He lifted his fork to take a bite of lasagna, but hesitated. "I think I'm more settled now. I don't look at my life the same way anymore. I started making long-term goals."

"What kind of goals?" I twirled spaghetti onto my fork and ate it.

I listened to him lay out his life plan which included his acceptance to grad school. He made it a point to tell me he'd be around for another two years. I realized this guy was nothing like Matt had described. He was strong. He was sensitive. He was smart.

After Robert paid the bill, he got up and extended his hand. "Do you need to go home now?" I ignored his gesture and stood up.

"No, I still have time." I wanted to be with him as long as possible.

"Good. I have one more place in mind." With his hand at my waist, he led me out to his car.

"Where?"

"Surprise. But first I have to lower the top." He winked and a grin slowly spread across his face.

The wind blew through my hair while he drove in a direction unfamiliar to me. The further we drove, the lights of the town faded. All of a sudden, the stars brightened and filled the cloudless night sky. He turned along a winding road that ended at the top of a hill. At the crest, I looked out over the town and college campus, all lit up. The lights flowed up to meet the stars. They were everywhere. The sight took my breath away.

A few other cars were parked along the street. Their steamy windows gave me a good idea of what Robert had on his mind. He pulled onto the grass and parked away from the others.

I admired the sight presented before and above me. "Where are we? It's so beautiful."

"You haven't been here before?"

"No. Is this like...'Lovers Lane'?" My voice faltered.

"Yep. It's known as 'Make Out Ridge.'" He used a slight impish tone.

I whipped my head toward him and frowned. "Why did you bring me here?"

He held up his hands. "Hold on. Look at my car." He motioned around the inside of his vehicle. "Do you think we could do anything in this small space? And with the top down."

I observed our surroundings. "I...guess not. So why?"

"I enjoy talking to you. I like spending time with you." He glanced around. "I thought this would be a nice quiet place to do that." A sliver of a smile spread across his face. "You have to admit..." He stretched his arms out in front of him. "You can't tell me this isn't breathtaking."

I swallowed hard and stiffened, without responding.

"The top stays down. Your virtue is safe. Okay?"

I shrugged and nodded.

We sat in silence, staring up at the flickering points of light.

His voice cut through the air. "You know...I think we're meant to be together."

I swung my head toward him, unsure if I heard right. "What?"

He adjusted his body to face me. "What do you feel when I touch you?"

I chewed on my bottom lip. I couldn't answer that question. I couldn't admit he made my senses go haywire every time we touched. "I...I don't know what you mean."

"Do you feel anything? Does it feel...exciting when I touch you?"

I couldn't believe he expected an answer. What kind of a question was that for a first date? "I like it. Is that what you want to know?" I wrung my hands together in my lap. "Tell me what you feel?"

He sucked in a breath. "At the Delt jail, when I touched your arm, I got this tingly feeling that ran through my fingers. Then when I kissed you, my body went nuts. It was like you jumped into my soul." His glacier irises darkened. "It feels like you're a part of me. I swear our hearts are beating as one."

My mouth fell open. My heart started to race. He described my experience. I swallowed hard. "Robert. I feel the same."

He leaned over and stroked my face. His touch thrilled me, but when his lips pressed against mine, intense feelings of desire rushed over me. I threw my arms around his neck. A flash of heat radiated throughout my entire body. My muscles constricted and my back arched. His body tensed and his hand slid up my neck, his fingers knotting in my hair, pulling me closer. His lips moved against mine. I prayed he'd never stop. When his tongue pressed between my lips, I parted them and his tongue plunged in, exploring then caressing and twisting around mine. When I pressed my hand against his chest, I felt his heart hammering to the pounding beat of mine.

Tantalizing liquid heat surged through me until he abruptly pulled away. Robert fell back into his seat and sucked in air then released it slowly. "Holy shit, Belinda." He shoved his fingers through his hair. It sifted back over his forehead. "I have never experienced anything like this before." He let his arms fall and he sighed.

I sat boneless in my seat, dizzy with my heart racing. "Me either."

I turned to watch him and then reached to trace his lips. Robert leaned toward me again, crushing his mouth against mine in an urgent and demanding kiss. My fingers locked in his hair, holding him close. I slipped my tongue into his mouth to savor his taste. Our tongues explored one another making him groan. I hummed while he swept his through my mouth. The feeling thrilled me. I didn't want it to end, but I had to take control. I pushed him away.

"What's wrong?" He leaned back, catching his breath.

"Nothing. Just an early class tomorrow. I need to go home." I knew if I stayed any longer, it would be very easy for me to give in, even in this confined space. I wasn't ready to go there. And there still was the matter of Lora.

We peered at each other, moving our lips closer with every frantic breath. I was afraid I would find myself lost in his embrace, unable to escape if we made contact again. But, I didn't want to stop.

He moved in and gave me one quick kiss. "Okay." Then he fell back into his seat. "Seatbelt."

"Yeah...seatbelt."

We didn't dare hold hands on the way home. On some level, I suspected he knew that was dangerous.

Our walk to my front door was as quiet as the drive back. On the porch, I turned toward him. "I had a great time." I took a step closer, putting my hand on his firm, warm chest.

"Me, too. But this needs to be goodnight." He took a step back. "I'll wait 'til you go in." He lowered his head.

He seemed different, withdrawn.

Why hadn't he mentioned seeing me again or calling me later? Did I do or say something wrong? Was this the end? But how could it be after all that had just happened? He made no attempt to come closer, so, I had no choice but to say, "Good night," and leave him standing on the porch.

I ran upstairs to talk to Abby, but she was asleep. I undressed and crawled into bed, but sleep evaded me, wondering what went wrong or was it just my imagination.

Around three a.m., I sat at my window and stared up at the stars, just thinking about Robert. I imagined him standing in the yard the first night we'd kissed. He had crept into my soul, and I didn't know how to get him out, nor was I sure I even wanted to.

When morning came, I was too tired and sleepy to get up. I told Abby I planned to skip my morning class and would explain later. I turn my cell off and drifted back to my dreams of being with Robert.

CHAPTER 7

"BELINDA. BELINDA, WAKE up," I barely heard Abby call out. "Are you going to class today?"

"What?" I rolled onto my back.

"Are you going to class today?" she repeated a little louder.

"Of course." Sitting up, I stretched and let out a big yawn. "Why wouldn't I go?"

"You didn't yesterday." She stopped brushing her shoulder-length, auburn hair. "I couldn't reach you all day and when I got home, you were passed out. You were still asleep after I got back from Brent's." She gave her hair another stroke. "I even checked your pulse to make sure you were alive."

Confused, I turned toward her. "What do you mean I missed my classes yesterday? Today's Wednesday."

She shifted around with a dazed look on her face. "Seriously? No, it's Thursday morning." She turned back to the mirror. "That must've been one helluva date." With a half-turn, she grinned at me. "So, when are you going to tell me all the juicy details about Mister Gorgeous?"

My head spun like when your brain is trying to wrap itself around something that isn't right. "Did I really sleep a whole day?"

Abby slipped on her flats. "So, how was your date?"

"I thought it was great. He's nothing like Matt described."

Abby checked her hair, fluffing it. She stopped in mid-fluff. "Really?"

I pulled my knees up to my chest and wrapped my arms around my legs, then started to give her a brief rundown of the night. The main portions of our dinner conversation came first. I described the hurt I saw in his face over the rumor I'd heard regarding his reputation. "The last thing we talked about was our sexual experience and I admitted I was a virgin."

Her hand flew up, splaying fingers over her mouth. "Why did you tell him that?! The first rule of dating is never give out too much information. TMI! Oh, Belinda, tell me more."

I hugged my knees. "He kinda guessed."

Abby plopped, stomach down, on my bed and rested her head in her hands. "Then what happened?" She waved her hand in a circular motion to encourage me to continue.

"Then, he took me to 'Make Out Ridge.'"

Abby's eyes popped wide.

"Oh Abby, when he took me in his arms and kissed me, I thought I'd die." She listened, hanging on every word. "There's something else. I never felt this before. The only way I can describe it is…I feel this very enjoyable buzz, like an electrical charge racing through me. It intensifies when we really get into it. He described almost the same thing." I studied her face, hoping she didn't think I was crazy.

Abby sat there for a few seconds. "Oh." She looked at the clock. "We need to talk about this. I need more details, but I have to go." She gathered up her books. "Are you doing anything Saturday night?"

"Nothing."

"Plan for a girls' night in. We need to do some serious talking before you get into any more trouble." Abby shook her finger at me and walked out the door.

I turned in bed to gaze out the window. It was like I'd never dated before when I was with Robert. I thought I was doing so well with the dating cues Abby had taught me. I'd managed to maintain control over those other dates, but Robert was so different.

∽

After class, I meandered along the path to the library, inhaling the fresh spring air and soaking up the warm rays.

"Belinda, hold up." Matt ran to catch up. "Haven't seen you lately. Are you free tomorrow night to go to a party with me? My date canceled and I need a fill-in."

"Sure." After all, what else did I have planned? Robert didn't say he'd call when we said good night. He probably had a weekend plan with Lora. For all I knew, my relationship with him ended before it even started.

"You look upset. What's wrong?"

"Long story." I waved him off, but Matt had a knack for reading my face.

"Come to the Cave and tell me about it. Maybe I can help." He reached for my hand.

I brushed it off. "Okay, but you're not going to like my story."

I sat with my back to the Delt area and didn't even look to see who was there. Scooting his chair closer to me, Matt draped his arm around my shoulders. "What's wrong? Tell me." He sounded sincere.

Lashes lowered, I huffed. "Pennington…I went out with Robert Pennington." I looked up at Matt and noticed his eyebrows drawn and his lips compressed. "I thought we had a good time, but he just left after the date."

"You're too good for him."

"You think so? I nodded toward the Delt table. "Do you see him?"

Matt glanced behind us. "Nope, but the other one is looking this way."

"Garrett?"

"Yep, and now Pennington just slithered in." He faced me and butted my shoulder. "Play along with me." Before I could say anything, he pulled my chair out and turned it toward him. He placed his hand behind my head, pulling it forward then leaned in and kissed me. And not just a peck. What was Matt trying to do? Ruin what little chance I might have left with Robert, if any.

I pulled away and picked up my books as I stood. "I have to go."

"I'll walk you to class."

I ignored him and hurried to the exit. Why on earth did Matt feel compelled to embarrass me by trying to make me look like a player?

Outside on the sidewalk, I heard, "Hey, Belinda. Wait up."

I spun around to face my idiot friend. "Why did you do that?"

Matt's face read all kinds of confused. "Do what? Show Pennington, he's not the only one who can be a player."

"I'm not a player. I wouldn't even know where to start even if I wanted to," I huffed and started power-walking to my next class.

Matt caught and then walked backward alongside me. "I'm sorry. I just thought I was helping."

"Well, you didn't. In fact, I had a really nice time. Robert was the perfect date." *Until the end.* "He didn't act at all like a player."

He shook his head. "Yeah, like you would know."

Matt was right. How would I know what a player acted like on a date? I had nothing to base any of this on.

In front of the Fine Arts building, he halted. I tried to walk around him. He grabbed my arm. "I'm sorry if I upset you." His hand fell to his side. "I guess this means I blew my chances of you going with me to the party."

A groan escaped my throat because my pursed lips refused to let it out. I should've been mad at Matt, but his intentions were good and I really had nothing better to do. "What time tomorrow night?"

A broad smile stretched across his face. "I'll pick you up at seven. Oh, I almost forgot. It's a pajama party."

"Okay. Sounds like fun."

"I have a pair of leopard print men's pajamas. You wear the top and I'll wear the bottoms."

I looked at him puzzled. "Any top for you?"

He laughed. "You'll have to wait and see. And you? Any bottoms?"

I hiked an eyebrow and strutted away, not responding.

"I'll bring the top to you tomorrow. Meet me in the Cave at ten."

I just gave him a wave of acknowledgment and headed for class.

The sun was setting behind the trees as I approached the front of my house after class. I saw the signature blue BMW parked next door, but no Robert. Thank heaven. I didn't need trying to explain Matt's kiss. I quickened my pace and headed for the porch. About to unlock the door, I heard my name being called. My shoulders sank. "Great," passed my lips in a whisper, but I turned to see Robert jogging across the lawn. He wore a pressed, light blue oxford shirt and jeans that fit very well. He always looked so perfect and handsome.

"I've been trying to call you."

"You have?" I fished my phone out of my purse. "It's turned off. I'm not used to using this thing."

"You turned it off? Why?" His brow furrowed.

"So I could sleep. I slept all day yesterday."

"Oh." He placed one foot on the bottom step of the porch. "That explains why I didn't see you. I saw you with Matt today. Garrett said you looked upset earlier. Is everything all right?"

I straightened my back and lifted my chin. "I'm fine."

He cocked his head, looking a bit surprised at my tone. "What's wrong?"

I huffed. "What are you doing here?"

He shoved his hands into his pockets. "I came to see you."

I didn't know how to answer. Where was Abby when I needed her? "About what?" I stiffened a bit more. I wanted to be sure he knew I wasn't happy.

His head flinched back. "I want to spend some time with you. If you're not busy."

Now, I was confused. "On the porch…you made it seem like you didn't want to see me again."

"No. That's not what I meant."

I clutched my books close to my chest. "So, what did you mean?"

He ran his fingers through his hair. "I had a lot to think about. The date was sort of…I was trying to process everything that happened—the kisses, our reactions."

"So, did you?"

His brow rose. "I think so." Robert came up the stairs and placed his hands on my shoulders.

Abby's voice kept repeating in my head, "TMI! TMI! TMI!" So, fearing I'd start my telltale rambling or stick my foot in my mouth, I just stood and let him talk.

"I know I feel really close to you, more than any other girl, and I definitely want to date you."

My heart skipped a beat. I couldn't believe what I heard. I guess I didn't screw up as badly as I thought. Abby's voice screamed, "Give it time. See what happens. Lora may just go away." I didn't believe for a second Lora would melt into the woodwork. I had a fight on my hands with that one.

I swallowed then took a deep breath, but more of a sigh came out.

"So, how about giving me a Mulligan."

My head tilted to the side. "A what?"

He chuckled. "You don't play golf do you?"

I shook my head.

"It's a do-over."

Abby's recent lecture *Take a Chance* filled my mind. I wanted to try. I wanted to feel his arms around me. I wanted that electric zing. I had nothing to lose except my life at the hands of Lora. I needed to step out of my comfort zone. "Okay. I'll give you…What did you call it? A Mulligan?"

His shoulders relaxed and at the same time, a smile spread from ear to ear. "Can we start tomorrow night?"

Butterflies swirled for a brief second before plunging to the bottom of my stomach. "I can't. I already have plans."

His eyebrows drew together. "With Matt. The Theta Kappa pajama party."

I winced. "Yes. How did you know that?"

"I just put two and two together. Tell him you changed your mind."

"I can't do that!" Although, Matt would probably do that to me if the girl he asked changed her mind.

"Okay, I thought it was worth a shot." He half-smiled. "I have a swim party to go to Saturday afternoon. How about coming with me?" Robert's manner was very direct, almost business-like. I guess he figured he'd better close the deal now or lose out. But, why was he asking me and not Lora?

"Sure."

"I'll pick you up about three."

"Okay."

He rocked back on his heels. "Do you have plans for dinner this evening?"

"Noooo."

"Good. I'll be back at six o'clock." He didn't even wait for a response before he walked away. A take-charge kind of a guy or just wanting to stake his claim. Either way, I had a dinner date.

I turned to open the door. A hand touched my arm and a familiar charge passed through me. I spun around.

"Are you free now?" His hand stayed in place.

I couldn't think. The spark scrambled my thoughts. "I guess so. Why?"

He squeezed my arm a little tighter. "Why not?"

I wiggled my arm free. I needed to think clearly. My recovery time took a few seconds. I went to work reviewing what I needed to do for the next day. One missed day because of this guy was enough. "All right. But." I held up my forefinger. "I can't be out late. I have to study tonight."

"All right. I could get some studying time in myself. It's a bit early for dinner, so how about we hit the library first?"

My heart lifted. "That would be perfect."

"Give me your books." He stacked my books in one arm and then laced his fingers with mine. Even the slightest touch from him excited me. It took all I had to keep walking. I just wanted my lips pressed against his. He looked at our hands, gripped a bit tighter and I swear he puffed out his chest.

"Almost done there?" He snapped his book shut. "I hear a plate of lasagna calling my name."

I cupped my ear. "I don't hear anything."

He smirked and shook his head.

"Yep. I just finished." I arranged my books in a stack. "I guess that means Italian. Where are we going?"

"Back to our old haunt, Uvabianca Bistro."

I nodded and reached for my books. "Good."

"No, ma'am. No girl of mine carries her books."

Girl of his? A second date didn't constitute his girl. Damn dating cues. I couldn't figure out what he planned, one or two girlfriends. And why me? Inexperienced me? *Because of these strange reactions we feel? So confusing.*

During the drive to the restaurant, I figured I'd take a stab and do some digging to feel him out. I turned to face him. "I know I'm not the typical girl you're used to dating. And if you'd rather be with Lora, you can take me home. I'll understand."

He exhaled in a big gust. "What? If I wanted to be with Lora, I would've asked her. Where is this coming from?"

I'd put my foot in my mouth again, but it didn't stop me from continuing. "I guess I'm curious about why I heard that rumor about your reputation." *And Lora.*

"My reputation? Damn that rumor!" He hit the steering wheel and darted his icy blue eyes in my direction. He took in a deep breath and exhaled. "Look, I want to date you. You're not like any other girl I've dated." He reached over and clasped my hand. "You're very different."

The surge heated my skin. He grinned and lifted our hands. "And I want to find out what this is about."

I got his point. "Okay." Nothing else came out. He released my hand. Why couldn't I keep my mouth shut? It was like I had diarrhea of the mouth around him. Maybe I should just stay home on Saturday with Abby for "Girls' Night" instead of going out with him. No way.

I glanced over at Robert. He appeared to be mulling over our conversation. His head slightly shook and a muscle flinched in his jaw.

After killing the engine at the restaurant, he leaned over and pressed his soft lips against my cheek. I felt that all-too-familiar sensation and turned to kiss him. Our lips met and a discharge of what felt like electricity darted up my spine. I put my hand on his chest. "I thought the lasagna called to you?"

He grinned, then exited the car and came around to help me out. I took hold of his hand. He pulled me up into his arms and kissed me, hard and full on the mouth. The zingy surge tantalized my nerve endings. I pushed away and started walking while shaking my finger at him. He hesitated but complied by walking next to me.

Robert didn't just take a seat like most college guys. He stood behind my chair until I was seated. Then before he left he whispered in my ear, "Would you like a drink before dinner?"

Dang, this guy had manners. "White Zinfandel. Please."

As soon as he sat, he got the attention of a waitress and placed our order. With the drink business out of the way, he crossed his arms over his chest and relaxed back into his chair. "So tell me, what's your major?"

I rested my elbows on the table and propped my head in my hands. "Art and Education."

"Double major. Why did you pick those two?"

I explained how I liked to draw and paint and appreciated the many aspects of the art world. I told him I thought teaching would be fun and felt the combination of both fields would be a good fit for me as a career.

Our drinks arrived and I took a sip of my wine. "So, what's your major?" On our last date, we talked about superficial stuff. The small talk two people eating together for the first time do. My faux-pas had halted most of our dinner conversation, so, this was my opportunity to dig deeper.

"Business Management and in two years, I'll have my master's." Robert rested his crossed arms on the table. He became very serious while he divulged his reasons for his major. It was a family decision. His grandfather had started the financial firm, and, with his passing, his father took over. Robert was expected to do the same. He further divulged he looked forward to passing the business to his son someday.

"So, you plan on having a family?" I relaxed into my seat.

"Yeah, isn't that what everyone wants." He made a goofy face. "To have a bunch of mini-mes running around." He leaned back with his arms still crossed over his chest. "I have good parents. They taught me well, and I think I would make a good father."

I fixed my gaze on him. "What about a good husband?" I really wanted to see how he answered this one.

He delayed his answer as if he had to ponder it. "I think I'd make a very good husband to the right woman." He hiked an eyebrow. "Are you game?"

I shot up straight in my seat with a slight flutter in my belly. "What? Did you just ask me to marry you?"

Robert started snickering and broke into a huge smile. Under the smile came a chuckle. He covered his mouth with his hand, trying to control his muffled laughter.

"I'm glad I amuse you so much. Besides, I wouldn't marry you anyway, at least not with such a lame excuse for a proposal. You'd have to give me a big rock for my dainty finger." I gestured, wiggling my fingers in front of his face. "Then, you'd have to get down on your knee. No, mister, I get the whole nine yards or no deal." Dramatically, I crossed my arms and raised my nose in the air. I peeked over at Robert.

He just sat there with his arms crossed over his chest, shaking his head. "Did you ever think about changing your major to Drama?"

I wadded up a napkin and threw it at him.

After talking for the next hour about anything and everything, and several drinks, he asked, "Are you ready to eat? We need to stop drinking on empty stomachs."

"I agree." My wine was starting to make me feel a little light-headed.

Robert asked the hostess for two menus. She stood over Robert's shoulder and pointed out a few menu items he might consider. Watching her, I realized what Garrett meant about Robert being a magnet. She turned to putty and giggled a few times. If he noticed her reactions he never let on. He politely thanked her and then asked what I wanted. He placed our order and turned his full attention back to me.

"I'm looking forward to our date Saturday."

"So am I."

He paused and stared at me. His next statement bewildered me. "Have you ever thought about modeling?"

"NO!" I leaned up against the table. "I don't think I'd be able to strut down a runway with people watching. Kind of unnerving." My mind flashed back to my hideous display in modeling class. No, that was one episode I never wanted to repeat.

"I think you'd be a good model. Your long hair would be a great feature. I really like it. Don't ever cut it." Robert reached across the table and gently fiddled with a few strands. "It's so soft." He then relaxed back into his chair.

"I don't plan to. I hated my hair when it was short."

Our conversation drifted from subject to subject effortlessly as our food arrived and we ate. He had a good sense of humor. I found myself opening up to him, telling him things about myself that I'd never shared with another person. We talked until we were the last people to leave the restaurant.

It was a convertible type of night. Not a cloud in the sky. In the east, a full moon hung. Yeah, perfect convertible weather. We drove off with wheels squealing. I gave him a disapproving look but had to giggle because he was just being such a guy.

Parked in front of my house, he reached over to pull me closer. I leaned away. "I can't. We'll end up taking too long." Robert smirked and hopped out. He opened my door and offered his hand. Without thinking, I took it. He pulled me up into his arms and captured my mouth. I melted.

Tenderly, he ended our kiss. He kept his eyes closed and his breathing was heavier than usual. I watched him as he stood there in his moment of silence—statuesque in the streetlight. Slowly his eyelids lifted and then he walked me to my front door and kissed me very sweetly on my lips.

"I had a nice time. Thanks for dinner." I placed my hands on his shoulders and reached up to kiss him.

He pulled back, avoiding my advance. "Good night. I'll call you later."

I didn't release him right away. My heart thumped. I exhaled. "At least this time there's a follow-up plan."

Robert smirked. "Yes, there is and thanks for the Mulligan."

"Your welcome."

"Go on. Get inside."

I ran upstairs to tell Abby about my day, but she wasn't home. Falling asleep was difficult. I was worried about whether or not I was making a big mistake because I didn't know if Lora was still in the picture.

CHAPTER 8

WE WERE RUNNING late the next morning and there wasn't time to tell Abby about my date. In her consistent fashion, she wanted all the details. After class, I filled her in while we meandered to the Student Center. The most fun I had was watching her mouth drop open when I told her Robert proposed to me.

"Are you going out with him tonight?"

"No, I'm going with Matt to the pajama party, but I'll see him Saturday afternoon. We're going to a swim party. I guess our date for girls' night is off." I checked out Abby's face as we walked up the steps. She seemed unfazed.

"That's okay. We can get together another night." She stopped. "But only if you promise to tell me all the details. I'm crushing on Mr. Gorgeous."

I rolled my eyes and walked into the Student Center.

Brent was sitting at a Theta Kappa table waiting for Abby as we walked in. Robert caught my glance toward the Delt tables and crooked a finger to come over. I shook my head. His lower lip poked out. He looked adorable and my heart fluttered. At the table, to make my staring less obvious, I flipped my hair over to the side that faced everyone behind me. Then I placed my elbow on the surface and rested my chin on my hand. His face softened. I could see Robert and he could see me.

Robert's posture stiffened. His gaze shifted away from me then moved back. Before I could turn and look, Matt surprised me by wrapping his muscular arms around me from behind. I gave Robert a fleeting glance. He didn't look happy.

Matt shoved a plastic bag into my hands. "Here."

I pulled out a crumpled pajama top and held it against myself. The top was about ten inches above my knees. Across the pocket was embroidered Wildcat. I laughed, fingering the stitching and felt my face heat up. With a subtle glance in Robert's direction, I winked. Robert responded with a forced half-grin.

Matt rambled about something until it was time for Abby and me to leave. Sometime, while I was distracted by his raving, Lora came in. She was sitting next to Robert, running her hand through his hair. I tried not to stare. I didn't want him to think I was jealous, but I was.

As we passed, I glanced toward Robert. He looked my way. Time became suspended as I scrutinized him. Our gaze seemed to last forever, but it really only took a few seconds. Lora grabbed his chin, turning his face toward hers. I guess my question had been answered. He planned on dating both of us. I knew I had no right to be envious, but I wished I was in her place.

My stomach remained in knots. I had two hours to finish my art assignment and turn it in before the end of class. The project didn't require much brainpower, which meant too much time for me to think about Lora showering her affections on Robert. Fighting with myself to keep on task, the professor's dismissal came as a welcome relief. I hurried to turn in my work. I had one thing blazing through my head, Robert. Gathering my things before I turned to run out of class, I glanced at Abby. "I'm going back to the Cave to see Robert."

She managed to grab my arm. "Don't be too eager." I nodded my understanding.

Almost to the Student Center, I came to a screeching halt. Robert and Lora strolled out of the building. He had his arm draped over her shoulders. I dashed behind a brick column, sure they hadn't noticed me. I peeked out to watch them. He smiled at her comments and didn't look like a guy who had any intentions of only dating me. They looked like I imagined we appeared together, at ease. Did Robert make all the girls he was with feel comfortable? Was I like all the other girls despite what he said? My stomach flipped. Lora gazed at him with a look of admiration. Robert stared ahead. I turned my back against the column, tilting my head back to avoid being seen as they passed. My need to run became unbearable. When they were out of sight, I ran home to the safety of my room.

Abby was napping. I decided to do the same. The sight of Robert and Lora together kept repeating like a broken record. Sleep came, but it wasn't restful.

A gurgling in my belly woke me. It only took a few seconds before Robert invaded my mind again. The thought of him made me smile until the memory of how nonchalant Lora and he looked made my heart sink like an elevator dropping out of control. I lay in my bed, tormenting myself when a loud rumble from my stomach interrupted. I sat up and looked at Abby. She was on her bed painting her toenails. "How does pizza sound?"

"I don't know. I've never heard a pizza make a sound." She giggled at her lame joke. "Sounds great to me."

We ordered our usual.

While we waited for the food to arrive, we started getting ready for the pajama party. I was preoccupied and still upset until Abby spoke up. "Did you see Robert?"

I heaved a sigh and plopped on my bed. "Yeah. He was leaving with Lora."

She stopped buttoning her pajama top. "You sound upset. Why?"

I shrugged. "I guess I am. Abby, why is this bothering me so much?"

She sat next to me and folded her hand around mine. "Forget about him tonight. We're going to a party. Keep things light and let's go have some fun." After a gentle pat on my hand, she stood up and headed to the closet. She came out holding my outfit, the pajama top. "Now get ready." She tossed it at me.

"Okay." She was right. I needed some fun.

Abby and Brent were also sharing a pair of pajamas. She wore the blue and white striped top with white tights. The Wildcat top and black tights completed my outfit.

Brent arrived first. He honked his horn. Abby picked up her purse. "See ya at the party."

I watched from the window. She met Brent halfway across the yard and jumped into his arms. I admired her. She always seemed so comfortable with the opposite sex.

When Matt arrived, I opened the front door and placed my hand on my hip and struck a pose to show off my outfit. Matt had on the leopard bottoms and a black muscle t-shirt. His well-formed upper arms did him justice as he struck a bodybuilding pose and bulged his bicep. We both laughed. I even managed to forget about Robert and Lora, but that was short-lived.

Over Matt's shoulder, I caught a glimpse of the signature blue BMW pass by with two people inside. Like a shot, Robert and Lora were back on my mind and I wondered if she was the other person in his car.

The party was a great distraction, and, to my surprise, I enjoyed myself. When Matt took me home, he walked me to the front door and planted a juicy kiss on my cheek. "Thanks for going with me. I had a great time."

"I enjoyed it too." I guess he was trying to be funny by slobbering on my face. I wasn't amused. I wiped the spittle off with the sleeve of the pajama top and smirked at him before heading inside.

The soft pillow gave me hope that sleep would come fast. That was not the case. Thoughts of two people in the blue Beamer crept back into my head.

CHAPTER 9

NINE THIRTY SATURDAY morning, I just lay in bed imagining what my evening with Robert would be like. The reality of what I'd seen last night invaded my fantasy. *Was that Lora with him*? I couldn't be upset. After all, I had been with Matt. I shook my head to clear all the negative thoughts, determined nothing would spoil my date with Robert. Not even me.

Time was my enemy. I needed to keep myself busy, so, I rummaged through my dresser for my bathing suit and cover-up. My suit was a seafoam green bandeau-style two-piece, not an itsy-bitsy bikini. The cover-up was a two-piece terry cloth set, shorts and jacket in the same color. I decided to wear my mules and hoped I'd be above par compared to the other girls attending.

Why did our next date have to be so challenging? I hated the thought of a bunch of scantily-clad females strutting around Robert and didn't need the competition. STOP! I clasped my head and shook it to get those thoughts out.

Thank heaven Abby woke up and halted my fixation. "I'm hungry. Let's go grab something to eat." She jumped out of bed and dashed around the room. She had entirely too much energy in the morning. I liked to linger and wake up slowly, but not Abby. She hit the floor running.

"Me too. How about pancakes?" I loved pancakes.

We decided to go to our favorite diner up a block, across the street on Main. The traffic light prevented us from crossing right away. That's when I saw the blue roadster fly by. I clearly saw Robert, but couldn't make out the passenger. My heart sank and my thoughts went berserk. Did he spend the night with Lora? The thought made my stomach churn.

The aroma of my favorite breakfast almost made me gag when I opened the door to the diner. I managed to order my food without drawing any attention from Abby and then descended into my own world of torment.

She snapped her fingers in front of my face. "Belinda, pay attention."

"Two heads last night, two heads this morning. Who was with him? The same person?"

Abby leaned forward and steepled her fingers. "What are you talking about?" Abby threw her hands into the air. "Oh, never mind. I'm sure this has something to do with Robert and Lora."

I slumped back in my seat. "When I was leaving with Matt last night, Robert drove by and there were two people in the car. Then when we were standing on the corner, I saw the Beamer, and I'm certain I saw two people."

"Could you see who was with him?"

I shook my head.

"Quit thinking about it. You're going to drive yourself crazy. You know he lives with a bunch of guys at the frat house. It could've been one of them."

"You're right. Today is my day with him." I attempted to brush off the feelings, but my nagging thoughts still haunted me while I forced myself to eat.

The pancakes did the trick, and they were great comfort food. Abby and I rolled ourselves out of the restaurant, very satisfied.

We were about to cross the street, in front of the house, when I notice the roadster parked next door.

Abby spotted it too. "Well, are you going?"

My first impulse was to run over there, but I managed to maintain control despite my jittery nerves. "No, I'll see him at three."

"Good choice. Don't be eager." Abby headed upstairs in front of me. "I hear music coming from the room."

I rushed past her. The tune stopped just as I picked up my cell off my bed.

She followed and stood next to me. "Who was it? Robert?"

"Yep." I flopped down on my mattress, scrutinizing the phone.

"Are you going to call him back?" Abby sat on her bed, facing me.

"Nope. If he wants to talk to me, he can call back." I tossed it back on the bed and stared at it, wishing the stupid thing would ring.

"Playing hard to get, huh?" Her smirk reeked with satisfaction.

I controlled my impulse to pick up the damn thing and return the call.

The clock read twelve noon. Now, along with my torment, I had to kill time. I thought about sitting and reading under the oak tree. Instead, I chose to stay indoors and keep myself busy by taking a relaxing bath, painting my nails, and anything else to keep myself occupied.

Time crept by. I couldn't stand it any longer, so I got dressed. With my suit on and my hair braided, I strutted out of the bathroom. Abby was lying on her bed reading a romance novel. She looked up and chuckled as I stood in front of the full-length mirror. Twisting and turning, I kept checking myself from every angle. I wanted to look my best and make a lasting impression on Robert.

The girl in the mirror was someone who was told she was attractive, but, inside her lived a girl who couldn't convince herself of it.

"You look terrific. You'll keep his attention, along with all the other Delts. And you'll have all their girlfriends wanting to strangle you."

Shifting my weight from side to side, I ignored her warning about my possible demise. "Does it really look okay?"

She sat up on her folded legs. "Definitely. You need to quit seeing yourself as the old you. Focus on what you see in that mirror."

"It's hard. I was that invisible person for so long it's hard to believe what I see is me."

The first few bars of "Forever in My Mind," my favorite song and the ringtone I assigned to Robert, played from my cell again. I walked over to my bed, then took a deep breath before answering with attitude. "Hello, Robert."

"Hi. I saw you and Abby on the corner this morning."

"We were on our way to breakfast."

"Is three o'clock still okay?"

"Yes!" I wasn't about to tell him I was ready now. He didn't deserve the satisfaction of knowing I was eager and he had me twisted in knots.

"Is everything okay? You sound—"

"Yeah," I interrupted. "I'm fine. I'll see you then." And, with a push of a button, the call ended.

Folding her arms across her chest, Abby looked up through her lashes, furrowing her brow. "Be nice." She reminded me that I didn't have any claim on him, and I also had a date last night. In only a pajama top no less.

She was right. I needed to be nice if I wanted to keep him around. He could have any girl he wanted, so why should he put up with me and all my insecurities? My insides tensed and my stomach roiled.

The digital clock, next to my bed, assaulted me with every passing minute, a constant reminder of how much time I had left until Robert's arrival.

I sat close to the window. At three o'clock sharp, Robert pulled into the driveway. My heart skipped a beat. When the doorbell rang, Abby mumbled, "Keep it light. Be nice, have fun, and strut your stuff."

I huffed and grabbed my bag. "See you later."

At the front door, I paused, took in a deep breath and plastered a broad smile across my face as I swung it open. I'd hoped my expression would camouflage the torment I'd been placing on myself over this damn date.

There he stood in his trunks and an unbuttoned sports shirt which displayed the most attractive six-pack of golden, taut skin.

I just stared, speechless. Be still my heart. I thought I'd faint right then. I started to think a swim party may not be the best idea. There was just too much-exposed skin between the two of us.

"Belinda, eyes up here." He took off his sunglasses and flashed me a drop-dead smile. "Aaah, you look great." A slight crook formed on his mouth when he gave me the once-over. He pulled my braid. "I like your hair."

He made me uncomfortable and I thought about pulling my cover-up closed, but stopped myself. "Thanks." I gave him a quick kiss and made a conscious effort to avoid his chest. Nevertheless, the thrill of arousal welled in my soul. I maintained control and then headed down the steps toward the car.

The first part of the drive felt awkward with neither of us saying a word. I was dying to know if he was with Lora last night, but I was too chicken to say anything. Luckily, Robert broke the silence. "Did you have fun last night?"

"Yes. Did you?" I barked, watching him.

He briefly darted daggers my way.

"I saw you with Lora." I took a wild guess.

"We just went out to eat and to a movie. Then I took her home." His defensive tone matched his blanched grip on the steering wheel.

I twisted in the seat more toward him. "Well. Did you have fun?" Of course, I wanted to fish for more information. It upset me he went out with her last night, after all he had said to me the previous night, but I had to keep myself calm. I didn't want him to know how much his relationship with her drove me nuts. "Monster" raised her head. Jealous? You bet I was jealous. Matt and I were friends, but we were never intimate and that made our relationship different.

"No!" he spat out and glanced at me with a frown. "I kept thinking about you in that damn short top at the pajama party with him."

I flinched at his tone. I didn't know what to say. His response shocked me, so I kept my mouth shut the rest of the way.

In the past twenty-four hours, I had managed to make myself miserable thinking about all the scenarios that could play out in my story with Robert. This was a flaw of mine. I always stirred up turmoil within myself. I had to work at keeping things light. Most of the time I succeeded, but, with him, my mind went into overdrive and I had to stop.

We drove up to a two-story house surrounded by huge pine trees. "What are their names? I forgot."

He killed the engine. "Russell and Cheryl."

"Russell, Cheryl. The man is Cheryl and the woman is Russell?" He looked at me like I was crazy, but I managed to keep a straight face. Bursting out with a short laugh, more like a grunt, he understood my attempt at a joke to break the ice. After all, I needed to keep it light.

We walked around to the backyard where a crowd had gathered on a nice-sized patio. Robert introduced me to Russell and Cheryl, a very pleasant couple. We shook hands and I used their appropriate names. I nudged Robert and smirked. "Got the names right." We laughed. Laughing felt good.

We claimed two lounge chairs next to the pool. I looked around at the other girls to check out their bathing suits. Most were modest like mine, except for two that were embarrassing to look at. Feeling a little more confident, I removed my jacket and shorts. Someone yelled, "Robert, she's HOT!" I glanced around and stopped on Robert.

Robert didn't help. He stood staring at me with his arms crossed and a hint of a smile on his face. "WOW! You do look hot."

My discomfort level soared. I didn't like displaying myself like this in public. I started to reach for my cover-up top but stopped. Abby's voice screamed in my head until I had no alternative but to, "Keep it light."

"Thanks." Even his stare made my skin prickle and I wanted so badly to crush my lips against his, but I didn't dare. A slight breeze filled the air with his scent. I needed a diversion.

Water! The water could be my concealer. I stepped out of my mules, strolled to the deep end of the pool and dove in. When I broke the surface, Robert was seated on the edge at the shallow end. I scanned around. No one but Robert was watching me. This would work and when I got out, I'd have a big towel to wrap up in.

Being the only one in the pool, I decided it needed more people and it would start with Robert. So, I swam toward him.

"Help me out." I extended my hand. The second he took it, I gave him a yank. He hit the water with a splash and went under. I took the opportunity to escape and looked back to see his devilish grin.

"You're in for it now." Lunging toward me, he missed.

Halfway across the pool, Garrett popped up and scared the daylights out of me. My first reaction was to dunk him, but he took off. Bound to pay him back, I went after him.

When I came up for air, I fully expected to see Robert closing in. Instead, he had stopped to talk...no, flirt...with the two scantily clad girls sitting on the edge with their feet dangling in the water. With them leaning toward Robert, they looked like they were about to fall out of the tiny fabric triangles. I felt as green as my swimsuit and let "Monster" out of her lair. My blood bubbled.

I climbed out of the pool as my "Flight or Fight" response kicked in. I hated confrontations. I snatched up my towel and marched toward the best place to hide, the house.

Garrett yelled, "Hey, where you goin'?"

I ignored him and flung open the back door.

Cheryl was bustling around the kitchen prepping food.

"Can I help you?" I stood along the edge of the island.

"Don't you have a date out by the pool?" She picked up a towel and began to wipe drops of water off a washed bowl.

"Robert's preoccupied right now." I guess I looked like a soaking wet puppy dog with my wet hair.

She stopped wiping the bowl. "Oh." Her tone filled with understanding. "Girls always flock around him and he's too nice of a guy to be rude to anyone. Don't let it bother you. He came with you."

But it did bother me. Big time. He brought me and flirted with them. How would he like it if I did the same to him? Except, I'd never do that to him or any date. I'd bet she didn't know he was cheating on Lora.

Cheryl slid the bowl across the island countertop. "Here, put the chips in this."

The back door opened and Robert peeked in. "Belinda. Why'd you come in here?"

"You were *obviously* busy," I hissed. "So I came in to help Cheryl." I couldn't give him the real reason, that I was jealous and let "Monster" escape her hole.

He grimaced and extended his hand. "Sorry, come back out with me."

"No, I'm helping. You go talk to your girlfriends." I poured out the chips.

He appeared perplexed by my attitude. He turned his attention to Cheryl. "What can I do to help?"

Cheryl studied the two of us. She handed him a tray of food and told him to put it on the table outside. Turning toward me, she handed me another and said she'd finish the rest. "Go be with him." Her eyes grew larger to emphasize the point. "He's not doing anything intentionally."

Oh, really! "Then why do it at all?" I took the tray and marched out.

Reluctantly, I followed him to the table where we left the trays.

Robert slipped an arm around my waist, and then lifted my chin. "Sorry, I upset you. It won't happen again." Pressing his lips to mine, I got a shooting feeling up my back and pulled away. He understood and raised his hands. He took a step back, giving me more room.

I thanked him with a nod.

"I missed you Friday," he said as we walked to our lounge chairs.

"I headed to the Student Center to see you, but you were leaving with Lora." I didn't want to tell him I watched him put his arm around her and how it made me feel.

"Her class is in the building next to mine." He stared into my eyes, commanding my attention. "Look…I know you're having fun dating around, but I don't like it. I don't want to share you with other guys."

His statement stunned me and I heard myself responding, but it felt right. "I feel the same way. I…I don't like seeing you with other girls." I wanted to add, especially Lora. I pointed out, "You know, I can do what you do. We don't have any ties on each other."

He scowled and shook his head, seeming to understand what I meant. He led me to the pool and we waded to the deep end.

I wrapped my legs around his waist and my arms around his neck, fusing myself to him.

His arms encircled me. Only our heads remained above the water. His lips touched mine and my body quivered. When the kiss became more intense, he took us underwater. We came up gasping.

Robert brushed a few loose strands of hair behind my ear. "I love how we respond to each other. I get this very pleasant buzz when I touch you. But when we kiss, it's like every part of my body comes alive."

I could tell.

"You can't imagine how…how hard it is to stop." He reached up, placing his hand on the back of my head and pulled my face close to his. "Belinda Davies, I'm in love with you." He leaned away, never releasing my head or looking away.

Abby's Keep it Light speech entered my head. Were we moving too fast? Did I want to slow down? Hell no. I fell in love with him the first day I saw him. I wanted to be with him the rest of my life. So, to hell with Abby's speech. And Lora.

Heat swept through my veins as his words filled my ears. "I love you, too." I pushed a hand against his chest. "But what about Lora?"

His dark intense eyes still held mine. "I ended it last night." He placed his lips to mine, then pulled my head closer, crushing our mouths together. With a searching tongue, he explored my mouth, heightening my lust for him.

The rush of adrenaline caused my girl parts to tingle. I almost forgot we weren't alone when Robert took us underwater. We remained lip-locked for as long as we both could hold our breath.

When we surfaced, I pulled away and raised my hands, backing up to give me more space. He acknowledged the gesture with a nod. My heart beat like I'd run a marathon. Taking short, ragged breaths, I mouthed, "I will always love you," before turning to swim across the pool to where Garrett sat on the edge of the shallow end.

Robert caught up and stood behind me with his arms wrapped around my waist, resting his head on my shoulder. I shivered. "Garrett, I never thanked you for stepping aside and letting Belinda and me date. I owe you, bro." He squeezed a bit harder. "I'm in love with this girl."

I turned to face Robert. "Are you sure? We've only known each other a few weeks."

"I've never been more positive about anything in my life. You're on my mind constantly. As I said before, I don't like sharing you." He gave me a slight tug. The heat from his body warmed me despite the coolness of the water.

My heart soared and I planted an open mouth kiss on his lips. My body reacted and we collapsed back, underwater until we bobbed up chuckling and gasping for air.

"Would you accept a sweetheart pin?" he whispered in my ear.

Again, without giving his question a second thought, I responded in an almost inaudible voice. "Yes. Absolutely."

Garrett, still perched on the edge of the pool, watched the show unfold in front of him. In our threesome cocoon, I said, "He wants to pin me. Am I dreaming?" Garrett only shook his head. A little voice in my head warned me, keep it light. I dismissed it. I didn't care. I loved him.

"Garrett, let's keep this a secret right now. I'll arrange for a pinning ceremony." Robert looked at me for approval. I had one stipulation. I wanted to tell Abby and bring her. Robert made me promise she would be the only one I'd tell for now.

Russell announced, "Hamburgers are ready. Come and get'em." The hungry partygoers converged around the tables, picking out their choices of the available foods. During the meal, Russell changed the tone of the music. His selections were more romantic and suitable for conversation.

The three of us sat on our lounge chairs and ate. Curiosity got the better of me. "Garrett, why didn't you bring a date?"

"I haven't met anyone else I'd like to date." He looked at me and half-smiled, and then wolfed down a bite of hamburger.

I swallowed my bite of food. "You know, I think you'd like my roommate, Abby. She's dating someone, but I don't think it's serious. I'll talk to her about you. Is that okay?"

"She's pretty. You've seen her with Belinda at the Theta Kappa tables." Then he described Abby to Garrett with just a hint of too much enthusiasm. "She's got a good build and auburn hair. Nice green eyes, too."

I stopped eating and glared at Robert.

He responded innocently. "What?"

Garrett laughed. "You two sound like an old married couple, and, yes, talk to Abby."

After the used plates found their way into trash cans, Russell changed the music to a lively tempo. The beer, wine, and anything else the frat brothers snuck in flowed freely, and the excitement of the night heightened. The swimming pool lay abandoned with the guests utilizing the dance area, moving to the beat of the music.

A slow song started. I reached for Garrett's hand and pulled him up to dance. "Robert thanked you. I also need to thank you for bringing us together."

He tightened his grip around my waist and glided me around to the music. "If things don't work out, I'll be here for you."

"Not if you and Abby get together." I smiled up at him as his gaze darted over my shoulder and his face contorted. "What's wrong?" I turned at the waist. The bikini girls each had one of Robert's arms, trying to pull him out of his chair. He resisted, shaking his head. I wondered if this was something I'd have to get used to. I'd really have to keep Monster under control and trust him. They finally gave up.

He winked and saluted.

I nodded and smiled.

The song ended and a hot tempo piece started. Robert jumped out of his chair and took me out of Garrett's arms. "This is my dance." Just like the first time, we moved together in a tandem rhythm.

∞

The car came to a halt. As soon as the engine died, Robert twisted toward me and blurted out, "Stay with me tonight."

That little statement set off a huge alarm, rendering me speechless. He didn't know how hard it was for me to say no to his advances. My mind said no, but my body screamed yes. Maybe the time to show him how much I loved him had arrived, but not tonight. Surprising him the night we're pinned would make the event more special and memorable. This decision needed more consideration. It was a big step and I didn't know if I was ready.

"I can't. I'm not staying in a frat house and taking the 'walk of shame' in the morning." Then it dawned on me. If I surprised him by giving in after the pinning, our only other options would be his car or a motel. No way!

"Yeah, you're right." Robert hit the steering wheel with both palms. "I need to move into an apartment."

I didn't need to worry. It'd be impossible for him to find an apartment mid-year in this college town. This would take him some time. Nope. My virtue was safe until I was ready.

With a silly grin on his face, he moved the steering wheel out of the way and invited me across his lap. I made him button his shirt before maneuvering myself into his arms.

In no time, fog formed on the windows from our heavy breathing. Robert rested his head back, filling his lungs. "I need to go. I'll call you in the morning." He helped me out of his car and walked me to the door. "I love you." He gave me a quick, gentle kiss. "Good night."

"I love you, too. Good night." I hugged him. Against every fiber of my soul, I released him and went into the house.

Abby looked up from the novel she was reading in bed. "How was the party?"

I could hardly contain myself. I threw my stuff on the bed and jumped on hers, folding my legs underneath me. "Unbelievable! Great! Terrific! You'll never guess what happened! But first, how would you like to go out with Garrett sometime? He's a senior and he'll be going to grad school, so he'll be around for at least two more years. He's not dating anyone in particular, and he said he'd like to go out with you. You interested?"

"Sure. From what you've told me, he seems nice and he's cute. Besides, things with Brent are tanking. It's time for a change.

"Well, this is great timing then. Now for the unbelievable news." I stalled to add more effect. "Robert said he's in love with me and we're getting pinned. I'm so excited," I shrilled, bouncing up and down, and bubbling over with joy. "I'm crazy about him and he feels the same."

Abby sat with a dumbfounded look on her face. It seemed to take her a few minutes to grasp what I'd just rattled off.

"Do you want to come to the ceremony? I'm not sure when it is. I'll let you know later."

She looked down at the bed. I could tell she was trying to figure out what happened to the "keeping it light" part of my relationship with Robert. Then she looked up. "You bet I want to come. Who cares if you can't keep it light. I'm so happy for you." Our cheeks squished together when she placed her arms around my neck. "Ah, what about Lora?"

"It's over."

CHAPTER 10

BURNING EMBERS IN my heart made my body hum. I relived every wonderful second of yesterday evening. He loved me and I loved him. I found it hard to believe all of this was happening.

At 10:30, the familiar sound from my cell indicated I had a text message from Robert. You awake? I replied yes, then lay back on the bed and waited while tiny wings circled inside my belly.

Within seconds he responded. He asked me to meet him in thirty minutes at the frat house to help him move to an apartment.

I shot to a sitting position and reread the text to make sure I hadn't misread it. How on earth did he get one so fast? I could be in BIG trouble. Was I ready to give in? I didn't know if I'd be able to control myself if we had a bed and privacy at our disposal. He had to be moving in with someone else, and a roommate could always be used as an excuse for not spending the night. I decided I had nothing to worry about.

I slipped out of bed, pulled my hair back into a ponytail, and threw on shorts, a knit top, and sneakers. I tiptoed around trying not to awaken Abby. I left her a note, picked up two large suitcases for packing, and flew out the door to my car and left.

"You're late." Robert pointed to his watch and grinned. "It's been thirty-three minutes." His strong hands grasped my waist and he swung me around, then kissed me tenderly on the lips. I took in the pleasant sensation of his touch. "Let's go for breakfast first."

"Good. I'm starving. I didn't get to eat much last night. Someone kept me busy with other things," Just joking, I poked him in the side on the way to his car. I was dying to know about the apartment but decided to wait and see if he offered the information.

"What do you want?" He started the engine.

"Pancakes. I love pancakes."

"As much as you love me?" he teased. "Pancakes sound good to me, too."

Robert ribbed me relentlessly about my grumbling stomach until the food arrived. I took a few bites. He hadn't said a word about his new place, so, I started the conversation. "How'd you get an apartment so fast?"

He swallowed. "I remembered Paul wanted to live in the frat house. He was there last night when I got home. I asked if he'd be interested in swapping and he said yes. So, we decided to switch today."

"Are you going to have a roommate?" I forked another bite, praying he'd say yes.

"Nope. I have the whole place to myself. That is…unless you're interested." I slowly turned my head toward him. He looked at me, rocking his eyebrows in a rapid motion. "We'll have all the privacy we want."

My heart skipped a beat. I swear his irises turned deep ocean blue. He expected an answer. *Oh, God.* My earlier fears were coming true. Now, I had a real problem. The roommate excuse just flew out the window. I wouldn't be able to say no to spending the night. Shoving a bite of pancake into my mouth, I chewed as long as I could to give me more time to think. I glanced over at him. He waited patiently for me to swallow. Robert wasn't joking around like he did on the first date. When I couldn't chew any longer, I just swallowed and sat there. I really didn't want to address the awkward suggestion about us living together, and he seemed to have figured it out. He dropped the subject and smirked then took a bite.

I cleared my throat. "I brought two large suitcases you can use."

"Thanks for helping. My car doesn't hold much. It would've taken all day moving a few things at a time. With your car and help, we'll finish faster. Then I can spend more time with you."

"Glad to help." I lifted my forkful of syrup-laden pancake. "Where is this place?"

"Close to campus. Within walking distance. I think you'll like it."

When we arrived at the frat house, there was a stack of boxes piled in the hallway. I assumed it was all of Paul's stuff. Earlier, Robert had told me he had helped him vacate his apartment.

We packed all of Robert's belongings and loaded everything into the two cars. Robert's car was a joke. He put the top down to load more stuff in the passenger seat. He barely fit, leaning over into the driver's side door.

Thank heaven the apartment was only a few blocks away. We pulled up in front of a large Victorian-style house. Robert tossed me the keys. "My place is the first door to the right." He started unloading boxes.

I took hold of the two suitcases and wheeled them up the sidewalk, admiring the house. It was rather impressive with its huge wraparound front porch. Rocking chairs flanked the front door, which had ornate etched glass windows surrounding it.

Robert's apartment came furnished. A decent-sized room served as the living, dining, and kitchen area. To the left of the kitchen were a small but adequate bedroom and bathroom. The stained wood trim created a warm feeling that blended with the hardwood floors.

The living room area had a wood-burning fireplace. It would come in handy for those cold days and romantic nights. The updated kitchen came with everything needed to cook a meal.

It was a place I could feel comfortable in. It was a place I could call home, but it wasn't mine. It was Robert's. I came here to help him move in and, from the looks of things, give the place a good cleaning.

I walked around, checking things out, and noticed a vase decorated with a red bow sitting on the table in front of the windows. It held a single red rose. Next to it laid a handwritten note with small red hearts drawn on it. It simply read, *To New Beginnings, Love Robert*. My pulse jumped. This was the sweetest thing anyone had ever done for me. No one had ever given me flowers.

The door flew open. Robert stomped in juggling several boxes in his arms. "Good, you found it. I hope you like it."

I clasped the note close to my heart. "I love it as much as I love you."

He stacked the boxes by the door. I threw my arms around his neck. We kissed. That familiar electric sizzle rushed up my spine. I didn't want to let go, and, I could tell, Robert didn't want to either.

Things could've gotten out of control, but I didn't let it. "While you're unpacking, I'm going to clean the kitchen and bathroom." I patted his chest and took a few steps back. "Go get the rest of your stuff out of the cars. It's supposed to rain."

He whispered, "Later," and attempted to pull me close again. I put my hands on his chest, holding him off. Tilting my head, I raised an eyebrow to let him know I meant business. He complied with a sigh and walked to the door. With a hand on the knob, he turned and mouthed, "Later." This time it held a totally different meaning.

I found rubber gloves and a cleaning solution under the kitchen sink and started to work. With the gathering clouds growing darker, Robert rushed to get everything unloaded before the forecasted evening's rain started.

Robert puffed, stacking the last load from my car. "You don't need to do that. Relax. You're not here to be my maid."

"Oh, yes I do. Have you seen everything in here?" I rubbed my glove-clad hand over the kitchen counter and made a face at the grime I lifted. "I even had to wash all the dishes."

Robert smiled and shrugged his shoulders. "I don't cook. It wouldn't bother me."

"Ew."

I finally finished cleaning at about 5:30. "Your maid is starving and exhausted." Sighing dramatically, I peeled off the rubber gloves and tossed them in the trash can. "I never want to see those things again."

Robert stepped out of the bedroom where he was unpacking his clothes. "What are you hungry for?"

"I'm too tired to go out. Just order anything."

I walked into the bedroom to help unpack. I took some t-shirts out of a suitcase and walked over to the dresser to put them in. When I opened the top drawer, Robert told me to put them in the third drawer down. I placed them in the drawer as instructed. I picked up some of his shirts he had on hangers and walked over to the closet. He told me to place the hangers on the right side. The whole left side remained empty.

With everything done, the two top drawers of the dresser remained empty and the left side of the closet had nothing hanging in it. His place. His clothes. He told me to go relax while he finished unpacking his stuff in the bathroom.

Rain beat against the windows in a rhythmic pattern. The thick black clouds made the evening sky darker than usual. The only lamp on in the living room cast a dim glow, giving the room a warm and cozy aura. I let my hair out of the ponytail and went to the couch to stretch out. The well-worn leather was comfortable and clean, thank heaven. It didn't take long to fall asleep.

"Belinda. Angel. The food's here. Wake up."

My eyelids fluttered then opened. *Angel*? I was confused for a second. Who called me Angel? Robert knelt next to me and gently brushed strands of hair away from my face. "How long did I sleep?"

"About an hour. Sit up." He sat down and pulled me back so my head rested on his lap.

It was spring and with the rain, the night turned cool. Robert had lit a fire in the fireplace. The faint smell of burning oak filled the room. I looked at his face and studied his striking features in the dim light of the flickering flames. I reached out to touch his cheek and ran my fingers down the side of his face. Sensual awareness moved me. Robert bent over to kiss me. Unsure of where a simple kiss could lead, I put my hand on his chest to stop him. "I'm starving."

He stopped in mid-bend. "Okay. We wouldn't want our food to get cold."

We ate in front of the fireplace and drank most of the bottle of wine Robert had picked up earlier. We talked and laughed, asking each other questions about one another. After we ate, I lay on the couch with my head on his lap watching the mesmerizing flames flicker and dance as he stroked my hair.

"Thank you for all your help." His voice sounded soft and tender.

"My pleasure. I enjoyed it."

After several seconds, the dreaded question came out of his mouth. "Will you stay with me tonight?"

I hesitated and stopped breathing with a small gasp. His hand stopped stroking my hair. Feeling him looking at me, I had to ask myself if I could keep my hands off him. I rolled onto my back. "I don't think that's a good idea. I'm not ready." My breath seized. I never wanted anything more in my life.

His fingers brushed the side of my face. "Can we just sleep together?"

Could we do that? "Just sleep?"

"Yes."

A volcano erupted in me. Could I be in the same bed? I'd have to muster all the strength I had, but I couldn't bring myself to say no. "Okay. But I don't have any clothes for tomorrow or my books."

"Let's go get them now." He shifted his position like he wanted up.

Rain pounded against the windows. "Maybe we should wait for the rain to slow down."

"No. Now's good."

I sat up. "You're a little eager, aren't you?"

"Who me?" Robert grinned. "Come on, let's go." He jumped up, hauling me with him.

By the time we reached my place, the rain had slowed to a sprinkle. Robert waited in the car while I ran in to grab everything I needed. Abby wasn't home, so I left an updated note.

At his apartment, I threw my stuff on the bed and headed for the bathroom. "I get the clean shower first."

"Can I join you?" I slammed the door in his face and locked it. Message delivered loud and clear.

Warm, relaxing water cascaded over me, washing the soap and grime down the drain. I reached for one of his plush towels and started rubbing it all over my body. The softness set my mind in motion, imagining it was Robert's hands. Goosebumps prickled my skin and my lady parts raged. Wow. I dropped the towel and got my mind back on track. Something to wear. I dug in my bag for my jams. Nothing. I dug again, moving the contents from side to side. Nothing. I dumped everything on the floor and rummaged through the pile. Damn. "Robert, I forgot my pajamas. Can I borrow one of your t-shirts?" I shouted from behind the door.

"Sure, help yourself."

"What?" Surely he wasn't going to make me parade around in a towel. "Can you, please, get me one?"

"NOPE. You know where they are."

He is. "Robert Pennington Junior. *Please* get me a t-shirt."

Again, a simple "Nope."

I picked up the towel and wrapped it around me, took a deep breath, and opened the door. Robert lay on the bed looking through a magazine. I tiptoed quickly over to the dresser. He didn't move. I snatched a t-shirt from the drawer then ran back into the bathroom. The tee barely covered my ass, but I had to live with it. I picked up my stuff and opened the door.

Without looking up from his magazine, Robert pointed to the chest of drawers. "Put your things in the first two. They're yours."

I froze and stood silent for a moment. As instructed, I padded over and placed my clean clothes in the top drawers. I turned around, but, before I could say anything, Robert proclaimed, "My turn." He jumped off the bed and headed for the bathroom, shutting and locking the door. That made me giggle.

I crawled between the fresh, clean sheets, laying claim to the right side and fell asleep within minutes.

The movement of Robert crawling into bed behind me stirred me. His strong arm reached over and pulled me close. Warmth radiate to my back. He whispered, "Sexy t-shirt. It never looked better."

"I thought you were too busy reading to notice."

He kissed the back of my head. "I took a peek while you were putting your things away. I did, however, prefer the towel look more." He tugged me closer and gave me another kiss. "Good night, Angel."

Angel? I felt a slight shiver inside. I slept all night, better than I could ever remember, and Robert kept his promise.

∞

In a light sleep, I felt the sensation of warm lips brush kisses up my neck. And then I heard a soft, loving voice. "Wake up, Angel. How did you sleep?"

I stretched. "I've never slept better. Do I have to get up?"

"Come on." He pulled me up off the bed and pressed me against his warm, bare chest. "You feel so good." His voice deepened. "Now, get ready." A quick slap on the butt made me jump as he left for the bathroom.

His abrupt departure yanked my heart from my chest. I had to steady myself to keep from losing my balance. Lying back on the bed to regroup for a few minutes, I wondered how long I would be able to resist him.

We stepped onto the porch and caught sight of the sun coming over the buildings. The morning was clear and crisp. Taking a deep breath, I allowed myself a few moments to enjoy the fabulous spring day. Raindrops still clung to the leaves of the trees from the showers during the night. As we walked arm in arm along the sidewalk, they splattered on our heads. We laughed and tried to dodge our attackers from above, weaving from side to side.

"Where are we going, anyway?" One splattered on my cheek.

"For my favorite breakfast." He wiped the drop away with his thumb. I shivered.

I realized we were heading to the bakery the second we stepped onto Main Street. The aroma of the pastries hit me well before we arrived. In front of the store, Robert threw his arms up. "TA DA! Blueberry bagels and coffee." He was such a goof with a good sense of humor.

Robert swallowed his last bite. "Oh. I almost forgot to tell you, the pinning ceremony will be at the frat house before our meeting tomorrow evening at 7:30. The ceremony doesn't take long. I'll pick you and Abby up at 7:15."

After breakfast, we headed for campus and began our busy day of classes.

I saw Robert a few times during the day, but he never asked me to spend the night again. Maybe he had other plans.

At the end of the day, Abby and I headed for home to work on an assignment. We made it halfway before she freaked out and jabbed me in the shoulder with her finger. "So! Did you stay at the frat house last night?"

"No, his apartment." I laughed inside.

"His apartment?" Abby's hands flew to her mouth while I explained how Robert acquired his love nest in less than ten hours.

She hip bumped me. "Well. What else did you do?" She bounced on her toes like a child getting a new toy.

I knew what she wanted, but I wasn't ready to give her that information yet. "Besides helping him unpack, we ate dinner."

Abby shot a piercing glare my way. "Belinda." Her voice squealed in a high pitch tone. "Did you seal the deal?" She stopped, refusing to take another step. "Come on, Missy. Give it up! What else did you do?"

I laughed aloud. "Nothing else happened. Robert was a perfect gentleman. He promised he wouldn't put any moves on me and he didn't." Little did Abby know, tomorrow might be the night Robert and I would take our relationship to the next level. I hadn't fully decided, but the thought of the unlimited possibilities of our love made my knees wobble.

Abby hit my arm. "I don't believe you! Tell me all the details."

"Ouch! When we get home. We have to be comfortable." Before she would move, Abby made me swear. I crossed my heart, but, boy was she going to be disappointed. "By the way, the pinning ceremony is tomorrow evening. Can you still come?" I glanced at her. "I can introduce you to Garrett."

"Yes, of course. I wouldn't miss it for anything."

The minute we arrived in the room, Abby started in on me. "Okay. Now for the details." She dropped her books on the floor and jumped on her bed, sitting cross-legged, anticipating what I wasn't going to tell her.

I felt bad for leading her on. "Abby, there really isn't anything more to tell you. He was a gentleman. Really he was."

Abby fell back on her bed. "I hate you." She picked up a book and dove into her studying. I laughed but did the same.

Later and with no word from Robert, Abby and I decided to take a break from our homework and go eat.

We were walking back when she nudged me and pointed toward the house. Robert was in his car with the top down, just waiting. Abby walked by and gave him a quick wave.

He hopped out. "I've been trying to call you."

"I haven't heard my cell." I retrieved it from my purse. "It's dead." I gave the phone a shake. "If you haven't figured it out yet, I'm not used to this thing."

He huffed and wrapped his arms around me. "Stay with me tonight?"

I shook my head. "I can't. I'm working on an assignment that's due. I'll see you tomorrow evening at 7:15."

He squeezed tighter. "I liked holding you last night." He pulled back and scanned my face. "I'll miss you."

"I'll miss you too, but I have to get back to my assignment. I need to go." I ran my hands up the back of his neck and into his hair. He hugged me close and kissed me. Kissing gave me more of a thrill than just his touch alone. I shuddered and pulled away. "Good night. Love you."

"Love you, too, Angel."

About to slip into his car, he turned back. "You sure you won't come?"

I bit my lip, resisting the need to run to him. Instead, I shook my head.

He pointed a finger. "Charge that phone."

I nodded and walked to the front door. My insides screaming, "Robert, I want you!"

CHAPTER 11

AFTER AGONIZING HOURS of classwork and growing anticipation over this evening's event, it seemed like Tuesday afternoon would never end. Abby and I hurried back to the house to prepare for the pinning ceremony.

By 6:30, I was ready in my light blue strapless dress. The three-inch white heels added a nice touch. Abby wore her hot pink dress.

I paced the room, chewing on my lower lip. "Abby." I stopped and faced her. "I don't know anything about this ceremony. Do you?" My stomach churned. What if my plans backfired?

"Nope. Not a clue." She pursed her lips, shaking her head. "Sit down and relax. Everything is going to be fine."

I shook my head and continued with my nervous walk. My mind wouldn't shut down.

My faithful digital clock finally read 7:15 just as the doorbell rang. On the way downstairs, I pulled some hair forward so Robert couldn't see my bare shoulders. I didn't want him to notice until he started to pin me. I opened the door and froze at the sight of him. "WOW! You look so handsome." Wearing a sports coat, slacks, dress shirt, and tie, with dress shoes, he looked like he'd stepped off the cover of a fashion magazine.

Abby elbowed me in the ribs.

"What?" I looked at her and she nodded her head toward Robert. I realized they'd never met. "Oh. I'm sorry. Abby, I'd like you to meet Robert Pennington. Robert, this is Abby Curtiss."

Abby extended her hand. "Nice to meet you, Mr. Pennington. I've heard a lot about you."

Robert politely took hold of her hand. "Nice to meet you, Ms. Curtiss. I, likewise, have heard nothing but good things about you." Now the two were playing the introduction past where it needed to go. I rolled my eyes.

A smile grew across his face. "You two look absolutely gorgeous. I'll have a beauty on each arm." He turned and extended his elbows. "Ladies."

The minute Robert and I walked into the frat house, Michael, the Delt chapter president, made an announcement. "May I have everyone's attention?" A hush came over the group. "Everyone, please gather in the living room." Once the group assembled, Michael continued. "It's my pleasure to announce that Robert Pennington is pinning Belinda Davies this evening." The sound of muffled voices erupted and a room full of eyes followed us as we joined Michael for the ceremony.

Robert and I stood facing each other as the chapter president began talking. Nervous and mesmerized by my boyfriend, I didn't hear a single word. Luckily, the ceremony didn't take long. Then Robert showed me the pin. He pushed my hair behind my shoulder. A wide grin spread across his face as he shook his head. Robert pinned me without any problems, but his fingertips slid under the bodice and grazed my breast. I felt a sizzle all the way to my toes. I quivered.

Oh well, so much for my Plan A. I hoped I'd do better with Plan B.

After he secured the sweetheart pin, he grasped my hands. At first, I didn't understand. When he reached over to kiss me, I glued my lips to his. The kiss was passionate enough without me entwining myself around him. Robert maintained his grip the entire time. After a few seconds, he ended the kiss and released my hands.

I whispered, "I'm sorry," and hid my burning face in the hollow of his shoulder.

He nuzzled my hair. "Nothing to be sorry about. We handled it."

The moment came to an end when the fraternity brothers rushed in. Some hugged me while others shook Robert's hand. I heard "lucky" and "Lora" mentioned several times.

After things settled down a bit, I found Abby surrounded by a group of Delts. "Hey guys, I need her to come with me."

Grasping Abby's arm, I led her over to introduce her to Garrett. "Garrett Barnett, this is Abby Curtiss." They smiled at each other, and by the way, Abby looked at him, I knew she was impressed.

Michael made an announcement the meeting was about to start. Robert handed me the keys to his car. "Come back in forty-five minutes."

My heart jumped. "You're letting me drive your car?"

He shrugged. "Sure, why not?"

Now butterflies erupted. "Great! Come on, Abby, we're goin' cruisin'."

"Be careful."

"I promise it won't end up on the scratch and dent aisle." I held the keys above my head and gave them a jingle.

"I don't care about the car...only you." He kissed the top of my head.

How sweet. I promised I'd be careful. I took Abby by the hand and we dashed to the car.

I slid into the driver's seat. "Abby. I won't be home again tonight."

"Having another sleepover?" She closed her door.

"No." I swallowed hard and inhaled. "I think I'm ready to take the plunge." I was in love, and, if everything worked out, tonight would be a perfect time to execute Plan B and elevate our relationship to the next level.

∞

Driving the Beamer around campus was fun, but the need to quench our thirst became a priority. So, we stopped for sodas at the local drive-in. While we talked about my plans for tonight, a convertible parked next to us. I glance past Abby at the girls in the vehicle. My mouth fell open. There sat Lora, staring at me with a look that could kill. If she didn't know before that something was going on between Robert and me, she knew now with me in his Beamer. By tomorrow, the rumor mill would have confirmed the pinning. I froze and returned her glare.

Abby looked around to see what I was staring at. "Oh, shit!" She swung her head back toward me. "Is that Lora?"

"Yeah, let's get out of here." Lora never released her stare. I don't know what possessed me or why I even felt the need to do what I did next. I guess it was that look of disdain she gave me, a look that was all too familiar from my high school days. As I backed out, my dress bodice was in Lora's full view. I pointed to the pin. The look on her face was priceless and paid me back for all the ridicule I had taken for years.

Abby's jaw unhinged when she realized what I did. "Belinda, I never thought you had it in you."

We drove straight back to the Delt house. Robert and Garrett were standing out front, talking. Robert walked over to the car and opened my door. "Did you have fun?"

"Yeah, we enjoyed ourselves." I shot a big-eyed glance at Abby. I chose not to tell him about my encounter with Lora. I figured he'd have to handle her all by himself.

He pulled me close and bent over to my ear. "Stay with me tonight."

A warm sensation rushed over my skin. "Okay, but we have to make a quick stop by my place."

I turned toward Abby when she said, "Garrett is taking me home." She gave me a quick thumbs-up when he wasn't looking. I hoped things worked out for them. I liked the idea of two best friends dating two best friends.

Robert stayed in the car as I ran upstairs to pick up some clothes and books. Abby wasn't there, a good sign. So, I left a quick note on the desk. *See you in class. Mum about Lora.*

"Now, time for Plan B." I filled my lungs and almost forgot to let the air out. I raced down the stairs back to my love and then we drove the few blocks to his apartment. My heart pounded the whole way.

I tossed my things on the couch. Robert took off his jacket and tie and laid them on a chair and then flipped through his mail. I walked toward him and wrapped my arms around his neck. The manly scent of his aftershave, musk with a hint of spice, filled the air. I savored the fragrance then slid a hand up into his hair and pulled him down to my lips. The mail fell to the floor and scattered around our feet. His arms wrapped around my waist, tugging me close. He deepened the kiss. I trembled. This time I reached behind me and pulled his hands in front of us as I ended the tender moment. He was about to say something, but I put my finger across his lips. I nodded toward the bedroom. His eyes widened, and, for the first time since we'd met, he said nothing and followed.

I turned and started to unbutton his shirt.

He grasped my hands and frowned. "Belinda, we don't have to do this now. I didn't pin you so you'd have sex with me."

My face flushed hot. "I want you to make love to me. I want tonight to be a memory I'll always cherish."

"Angel, I didn't expect this."

I rubbed my hands over his chest. "I started taking the pill after we began dating." A look of astonishment came over his face. "I wasn't sure I'd be able to resist you. I wanted to be ready." Gripping the back of his neck, I pulled him close and kissed him. My neurons went crazy. He pulled me closer and took control of the kiss. My heart hammered and the kiss melted me into his body.

Robert pulled away. "You know that's not enough and I hadn't planned on this happening tonight. Let me check." He went to the nightstand, opened the drawer and pulled out a small open box. A big, adorable smile spread across his face as he turned the box upside down and dumped foil packets on the bed.

I pointed at each little square, counting. "Is five going to be enough?"

His eyebrows winged high. "You're optimistic."

"You know I'm a virgin. How would I know?" I picked one up.

"Angel, five is plenty."

"Oh!" I tossed the packet on the bed with its friends. I grabbed Robert's belt and tugged him toward me.

He brushed a stray hair off my forehead. "Are you sure you want to do this?"

How sweet and thoughtful. I tugged him closer. "Positive." I nuzzled his neck then stepped back to remove my belt. I felt the heat rising in my body. "Very positive."

Turning my back to Robert, I coyly requested, "Unzip me." I wrapped my arms under my breasts to hold the dress in place. I felt the slide of the zipper down my back. Taking a deep breath to gather enough nerve to make the next move, I relaxed my arms just enough to let my dress slip down to the floor. I stepped out of it and just stood there. His hands rested on my shoulders and he turned me toward him. He pulled my arms down to my sides and gently brushed my hair aside. I stood there in only lace bikinis and high heels. I shivered inside and heat rushed across my face.

He studied me from head to toe, briefly concentrating on a few areas. "You...*are* the most beautiful girl I've ever seen." His dark, hooded eyes were both sensitive and seductive at the same time, if that's possible.

I took a deep breath and finished unbuttoning his shirt, revealing his muscular chest and abs. Unable to resist touching them, I inched my hands up, kissing his body along the way. His chest rose sharply with a deep breath. I slipped the shirt over his shoulders and it slid to the floor.

He watched my every move, making heat prickle over my face. I unbuckled his belt as he started feathering kisses down my neck. My pulse jackknifed below my ear and a wave of heat flashed throughout my body. My head fell back in submission. I hummed and trembled from his touch. He laid me on the bed and removed my high heels, one by one. He slipped off my bikini's and began kissing each place his hands explored. I gripped the sheets when the electric feeling intensified, shooting up my spine. My back arched. My body stiffened.

In one fluid motion, he undressed, tore open a packet, and rolled it on. Then he crawled up, placing sucking kisses along the way, and hovered over me. Goosebumps raced over my skin as I shivered. I threw my arms around him, pulling him close. Skin touched skin. The heat of his body made mine cry for more. He captured my mouth and settled between my thighs, making my lady parts clench with need.

The sudden discomfort startled me. I gasped and tensed.

He froze. "Are you okay?"

"Yes. Don't stop." His concern made me love him even more, and I relaxed into the passion overwhelming me. His lips claimed mine once again. A soft groan escaped from deep in his throat. Being connected to him was like we were two halves of a whole, fitting perfectly, moving together in a rhythmic motion. I had never felt so loved. It was pure ecstasy!!! With one steady motion…our souls joined as one.

With four empty packets on the floor, I didn't want it to ever end. He turned onto his back and his chest rose up and down in rapid motion. "Never in my wildest dreams did I think it would be so…mind-blowing."

"I'm gathering you're enjoying this."

He was still breathing hard when he looked at me. "Yeah. Absolutely. It's beyond words." He pulled me close to his side. "Aren't you?"

I slid on top and straddled him, pressing my rotating hips against him. He sighed. "Ooo…Aaah…Angel."

I kissed his forehead, then his nose, and then his lips. I raked my fingers over his well-defined muscles, kneading them, increasing my awareness of him. His hands began roaming my body. Craving more of him, I ripped open packet number five.

CHAPTER 12

SOMETHING LIGHT AND velvety glided all over my face and neck. Lifting my eyelids, I gazed at my handsome boyfriend with a single red rose in his hand. "For you, my love." With his other hand, he stroked my face, down my neck, and over my body. His feathery touch sent chills racing through me. I trembled.

He shook his head. "We need to get moving or we'll be late for our classes."

I locked my arms around his neck. "Thank you for the rose." My breathing erratic, I wanted more of him. "Do we have to go?"

He reached down and retrieved a discarded foil packet. "If I stay here we'll need more of these."

"Can you stop and pick up a box today?"

Robert nodded. "Definitely." He gave me a quick peck on the lips. "Come on. Get up. We can't get in the habit of skipping class." He pulled my hands from around his neck. "What time do you have to get out of here?"

"My early class was canceled. I don't have to be there until one."

"Okay, I'll shower first and you, lucky lady, can fix us some breakfast." He fiddled with my hair. "Any regrets about last night?"

"No. Not at all." Memories that would be with me forever flooded my mind. Connected, I felt complete. That it wasn't just him and me anymore, but us as one. It felt so right. "It was wonderful. Will it be like that every time?"

"I hope so." He winked. We'll see what happens tonight." Robert laid the rose on the pillow next to me and headed for the bathroom.

Seeing him in all his naked glory gave me a hot flash.

At the bathroom door, he hesitated and shot a glance at the pile of foil packets crumpled on the floor. "On second thought, I think I should pick up a few boxes."

"Good idea." I put on Robert's shirt, picked up my rose and went to the kitchen. I placed the rose in the vase and decided to dry the wilted one. At the front door, I eyed Robert's gym shoes and borrowed a lace. I tied it around the stem of the rose then hung the flower upside down, tying the other end of the lace to a knob of one of the upper kitchen cabinets. There it would remain until it dried enough to place it in a box. I stepped back to admire my handy work. Then I started breakfast.

Robert came in and stopped in his tracks, pointing to the hanging rose. "Should I take that as a warning?"

I giggled. "No, it's a girl thing. I'm drying it." I walked over, put my arms around his chest, and looked up at his apprehensive face. "I want to save them. Then when I need a reminder of how much you love me, I'll have them to look at if you're not around." I gave him a gentle, well-placed kiss on the lips and my body heated in seconds. Robert wrapped his arms around me, tightening his hold. The kiss lingered.

He leaned away from me. "Angel. As much as I would love to take you back into that bedroom, I need to eat and leave for class."

With a sweep of my hand, I pointed to the table. "Your breakfast is served, sir."

Robert peered at the dangling treasure. "What do you do with it after it's dried?"

"I'll find a box for them. It will be my treasure box of love reminders." In a sexy voice, I emphasized the word "love." Robert just shook his head.

Over breakfast, we planned our day. I would spend the night with him for the third time. He decided he'd walk to class and I'd take the car to pick up what I needed from my place. After his class, I'd pick him up so we could have lunch at a restaurant off campus.

"I guess that settles it." Robert gathered his books, gave me a kiss on the top of my head and headed for the door. Just before closing it, he said, "I really like having you here."

∞

It was a glorious spring day to drive around campus with the top down until I stopped for a red light on Main Street. At the corner, waiting to cross stood evil-eyed Lora. Our eyes collided. She never took her glare off me as she made her way across the street and stopped. I was afraid she'd approach the car and strangle me. Hatred consumed her face. My heart sped up. My mouth went dry. The second the light changed, I floored the accelerator. I glanced in the rearview mirror. Lora never moved. The turn onto University Drive broke our line of vision. Why in the world was he ever with her?

Arriving a few minutes early gave me time to recoup from my brief encounter with the witch. I had a hard time getting her out of my head. I knew what it felt like being ignored when I was growing up, but being hated by someone was a new experience. I thought about telling Robert but decided to keep it to myself. I wasn't going to let my insecurities get in the way of our budding relationship.

Robert leaped into the car without opening the door. "Hey there, Angel. Where we having lunch?" The tips of his mouth curled up and washed away anything left of my Lora encounter.

∞

"Meet me in the Cave." Robert leaned against the wall next to the door of the lecture hall.

"Okay." I went to give him a kiss, but he sidestepped away.

"Not in public, Angel." He cupped his hand over the side of his mouth and murmured, "I don't think I'd be able to stop with a kiss." He gave me a long pleading look and then winked. I just shook my head and walked into class, but I knew exactly what he meant. I didn't know if I could've stopped either after what I'd experienced last night.

The clock ticked down. Every second closer, my heart jumped. With my books already packed and one foot in the aisle, I jumped up the second the prof dismissed the class and hurried to the Student Center.

"Belinda!" Matt ran up beside me just outside the Cave and zoned in on the pin immediately. "A Delt sweetheart pin. Do I dare ask whose?"

A flutter came over me. "Robert—"

"Pennington?" He grasped my arm and led me to the Theta Kappa area.

Robert watched us from where he sat with the Delts. I half glanced at him.

"When did this happen?" Matt pointed a finger and grimaced.

"Last night." I wiggled away from his grip. From the corner of my eye, I saw Robert start to get up. I gave him a stern look and shook my head for him to stay put. "I love him. He loves me. It just happened."

"You sure he loves you?" He set his books on the table.

"He says he does and I believe him."

"Be careful. I don't trust him." The muscles of Matt's jaws twitched.

"I'll be careful, but it's really none of your business." I didn't wait for his response. I turned and walked away.

When I reached Robert, he pulled me down across his lap. "Why were you over there?"

I rested my head on his shoulder. "Matt wanted to know about my pin."

"And?"

I picked at my thumbnail. "He warned me to be careful."

Robert lifted my chin so our eyes met. "Did he put doubts in your mind? I'm not going to hurt you. You'll always be a part of my life. I love you." He kissed my forehead, and a warm thrill stirred inside me.

"No, I trust you." I lay my hand over his heart.

He nuzzled my ear. "Move in with me."

I shook my head. "I can't. My parents would disown me."

"You're practically living there now."

"That's different. I'm not moved in and they don't know. Sorry."

"I love holding you when you sleep." He squeezed me. "Okay. I can wait, but I won't like it."

I stayed on his lap with my head on his shoulder. With his arms encircling me, he moved slightly from side to side in a rhythmic motion. I don't think anyone would've noticed, but I felt the sway and the beat of his heart. Neither of us said anything for several minutes. I felt safe and loved in his arms.

Robert's voice broke my safety-net bubble. "It's time to leave." He picked me up by the waist and planted me on my feet, then linked his fingers with mine and walked me to class.

The prof dismissed class a few minutes early. I ran to wait for Robert at his car. When he saw me leaning against the trunk of the Beamer, his signature smile spread across his face. He gave me a quick kiss on the cheek, which surprised me. I guess he figured since we'd be going to the apartment, he had nothing to worry about. Of course,

I reacted. I took him by the collar and pulled his lips close to mine. I stopped just millimeters away. Heat radiated from his parted lips. His breath brushed my cheeks. Then, ever so gently, I pressed my lips to his. Sparks ignited every nerve. I clenched his collar tighter to keep my lips on his, but he stepped back.

"Naughty girl." He opened the door for me. "Let's go home."

I really liked him calling his place *our* home. His twinkling eyes roamed my face.

"I stopped at the pharmacy earlier, and we're all set." He pointed to a small brown paper bag on the passenger seat.

I hated to be the bearer of bad news. "We can't go home. Remember, you have a game." I looked at my watch. "In about fifteen minutes."

The lust in his eyes faded away.

"Damn. I forgot. Let's go." He gestured for me to get into the car. I started to move past him, but he put his arms around my waist and pulled me close with a tug. "But after the game…you're mine."

"Um. I'm afraid not. I have to study for a test tonight. I'll use the bedroom so you can watch TV."

He tsked and heaved a sigh. "Okay."

∽

Robert walked over to his brothers at home plate and I went to stand in my usual spot so I could see his face during the game.

The Delts were playing the Omega Tau's.

It was an exciting game. I jumped and screamed until my voice was sore.

In the last inning, from across the field, I saw Lora with the girls from our encounter at the drive-in. They were glaring at me. Her eyes were slits, almost closed. She didn't even try to conceal her hatred. But what bothered me the most was the crazy, scary way she glared at me.

I ignored her and focused on the tied game. Robert stepped up to bat. He hit the ball to center field and took off running. He ran the bases before the Omega Tau's could throw the ball back for an out, finishing the game with a Delt victory.

I sprinted across the field to join my hunk of a boyfriend. Sweat trickled down his face. His soaked t-shirt stuck to his muscled chest. He panted with every breath. His mouth stretched into a knockout smile and I flung my arms around his neck, planting my lips on his. In an instant, my feet went airborne as he swung me around.

"Did you see that? We won."

I threw my head back and let out a laugh. "Put me down. I'll get dizzy."

He controlled my slide back to earth but never released me. He rested his forehead against mine and pecked my nose. "I'm in need of a shower and you need to study. Let's go home." He gave me another peck, this time on the cheek. "I have to get my bag. Wait here."

I stepped off to the side, out of the way of the others leaving. At the edge of the field, I noticed Lora standing with her arms crossed over her chest. She stared with her icy glare for a few minutes then turned and stomped away. A chill ran up my spine in a bad way.

Robert jabbered non-stop about the game on the way to the apartment. About a block away, he said, "Let's get some burgers before we go home. All I want to do is eat, shower, and relax with you under me. If that's all right with you?"

"That's fine. But remember, I have to study."

When we walked into the apartment, I headed straight for the bedroom. He followed—pharmacy bag in hand.

"I need something." He wrapped his arms around my waist and pulled me close, his lips touching mine. I gasped as my body was given a kick-start.

It was hard, but I pulled away. "I need to study. This has to wait 'til later."

"If it has to, but a kiss was all I was after." He grinned.

I pointed to the door. "Out!"

"Can't, need a shower, and I have to put these away." He opened his nightstand drawer and deposited the contents of the bag then walked to the bathroom. "Would you like to join me? I could bring one of those with me." He winked. I crossed my arms over my chest and tapped my foot. "Guess not, but I'll leave the door unlocked just in case you change your mind." I picked up a pillow and flung it at him. His instincts were too fast. He managed to close the door before the pillow made contact.

A little after midnight, I gave up. My eyelids drifted shut every time I tried to read a word.

Robert had stayed in the living room and fallen asleep. I knelt next to the couch and traced a finger over his lips. "Robert, come to bed."

He grabbed me around the waist and pulled me over on top of him.

"Baby, we were up late last night," I began, hoping to soften his disappointment. "And you must be tired from the game. Would you mind if we just went to sleep? You know we're both exhausted."

He huffed out a big sigh. "Ooookay."

I don't know if he was being cooperative or relieved, but he followed me to the bedroom. He slid in next to me, and I cuddled at his side. He kissed me. "Love you. Good night, Angel."

"Robert. Why do you call me 'Angel'?"

He nuzzled my hair. A half yawn escaped. "Why? Because…it was like you descended from heaven into my life. You…just appeared one day." He tightened his arm around me and snuggled closer.

"Oh." That was the sweetest thing anyone had ever said to me. "I love you, too." My heart soared.

CHAPTER 13

I NEVER IMAGINED anything could've prepared me for the wonder of waking up every day beside the man of my dreams. Often, I would stare at him, wondering how I'd been so lucky to hook a guy as gorgeous and wonderful as him.

The next morning, reality took hold. Robert and I rushed around the apartment.

Breakfast consisted of a ride to the bakery for blueberry bagels and coffee. We didn't even have time to sit and talk. It was grab-and-go.

Both of our schedules were packed. My Art History exam had me concerned. Usually, I had enough time to study several days before a test. This week Robert kept me too busy.

"I won't be coming to the Cave after class," I told Robert, opening my door. "I'm going to the library to review. I'll come after my test."

He gave me a quick, "Love you. See you later." I barely had time to close the door before he drove off.

I didn't pay too much attention in my first two classes. My mind kept wandering to my upcoming test. The second we were dismissed, I rushed to the library. Abby had the same test, so I hoped she'd be there and we could quiz each other.

A sigh passed my lips. Abby never failed me. "Hey, I'm glad you're here. I need help studying." I sat next to her.

Abby looked up from the Art History book. "Hey, stranger. Where've you been the past few nights?"

"I've been kinda busy." A twinge of warmth flashed across my face.

She leaned in close. "So, did you do it?"

Biting my lower lip, I ignored her. "I need to review for the test right now. Will you help me?" I stuck my lower lip out, but Abby didn't waver. She wanted more. I rolled my eyes. "Okay. Okay. I promise I'll fill you in later."

She flipped a page. "You swear, or I won't help you."

"I promise or my name isn't Belinda Davies." She nodded. I opened my book and we started reviewing and quizzing each other.

The test was long and harder than I expected, so it made me late to meet Robert.

The minute I entered the Cave I froze. He wasn't alone. Lora was sitting across his lap and they were kissing. "Oh. Shit!" How stupid could I be? Matt had told me the truth. Robert got what he wanted, and now he was back playing the field. I bet Lora and her friends were getting a good laugh at my expense.

"Monster" raged. I whirled around and hurried out. Outside, I cried so hard I could barely see. I needed to run and hide, like I had in the past. Garrett called my name. I bolted behind the building next door. Then I heard Robert calling. They sounded close.

Through my veil of tears, I focused on the wooded area behind the student parking lot where I usually rode Beau. I made a mad dash to it. I knew I could find someplace to hide in there. My emotions were too raw to face him right now.

Their voices faded the further I ran into the woods. I pushed aside low hanging branches that slapped my face and stumbled over rocks. A protruding root caught my foot. Pain shot through my ankle. I toppled to the ground, face-planting in the dirt.

I tried to stand, but the pain caused me to fall again. I scooted under a nearby bush, so the drooping branches could conceal my location if they looked for me in here. I lay curled in a fetal position crying. My cell rang. It was Robert. I didn't answer and shut it off so its sound couldn't be used to track me. Sobbing, I had trouble catching my breath. The picture of them kissing looped through my head.

Leaves rustled in a nearby bush. I swung around. Nothing, but the noise made me realize the light was fading. The stillness of the air offered no further calls from Robert or Garrett. The dim light made the familiar woods look different. I lost my sense of direction. A pounding in my chest followed by tension in my neck told me I needed to find my way back to the parking lot and call Abby.

I struggled to stand then picked a path and started hopping on one foot from tree to tree. The pain and the effort it took exhausted me. Luckily, I picked the right route and finally made it.

I sat just inside the tree line, out of sight, and called Abby. She didn't answer, so I left a text. Call me. I need your help and don't talk to Garrett or Robert.

My ankle throbbed, making tears well up. Abby didn't respond to the text. Tears rolled down my cheeks and I struggled to keep my hands from shaking.
The veil of fluid over my eyes made it difficult to see the numbers, but I managed to press her speed dial. This time she answered.

"Abby, did you talk to Garrett or Robert?"

"No, I haven't. What's wrong?"

"I need you to come pick me up. I've sprained or broken something in my ankle. I can't walk. Are you at the house?" I could barely talk between sobs.

"I just got in. I had my phone off." She paused. "Where are you?"

"Just inside the wooded area behind the student parking lot. Can you come get me now? My spare car key is in the second drawer under my pajamas."

"What's going on?"

"Just come get me. I'll explain in the car." I flinched from the pain.

"Be there in a few."

The parking lot only had a few cars left in it, and the lights were just bright enough for me to spot my CR-V approaching. I flagged Abby down and hopped into the passenger seat.

She looked me over. "You're a mess."

I swiveled the rearview mirror to take a look. Mud mixed with tears streaked my face. Leaves littered my hair. Grime covered my jeans and hands. Wincing in pain, I reached down to rub my ankle. "My ankle is killing me."

"I'll take you to the Emergency Room." She floored the accelerator. "Now, what happened?"

"I saw Robert kissing Lora. I'm so stupid. I shouldn't have slept with him." I lowered my face into my hands.

"Belinda, I'm so sorry." She squeezed my shoulder.

I let my hands drop to my lap. "He said he loved me. I trusted him." The sharp stab in my chest was as bad as the pain from my throbbing ankle. I couldn't tell which was worse.

"This isn't the time to talk about Robert. Let's get your ankle taken care of, and then we can talk when you're not so upset." Abby seemed to be doing her best to try to comfort me.

She helped me into the ER. The nurse did her handy work on the leg of my jeans by splitting it to the knee. The x-rays revealed a sprain and after an ace wrap application, I received a pair of crutches. The instructions given were for no weight-bearing for the next week and to make an appointment with the orthopedic doctor.

I hobbled out on my crutches to the parking lot. Crutches first, then foot. Crutches first, then foot. The routine was exhausting. So, I stopped to rest, only to see Robert walking toward me. How did he know where I was? Abby was with me the entire time, except when I had x-rays done. She must have called.

The blood in my veins boiled from the double betrayal and the sight of Robert. "Go away! I don't want to see you!" I pulled off my sweetheart pin and threw it at him.

He stopped and his shoulders slumped before he picked it up. "Angel, I need to talk to you. Please, let me explain. It wasn't—"

I put my hands over my ears and repeated, "LA LA LA LA LA," while trying to stay upright on the crutches.

He reached out and pulled my hands down. I nearly toppled over but regained my balance and jerked away. "Don't touch me! Leave me alone!" Tears streamed down my face. "You got what you wanted, just go back to Lora! Go away!"

He grimaced, shaking his head. "Angel, please let me explain."

"Go away!" I yelled again, sobbing.

He dropped his head and fiddled with the pin. "Abby, take her home." He walked to his car and left.

We drove home in silence. I felt so stupid for believing him. It felt like I'd been kicked in the stomach and ached all over.

"Belinda, let him explain. Garrett said it wasn't Robert's fault. It was Lora's."

"I don't want to hear excuses. It didn't look like he was trying to avoid it or push her away. I don't want to talk right now. Okay."

We parked in the driveway, and I was making my way along the walkway when Robert's car pulled in behind mine. He rushed toward me.

"Go away!"

He kept pace with me as I struggled with the crutches.

"Please, listen to me."

My tear-filled eyes widened. "Why should I." Then I stumbled.

Robert caught me by the shoulders.

I pulled away and wobbled. He again took hold of my shoulders. I raised my head to see his eyes. "Why?" Tears streamed down my cheeks. "Why?"

He swallowed hard. I let him wrap his arms around me. His voice cracked as he nuzzled my hair. "It wasn't my fault. She plopped herself in my lap and kissed me. She caught me off guard. I was expecting you, and, when I realized it was Lora, I stood up and told her I was pinned to you." He took my head in his hands. "I love you and only you." His face was awash with concern. "Come with me."

I took a deep breath. My pulse slowed. I wanted to believe him. I shook my head. "I'll sleep here."

"Angel, please. I just want to talk."

"Well, we can talk here and now."

Robert looked past me. "Abby, some help here."

"Belinda. Be sensible. You need to get off those crutches and elevate that leg. You can't do that standing in the front yard. Go with him and talk."

I pursed my lips. Abby was right. I took in a long breath. "All right."

We didn't say anything during the ride, but he kept glancing over at me. In my mind, I compared what I had seen with what he'd told me. I hadn't seen the complete incident. He'd never lied to me before, but I hadn't known him that long. Garrett had verified his honesty. Lora hated me. Maybe she and her posse planned everything. Hell, I didn't know what to believe.

I let him carry me into the apartment and he sat next to me on the couch. He took the pin out of his pocket and tossed it on the coffee table.

"I thought you broke it off with Lora."

"I did. The same night you went to the pajama party."

"Then why didn't you push her away?"

"I told you. I thought she was you. The minute I realized it, I got her off my lap and stood up. You didn't see that part, did you?"

I shook my head, way too embarrassed to admit I let "Monster" out. The pain from my ankle screamed at me. "I need to put my foot up."

He jumped to his feet and disappeared into the bedroom only to emerge with a pillow and placed it on the coffee table. "Here, rest it on this." Then he made sure it was under my ankle. Once all the fuss was over, he asked, "What did you see?"

I hung my head. "You two kissing. I didn't stick around to see anything else."

"Do you believe me? If not, we can call Garrett. He saw the whole thing." Within seconds he had his phone in his hand ready to dial.

I studied his face, full of hurt and worry. "I believe you."

A gush of air escaped him. "Thank you." He inched closer to me. "I want to talk about something else." He cupped my chin. "Angel, promise me you won't run away like that again. Confront me next time something upsets you." His brow furrowed. "Where did you run? I looked everywhere."

"The wooded area behind the student parking lot."

He grimaced. "What if you were knocked unconscious? You could still be in there. Who knows what's lurking out there? Who knows how long it would've taken to find you, once someone even thought to look in the woods. Please don't do that again." Robert's voice wavered and his hands trembled.

Seeing him this upset made me start crying all over again. I didn't like seeing him this way. Through my tears, I stammered, "I...I'm sorry. I didn't think you cared anymore. I just wanted to get the hell out of there."

Robert wiped away the tears running down my cheek. "Angel, I love you. I will always care about you." He pulled me across his lap, cradling me in his arms, then nestled my head against his chest. He held me tight as he kissed the top of my head and started the rhythmic motion like he had in the Cave.

I felt myself relaxing. "Monster" went to sleep. The gentle sway of his body and his regular heartbeat could've put me to sleep, but the throbbing pain in my ankle caused me to stiffen. "Robert."

"Hmm."

"I need a pain pill. Would you get the bottle out of my purse?"

"Have you eaten? You shouldn't take pills on an empty stomach."

"Not since breakfast."

"You need to eat. What do you want?"

"I don't care, anything quick." I was too absorbed in my own self-pity. I knew Robert was upset with the whole situation, yet he had a gentleness and a strength about him that made me feel everything was going to be all right. I believed his story about Lora. She hated me. Unfortunately, I fell into her trap. A shooting pain forced me to rub my ankle. A clump of dirt fell on the couch cushion. I studied it and then my clothes. "I need to shower and change."

"I'm almost done. I'll help you with the shower after we eat."

"But how am I going to with this ankle wrapped. How am I going to get to my classes? I've screwed everything up."

He came back and handed me a plate with a PB&J sandwich and a glass of milk, and then sat next to me with his. "We'll figure something out. The showering problem is easy to fix. I'll wrap it in a dry-cleaning bag and tape it." He took a bite of his sandwich and washed it down. "When I broke my arm my Mom wrapped my cast the same way. It worked like a charm."

I took the last bite of the sandwich and before I could swallow, Robert handed me a pain pill and my milk. "Angel. Are you ready for that shower?"

After a nod, I found myself in the air in the arms of a guy I knew loved me. He sat me on the bed, helped me out of my jeans, and wrapped my ankle. The pill started to work and I relaxed. Again, I floated in his arms to the bathroom where he positioned me on the built-in bench of the shower. Then he made sure I had everything I'd need.

"Thanks." I must have looked horrible.

"Yell if you need anything. I won't be far." He closed the door.

Exhausted and not wanting to move, I just sat there. I finally mustered some energy and took off my remaining clothes. I let the warm water flow over my aching muscles. It felt so good I didn't want to leave, but the cooling water forced me to finish. I maneuver over to the sink and removed the remaining mascara from my puffy eyes. They were beyond help. Nature would have to take its course there.

I staggered to the kitchen on my newfound friends, my crutches, and sat at the table. In the middle stood my vase with a red rose. I pointed to it. "When did you get that?"

"After Abby called, I knew how upset you were. So, on the way to the hospital, I stopped and picked it up." He walked over and sat down.

"It's pretty. Thank you."

"Will this one end up at the end of a rope like the others?"

I giggled. "Yes. All of them will."

"So, you think there will be more?" He chuckled.

His sense of humor never stopped to amaze me. Plus, he seemed to enjoy bantering as much as Mom and I did. "If you intend to keep me around, there better be a bunch more." I reached over and poked his nose.

He grabbed my hand and kissed my knuckles. "I'll see what I can do about that."

I stood up and wobbled on my good foot. "I'm going to sleep. I'm exhausted. Can you hand me the crutches?" He came around and swept me up into his arms and carried me to bed.

I was half-asleep when the warmth of his body touched my back. His arm reached around and pulled me close. "Good night, Angel, my love." His soft, warm lips caressed my neck. A slight zing shot up my spine.

Too tired to respond, I drifted to sleep.

CHAPTER 14

FRIDAY, BEFORE LEAVING for class, Robert pointed to the coffee table. "Haven't you forgotten something?"

I saw my sweetheart pin. "You still want me to wear it despite everything that happened yesterday?"

"Of course I do. Yesterday is in the past." He half grinned. "Let's leave it there."

At the Fine Arts building, I located the handicap ramp. It appeared to be a block away from the door and just as long. Taking a deep breath, I hobbled toward it.

Robert stayed right by my side until he noticed the ramp. "That sucker is all the way over there. Hang on to the crutches." He swooped me up into his arms. At the door to my class, he put me down, made sure I was steady on my feet, and then carried my pack to my seat. "Wait for me by the door. I'll be back ASAP after my class."

I barely got, "Okay, thanks," out when he raced out the door.

My throbbing ankle made it difficult to concentrate on the lecture, but I muddled through to the end.

Robert was leaning against the wall when I exited. "Just help me to the library. It's too far to the Student Center."

"Okay, but I'm staying with you." He reached for me.

"No." I pulled away. "You don't have to. Go visit your friends."

"Nope, I'm not leaving you. I have some studying I can do."

Robert took my backpack to make it easier for me to maneuver. But, one look at him told me, I was still too slow.

"Crutches." He scooped me up in his arms. In no time, we were in the library.

Robert found an empty table near the first row of stacks and helped me settle in. He took a seat next to me and spoke in a hushed tone. "There's a party at the frat house this weekend. We can go if you want to, but I think we should stay in so you can keep your leg elevated. We can relax in bed and do some studying." He raised an eyebrow and smirked. "Angel, we still have those unopened boxes in my nightstand."

I giggled. "Staying in sounds good to me, but I want to start studying first." I winked. "You know which subject I mean."

He beamed and gave me a thumbs-up.

After our last class, we headed to the Student Center. I insisted he put me down at the door so I could use the crutches. I was self-conscious enough. Robert carrying me around outside was fun and people didn't seem to pay any attention. But in the building, it was more obvious. In there, I just wanted to be a girl on crutches.

Desperately needing to use the restroom, I headed for the one nearest the Cave and mouthed to Robert, "Ladies Room."

He nodded and leaned against the wall. "I'll wait here."

In front of the mirror, two girls were primping and talking when I hobbled into one of the stalls. One said, "I can't believe he pinned some girl after only knowing her for a few weeks." It took no time for me to figure out who they were gossiping about.

The other one uttered, "Lora is really pissed. They've been dating for almost two years and he's never even mentioned pinning her."

The first girl sneered, "Lora heard that his new girlfriend trapped him by getting pregnant. He's doing the honorable thing."

The other girl harrumphed. "Really. I'll bet they don't get married. He probably doesn't even love her."

I made my way to the sink to wash my hands. They continued their gossiping. I smiled and eavesdropped on their speculations. Unable to contain myself any longer, I chimed in, "I heard him say he loves her."

Their mouths dropped open. Halfway out the door, I stuck my head back in and finished with, "And I'm *not* pregnant."

Robert remained right where I left him. "What's this about pregnant?"

I looked over my shoulder at the two girls coming out of the restroom. Dumfounded expressions swept over their faces. I grinned and flashed them a wave.

Robert nodded toward the bug-eyed busybodies. "What's up with them?"

"Lora is spreading a rumor that I'm pregnant. I told them I wasn't." We gave a glance back in their direction. They hadn't moved. Robert flashed them his signature smile and gave them a gentlemen's nod.

"I hope that rumor doesn't get spread around." His face went solemn. "Lora is being such a bitch."

Crutches then step. Crutches then step. The Delt tables looked miles away.

"Let me just pick you up."

"No."

"Hmmm. Note to me. You're stubborn. Good to know."

I huffed, but persisted and finally reached our destination.

With the ritual over of making me comfortable, Robert sat. He placed his elbow on the table and rested the side of his head in his palm. He gestured for me to do the same. We sat there face to face enveloped in our own world. "I've been mulling something over." His mood, reserved. "I'd like my parents to meet you."

I leaned back and placed my hand over my heart. "Really?"

"Yes, really." A smile slid across his face.

"Okay. When?" Life was moving so fast with him—just another reason why butterflies had taken up permanent residence in my belly.

"We can decide that later. We need to check our schedules first. I know I have a couple of games coming up."

I opened my mouth to say something, but Garrett dropped into the chair across from us. "Am I interrupting anything?"

Robert motioned for him to stay seated. "We were just finishing up."

Garrett darted a glance between us. "I need to ask you something." He wrung his hands. "Um. I really don't..."

Robert gestured with palms up. "What is it, man?"

Garrett huffed. "Belinda, are you pregnant?"

Robert laughed so hard he couldn't contain himself.

I nearly gagged. I looked at Garrett then elbowed Robert in the side. "So much for the rumor not spreading." I tsked, "Lora is not happy about us and she started the rumor."

Garrett exhaled. "I'm glad to hear that."

Robert came up for air from his laughing spell. "Since I knocked her up, I have to take her home to meet the parents."

I punched Robert in the arm. "That's not the reason we're going."

Garrett held up his hand. "Okay, I get that there's not going to be a Robert look-alike running around anytime soon, but what's this about meeting parents?" He panned from Robert to me and back again.

"I'm taking Ms. Davies home to meet my folks." He reached over and placed his arm around my shoulders and pulled me close, obviously very smug about his decision.

Garrett leaned back hard in his chair. "You're the first. I've known him since our freshman year. He has never taken anyone home to meet Mom."

Wow! I couldn't believe it. I'd be the first to meet his parents. I guess he does love me.

"By the way, how are you doing?" He pointed a finger at me. "You had me and Robert so worried. We looked everywhere for you."

"Sorry, but I'm fine. Just a sprained ankle." I rested my head on Robert's shoulder. "I'm tired and my ankle is throbbing. Can we go home?" Home. That word gave me warm fuzzies every time. My stomach growled. "I'm hungry, too."

"What are you hungry for? How about your favorite?" He arched an eyebrow. "Mexican food? We can stop on the way home for take-out."

"That would be great. I can take a pill and prop my foot up while we eat."

"Garrett, we'll see you later, but you'll be watching us for a while as Gimpy—he nudged me—makes her way out of here." They both laughed at my expense. "Angel. The minute we hit the steps it's airborne for you again."

"Fine," I huffed.

Over dinner, we looked at our schedules and decided we'd leave next weekend for the visit home.

Robert cleared the trash and put the leftovers in the frig. "You sit there and relax while I shower. I'll be back shortly."

"Take your time." I started to curl up on the couch and noticed a white box with a card on the end table. It read, *To my beloved Belinda, my Angel. Love, Robert.* I opened it and found a decorative wooden box with a hinged lid. Inside, was a single red rose, along with a new package of shoelaces, and another note, *For Your Keepsake Roses*, followed by several hand-drawn hearts. Sighing, I put the box on the coffee table then lay down. The exhaustion from the day before, the physical strain from the crutches, and the pain meds proved too much for me. I fell asleep.

I felt the rhythmic motion of Robert carrying me to the bedroom. With my head against his chest, I heard the sound of his beating heart echo with every footstep. The motion and the heartbeat relaxed me even more. He set me on the edge of the bed and then helped me undress before I lay down. He pulled me to his side, my body draped over his, and held me tight. Before drifting into oblivion, I thanked him for my new rose and treasure box. "I love it as much as I love you."

He kissed the side of my head. "Good night, Angel. Now, can I have my shoelace back?"

"Yes, Baby." I drifted off into a deep sleep, wrapped in my lover's arms.

Saturday morning the smell of fresh coffee filled the room just before the door opened and Robert appeared carrying a tray of food.

"What's all this?"

"Breakfast." He presented the array. "I made my special scrambled eggs, toast, bacon, OJ, and coffee. I hope you like it."

The aroma made my mouth water. "I thought you said you don't cook."

"Just because I don't cook, doesn't mean I can't. Besides, why should I if I can get other people to do it for me."

He placed the tray on the bed and scooped up a spoonful of egg. "Here. Tell me what you think."

The minute the spoon hit my mouth the tantalizing taste erupted. "Oh, my gosh. Those are the best eggs I've ever tasted. Give me the plate."

We spent the rest of the weekend relaxing in bed, watching movies, and actually studying. Robert never left my side. However, every chance we got, we indulged in our newest interest—human anatomy.

Several times, I caught Robert staring at me and he'd just half-smile. Something was bothering him. I curled up over his side, and he wrapped his arms around me. He seemed deep in thought, gazing at the ceiling.

I tilted my head back. "You look upset. What are you thinking about?"

"You." He turned his head and stared down into my eyes.

"Me? About what?"

"You got hurt because of something I did." He tightened his hold on me and kissed my forehead.

"And because I didn't stick around to get the facts." I pushed away and propped myself up on my elbow so I could look him in the face. "I have to take some blame here and I promised I'd talk to you before jumping to any conclusions." I tried to comfort him by running my hand gently down the side of his face.

"You better. I don't know what I would do if you got seriously injured because of me." He was very solemn as he reached up to stroke my hair.

I needed to change the subject to cheer him up. "Are we going to Sugar Land on Friday or Saturday?"

"Saturday morning. I don't want to sleep without you for two nights. I assumed you'd be staying with your parents?"

"Yeah, but I sleep better in your arms." I leaned over and our lips met. For the next hour, we practiced our new home study course—each other.

CHAPTER 15

IT TOOK SEVERAL hours to drive to Sugar Land. The closer we got, the more nervous I became. I was out of my league with Robert. What would his rich parents think of me—common everyday me?

"Do you think your parents will like me?" I shifted again in my seat.

"Don't worry." He reached for my hand and gently rubbed his thumb in circles. "They'll love you as much as I do. Relax. Just be yourself." He squeezed my hand. "What if yours don't like me? What have you told them?"

"Only, that you're the sweetest and most handsome guy I ever met who makes me very happy."

"So, I'm Mister Wonderful, huh? No pressure there!" Robert let out a snort. "Since I started college, I've never been taken home to meet a girlfriend's parents. This is new territory for me, too."

"Do I sense fear? I squeezed his hand. "My parents don't bite, and they've had all their shots." He gave me a dirty look.

I tried to turn in my seat to face him, but my new support boot took up too much space. "This thing is too big. And ugly."

Robert let out a chuckle. "It's better than the crutches and it shows off your great fashion sense."

"Oh, be quiet. You'll miss carrying me around. As for the fashion part, I don't think so." I attempted to adjust the damn thing.

"To tell the truth, you were getting a bit heavy." He winked.

"Don't you even go there, Mister."

He jabbed me in the ribs. "I'll miss it. I liked taking care of you."

"Hands on the wheel." This guy didn't fit Matt's warnings at all. In fact, he was just the opposite and he loved me. Silly, plain me.

White fluffy clouds drifted across the big, blue sky making this a perfect top-down kind-of-day and a great day for a road trip. We made our way through Houston and to the southwest side to Sugar Land. It's a bedroom community, with modest to estate subdivisions. Robert's parents lived in one of the estate neighborhoods. I, on the other hand, lived in the modest category.

He turned off the main highway and down what could've been a country road. Even though I'd lived in Sugar Land since high school, I never knew areas with such large houses existed. We drove down a lane that curved back and forth. The trees along the sides of the road hid many of the massive homes from full view. I bobbed my head from side to side, trying to catch a glimpse. Robert made one last turn. "There it is." He pointed to a huge mansion.

"Oh. My. God! Your house is fabulous." The enormous brick-and-stone Tuscan-style house sat at an angle on a corner lot with a circular drive.

Robert parked and came around to my side of the car. He reached in and just lifted me out.

"What? Now, I'm not too heavy."

"I'll survive this one last time." He flashed that perfect set of teeth.

I slapped his shoulder. "Rat."

He punched the doorbell with his elbow.

"Don't you have a key?"

"Sure I do, but it's in my pocket. My hands are occupied right now." He bounced me up a few times.

"Do you want me to reach in and get it?" I smiled, giving my eyebrows multiple lifts.

He looked me squarely in the eye. "I dare you."

I reached into his pocket, wiggling my fingers with every millimeter of progression. His face and body movement told me he liked it a bit too much. I lost my nerve and pulled back. "Well, you could put me down and get it."

"Chicken." He smirked.

About to plant a smacking kiss on his lips, I noticed an attractive lady appear in the doorway. "Robert." She smiled. "Did you forget your key?"

"It's in my pocket. I didn't want to put her down."

She opened the door wider. "You must be Belinda. Welcome to our home." A man who was obviously Robert's father joined us.

Robert set me down. "Mom, Dad, I'd like you to meet my girlfriend, Belinda Davies. Belinda, this is my mom and dad, Sandra and Robert Pennington."

Robert's parents had this air of sophistication. They wore designer clothes. His mom's hair and make-up were perfect. His dad—well, he looked a lot like Robert, just older. I couldn't imagine what they must've thought of me with my braided, wind-blown hair, dressed in blue jeans, a knit top, one tennis shoe, and all that topped off with my designer savvy boot. Nope, I definitely didn't fit in their league.

Sandra cupped my hand in hers. "It's so very nice to meet you. Call me Sandra." Heat radiated around my hand. "Robert never brings young ladies home for us to meet." She frowned at Robert then glanced at my boot. "What happened to your foot?"

"Oh. I sprained my ankle."

Robert stuffed his hands in his front pockets and pursed his lips.

His dad raised a brow. "Robert, are we missing something? Did this involve you?" He nodded his head in the direction of my new fashion statement.

"Yes. It's a long story and I'd rather not think about it, okay?" Robert grimaced, shaking his head.

Mr. Pennington moved behind his wife and placed his hands on her shoulders. "Welcome, it's nice to finally meet you. You can call me Rob."

"It's nice to meet you too sir." I nodded at Robert's mother. "Both of you."

"Well, let's not stand here in the foyer." His mom motioned for us to follow them.

I looked around the room. "Your home is lovely." A horseshoe-shaped stairway wrapped around either side of the room meeting in the middle, forming a balcony on the second floor. There were matching ornate Bombay chests on either side of the stairs flanking the entryway to the formal living room. An oversized, cobalt blue vase sat on each chest. A magnificent crystal chandelier hung in the middle of the towering ceiling. I could see what looked like a study off to the left behind two closed French doors. On the right, an open arched doorway led into the dining room which hosted a grand oval table and ten chairs.

In the family room, Robert led me to the couch. "I'm going to go get my duffel out of the car. Make yourself comfortable. I'll be right back." A twinge in my chest made me very aware he was leaving me alone with his parents.

"I fixed the guest bedroom across the hall from Robert's for you." Sandra positioned herself on the edge of the chair across from me. She sat with her legs crossed at the ankle. Her hands clasped on her knee. I imagined a photographer standing behind me ready to snap her picture. So elegant, and, yep, I'm so out of their league. I tugged at my tee to straighten it and brushed a few flyaway hairs from my face.

"Oh, I'm sorry. My parents are expecting me home tonight. But I appreciate your thinking of me."

"Can you join us for dinner? We were planning to take you both out for your favorite, Mexican food."

"That would be great."

Robert returned and announced, "I'll be right down. I'm going to stash my stuff."

His mother excused herself. Rob sat in a chair next to the couch. The twinge hit harder. I shot a half-smile toward him. Neither one of us spoke. In the awkward silence, I looked around the room, my way of dealing with the mounting tightening in my chest. I assumed they had the interior of their home professionally designed.

Someone had to say something, so I just jumped in. "Your home is beautiful."

Rob swung his head toward me and let out a sigh, then scooted forward in his chair. "Thank you. My wife did it all."

"Really? Is she a designer?"

The familiar upturned corners of his mouth appeared. I saw Robert all over Rob's face. "Yes, she is. I'm sure she'd like to give you a tour later."

"I'd love that." The tightness turned into a flutter when I imagined what other decorating secrets the rest of this palace held.

Another awkward pause pursued. This time he broke it. "Robert has told me a lot about you, except…" He nodded toward my boot. "What did he do?"

"Umm, it's nothing." I shrugged my shoulders. "My fault really. I overreacted."

His dad gave me a curious look. "Overreacted?"

"Yes, I mistook something I saw." I looked down at my hands clasped in my lap, face warming. My heart rate sped up. I thought changing the subject might help relieve my emotional discomfort. "So, Robert has told you about me?"

"Robert and I have a good relationship in that respect. We talk often and he confides in me. That's why I'm surprised he didn't tell me about your injured ankle."

Crap. The ankle again. I bit my lip.

Rob's face softened. He leaned forward and rested his forearms on his knees. "Tell me what happened." I heard Robert in that gentle voice.

I nodded and dove into the story of my unfortunate accident. When I finished, I showered Robert with all kinds of praise for the wonderful care and attention he'd given me. I painted a picture of his perfect son and attempted to make sure Rob knew this whole mess was entirely my fault.

Rob took a deep breath, releasing it loudly, and sat back in his chair.

Sandra and Robert walked in. They'd been gone for a while. Whatever they were doing upstairs seemed to put him in a good mood. "What have you two been talking about?" Robert asked.

His father stood up from the chair and walked over to him. "Her ankle."

Robert's smile vanished. His mouth opened slightly as he looked at me, head cocked.

Rob laughed and put a well-placed hand on his son's shoulder. "Don't worry. She didn't sell you out. In fact, she sang your praises." He then followed that with, "She's a keeper." He panned between his son and wife. "What were you two up to? You were upstairs for quite some time."

Robert shifted his weight and pushed a hand in his pocket. "Same as you...just catching up." He turned to me. "Let's get you home so we'll have some time to visit with your parents before we go out to eat." He reached for my hand and directed me toward the front door. "I'll be back in a little while."

"See you later." I waved.

I stared out my side window. "Your parents are so nice. I really like your dad." I paused and gazed at him. "Robert, I don't fit into your sophisticated lifestyle. I feel out of place. Y'all look and live like royalty."

Robert huffed and pulled to the side of the road and stopped. He leaned over and gently ran his fingers down my cheek, keeping them at my chin. "I love you the way you are—sweet, kind, generous, caring, loving. I could go on and on. You fit in just fine and my parents will see that as well."

I hugged him. "I love you. You make me feel so special."

"You are special. So, no more of this 'I'm not good enough BS.' It's me that's not good enough for you."

I scrunched my nose. "Yeah. I'm the one who's too good for you." I poked a finger in his rock-hard chest. "And don't forget it." I let out a giggle, but in my heart, I knew that wasn't the case.

∽∾

My home was a two-story brick house that would've fit into the Pennington's two-plus times. Robert helped me to the front door and I rang the doorbell. "Where's your key?"

"I don't have one. I usually have my garage door opener, but it's in my car." I nudged him in the side and giggled.

Mom opened the door and welcomed us in. Dad joined. "Mom, Dad, this is my boyfriend, Robert Pennington. Robert, this is Dora and James Davies."

Mom glanced at my foot. "Nice fashion statement." Then she turned to lead us to the family room. "At least you're on the mend."

We sat and visited for a while before Mom stood and offered to make some snacks. I volunteered to help her, figuring this would give my father and Robert time to become more acquainted.

The kitchen island gave me a perfect view of the two most important men in my life. I had no clue what they were talking about, but, whatever it was, they both had a vested interest in it.

Mom placed the last cracker next to the cheese and started to pick up the platter. I grabbed her arm. "They're talking about something, and I don't want to interrupt."

Mom glanced into the den. "Okay. Let me know when."

Seconds later the discussion ended with them standing and shaking hands. Mom and I looked at each other. I shrugged.

She took the handshake as her cue to announce, "Snacks anyone?"

She gracefully moved into the family room with the tray of food. Mom was so much the homemaker and seemed out of place in her jeans. She should've been wearing a crisp, starched, collared dress, fitted at the waist with a full skirt covered by an apron. She acted like a mother I'd seen on a rerun of a '50's TV show.

"Please. Sit down." She placed the tray on the coffee table.

Now, it was Mom's turn to ask twenty questions. She fired them off in rapid succession, and, to my amazement, Robert kept right up and politely answered each one.

In a well-timed pause, Robert stood up and turned toward my parents, taking in a deep breath. "Mr. and Mrs. Davies, I know this is all happening rather quickly, but I'm hoping this will prove to your daughter how much I love her and want to be with her forever."

I gazed at Robert. *What's going on?*

"I'd like to ask you for her hand in marriage."

With his last words, my breath caught and my heart hammered almost out of control. My mouth went dry. I froze, still staring at him.

"Belinda." My mother drew my attention, but Dad reached over placing his hand on hers, a request for her to remain quiet. She sat back in her chair. Her gaze shifted from Dad to me. From my father's reaction to Robert's request, I now understood what their conversation had been about.

My father sat back in his chair. "You know my answer." She just stared at Dad with his hand still on hers. "The young man asked me politely a few minutes ago. There wasn't time to talk it over with you." He smiled at her. "So what do you think?"

Mom looked at me. I'm sure she could judge my anxiety level. She knew I loved him. I bit my lower lip. She addressed Robert. "Young man, the subject of you has dominated most of Belinda and my phone calls. I know marrying you would make her very happy." She waved a hand in the air. "You have my permission."

Robert pulled something out of his jeans pocket, clutching it in his hand. He knelt on one knee and reached for my hand.

I tingled from the gentleness of his touch. My pet butterflies in my stomach started to flutter their wings.

"Belinda Davies, I love you with all my heart and promise to love you forever. Will you marry me?" He opened his hand.

Tears of joy blurred my vision and I didn't hesitate to give my answer. "Yes...yes, I'll marry you!"

"This was my great-grandmother's engagement ring."

I stared at the three diamonds mounted in a silver-colored setting. Its mesmerizing beauty left me speechless.

"My grandmother and my mother wore it as their engagement ring." He slid the ring onto my finger. "I've been told all who have worn it have been happily married. They thought of it as a good luck charm. Mom wanted me to give it to you."

I fingered the jewels. "I love it." I flung my arms around his neck and kissed him. My heart bursting.

"Did I get it right this time? To your satisfaction?"

"What?" I pulled back, puzzled.

"Our first date?"

I remembered the scene at the restaurant when I questioned how Robert had asked me to marry him. I laughed. "Yes, it was perfect."

My father cleared his throat. "We only request one thing—that you graduate from college before you get married. You need to finish your education. Robert gave me his word when we talked. Can you give me yours?"

Robert sat next to me. "Dad, I promise I'll finish."

"He's a senior. You're a junior. He's graduating," Mom pointed out.

"He'll be working on his master's for the next two years, starting this summer." I reached for Robert's hand. "We'll only be apart during the summer, and I'll go visit him often."

Robert shifted and leaned in to address my father. "Sir, I promise she'll graduate."

"Young man, I'm holding you to that promise, and you better keep her happy." Dad glanced at Mom for approval. She smiled and nodded.

Robert stood up and extended his hand to my father. "Sir, I'll do the best I can to ensure both." Dad stood and returned the handshake. I knew he impressed my father. Heck, Robert impressed me.

"You'll have to excuse me, but I need to head back home to visit with my parents." He turned to me. "I'll pick you up at 7:30."

"Oh, Mom, Dad, I forgot to tell you. Robert and I are going to dinner with his parents tonight if you don't mind. Maybe we could have lunch here tomorrow so we can talk more." I knew my parents would want more time with us, in light of Robert's surprise proposal.

Mom nodded. "Of course. Lunch tomorrow would be just fine."

"Okay, 7:30 it is." I started to stand to see Robert to the door.

"You just stay seated and off that foot. I'll see you in a little while. Mr. and Mrs. Davies, it was very nice to meet you." Robert headed for the front door with my father following.

Dad returned and shoved his hands in his pockets. He paced back and forth. I grew up with my father's pacing habit, his ritual when something concerned him. "He seems like a nice guy, but aren't you two rushing this? You've only known him for—what—about a month?"

"Mom, Dad, the first time I saw him, I knew I had to meet him. The first time he touched me, I knew I had to date him…to get to know him…and the first time he kissed me." I briefly closed my eyes. "I knew he was the one. I'm in love with him."

My mother had been fairly quiet to this point. "All right, we just want you to be sure…to be happy. Honey, I don't want you making a mistake."

"I'm not. I've never been more positive about anything in my life."

The doorbell rang at 7:30 sharp. I hobbled to the door. Robert stepped in and swept me up into his arms. "What are you doing answering the door?"

"Waiting for you." I gave him a peck on the cheek. "I missed you."

"I missed you too, Angel."

The second we walked into the restaurant, his mom jumped up from her seat. "Let me see it!" She reached for my hand. "Do you like it?"

"I love it. It's exactly what I would've picked."

Her arms went around Robert and she laid her head against his chest. In a natural gesture, he embraced her. Next, her arms encircled me and she whispered, "Welcome to the family."

The waitress took our drink orders and passed out the menus. Then Sandra reached over and cupped my hand. "So, when is the wedding?"

"I told my parents we'd wait until I graduate."

"Oh…well, that's perfect. That will give us a year to plan a big spectacular wedding. There's so much that we'll need to do. I can start a guest list. I'll need your mother's phone number so we can coordinate."

Big spectacular wedding?! I looked at Robert. He saw the pleading in my eyes and interrupted his mother. "Mom. Belinda and I haven't discussed wedding plans yet. We just got engaged. We don't know what we want. There's plenty of time to decide, and we'll give you all the notice you need." Under the table, I gave Robert a gentle "thank you" squeeze on his thigh. He patted my hand.

The group settled in to get the meal underway and to give Robert's parents' time to size me up a bit more. Despite their sophisticated ways, I found them to be friendly and caring.

Enjoying a bite of my tres leches, I noticed a man approaching our table.

"Please excuse my intrusion, but I couldn't help noticing what an attractive couple you are." He looked at me. "I'm Frank Johnson, of the Johnson's Modeling Agency.

I'm always looking for fresh new faces for advertisements and commercials. If you think you'd be interested, here is my business card." He handed it to me. "Again, please excuse me for interrupting." He nodded and left without waiting for a response.

We all glanced at each other amazed. I studied the card. Robert's father told him it wouldn't be a good idea since he'd eventually be running their company and a seemingly innocent ad could tarnish the company's image.

"I'm not interested. I think he was mainly interested in Belinda." Robert smiled at me. "See, I told you you'd make a good model." He snitched a bite of my dessert and winked.

I chuckled to myself imagining a picture of Robert, the future head of the Pennington Financial Firm, plastered across billboards in only men's briefs.

As for me, no way. I learned my lesson the first time and never again. One disastrous practice walk down a runway gave me all the modeling experience I ever wanted.

"I'm not interested. I don't have time for that now. I have school and a wedding to plan." My first impulse was to toss the card on the table and leave it. Instead, I slid it in my wallet.

My ankle started to remind me of its existence. I leaned over to Robert and asked if he could take me home. I knew a pain pill and elevating my leg would relieve my growing agony. We said goodbye to his parents. On our way out of the restaurant, Mr. Johnson nodded and made a "call me" sign with his left hand. I just smiled, knowing that would never happen.

Without Robert next to me, I tossed and turned all night. Relief finally came when light started to fill the room. I dragged myself from the bed to clean up and dress, then I made my way downstairs. At mid-stairs, a mouth-watering aroma filled my nostrils. I stopped and lifted my nose to inhale a healthy sniff. "Mom's pancakes."

"Good morning. Did you have fun last night? Orange juice or coffee?" She started with her rapid-fire questions while flipping a pancake.

"Both." Mom had a habit of asking too many questions at once. This made it difficult to answer everything, but it did have its good points. I could select what I wanted to answer then go on to the next set of questions. I sat at the table across from my dad, who had his nose stuck in the Sunday newspaper as usual. Mom brought me the orange juice and coffee, followed by my plate of pancakes.

"Mom, come sit down. I have something to ask you both." To my surprise, my father lowered the newspaper onto the table. Mom sat next to him.

"Can I go to summer school and take a class to lighten my fall schedule?" *Please say yes.*

Mom crossed her hands in front of her. "Don't you mean so you can be with him?"

She knew me too well. "For both reasons."

"We didn't budget for summer school. It won't hurt you to be away from him for a few months." Dad scooped up a bite of his pancakes then picked up the newspaper and leaned back, giving it a quick jerk to make it rustle. I grew up knowing that usually meant he'd had enough talking for now.

That didn't stop me from trying because his hearing was perfect. "I can find a job to pay for my rent and food. You'd only have to pay for the class." I wanted to be there with Robert.

"We'll think about it and let you know." Dad's grumbly voice emerged from behind the newspaper. I knew pressing my father would only make him more determined. I dropped the subject and filled my mouth with Mom's pancakes. They were the best in Texas and the one thing I missed most.

After breakfast, I gathered some things I wanted to take back with me. I had to limit my choices. Robert's car could only hold so much. I moped around my room, trying to kill some time. There was a knocked at the door and Mom asked if she could come in.

She sat on the edge of the bed. Mom had always been in my corner when I was troubled. I could talk to her when there was no one else to turn to in high school. She was my cheerleader. She loved me with a mother's love, a kind that is given unconditionally.

"You really love this boy, Belinda?"

I sat next to her. "I feel complete with him. It's like I found a missing part of me. Mom, I don't want to be away from him."

She smiled in that familiar way that comforted me so many times as a child. She took my hand in hers, patting it. "Oh, young love, how I remember." She shifted her weight to face me. "If he really loves you, he'll wait for you."

I looked at her with a straight face. "*Moooomm*, how cliché." We both burst out laughing. She knew how to get a good laugh out of me. My heart lifted.

"Honey, I'll see what I can do. I'll talk to your father."

I hugged her neck. "Thank you. I love you."

Her soft voice filled my ear. "I can't promise anything, but I'll do what I can." I tightened my hug at the news of the sketchy promise. "Okay, enough. You need to come downstairs and help me with lunch. Don't you want to show your fiancé you're a good cook?"

"Nooo! Then he'll expect me to cook all the time. What he doesn't know won't hurt him."

Mom flashed a smile and patted my back. "Good job. I taught you well, never let them know everything." We burst out laughing then headed downstairs.

Robert arrived promptly at 12:30. With a lunge, he swept me up in his arms and gave me a stirring open mouth kiss. My eyes widened with longing, but I knew a kiss like this was pushing our limits. He nuzzled my hair. "All this touchy-feely stuff is driving me nuts. I can't wait 'til tonight."

I threw my head back and giggled. "Me too." Over his knit shirt, I felt his hard chest as I rubbed my hand over his pecs. A stir started deep in my belly and I knew it wouldn't take long for that sensation to intensify. I gave him a quick pat. "Come on. We're ready to eat."

Dad and Robert talked about a variety of subjects over lunch. He seemed to know instinctively what my father's interests were and hit on most of them.

Robert asked for another slice of the spinach quiche. "This is very good, Mrs. Davies. I'd like to have this recipe."

"Oh. Do you cook?" Mom looked innocently at him, taking a sip of juice.

"I dabble." He stuffed another man-size bite in and glanced over at me.

"Well, Belinda made this, so I'm sure she can share the recipe with you." She smirked at me.

My eyes grew wide. I glared back. She enjoyed bantering with me. It was her favorite sport. I have to admit, I liked to return the teasing right back to her. "Moooomm!" I squealed at her.

She just smiled at me as if to say, *What did I do?*

Robert scrutinized the two of us then elbowed my arm. "Have you been keeping secrets from me?" He popped another bite full into his mouth. "Hmmm. Delicious."

I looked him straight in the eye. "Just because I don't cook, doesn't mean I can't. Besides, why should I if I can get other people to do it for me."

Robert paused and then exploded into laughter. "I'll get you back for this, I promise."

Mom and Dad looked puzzled. I waved my hand in dismissal. I leaned in to exaggerate my displeasure with her. "Inside joke and thanks, Mom."

∞

"I don't think you need to carry me anymore. My ankle feels better."

"You're too slow with that boot." He darted around campus in his usual manner. He raced into the Fine Arts building, up the stairs, and then into my classroom. After scanning the room, he located Abby and put me down in the seat next to her. "Stay right here until I get back."

"Yes, Master." I liked feeling his arms around me, squeezing me tight. Even though it wasn't necessary, I didn't insist he stop.

He leaned over and kissed me tenderly on the head as he stroked my hair. Robert winked and turned toward Abby. "Keep her out of trouble. I have a lot invested in her."

Abby nodded. "Hmmm. Like I can."

After I settled in, I flashed my hand in front of her, but she didn't notice. So, again, I waved my hand, with more exaggeration, in front of her nose.

Her eyes crossed. "Belinda! You're engaged?!" She smiled and bounced in her seat. Abby clutched my hand and stared at the perfect diamonds that represented Robert's latest symbol of our love.

"Uh-huh." I rested my head on her shoulder so we could admire the perfect ring sitting on my finger.

"Tell me all about it. When? Where?" Just as she asked her questions, the professor started his lecture. Abby's excitement diminished to disappointment.

The minute the professor finished the lecture, Abby snapped her head toward me. "Okay, start talking."

So I started from the beginning, telling her about our perfect weekend. Abby hung on every word with her usual enthusiastic nature. "So, when is the wedding?"

"I told my parents we'd wait until after I graduate."

Abby's brow furrowed with concern. "Isn't Robert graduating? What are you going to do with him gone?"

"Robert's going to grad school here. He's starting this summer."

"So. You'll still be apart."

"No, we won't." I pulled her close and delved into my plan and explained if my Mom managed her part, this summer would never be an issue.

"You go." We high-fived. "By the way, are you and Robert going to the Delt formal?"

"What? What formal? He hasn't mentioned it. When is it?"

"It's in two weeks." Abby looked like she'd let a cat out of the bag.

I did my best to act like nothing was wrong. "I'll have to ask him. Are you and Garrett going?"

"Yep. I was hoping you and Robert had planned on it, too." She bit her lower lip. Abby couldn't hide her emotions. Instead, she wore them on her sleeve.

Robert, with his signature smile flashing, arrived to retrieve me. "Hey, ladies." He reached over and kissed me.

Our drive home was quiet. I couldn't stop wondering why he hadn't asked me to the formal. Did I embarrass him somehow? Why didn't he want to take me? I took a deep breath, swallowed hard and let the question rip. "What's this I hear about a formal in two weeks?" I held my breath, hoping for the response I wanted to hear.

"Uh. I forgot about the Spring Formal. Something has been keeping me preoccupied lately." He moved his brows up and down. "Do you want to go?"

I exhaled. "Of course, I do, silly. I'll have to call Mom and ask her to send me a dress. It might need to be altered, but I'm sure she can handle that."

"Then it's settled. We'll go."

The next few days passed rapidly. My life with Robert couldn't have been more perfect. My ankle kept improving with exercise. I even surprised Robert with a few home-cooked meals. On one occasion when he came in late from class, I had a romantic dinner planned. Timing his entrance perfectly, I smiled and walked out of the kitchen wearing nothing but a bib apron, carrying our plates of food. "Dinner is served." He must have liked my outfit. Dinner was microwaved much later that night.

Chapter 16

MY ANKLE HEALED. So, with my two functioning feet and in matching shoes, I decided to surprise Robert by meeting him when he came out of class. I ambled along, admiring my ring every now and then. I loved how the sunlight made it sparkle. Yep. My life was pretty great.

That is until I rounded the corner of his building.

I jerked to a halt. Several feet in front of me stood my fiancé and Lora. Embracing? Kissing?

My heart stopped beating. She had her arms wrapped around his neck and his hands at her waist. Oh my God! Not again. I wanted to hurl. Tears flooded my eyes and streamed down my cheeks. *Confront him*, he had told me.

So, without any hesitation, I rushed over and grabbed Lora's arm and ripped her off of him. Then I spun around and slapped Robert across the face so hard my hand went numb. I screamed, "I trusted you! Liar! Cheater!"

He held his cheek and said nothing.

"Monster" reared her head and charged out of her lair. I turned and ran back down the side of the building toward the parking lot, sobbing. My tears blinded me.

I heard Garrett yell, "Belinda, watch out!" A well-placed hand reached out and yanked me back as a car flew by.

"Garrett. No!" I shoved at his chest, still wanting to get the hell out of there.

He wouldn't let go. "No! You're too upset. You almost *just* got hit by a car."

I swiped the tears from my cheeks and scanned in the direction where I left Robert. He wasn't following me. I sniffled. "Do you have your car?"

"It's over there."

I grabbed his arm and we headed toward my escape.

Tears streamed down my cheeks the whole time we sat on the couch. Garrett didn't say anything. He just put his arm around my shoulders and let me cry.

My cell phone played a familiar tune. I scowled at my purse, knowing it was Robert, but I wasn't ready to listen to his excuse. So, I retrieved it and pressed the off icon. Garrett's cell rang. "Don't answer it," I spat out. "I don't want to talk to him." My insides had been ripped out, and my heart still had Robert's foot on it.

Garrett shrugged his shoulders and didn't answer the call. He cupped my chin and turned my head to face him. His fingers wiped at my tears. "Belinda, This could be Lora's doing. You need to talk to him and get his side of the story."

"No! They were lip-locked." I grabbed a pillow and crossed my arms over it. "He wasn't pushing her away. I can't trust him. I'm an idiot for believing he loves me." Hardheaded I refused to believe I was wrong again.

"No, you're not. I know he loves you."

Garrett's cell rang again. This time he turned it off. "Feel like watching a movie?"

"Yeah. Sure. Just don't make it a romance." I cradled my head against his chest, then tucked my legs up on the couch.

"Right."

The motion of Garrett carrying me stirred me from my sleep. I didn't even remember the end of the movie. He placed me on the bed, covered me with a blanket, and then left the room.

From the living room, I heard him talking to someone on his cell. "Yes, I have her at my place." He paused. "No, leave her here——. She's asleep. She almost got hit by a car, for chrissake. What were you thinking, kissing Lora?" He paused again. "No, I won't let you in——. No Robert, let her calm down——. I'll try to get her to talk to you later."

I turned over into a fetal position, feeling confident Garrett would keep Robert away from me, for now. I was emotionally exhausted. Sleep came, but it was fitful and plagued with disturbing dreams.

When I awoke, the vision of Robert kissing Lora and its aftermath engulfed my memory. I didn't want to think about it or cry anymore. I stumbled into the living area, where Garrett sat on the couch, and noticed light coming in the window. "What day is it? Is it still Friday?"

"No, it's Saturday. I just let you sleep." He walked over and hugged me.

It felt good having someone with me when I felt so dreadful. "Why couldn't it have been you I fell in love with?"

"I wish it had been." He squeezed me again and let out a big sigh. "But I'm just not the one who's meant to be with you."

Our relationship had been sealed when I started seeing Robert. Garrett would always have a place in my heart and my life, but would never be my love.

"You hungry?"

"Yeah, a little."

Garrett walked toward the kitchen. "How about a ham and cheese omelet and toast?"

"Okay." I sat on a stool at the counter and rested my head on my arms and watched Garrett whip together breakfast. We talked, but we avoided the subject of Robert.

The meal was just what I needed. "Thanks, that was delicious. And thanks for your help. I really appreciate all you've done for me."

"Anytime. It would've devastated Robert if something had happened to you. Not to mention how I'd feel." He reached for my hands. "You mean a lot to everyone."

"Except Robert." Tears began to well.

He looked at me with a shocked expression. "Belinda, you're all he talks about. How he can't imagine living without you. You need to talk to him. He's been calling all morning. He's freakin' out."

"I can't!" Robert's foot was still grinding away at my heart, pressing so hard the pain was almost unbearable.

We sat on the couch, and I lay down with my head on his lap. He ran his finger through my hair. It was very evident that my reaction to Garrett was so different from Robert's. When Garrett touched me, it was soft and tender, but no zing. But with Robert, it was stimulating. It always triggered a ravenous urge to kiss that would make every inch of my body feel like it was on fire and he was what I needed to satisfy my urge. The more he kissed me, the more I needed him. Our love was different from anything I'd ever experienced. There was a sensitivity I felt with Robert. He made me feel as if nothing could hurt me, until he did. Garrett continued to stroke my hair, and I started to drift.

I woke up and checked the time on my cell—4:20. Garrett had also fallen asleep. I tried not to disturb him but failed. "Sorry, I didn't mean to wake you. I guess I should go home. Would you drive me?"

Garrett yawned and stretched. "To his place?"

"No. Mine."

∞

Abby must have heard us pull into the driveway because she was waiting at the top of the stairs. "Garrett told me what happened. I wanted to come over there, but he said you needed some time to calm down. Jeez, Belinda. I'm so glad Garrett was there." She turned and walked into our room then spun around, inches from my face. "You need to control your 'Monster.' You could've been killed this time." Seconds later she flung her arms around my shoulders and hugged me. "I've been so worried about you."

The arms of my friend comforted me. I didn't have time to return the embrace. Abby pulled away and tossed out another question. "Have you talked to Robert yet?"

I shook my head and ran a finger over the diamonds of my engagement ring. Abby wrapped her hands around mine. "Belinda, don't go making any hasty decisions. You need to hear his side of the story. Maybe Lora caught him off guard again." She stared into my eyes, tightening her hold on my hands.

"It didn't look that way to me. But, I sure surprised him." I slid my hands from hers and fingered the ring again, but didn't take it off. I plopped crossed-legged on my bed and faced her.

"What do you mean?" Abby joined me with a bounce.

"I slapped him across the face so hard he probably still has my handprint on his cheek. He told me to confront him next time something upset me...so I did." Tears welled and started to trickle down my cheeks. "Abby, what am I going to do? I can't keep going through this. It hurts too much."

She put her hand on my shoulder. "I know you don't want to hear this, but you need to talk to him." She patted my back. "Let him explain. You know Lora hates you."

"I can't, not today. Maybe tomorrow."

Tears poured down my face. It felt good to be held, but I'm sure I soaked Abby's neck. I reached for the box of tissues and knocked my purse over. My cell phone fell out. Abby and I looked at it, then each other.

"Go ahead," She shoved it to me. "Check it."

I had a lot of voice and text messages from Robert. They all said the same thing. He claimed what I saw was just a misunderstanding and pleaded for me to let him explain.

My cell started singing. "It's him." I tapped the end-call icon and tossed it on the bed. My stomach growled. "I guess it's trying to tell me something. Are you hungry? But, I don't want to go out and risk running into him."

"We could just order our usual. Pizza would be okay with me."

"That's fine. Would you order it? I'm going to take a bath." I imagined I was a sight. I hadn't bathed for over a day or changed clothes.

"Sure, I'll let you know when it's here."

The bathtub, a real soaking type, was an antique claw-footed tub, one nice benefit of living in an old house. I lay covered with Cherry Blossom bubbles, trying not to see a repeat of the kiss that seared my mind, but I finally gave up. I'd just finished putting on my pajamas when Abby called through the door that our pizza had arrived. But that wasn't all. Robert was at the front door.

"Belinda, he wants to talk to you. Go downstairs."

I wasn't ready to face him yet. I walked out of the bathroom straight to our open front window and yelled, "Robert, go away! I don't want to talk to you right now! Go!"

"Belinda, please, let me—" I slammed the window closed and walked away. A few minutes later, I heard squealing wheels.

Abby and I sat quietly on my bed and ate our pizza until she broke the silence. "If you want to talk about it, I'll listen. Maybe I can help you through this." Her cell rang. She rolled her eyes. "Of all times for this thing to ring."

Abby glanced at me. "Hello." She whispered, "Garrett," then listened a few seconds more. "She seems to be doing okay. We're eating right now." She scrunched her brow. "He is? She'll be glad to hear that." She nodded. "Yes, I agree." She smiled. "I'll see you tomorrow. Good night."

Abby was almost too giddy. "Robert is really upset that you won't talk to him." She bounced and made the pizza teeter on the edge of the bed. "Ooops." She caught it and continued. "He said Robert was coming over to his place so he needed to reschedule."

"Were you supposed to go out with Garrett tonight?"

"Yeah, but we agreed I need to stay with you." She took another bite of her slice of pizza.

I let out a sigh of relief. "Thanks, Abby."

"Let's make this a girls' night in. We need to do something fun." Abby walked to the closet. She brought out a bottle of wine and some paper cups. With them held up and strutted back toward her bed. "This should help. And some singing. You game?"

"Sure, pop the cork." I smiled. My thumbs got busy as I searched my playlist and started the music.

"It's more a twist-off," she joked, rotating the cap. She poured us each a cup of White Zinfandel. "I have another one of these if we run out."

We sang and danced to several songs while keeping our cups filled. I began to relax and my thoughts of Robert faded.

Abby and I were in full swing with our makeshift karaoke when our landlady peeked into the room. "Hey girls, you're being a little noisy."

"Sorry, Mrs. Evans." Abby pointed to me. "Fiancé problems."

"Oh. Are you all right, dear?" Mrs. Evans' expression came across as a caring grandmother.

"I'll be fine. I'm drowning my woes." I held my cup out toward her. "We have another cup. Would you like to join us?"

The corners of her mouth tilted up as she walked into the room. "Sure, I'd like that." Mrs. Evans ambled over to an upholstered wingback chair. She paused then gently ran her hand along the top, smiling like she had a pleasant memory. She sat in it and rested her head against the back. "Mr. Evans and I had our fair share of problems in the beginning. But, we hung in there and worked them out. We were happily married for forty-two years." She took a sip of wine from the cup I handed her. "Which one of you has the good voice?"

"That's her." Abby pointed to me.

"Continue singing. I'll just sit here and listen. Both of you seem to be having such a good time."

"But what about the noise?" Abby tipped the bottle to fill her cup, again.

Mrs. Evans raised her wine. "Who cares now? I'm up here too."

Abby and I lifted our cups to her and burst into laughter. "To a great girl's night in," Abby declared just before we all took a gulp.

Abby selected another song and the show continued. We jumped around with our air guitars and sang. With one bottle of wine under our belts and another opened, we had so much fun.

Exhausted and tipsy, Abby and I collapsed on the floor. Loud voices, engines revving up, and wheels squealing, filtered in from the frat house next door. Mrs. Evans walked over and looked out. "Doesn't your boyfriend drive a little blue sports car?"

"Yes, why?" Lightheaded, I weaved my way toward her.

"It's parked out front. He must be next door. Most likely he wants you to know he's near," she said smugly.

I peeked out the window. "Yep. That's it. He sure is upset. Huh, out partying." *Asshat!* F-bombs usually weren't part of my vocabulary, but one escaped. "Sorry." I took a good gulp of wine, emptying half the cup.

Mrs. Evans looked at me with a devilish grin that put a glint in her eyes. "When I was upset with my Sam, I used to pull pranks to get back at him."

She had my attention. "Like what?" I was game for anything.

"One time, I stuffed his car with crumpled newspaper during the night. I waited until he fell asleep, and then struck. I watched the next morning while he cleaned up the mess. He didn't come back into the house. He would've been late for work." She covered her mouth with her hand and let out a muffled chuckle. "I—" she winked "—just happen to have plenty of newspapers still in the recycle bin." Her face lit up when she lifted one brow.

"I'm in." Abby raised her cup from her reclining position on the floor.

"Okay, let's do it." I knew how much he loved that car. I'd be getting back at him without causing any real damage. "He should be home, not out partying."

Mrs. Evans told us to go to the back porch, and she would be there in a few minutes.

The back screen door creaked open. Mrs. Evans stepped onto the porch with two large black trash bags and sat on a chair. "Just crumple the newspapers and put'em in these bags. But, stuff in as much as you can, so you have enough to fill that little car." Her grin widened like she was having the most fun she'd had in a long time.

Abby and I hauled the two stuffed bags to the front door then peeped out the window to see if his car was still out front. The party sounded like it was in full swing. Since the house sat on the corner of Main Street and Elm, we had decided to take the direct path to his car to avoid being mistaken as burglars by the local cops. So, we grabbed the bags and dashed outside.

Mrs. Evan's stood guard peering through the hedge while Abby and I snuck along the drive. Luckily, the car was unlocked and the hedge offered cover for our covert operation. We did our deed and ran back inside.

Mrs. Evans joined us. "Are you going to stay up and watch?"

"I am. I wouldn't miss this for anything."

"Me, too." Abby jumped up and down, clapping her hands. "This is so exciting."

Yep. Way too much energy.

"Well, I'm off to bed. Thanks, girls, for a wonderful evening. Good night." Mrs. Evans shuffled toward her bedroom. "Let me know how this turns out. Keep the noise down," she warned in a playful voice at her bedroom door. Just before it closed, I heard her chuckle.

Abby and I dashed upstairs and turned off the lights. We lay across my bed on our stomachs with our heads propped up on our palms. We watched out the window and hoped the sheer lace curtain concealed us. The streetlight made it easy to see his car. Abby spoke first. "Do you think he'll suspect us?"

"I doubt it. He'll probably think it was the pledges."

Silence fell over the room. It was odd Abby didn't have anything to say, but the quiet was short-lived. "Are you going to talk to him tomorrow?"

"I don't know. Maybe." I thought about it for a few seconds. "No, I don't think so. He must not be too upset. He's partying."

"You let your 'Monster' out again. You should've stayed there and really confronted him and then told that bitch to keep her hands off." Abby never took her eyes off me. "Running doesn't solve anything. It could have put you in the hospital or killed you. He'd blame himself. You wouldn't want him to live with that, would you?"

"No. I panic and run without even thinking." Fear shot through my heart. "I'm afraid of losing him."

"Belinda, he hasn't left you. It's you who keeps leaving him."

I bit my lip but realized she was right.

Lying still on the bed and feeling the effects of the wine proved to be too much. We fell asleep.

∞

"Dammit!" and a few other choice words, woke me up Sunday morning.

I peered through the lace curtains. "Abby, get up."

She rolled over on her back. "What?" In mid-yawn, she stopped. "Who's doing all that cussing?" In a flash, she flipped onto her stomach. A smile as big as Texas spread across her face. "This should be fun."

This was the first time I'd ever seen Robert look a mess, not Mr. Perfect. His clothes were all rumpled and his shirttail hung out. His hair stuck up all over his head, but he was still gorgeous, and I knew I loved him despite everything that had happened.

Robert stomped around the hedge to the frat house. A few minutes later, he and Brian walked back to his car with big garbage bags. Robert opened the passenger door and started pulling out paper, handing it to him. Brian said something and glanced toward our house. Robert stopped and glared right at the window. His piercing eyes made my heart jump. I swear he looked right at me despite the cover of the curtains. He stared for a few seconds then returned to the mission. When they finished, Robert drove off and left Brian with the paper-filled bags.

Abby and I rolled onto our backs. She burst out laughing. I tried to laugh but grabbed my head on either side. "I can't laugh. It hurt's too much." The last thing I wanted to do was to get up.

Abby rolled out of bed. "You want something for that headache?"

"Don't talk so loud." I covered my ears.

"You're such a wimp."

I put my pillow over my head. "Just leave me here to die."

A few seconds later I felt a nudge of my shoulder. "Here take these. I'll go get us some breakfast but first I'll pick up your car at Robert's place."

I took the pills and glass. "How do you do that?"

"What?"

"Get up with so much energy and no headache."

She shrugged. "Practice."

The next thing I heard was Abby coming in with our breakfast. "I talked to Garrett. He wants us to come over for dinner. Will you go?"

"I guess. I have to eat."

Abby stayed with me for the rest of the day. We talked and laughed about Robert's reaction to our stunt. It felt good to laugh. It blocked out the hurt I had inside.

The afternoon was rather lazy. We laid on our beds and binge-watched reruns. I found it difficult to concentrate. My mind kept drifting back to Robert. Why couldn't he stay away from Lora? Did she kiss him? Did I not catch the whole event like the last time? Too many unanswered questions filled my head. During a sitcom, I dropped off to sleep.

∞

The scream never escaped my lips no matter how hard I tried. I shot up in bed. My heart hammered. I looked over at Abby. "How long have I been asleep?"

Abby had an alarmed look on her face. "About two hours. Are you okay? You look like you've seen a ghost?"

My hair was sticking to my sweaty forehead. "I had a horrible dream." I clenched my blanket. "I was at a party with Garrett and you. Robert came later, but he didn't know who I was." I flung my feet off the edge of the bed. "Abby, I don't know what I would do if I lost him. I love him so much. I couldn't live without him. I wouldn't want to either."

Tears streamed down my face. She came over and wrapped her arms around me.

"The dream seemed so real." My shoulders heaved along with my sputtered breaths.

She tightened her grip and started to sway . "Belinda, it was only a dream."

"I know. But what if I do lose him?"

Abby placed her hands on my shoulders and leaned back. "How this whole thing plays out is up to you."

I wiped my eyes. "I know."

Abby poked my stomach. "Good. I want to watch this next episode. I missed it the first time around." A broad smile spread across her face. She bounced back to her bed.

I had difficulty concentrating on the TV shows. The pain roiling in my belly moved its way to my chest. The fear of not having Robert in my life terrified me. The rational part of me warned to be cautious and think about my decision, but the emotional aspect overrode the practical. I was almost ready to forgive him rather than live without him. Relief came when we left to go to dinner. My mind would have something to do other than think about Robert.

∞

"Hey, you're just in time. I just got finished."

We were filling our plates when someone entered the front door. I turned around and there stood Robert.

I swallowed hard. My neck muscles tensed before I spun and barked at Garrett, "Why?" I pointed at Robert. "Why did you invite him?"

Garrett held his hands up, palms out in front of him. "This was his idea so he could explain to you what happened. I just agreed."

I dropped my plate on the counter. Food flew everywhere. I huffed and headed for the front door. I came within a few feet of the doorknob but Robert side stepped to block my exit.

"Belinda, listen to me!"

"I don't want to hear excuses." Ducking under his arm, I lunged for the knob again.

He grabbed me around the waist and lifted me off my feet, then headed for the bedroom. "Garrett, do you mind?"

"No, not at all."

I tried to push his arm away. "Put. Me. Down!" He ignored me. I looked at Abby. "How could you do this to me?"

"Because I love you and I know you love him. You're just being a mule."

Robert kicked the door closed and put me on my feet. I stood with my hands fisted at my side. "I wanna leave."

"Please. Hear me out." He stood in my path.

"Hear you out? So you can give me some lame excuse that I'll believe. Not this time."

His eyelids closed and his chest rose and fell. "My heart is breaking."

"And mine isn't?" I slapped his arm. "Look at me."

He opened his eyes and what I saw melted my heart. They had welled with tears. "I know you won't believe me, but Lora caught me off guard." He swallowed hard.

"You're right, I don't believe you. It's just another excuse to justify your beha—"

"Belinda...please, let me finish. She heard we were engaged and wanted to talk to me. She sounded really upset when she called, so I agreed to meet her. We were talking when she threw herself at me. That's when you arrived." He raised his hand to his cheek and rubbed it. "Man, you dazed me for a few seconds with that slap, and then you were gone. I was about to run after you when Lora grabbed me and was all over me again. By the time I got her off, she was crying hysterically. I saw you with Garrett and I knew he would take care of you. Lora was still trying to cling to me and I didn't feel right just walking away."

I jerked my head back and snapped, "You'd rather console her than me?"

He raised his hands, palms out. "No, no. There was so much going on I didn't know what to do first. Besides, I thought you'd be in class and wouldn't find out about our meeting."

My mouth dropped open.

A blank stare came over his face before he lowered his head, shaking it. He just stuck his foot in his mouth with that remark.

"Oh! So you think it's okay when I'm not around and won't know! How long have you been sneaking around with Lora?"

"Belinda, I haven't been. You know I'm with you every free minute!"

"Except when I'm in class and won't find out. I can't trust you." I started pulling my engagement ring off. "I wish I'd never met you."

His eyes were full of hurt after my last jab. He placed his hands on mine. "Don't say that. I swear I haven't. I wouldn't do that to you. Angel...I'm not prepared to live without you."

"So why not tell Lora to get lost and leave you alone?"

"I did, but she won't give up." He rubbed the back of his neck. "She's use to getting her way. It's like she's stalking me." He took a deep breath. "Sorry it took so long to end it, but...I've never had to break up with anyone before. Lora is the first."

His confession threw me off guard. "You're telling me you've never broken up with a girlfriend?"

He pursed his lips and nodded. "That's what I'm saying."

I sat at the edge of the bed. I understood me never having to break up with anyone. I never dated. Robert surely had girlfriends, different girlfriends.

"But you've been dating since High School? How?"

His chest rose and fell with a sigh. "May I?" He motioned toward the spot next to me.

"Sure."

He sank down on the bed, supported his elbows on his thighs, and then clasped his hands. "Time or distance always took care of the break-ups. I'm a one-girl-at-a-time guy."

His face appeared sad and remorseful, but it was his pleading eyes that touched my soul. "Go on."

"I was jinxed when it came to girlfriends. I dated Jen my sophomore year of high school. During the summer, she moved. The same thing happened in my junior year. My senior year, Cathy decided to go to a college out of state." He looked at me and nodded. "Are you seeing the pattern here?"

"Continue."

"I started dating Lora at the beginning of last year. She lives in Dallas and my dad had me working full-time at the office last summer so I never saw her. When we came back this school year, she wanted to pick up right where we left off. I was okay with that until I met you. Then everything changed." He filled his lungs and exhaled. "You turned my nice neat package of a life upside down and I don't want to let you go. You're a dream come true."

I didn't know how to respond at first. "What about Lora?"

"I did what I had to do. I told her I loved you and would never respond to any of her phone calls again."

We sat in silence. The thought of my dream from earlier flooded my mind. The pain of not having my love in my life felt so real. I never wanted to experience anything like that again. Somehow I'd have to overcome this. So, for now, I decided to forgive him.

I sighed and placed my hand over his. His shoulders relaxed and he let out a gush of air. "Thank you, Belinda."

I swallowed hard. "I have one more question." I slid my hand away. "Have you slept with Lora since we started dating?" I closed my eyes fearing the response.

His hand grasped my chin and turned my head toward him "Open those baby blues."

I exhaled and lifted my eyelids.

"The day I saw you on Beau in the Commons you entered my head and never left. Every time Lora came close, I saw you. I knew I couldn't be with anyone else."

All kinds of replies circled my mind, but only one came out. "Let's go home."

We walked out of the bedroom and explained to Abby and Garrett that we wouldn't be staying for dinner. Abby flashed a thumbs-up.

Robert pulled out of the parking lot and we drove toward his place. "I had a small problem this morning." He cocked his head in my direction. "My car was stuffed full of newspaper. I questioned several of the pledges. No one knew anything about it. Do you?" He gave me a little nudge in the ribs.

"Nope. Besides, do you really think the pledges would tell you? Anyway, it serves you right. You should've been home moping last night instead of partying."

"It was a good way to blow off some steam."

"Well, I'm sure the car stuffing will remain a mystery." Sarcasm colored my tone. I'd never give him the satisfaction of knowing Abby and I were the culprits. I shifted my foot back against the seat and heard what sounded like paper crunching. I picked it up. "Look, you left part of one."

"Yeah, I know. I thought I'd keep it. It has your address on it." He reached over and tapped it with his finger. "BUSTED," passed over his lips followed by a snicker.

With an exaggerated motion, I shoved it in my purse. I never took my eyes off of Robert and could tell he enjoyed my display.

He had a light playful look on his face. "Drama Queen."

I had a feeling I'd pay for my prank tonight.

I barely had time to walk in the door when Robert turned and wrapped his arms around me. I gasped at his spontaneous touch. Every muscle in my body tensed with excitement as he held me. He studied my face, not saying a word. With a slow deliberate motion, his lips found mine. His hands reached into my hair, pulling me close. I could hardly breathe. I reached for the buttons on his shirt. His lips traveled down my neck. Through heavy breaths, we peeled off each other's clothes and never made it to the bed.

CHAPTER 17

I WOKE UP to Robert gazing at me with a half-grin curving his mouth. "Good Morning. You look like the cat that ate the canary. Why?"

He brushed a strand of hair from my face and slid a finger down my cheek. "I missed you being wrapped around me. I didn't sleep very well with you gone." His finger moved across my lips, making them tingle. My breath caught. "Saturday night the alcohol helped, or should I say caused me to pass out on your neighbors' couch." He chuckled.

I couldn't believe how easily I forgave him, but he had looked so hurt and sorry, and I knew Lora would do anything to break us up. I slid over, draped myself over him, and lay my head on his shoulder. "Like this?" I tried to make my voice sound sexy.

"Yes, and I missed holding you tight to me. Like this." He gave me a squeeze that sent me into a twitter.

"And did you miss this?" I ran my fingers over his chest, down his abs to his navel and back up, while kissing down his neck.

He purred while he enjoyed my touch. "Yes, I missed that." Gently, he rolled me off and turned onto his side facing me. "That's enough. We need to keep our wits about us. We have some more talking to do this morning."

This was serious. Never in the past had he let us cut class.

I motioned toward him with my palm up. "Okay…you first."

Robert propped himself up on his elbow and fixed his eyes on mine. "Garrett told me you were almost hit by a car, but he caught you just in time. What if Garrett hadn't been there?" A frown furrowed his brow. "Angel, please don't ever run off like that again. We were lucky Garrett stopped you. If I'd lost you, I don't know what I would've done."

I ran my hand across his cheek. "I'm sorry I ran, but when I saw you kissing her, I thought my fears had become reality."

He reached for my hand, his eyes still locked on mine. "Belinda, I've never asked another girl to marry me, and I've never said I love you to anyone but you. Why do you keep running away?"

"I guess to avoid the pain of losing you." Tears built up in my eyes.

He winced and caught an escaping tear with his finger. "I know I didn't display the best judgment handling Lora. I know I hurt you and I can never take that back."

I placed a finger over his lips. "You've apologized. I don't need words. I need your actions to speak for you. Time will tell if you mean what you say."

He swallowed hard. "There's something I need to say."

I nodded.

"Do you understand how scared I was this last time you ran?"

"Robert, we've already talked about this. I thought we settled it."

He took a deep breath. "Not to my satisfaction." He repositioned himself and sat up. "You could've been killed this time and I don't know if I could've lived with that. Do you understand?"

He didn't look at me. I scooted to sit next to him and put my arm around him. "Baby, I've never really had to think about how my running away affected anyone. In the past, no one cared." I rubbed his shoulder. "I'm sorry."

"Okay. Apology accepted, but how do I know you won't run again?"

"Seriously?"

He spun his head toward me and furrowed his brow.

"Mr. Pennington, if you don't want me running, don't let other girls kiss you."

"And how do you propose I stop them?"

I stopped to study him. "I guess the easiest thing would be to move faster."

He chuckled then started laughing. "Are you serious? That's the best you've got."

I slapped his shoulder. "So, what are we going to do about this?"

He rolled on top of me. "I'll make a deal with you. I promise no other lips will touch mine except yours if you'll stop running. Do we have a deal?"

I hesitated.

He took a deep breath and raised his right hand. "Belinda Davies, I swear I will discourage all females from kissing me." He looked at me with sincere, thoughtful eyes and then held up one finger. "Ah, with the exception of my mother and grandmothers.

I chuckled. "Okay, you have a deal."

His mouth grew wider until I saw only a small portion of his teeth.

"Just so you know, the only kisses I thoroughly enjoy are yours, and I'm dying for one now." His head lowered until his lips crushed against mine.

We spent the morning expressing our love in the most affectionate way. This time it was different, more intense. The full force of our feelings for each other flowed through us. Our minds and bodies reveled in the passion we displayed.

That afternoon, we decided we should attend our classes. The sun-filled the sky, so we walked to the campus, enjoying our time together. We silently meandered with an arm wrapped around each other.

Robert cleared his throat. "I've been seriously thinking about something."

"What?"

"I think I have a summer solution. If you're game?" He stopped walking and turned toward me. "Let's get married right after my graduation ceremony."

My eyes popped wide open. I never expected that as a solution.

"My parents will be here. Just invite your parents to come to your fiancé's graduation. Afterward, we'll surprise them by driving to the Justice of the Peace and tell them we're getting married." His brow lifted. I motioned for him to continue. "That way you can stay here with me and if you want a break, forget about summer school. All your parents will have to pay for is your fall school tuition."

"Are you sure?" I froze where I stood. "What if my parents won't pay for my tuition after we're married?" I put my hand over my mouth. I couldn't believe I even considered his suggestion.

"I can't imagine they won't. They want you to finish your education and this way it will be cheaper." He rubbed his chin. "I could ask my parents for a loan if yours dig in." He cupped my shoulders. "So, is it yes or no?"

I didn't need to think about his proposal. I bounced on my toes. "Yes! Yes!" My heart thumped. I threw myself at him and planted my lips on his. My senses heightened, but he pulled away.

"Later." He smiled. "Let's keep this to ourselves right now."

Class was a waste of time. I didn't hear a word the professor droned. My mind kept thinking I'd be Mrs. Robert Pennington, his wife, in less than a month. We'd be together this summer and forever. When class ended, I rushed to the Cave. We arrived at the same time.

He half-smiled. "You're absolutely glowing."

"I'm so excited!" I gripped his bicep as we walked.

"Well, calm down, or the guys are going to suspect somethin's going on."

"Okay." I tried to contain my emotions, but it was so hard. I just wanted to yell out for the whole world—and especially Lora—to hear, *I'm going to be Mrs. Robert Pennington*! I filled my lungs and exhaled, then tightened my hold on his arm as we made our way to the Delt area and took a seat.

A few brothers were talking about an upcoming baseball game. Brian looked over at Robert. "Are you ready for the game today?"

Robert's brows pulled together. "That's today?" He grimaced.

"Yeah, we're playing the Kappa Psi's at 4:30." He looked at his watch. "In about an hour."

Robert looked at me. "The team needs me. You want to go?"

"Sure, I wouldn't miss it for anything."

⟨∞⟩

The crowd gathered on their respective team's side of home plate. Just before the game began, I gave Robert a kiss and retreated to my position on the sidelines that put me in his line of sight.

The game started with the Kappa Psi's up first. Robert ran onto the field, positioned himself at third base and waited for the first batter. The lead-off batter hit a line drive into the right-centerfield gap and made it to second base.

Robert was set and watching home plate. Then for some reason, and I can't imagine what possessed him, he stood up a bit and smiled at me. The next batter clobbered the ball. It shot like a bullet toward Robert and smacked his left shoulder, knocking him to the ground.

"Robert!" I ran onto the field. By the time I arrived, other team members were checking on him and a crowd began to circle around. He rolled from side to side, clutching his shoulder and wincing in pain.

In a flash, I hovered over him. "Robert, Baby, are you all right?" I'd never been so scared in my life. If he hadn't stood up a little, the ball could've hit him in the head. Now I truly knew what he'd gone through when I ran from him. The fear of losing someone I love so much scared the crap out of me.

"My shoulder is killing me." His teeth clenched.

Garrett appeared next to me. "Robert, do you think you can stand up? I'll give you a hand."

"I think so." Robert released his shoulder and extended his hand to Garrett. He struggled to stand, grabbed his elbow, and then pressed his arm close to his body. He stumbled forward but Garrett caught him by the waist.

"Belinda, I think we need to take him to the emergency room."

"I don't have a car here."

"We'll go in mine."

I wrapped my arm around Robert's waist as we walked. The hospital wasn't far, but the ride proved uncomfortable for him. Every time the car hit a bump, he'd wince and tighten his grip on his arm, letting out a groan.

In the emergency room, Robert called his parents and explained what happened. His mother's first reaction was to drive to the school, but Robert talked her into waiting until he received the final diagnosis.

The doctor checked and x-rayed the shoulder. No broken bones, just badly bruised. He gave Robert a prescription for the pain with instructions to keep the shoulder iced and immobilized until he saw the orthopedic specialist.

Garrett helped Robert to the couch and his last words before he closed the door to the apartment were, "Call if you need anything."

Robert rocked and gripped his arm to his chest.

"You need an ice pack and a pain pill." I went to the kitchen to retrieve the items needed to treat my patient.

I walked back with a bit of a swing to my hips with the hope I could distract him. Robert had unfastened the hospital gown and was examining his shoulder. "This hurt's like a son-of-a-bitch."

I sat next to him. "It's not pretty." I brushed my lips over his bruised, discolored, and swollen shoulder, feeling his warm skin twitch. Air rushed into his lungs. I pulled back. "Did I hurt you?"

"No. I liked it." He quirked an eyebrow.

"Robert." I would've smacked him, but he was in too much pain already. Instead, I shifted around and straddled him, then ran my tongue over my top lip. As I draped the ice pack over his shoulder, I bit my lower lip, letting it slowly pop out, trying to add some enjoyment to his painful situation.

Robert kept his eyes riveted on me.

Take this." I held out the pill and glass of water. He did as instructed.

I licked my lips again. "It's too late to cook something to eat. I'll order something in. Is that okay with you?"

"That's fine." He chuckled.

I made the call, moistening my lips the entire time.

He grabbed my hand and pressed his lips to my palm. When I shivered, he grinned. "I'm glad you're here, but you may not get much sleep. I'll probably be pretty restless." He glanced at his shoulder.

"I don't care. You took care of me. Now it's my turn." I leaned over and brushed my lips against his. I tensed up to control the sensations.

He frowned. "Don't do that."

"I had to. You're in no condition. Tonight, it's my turn to just hold you while we sleep."

"That'll be nice." With his head resting against the couch, he fixed his eyes on my face.

I ran my fingers through his hair. "You had me so scared today. Why did you turn and look at me?"

"I just lost my concentration. I was thinking about us getting married." He leaned his head over and kissed my palm.

"You need to pay more attention when you're playing. Thank goodness you stood up a little or it could've hit you in the head. Your brain would've been scrambled or worse." He chuckled. I clenched a wad of his hair and gave it a gentle tug. "That's not funny. I like your brain the way it is. It loves me." I rested my head on his good shoulder.

We sat in silence waiting for our order until Robert's fingers found their way under my t-shirt. Their touch sent a zing up my spine.

I pushed them away. "Robert. You're in too much pain. You need to relax."

"No, I'm not. The pain pill is kicking in."

I trailed my hand down over his zipper. "But then you might not be any good to me." I giggled.

The doorbell rang and I hopped up to answer it.

Robert managed to finish eating before his lids drooped and his head bobbed. "Come on, big boy. Time for bed."

I helped him get comfortable with pillows and a fresh ice pack after cutting the hospital gown off. Curling up next to him with my arm over his chest, I held him all night.

CHAPTER 18

TUESDAY MORNING, I found myself alone in bed. I sat up and scanned the room and called out, "Robert?" Concern arose that he had snuck out to class while I slept.

His head poked out of the bathroom. "Good morning." He walked into the bedroom, trying to put on his shirt, repeating, "Ouch. Ouch."

"Where do you think you're going?" I climbed out of bed—in the buff—and walked toward him.

Looking me over, he smiled. "Nice outfit. Uh, I'm going to class. I have a project due Thursday. I can't expect my partner to finish it. It's a major grade." He flinched again still trying to put on his shirt.

"Is this for your three o'clock class?" I reached for the shirt.

"Yes." He batted my hands away.

I propped my hands on my hips. "And doesn't Garrett have the same morning classes?"

"Yes. Why?"

"Then, you're not going anywhere." I carefully removed the shirt. His shoulder looked painful. The bruise had turned black, blue, and purple with a little yellow streaked through it.

He peeked at his shoulder. "Pretty bad, huh?"

"Yeah, and that could have been your head." The sight of the injury was an unpleasant reminder of how close the ball had come to his gorgeous head. "Where's the sling?" He pointed to the dresser, smiling. I reached for the sling and helped put it on his arm.

"Now get back in bed!" I ordered, pointing to it.

"Belinda, I need to go."

I shook my head and pointed again toward the bed. "No. Call Garrett and ask if you can get a copy of his notes later. I'll call Abby and do the same." I wasn't about to let him go anywhere. "I'll make sure you attend your afternoon class." He needed rest, a pain pill, and ice on his shoulder.

While he made his phone call, I refilled the ice pack then we both crawled back into bed. I made my call and then curled up over his uninjured side, and we fell back asleep.

A couple of hours later I woke up before Robert. I quietly slipped out of bed so I wouldn't disturb him. Throwing on my robe, I headed for the kitchen to make a late breakfast. I put on a pot of coffee, scrambled some eggs, and made a few pieces of toast. The smell must have awakened him because he appeared in the kitchen.

Robert's chest rose with a deep breath. "Smells delicious. I'm starving." He walked to the cabinet and reached for two mugs. "Do you want one?"

"Sure. Thanks, Baby." I finished putting the eggs and toast on our plates then carried them to the table and sat next to Robert. We picked up our mugs and clinked them together. He leaned his head over to mine. In unison, we said, "I love you."

∞

Robert said he had the pain under control if he used the sling, and assured me he wouldn't remove it. So, I dropped him off at his class, with the promise he'd call if he had any problems walking to the Cave afterward.

As planned, Robert met me at the Delt tables. He explained he had to meet with his project partner. He didn't know how long it would take, but he gave his word he'd call me for a ride home.

I headed to our place then settled on the couch and attempted to study, but fell asleep. I awoke to a dim apartment. The light coming in the windows confused me. I didn't know how long I'd been asleep. It took me a few minutes to determine it wasn't morning. I stretched over to the lamp next to the couch and turned it on, then reached for my cell. It read 6:20. I started to reread the same chapter but it put me back to sleep. I woke up about 7:45. No call from Robert. I washed my face, brushed my teeth and my hair, expecting a call at any time. Eight o'clock, still no Robert. My imagination started to go where it shouldn't. What was he doing? Who was he with? I studied my phone. Another twinge from "Monster" caused me to pick it up and text.

Me:	Where are you? I'm getting worried.
Robert:	Almost finished. Took longer than I thought. I'll be home soon.
Me:	I'll pick you up.
Robert:	Stay comfortable. A ride is arranged. Luv U.

I crawled into bed and reached for his pillow, pulling it to my face. Taking a deep breath, I caught a faint scent of Robert. I nuzzled deeper, taking another breath. His smell help ease my tension. I closed my eyes and drifted off.

I awoke to his lips pressed against mine, making me quiver. I threw my arms around his neck and pulled him to me as liquid heat raced through me.

He grimaced and pulled away. "Be careful."

"Oh, did I hurt you?"

"I'll be okay." He adjusted the sling.

I propped myself on my elbows. "What time is it? Where have you been? I was supposed to pick you up."

"Sorry. I got a ride home. It's 8:45. Are you hungry?"

"Yes, I'm famished." I was still annoyed, but my hunger was in overdrive.

"We stopped and I picked up lasagna and salads." He helped me out of bed.

"Who's we?"

"My study partner and I. I knew you'd be hungry so I brought the food home. It's on the kitchen counter."

I briefly looked at him. "Do you need to work on your project anymore tonight?" I wanted to make sure he didn't push himself too much for a while. That shoulder needed a chance to heal.

"No, but I have to meet with my partner tomorrow afternoon. It's due Thursday. I can't let her do the rest of the work."

I swung my head toward him. "Her?"

He swallowed hard and shot me a glance. "Yeah. My partner is a she. Her name is Erin Pennison."

I reached for the plates and stuffed "Monster" down. I wouldn't let her out.

"The professor decided who would work together. He just went down the list pairing everyone up." He exhaled a rush of air. "Angel, I had no choice."

I just nodded.

He poured us each a glass of wine while I dished out the lasagna and salads. We ate and cleaned up the kitchen with hardly a word spoken. He kept looking over at me but didn't say anything.

After filling the ice pack, I headed out of the kitchen. "I'll be in the living room with this. You need to ice your shoulder."

I turned on the TV. He walked to the couch and sat next to me. I placed the pack on his shoulder then laid my head on his lap. I surfed the channels while he ran his fingers through my hair. Nothing interested me, so I rolled onto my back and stared into his glacier blue eyes that focused on me. I loved looking into them. They had a calming effect as I thought about tomorrow.

"What are you thinking about? You're so quiet." His eyes peered deep into mine. "Are you upset with me?"

"No. I'm just thinking about what I should do tomorrow." I knew I needed to keep myself busy or my mind would drive me crazy thinking about Robert and Erin being together. Staying in the apartment alone wasn't a good idea. "I think I'll go visit Abby while you finish your project. I miss talking to her." I shut up again and thought through my plan which included Robert and me eating together, not him and Erin.

I sat up and checked the ice pack. "I want to make sure you're all right and not overdoing it." He assured me he was fine as long as he kept the arm immobilized. "I'll come by and pick you up when you're finished, then we can go have dinner somewhere." I stroked his cheek. "Promise you'll keep me updated?"

"I promise. It won't take long. We're almost done." He pulled me closer and kissed my temple. I laid my head against his good shoulder while he held me tight. "You're so beautiful. I see how other guys look at you. It makes me proud you're mine." He brushed his lips over the top of my head. "You have a way about you. Guys notice, but you don't respond to them."

I stroked my fingertips over his t-shirt covered abs. "I responded to you. Once that happened, no one else had a chance."

"But why?"

"Because when I saw you the first time, you left me breathless and my heart started racing. Your incredible eyes sucked me in. I felt drawn to you like there was some kind of connection between us. I'd never experienced anything like that before." I took a deep breath and released it. "I rode around that day trying to find you again. And then when you touched me—the sensations—I couldn't get you out of my mind. I just wanted to be with you."

He rested his cheek against my head. "The first time I saw you, I couldn't take my eyes off you. You mesmerized me, and my heart started sprinting. You stole my heart with your shy smile." He tightened his hold on my shoulder. "I asked around if anyone knew who you were, but no one did. I thought that maybe you were just a weekend visitor and I'd never meet you. When I saw you at the Spring Carnival, I knew fate had given me a second chance. So, I had you arrested. Your reaction to my touch had me concerned at first. I thought you didn't like it."

I interrupted. "Oh, no. I wasn't expecting that feeling or my reaction."

He inhaled. "I could feel this...this type of...the only way I can describe it is a pleasant...zingy sensation. And then when we danced, I felt your heart pounding." He kissed the side of my head, and I felt his breath stroke my hair. "And that first kiss in your front yard...If you hadn't left, I wouldn't have been able to stop."

I sat up and placed my lips close to his ear. "I left because I knew I wouldn't have been able to stop."

His words touched me. I don't think I ever felt closer to another human being than I did at that moment. I now knew he had a connection to me and we were attached on some weird level. I couldn't explain why. I didn't want to, either. All I knew was I loved him with all my heart.

"When we danced that first time, you muttered something about 'lost in the moment.' What did you mean by that?"

He bent his head over, shaking it. "I was imagining what it would be like to kiss you and have you naked under me."

I snickered. "Oh my gosh. You're so bad." My cheeks ran hot and I lowered my head. "I imagined the same thing."

He let out a hardy laugh. "My bad girl."

My face grew hotter.

"Are you blushing?" He reached for my cheek.

I swatted his fingers away and looked down.

"Angel."

I didn't raise my eyes.

"Angel. Look at me."

I did. His endearing face melted my heart.

"I'm glad we're having this talk."

"Me, too." My eyes moistened as I remembered the dream I had where Robert didn't know who I was. The thought made me cry. I looked up through my now tear-soaked lashes.

"Hey. What's wrong?" His thumb swiped away an escaping tear.

I couldn't tell him about the dream. "Nothing. I'm just happy."

"Angel, it's okay." He gave me a slight squeeze. "I love you. You are the best thing that's ever happened to me." He wiped more tears from my face. "I've got an idea. Graduation is close. Let's go apply for our marriage license next Wednesday after class. We can also ask about making arrangements with a Justice of the Peace."

"Okay." I sniffled through my smile and hugged him. He pulled back. Seeking my lips, he kissed me. In a flash, the zingy spinal feeling raced up my back. I closed my eyes, inhaled a deep breath and let the excitement slide over my body, rather than jump the bones of my injured fiancé.

CHAPTER 19

WEDNESDAY MORNING, I accompanied Robert to his follow-up appointment with the orthopedic doctor. As expected, the shoulder was only badly bruised, making him a baseball spectator for the rest of the season. The doctor encouraged Robert to start moving the shoulder. The sling would only be necessary if he needed to give his arm a rest.

Sitting in the Cave with Abby and Garrett after class, I leaned over and nudged Robert. "When are you supposed to meet Erin?"

He looked at his watch. "In about twenty minutes."

"Abby, I'm going home with you this afternoon. Robert has to work on a project. I'll treat you to a pizza." I raised my eyebrows. "Oh, by the way, I forgot to tell you we're going to the Spring Formal, too." Abby's face lit up. "Mom is sending my dress to the house. Would you watch for it and let me know when it comes?" I hoped my mother had worked her alteration magic.

"Maybe it's there now." Abby popped up from her seat and came halfway across the table. "Let's go see."

Abby never skipped a beat in the enthusiasm department.

"I need to get going. I'll call when I'm ready to be picked up." Robert kissed me on the top of the head and left.

I looked at Garrett. "Do you want to eat some pizza with us?"

"Sure. We can go to my place to eat first. Then I can study and avoid the girl talk." Abby pinched his arm.

"Ouch." He stiffened and gave her a stern look. "What's that for?"

"It's because you're such a guy." She reached over and gave him a sweet peck on the lips.

Garrett remained motionless for a few seconds, letting out a long sigh. "Do you think Robert would let you and Abby stay together the night of the formal?" I gave him a puzzled look. Groveling, he further explained. "Um, could you do it for Abby?"

"I don't know. Why didn't you ask him while he was here?"

He glanced at Abby, who nudged him. "I just wondered what you thought."

Abby stared at me and I got the message. "Okay, I'll ask him." I stared back at her. "For Abby."

I hoped Robert wouldn't object to the new arrangement that was meant to protect Abby's virtue, at least on the surface.

∽

We all hopped into my car to drive to Garrett's apartment. "I'm going to drive by our place first to see if the dress came."

Abby bounced in her seat. She was such a clothes hound and her excitement got me started. I squeezed her hand. Then we both swung our heads in Garrett's direction.

Garrett pursed his lips. "I guess so. Just make it quick."

I guess he figured the sooner we resolved the dress issue, the faster we could order the pizza. Garrett's main priority.

Abby and I sighed when we didn't see a package at the front door.

"Okay. No box. Time to eat," Garrett encouraged.

Abby held up her hand. "Hold on, buddy. Belinda, go inside to see if Mrs. Evans brought it in. We'll wait here."

"Okay." I ran inside and found the USPS box lying on the couch. I grabbed it and thought how silly it was for us to go over to Garrett's to eat pizza, and then come back before I could try on the dress. I knew we weren't supposed to have boys upstairs—this was at the top of Mrs. Evans' rule list—but I couldn't wait to try it on.

I leaned the box against the wall next to the door then went out to the car. "It's inside. Let's stay here and sneak Garrett upstairs." I looked at Abby's widened eyes, but knew she was game.

Garrett, however, needed convincing. "What about your landlady?"

"The worst thing that could happen is we get kicked out. Then, Abby would have to move in with you and I'd have to make it official that I was living with Robert."

He looked at Abby and smiled and, without a hint of hesitation, replied, "I'm in."

Abby whined like she was embarrassed, "Belinda!" Then she grinned and rubbed her palms together. "So how do we do this?"

"I didn't see or hear Mrs. Evans. I'll go in first to see if the coast is still clear." I pointed at Garrett. "When I give the signal, you run upstairs."

We all walked toward the porch keeping our eyes and ears open for any sign of our landlady. I walked in and scouted around. All was quiet, so I waved Garrett in and whispered, "Walk softly, but hurry." Then, Abby and I strolled up the stairs like nothing happened.

Abby ordered the pizza and I tore open the box, anxious to see my mother's handiwork. I dug into the package and pulled out the long, flowing, pale blue chiffon dress. First, I examined the top. My mother hadn't failed me. She had altered it to my exact specifications. "It looks nice. I hope it fits." I took the dress and laid it on my bed, and then methodically hand-pressed the wrinkles out. before returning to Abby and Garrett in our sitting room.

Garrett looked at me. "Try it on."

"Not until after we eat."

The huge closet was almost empty on my side. I began to rummage through my remaining clothes, gathering more to take to Robert's. It would be easier and cheaper to just move in with him, but I had to keep up the facade for my parents' sake. Mom might understand, but Dad, never. So, until I switched roommates by becoming Mrs. Robert Pennington—goosebumps rushed over my body at the mere thought—I'd keep my parents in the dark. I just finished pulling out a pair of silver heels to wear with my dress when I heard Abby announce, "Pizza."

After we ate, I cleaned up every crumb and demanded we all wash our hands, and then vanished into the bedroom. I put on the dress and silver heels then looked in the full-length mirror. To show off the full effect, the best I could, I pulled the sides of my hair up onto the top of my head and fastened them with an elastic band. I took one last look and exited the bathroom.

"Well, what do you think?" I twirled around so they could obtain a view of the back.

Garrett's eyes bugged wide and his jaw dropped. Words finally emerged. "You look stunning. Robert is going to love that dress on you."

"Does it really look all right? It's not too revealing, is it?" I tugged at the bodice. "Do you think it's too much?"

"No, it's perfect. You look gorgeous in it," Abby assured me.

"No…No…it looks just fine from where I'm sitting. I'd like to get a picture of Robert's face when he sees you in it." Garrett kept staring at me. Abby elbowed him in the ribs. Garrett twisted toward her. "What?"

Abby reached for him, cupping her hands on either side of his face. She stretched over and gave him a long, lingering kiss. When she pulled back, her face was full of adoration for him. Garrett just gazed at her with the most loving eyes as she warned, "Have fun looking, but remember, hands off. She's taken…and so are you."

He just smiled. "Yes, Babe."

They were so right for each other.

Point given, Abby turned her attention to me. "Wear your hair like that. I have some long, danglely rhinestone earrings that would be perfect."

Garrett's gawking snapped to a halt at the sound of my cell alerting me of Robert's call. "Hi. You ready?"

"Yep, we just finished. I'll be at the Admin in ten minutes."

"Okay, I'll need a few more minutes than that. I'm trying on my dress."

"Your formal?"

"Yes, they say it looks fine." I flashed a smile at them.

"They?"

"Um…Garrett is here, too."

"Are you at Garrett's?" Robert asked.

"No, we're at my place."

"So, we're going back to your place after you pick me up?"

"No, you can't come up." I rolled my eyes.

"Why?"

"Robert! After I pick you up, we're going home. Okay? I'll be there shortly."

Garrett and Abby caught the gist of my conversation. "So, he wants to come up, too." Garrett laughed. "Well, now I have to get out of here. Can you drop me off at my place after my escape?"

"Sure, but we need to pick up Robert first." I headed for the bedroom to undress. "You two better say your goodbyes while I'm changing. I'm leaving as soon as I'm finished."

After I hung my dress up and collected my other things, I called out from the bathroom, "You two ready to go?" No answer. "I'm coming out." I peeked into the sitting room. I had no idea why I even bothered to attempt to warn them. As far as they were concerned, I wasn't even there.

I rolled my eyes. Their arms and legs were everywhere. They never came up for air, and I wondered, if left alone, how long they would remain in an upright position. It was very clear how they felt about each other. They were both great people, good friends, and deserved to be happy.

I stood in front of the tangled mess and cleared my throat. "Garrett, I'm leaving now." In mid-kiss, Garrett glanced at me with one eye." I grabbed his arm to pull him away from Abby. "Come on." I waved to her. "I'll see you tomorrow." Pushing Garrett out the door, we made our way down the stairs and outside.

We swung by the Admin building to pick up Robert. I spotted him standing on the curb talking to a blonde with a very short, almost pixie-like haircut. As I pulled up, I caught a glimpse of her face before she turned and walked away. Robert opened the front door and motioned with his head for Garrett to vacate the front seat. He knew what Robert wanted—that he expected to ride shotgun. Garrett climbed in the back.

"Was that Erin?" I nodded in her direction as Robert climbed in.

"Yeah."

"Does she need a ride?"

"No. She's parked right there." He pointed then closed the door and immediately turned his attention to Garrett. "You got to go upstairs?" Robert frowned.

Garrett apparently decided to rub salt in the wound. "Yep, Belinda modeled her dress and DAMN! Wait till you see her in it."

"Really?!" Robert shot an unsmiling face in my direction. "When can I see it?"

I couldn't tell if he was grumpy because he was in pain or jealous because he was left out of our escapade. "Saturday." I tried to change the subject. "Did you finish your project?"

"Yes, it's finished." Without stopping to take a breath, he started again. "Why Saturday? I'd like to see it sooner, like tonight." He stared at me, still not very happy. I just tsked.

When we arrived at Garrett's apartment I turned around and gave him a stern look. The jerk knew he'd opened a can of worms. He just laughed. "See you later."

Robert wasted no time starting in on the dress again. He wanted to drive back to my place so I could pick it up. I put my foot down and told him he needed to wait, but he wouldn't let up. I didn't want to argue so I changed my tactics and used a more seductive tone. "Baby, I want you to get the whole effect. I want my hair and makeup perfect." My pouty face and fingering his shirt collar sealed the deal. "Garrett only saw half the picture. I want you to see all of it." Robert just rolled his eyes but accepted my reasoning. Trying to reposition himself, he winced and gripped his arm then laid his head against the headrest and closed his eyes. He let out a sigh and gave up.

Robert didn't fuss as I helped make him comfortable on the couch. "Do you need a pain pill?"

"I'm fine."

I still wanted to talk about our sleeping arrangements at the formal. "Baby, Garrett is going to ask you if it would be all right for me to stay with Abby Saturday night and you two share a room. She's not into sleeping with him yet."

A frown furrowed Robert's forehead. "I'll talk to him." He huffed. "So, he gets to see you in your dress, but I have to wait, and now I'm supposed to sleep with him as well?" His look told me how screwed up the situation sounded. "That's not fair."

"Yep, something for you to look forward to. You and Garrett should have fun together, at *night*." I giggled and gave him a quick peck on the cheek. "It's been a long, busy day. I'm exhausted." I yawned. "You relax on the couch. I'm going to take a quick shower. When I'm finished, I'll come help you."

Robert planted a quick, well-placed slap on my rump. "You're too bad."

I could tell he saw the humor in the situation.

After my shower, I gathered up everything he needed for his and took it to the bathroom. Robert had fallen asleep. I fingered his hair while admiring his face. His eyelids rose slightly. "Do you want to forget the shower?" He looked so comfortable and relaxed.

Forcing his eyes open, he looked around. "No, I need to get some heat on this shoulder."

I helped him up, and he put his arm around me as if he needed assistance walking. He had walked all over campus without me, but now he was unsteady? Go figure, but I didn't mind. I liked feeling needed by him. He sat on the shower bench where I helped him undress. I turned to leave but he pulled me close with his good arm. "I need someone to wash my back," he said with wishful eyes.

I just studied him and thought about what he requested before answering. "No, you need to let the water run on your shoulder. We don't need any of our acrobatics causing another injury to either of us." He nodded and released me.

I gave him a sweet kiss on top of his head. "I'll wait up. Let me know if you need help dressing." Somehow I knew he would, even though he was capable of handling the process himself. He always seemed to enjoy me dressing and undressing him, and I liked it, too.

CHAPTER 20

WITH EVERY PASSING day, my excitement grew and I couldn't wait for Saturday evening to arrive. My first fraternity formal! Robert made occasional comments about missing out on the first dress viewing. To make sure he didn't see the dress, I kept it at my place.

By the time Saturday afternoon arrived, I had packed and repacked my suitcase several times to make sure I had everything needed. That morning, I picked up my dress and hid it from Robert's view in a garment bag. I was so excited, but Robert didn't share my sentiments because he had agreed to Garrett's sleeping arrangements.

Abby and Garrett had arrived at the Dallas hotel just before us and waited in the lobby. After we checked in, the guys helped us with our luggage to our room. Robert sat down on one of the beds and started to lie back. I reached for his arm to stop him. "Oh, no you don't." I pointed to the door. "Both of you need to leave."

Abby immediately busied herself unpacking. I heard her spreading her stuff all over the vanity area. "You heard her." She stepped out of the bathroom then leaned against the door jamb. "Out." She nodded her head toward the adjoining door.

Robert and Garrett looked at each other.

Garrett spoke up, "We have several hours before we need to be downstairs. We thought we'd get some pool time in. You ladies interested."

"Sweetie, are you out of your mind? It's going to take Belinda and me a few hours to get ready."

"So what are we supposed to do while we're waiting?" Garrett pointed to Robert and himself.

Abby just shrugged her shoulders. I had a suggestion. "Robert, you could go to the pool. The exercise and water will help your shoulder." Then a thought hit me. There might be bikini-clad co-eds there to distract our guys and offer Robert an abundance of sympathy.

Silly me. What was I thinking? My bet was that every girl attending the formal would be busy doing the same thing we were—getting ready. I was pretty sure the pool area would be filled with guys all banned from their rooms.

We all decided to go for drinks in the bar before the dance. Abby marched to the adjoining door and opened it. "Out and don't bother us until we knock on this door."

"Yes, ma'am." Garrett saluted and left with Robert close on his tail.

"You two stay out of trouble," I added.

Abby and I primped for about two hours, doing everything from head to toes. I wore my hair with the front and sides pulled up on top and the back hanging down in curls. Abby's rhinestone earrings and a simple diamond drop necklace accented my neck and earlobes. My gown had an empire waist and was strapless with a sweetheart-cut bodice. The extra fabric in the center under the bustline added some fullness, allowing the body of the skirt to flow when I walked. Silver heels completed the effect, making me feel like a princess.

I was sitting at the desk putting on the final touches of makeup when Abby walked out of the bathroom. "You look beautiful." She made a few complete turns. "It's perfect." She moved her hands down the sides of her dress, smoothing it. The dress was a beautiful, aqua chiffon, off-the-shoulder gown with a fitted waist and an A-line skirt. Around her neck, she wore a strand of pearls that had matching earrings. Abby wore her hair hanging down and slightly curled under. She looked simply elegant.

"So do you. Robert's eyes will pop out of his head." Abby motioned for me to join her by the adjoining door. "You ready for the guys?"

I gave the bodice one final tug. "I think so." To assure her that she looked absolutely beautiful, I lightly squeezed her arm then knocked on the door. "Are you two decent?"

"Come on in." Robert had a slight tone of disgust in his voice.

Before opening the door, I turned to Abby. "You sure this dress doesn't show too much? I feel self-conscious."

"No! You look gorgeous. And sexy." She raised her eyebrows repeatedly. "You go first. I want to see Robert's face."

"Sexy is the part I'm uncomfortable with. That's not me." Adjusting the bodice again, I took one last look in the full-length mirror on the door.

Abby put her chin on my shoulder. "Maybe not the old you, but the new you, yes."

I opened the door and walked in with Abby following. Robert stood in front of the window looking out. As he turned, his mouth fell open and his eyes grew wide. Garrett took the opportunity to snap a picture of him.

"Do I look okay?" I pivoted around, waiting for his response.

Robert said nothing. His eyes just wandered over me from head to toe, making me feel more self-conscious as they stopped at the bodice. Finally he spoke. "You look absolutely...*gorgeous*."

And he was breathtaking in his tux. "So do you."

The tuxedo fit him perfectly. It accentuated his broad shoulders and narrow hips. For a rental, I couldn't believe how well it fit. He looked like a million bucks. I could've just stayed in the room, peeling it off one layer at a time. My heart hammered until Abby poked my arm and handed me her cell.

"Take our picture."

Robert reached for it. "Go stand next to your date." He raised the phone then lowered it. "Abby, you look awesome." He repositioned the cell and snapped the picture. "Garrett, we'll have the two hottest babes in the whole place."

"Definitely," he said, admiring Abby. Garrett pulled out the desk chair and sat in it. He asked Abby and me to stand on either side and give him a kiss on his cheeks. We obliged, stroking his ego while Robert snapped the picture. Next, numerous other pictures were taken, all of which Garrett or Robert photo-bombed whenever they could.

Robert walked over and stood in front of me. "Can I hug and kiss you?"

"Of course you can." I reached up for him. He carefully hugged me. The kiss, though, was sizzling and long. The quivering started. I ran my hands up the back of his neck and locked my fingers in his hair to pull him close, fantasizing about removing the layers of the tux. My back arched, adhering myself to him. My heart raced as he deepened the kiss, waltzing his tongue around mine.

If Garrett hadn't cleared his throat, we may have never seen the outside of the hotel room. "Okay you two, let's go." Garrett tugged Robert away from me.

"Hey, I was enjoying that," Robert protested.

"I know, and, to tell you the truth, so was I." Garrett smirked.

My eyes widened at Garrett's remark, somewhat embarrassed because Robert and I would always forget who and what was around us when we kissed. Abby came over to fetch Garrett. "Sweetie, leave them alone."

Garrett turned and swept Abby into his arms, dipping her down and placing a long passionate kiss on her lips. She went limp for a few seconds, and then wrapped her arms around his neck and hung on. He stood her upright without interrupting their exciting moment. After several short, sweet kisses, he stopped. Abby stood there mesmerized with her eyes closed. Garrett turned to Robert and me and gloated; "Now we're even."

Abby gave Garrett a love tap on the arm. He smiled from ear to ear. "Oh, Babe." Then he wrapped his arms around her. Over her shoulder, the goof rocked his eyebrows up and down at us.

Robert let out a snort. "And I have to stay with him tonight?"

Abby turned and said nothing, but I could tell the wheels in her head were working overtime. Would this be the night for Garrett and her?

"Maybe we'll let you have these rooms and we'll get another one." My ears perked up. However, that wouldn't happen. I was sure the hotel was full. So, with our fate sealed, we'd be apart tonight. The idea didn't appeal to me at all. I trusted Abby would do what was right for her, even if it meant separation for Robert and me. I had to respect her choice. She always respected mine.

Robert held his elbow out to me. I took it and slipped my key card into his pocket. He noticed. I winked and smiled as we stepped into the elevator. "Just in case."

The ballroom lobby bustled with ladies and men of all ages. We headed to the bar. It was situated in the back behind two huge doors with leaded glass panel inserts. As we walked in, I soon became very aware all eyes were looking at us. I wanted to yank up the bodice, but resisted, knowing it would draw attention to me.

"I love that dress and color on you," Robert whispered in my ear. "You look so exquisite. And sexy." He gave the top half of my dress a rapid glance.

"You're pretty hot yourself. How did you get a rental that fits you so well?"

"You don't. You have one tailored for you."

I should've figured.

Frat brothers with their dates, parents of frat brothers, and alumni were gathered around the bar. We drank and mingled until the headwaiter announced the ballroom was open for seating.

The room was very impressive. Round tables were scattered about the periphery of the dance floor in a horseshoe shape. A simple, yet elegant floral arrangement stood on every table. Around the base, a ring of votive candles added to the ambiance, and the dim lighting further enhanced the mood.

Our table was near the dance area, not far from the band. After seating Abby and me, the guys left for more drinks. While we were alone, I was tempted to ask Abby if she'd mind if Robert and I stayed together. I wanted so badly to be with him, but the right moment never happened before the guys returned, just as our meals were served.

Robert leaned close to my ear. "Angel, I'd like to tell Abby and Garrett about our wedding plans and invite them. Is that okay?" He pulled away and waited for a response. I smiled and looked at Abby. I couldn't imagine her not being there on the most important day of my life. I gave him a nod.

"Abby, Garrett, we have something we'd like to share with you, but you have to promise to keep it under wraps."

Abby looked at me with a look of sudden awareness. I wondered if she figured out our secret. I placed my hand on Robert's arm to get his attention so he wouldn't say anything just yet. I knew Abby's usual excited reaction to the news would give it away. "Abby, you have to promise you'll sit quietly after you hear what Robert has to say."

She blurted out, "I promise. I promise."

I looked at her to get another commitment that she'd control herself. "Okay, okay. I promise that, too. Now, what is it?" She leaned forward, closer to Robert. I took hold of her hands to further remind her to remain calm.

"Belinda and I are getting married after graduation." He wrapped his arm around me. "We'd like for you to be there with our parents. They don't know yet. We're surprising them. Will you come?"

Abby's eyes doubled in size. She ripped her hands from mine and covered her mouth. Little, muffled, whimpering noises came out. She lowered her hand and reached for mine, giving it a squeeze. "I wouldn't miss it for the world." Then she started to bounce in her chair.

"Abby, you promised."

She pursed her lips and flattened her hands on the table. "I know. I know. This is so hard for me."

I laughed as she struggled to keep her excitement under control.

"You know I'm here for you, bro." Garrett had a smile as wide as Texas across his face. "You two are meant for each other. But why are you keeping it a secret?"

"We can't invite everyone, just immediate family and you. We don't have time to plan a big wedding. I want Belinda here with me this summer, and the only way to accomplish that is to marry her."

"Belinda, just stay at school and live together. You're doing it now," Garrett pointed out.

A look of concern came over Robert's face. "Her parents wouldn't approve of that. They don't know we're practically living together. We want to keep it that way until we're married." He gave me a nudge. "Her father wouldn't stand for anything less, and I don't want to give him something else to be angry at me for. It's bad enough I'm breaking my promise by getting married before she graduates." Garrett nodded his head with understanding.

Soft music filled the air and people began to dance. "Can I have this dance?" Robert reached for my hand.

"I'd love to."

We glided around the dance floor. I felt myself float with every turn we made. Lost in his glacier blue eyes, I was unaware of anything or anybody around us. It was just he and I alone. His eyes never left mine. Time seemed to stop.

We were in our moment when the band started playing my favorite song, "Forever in My Mind." With my head leaning against his shoulder and my eyes closed, I quietly sang the words to him. They just poured out of me.

> Dear love, my only sweet true love.
> You've captured my lonely heart.
> My destiny is with you, love.
> I pray we shall never part.
>
> Our fate has been forever sealed.
> I'm bound by your gentle touch.
> By a true love that is so real.
> I love you so very much.
>
> My eyes met yours and I was lost.
> You found your way into my heart.
> We fell in love despite all cost.
> But shattered fate kept us apart.
>
> No matter where this life takes me.
> You're always there in my dreams.
> Each night I sleep, it's you I see
> Loving me in all the scenes.
>
> To gaze upon your loving smile
> With soft eyes of sparkling blue
> That guide me down the chapel aisle
> As I give my heart to you.

My eyes met yours and I was lost.
You found your way into my heart.
We fell in love despite all cost.
But shattered fate kept us apart.

Forever 'til the end of time
We will be what makes love bind.
As our world is in perfect rhyme
You're forever in my mind.

When the song ended, I kissed Robert on his neck and laid my head back against his chest keeping my eyes closed. I savored the moment until I heard applause. Still enveloped in his arms, I looked around as people faced us. "Why are they doing that?" I nestled closer to his chest.

He never loosened his grip. "I didn't know you could sing. That was beautiful. Everyone was looking around trying to figure out where the singing was coming from."

"They could hear me?" My cheeks warmed. "I thought I was singing to only you. I didn't mean for everyone to hear." I buried my face in his chest. "You were quiet at first. I even had trouble hearing you, but, as you got into the song, you sang louder with more feeling." Robert gave me a slight tug. It gave me a sense of security. "It was beautiful, and from the applause, I'd say everyone enjoyed it. They were trying to dance near us to hear you." He came close to my ear. "You have admirers."

Glancing around the crowd, I nodded, saying, "Thank you," for the unwanted attention I had brought upon myself. I reached for Robert's arm that never faltered from my waist and whispered in his ear, "Get me out of here." Without saying a word, Robert led me back to the table for a much-needed break and more wine. The hole we left on the dance floor filled with partygoers whose attention reverted back to themselves and off of me.

Once my nerves settled down, Robert and I returned to the dance floor. We never sat down again. We just took occasional breaks at the bar. Robert kept my wine glass filled and I gladly accepted each one. Abby and Garrett appeared to be enjoying themselves since their lips seemed to be glued together. I prayed that meant Abby wasn't going to be my roommate tonight. All this wine was making me feel amorous, and all I wanted was to love Robert until morning crept in to disturb our bliss.

Robert kept staring at me with those intoxicating eyes. We managed to maintain minimal contact. I was grateful for that. With the amount of wine I'd had, one kiss would have sent me over the top. I wouldn't have cared where we were or who was around as my reactions took over. Up to now, I had managed to keep my dignity and act like a lady. I wanted it to stay that way. Robert helped out all night. He was the perfect gentleman.

Robert gave Garrett and Abby a look of exasperation. Taking a deep breath, he glided us toward the dancing couple and demanded, "Okay, you two, I have to be with Belinda tonight. Do I need to get another room?"

Abby's cheeks bloomed hot pink. "No, I'll stay with him." She flung her arms around Garrett's neck and kissed him. They'd been doing a lot of that lately. I knew he would be in for the ride of his life tonight trying to maintain his virtue.

"Thank you, Abby." Robert wasted no time. He reached for my hand and led me out of the ballroom to the elevator. When the doors closed, he grabbed me and crushed his lips against mine. I returned his kiss with a feverish one. I wanted him and he wanted me. When the elevator doors opened, he folded his hand over mine and we ran to our room while he undid his tie and unbuttoned his vest. He reached into his pocket, pulled out my key card, and a foil packet. He quirked an eyebrow.

My mouth spread wide. "I love a man who comes prepared. I have three inside I put in the nightstand." I winked.

Inches from the door, he swiped the keycard. "If we run out I have more in my suitcase." He opened the door without skipping a beat.

My reactions to Robert's advances were more intense. We inched our way to the bed. Robert tossed the foil packet on the nightstand then splayed his fingers through my hair and clutched it, pulling my head back. He kissed every exposed area of my neck and chest. My heart accelerated. Blood rushed to my ears. I pulled back and tore at his tux, attempting to remove what was left on his body. I felt the zipper slide down my back. The dress fell to the floor. His hand grasped the back of my head and his mouth collided with mine in a hot, endless kiss. With his other arm wrapped around me, melding our heated bodies as one, we toppled over onto the soft sheets. He reached for the foil packet. I watched, my chest heaving. The second he finished, we were like wildcats—our bodies entwined, writhing, groping, devouring. This was not making love, it was raw SEX. We couldn't get enough of each other until we collapsed from satisfaction and exhaustion. Luckily, our pleasure outweighed the soreness in his shoulder.

Beads of sweat trickled down his chest as he rolled over on his back and pulled me close. "Oh. My. God! That was incredible!" He gazed at me with crazed eyes, in between his gasping breaths.

He pressed his lips against my shoulder in a quick kiss. "I keep thinking about you in that dress. You looked so sexy. I get aroused just thinking about it." He rolled over on top of me and started kissing my cheek, my neck, everywhere. My senses came alive, and, to my surprise, Robert started all over again, but this time we made warm, gentle love. Our newfound sensuality was wonderful. It drove us crazy as we made love again, and again, and again...

CHAPTER 21

A KNOCK ON the adjoining door awoke us Sunday morning. "Hey, you two, I need my stuff," Abby called out.

Still half asleep, I was wrapped over Robert's side. He pulled the covers completely over me. "Okay, you can come in," Robert shouted.

I pulled the sheet from my head before they entered, wondering how Abby faired last night. I couldn't wait until we were alone to pry her for all the details like she relentlessly did to me.

Abby and Garrett walked over to the bed. She took a seat on it, bouncing up and down before she settled in. "Belinda, everyone was talking about how gorgeous you looked in that dress."

"Really? I still think the top is a little too revealing."

Robert and Garrett chimed in, in unison. "No, it wasn't. It was perfect." Robert frowned at him. Garrett shot him a half-moon size smirk, full of white teeth.

I rolled my eyes. "Sheesh! Typical males—sex on the brain."

"I want to see you in it again." Robert flashed me an irresistible smile.

"Later, Tiger. Right now I think we need to call room service for breakfast." I became aware of the pain in my head as I repositioned, sitting up carefully so nothing slipped out by accident. "And something for a headache."

Abby fiddled with something gold hanging around her neck. It took my eyes a few seconds to focus. "Abby, come here." She scooted closer. "Move your hand." She complied with a grin on her face. "You're wearing a Delt drop!" I forgot about my throbbing head and gave her newest acquisition my full attention.

"He gave it to me when we came back to the room." She beamed. If she and I had been alone, we would've been jumping up and down squealing. However, the only thing between me and immodesty was the sheet and I was determined not to let Garrett get a peek at my lady parts.

Garrett had a half-grin. "Yeah, I don't want to share her anymore."

"Congratulations, Bro." Robert flashed a thumbs-up.

I leaned over and gave Abby a peck on the cheek.

"Hey, we're getting ready to check out. Robert, I packed your things in your duffel. You need to hurry if you're checking out by eleven."

"We're staying for a while longer." He rocked a brow. "Just bring my stuff in here, if you don't mind." Robert was bare-chested with the sheet draped across his lap, the only barrier between him and turning everyone red-faced.

Garrett disappeared from Abby's side, and then reappeared with the duffel in hand. "Well, I guess we'll let you get back to...." Garrett's voice trailed off into a knowing smile. Abby blushed and nudged him. He placed his arm around her and escorted her out of the room.

On his way back from locking the door, Robert pulled foil packets out of his duffle and picked up my dress. "Put it on." He had a naughty look on his face, standing there with the dress offering the only form of cover for his perfect naked body. He tossed the packets on the night table.

I slipped the dress over my head then turned for him to zip it. Slowly, I faced him with my hands at my sides fidgeting with it. His lustful eyes focused on the bodice.

"Don't move." His voice low, and husky.

His fingers feathered across the top of the fabric that outlined my breasts. My breathing quickened, making them heave. With the gentlest touch, he caressed my left breast. An electric thrill shot through me. My head arched back as each hand clenched fistfuls of dress fabric. His lips brushed kisses across my jaw, down my neck, over my shoulder, to each breast, and up the other side. All the while his hands explored.

With a slow even motion, he opened the zipper and the dress slipped, puddling on the floor. I threw my arms around his neck. He gripped me close, making our heated bodies rub against one another. Our lips searched until they pressed against each other.

He pushed me back onto the bed and stood at the foot with a big smile gracing his face. I heard the foil packet crinkle in his hand. Seconds later, he inched his way over me. "I hope you're ready." His body pressed against mine and our emotions exploded into the perfect rhythm of our love.

By three o'clock we walked up to the lobby desk. Robert slipped the room key across the counter.

"Ready for check out, sir?"

Robert nodded.

∞

With the top down, we flew down the highway. "I'm glad we decided to go. I had a great time. Did you?"

"Do you even need to ask?" He flashed a grin. "Abby and Garrett getting dropped sure was a big surprise. I'm his best friend, and I didn't see that coming."

Staring out my side of the car, more or less in a trance, I kept silent.

"Angel...Angel...Belinda..." He nudged my arm.

I snapped my head toward him. "What?"

"Why so quiet?"

I shrugged my shoulders. "I was just remembering last night and all that wild, crazy sex." I slapped his shoulder. "Didn't you enjoy it?"

"Of course I did."

I rested my head against the seat. "Which do you prefer? The hot, mind-blowing sex or lovemaking?"

He thought for a second. "I prefer making love to you, but, if you want wild, crazy sex, we can do that, too." Robert shot me a ravenous grin.

"Typical." I just laughed. but I could feel "Monster" twitch her tail, wondering about the girls who came before me.

Nope. "Monster" wouldn't be let out. The other girls didn't matter unless I let them. I reached over and stroked Robert's cheek. He took my hand in his and kissed my palm.

A zing hit me. My resident butterflies swirled. I wiggled my hand from his. "If we keep this up, we'll be pulling off the highway looking for another hotel."

He burst into laughter.

After Robert let the luggage drop on the living room floor, he swept me off my feet and carried me to the bedroom. He tossed me onto the mattress and straddled me, pulling his t-shirt off. "Well, which do you want first? Make love?" His eyes went sultry. "Or wild, crazy sex?" His eyes turned that deep ocean blue. He started tickling me, making me squirm and laugh so hard I could hardly breathe. "Well, which is it?"

"Robert I can't breathe." My words were muffled through the laughter.

"Which one?"

"Stop tickling me and I'll tell you."

He released my aching sides and sat back on his heels.

I beckoned him to come closer with a hooked finger. With his forearms on either side of my head, he was inches from my face. "I just love making love to you."

He placed a soft kiss on my nose. "I can't wait 'til you're Mrs. Robert Pennington. You know, we could probably get married this week."

I considered his proposition. "No, we need to wait." Just then my stomach growled loud enough for both of us to hear. "I'm hungry, are you?"

"Yeah, for wild, crazy sex!" he teased with a naughty look in his eyes.

I poked at him. "I'm craving pizza."

"Craving?" He gave me a curious look and became very serious. "Are you trying to tell me something?"

I waved my hands. "Oh, no! Wrong word. I'm hungry for pizza."

His smile started small but grew bigger. "You sure you're not up for some wild, crazy sex?" I pushed him off of me and got up. I gave him a stern look.

He heaved a sigh. "Just checking. I'll order our usual."

My pizza stuffed stomach magnified my exhaustion. "I'm going to shower."

Robert pulled me close. "Can I join you?"

"Sure, but no funny business." I grinned and shook my finger at him, thinking this shower was going to last longer than planned. But, it didn't. We were both pretty tired from the weekend's escapades. In bed, I curled up to his side and relived the formal— the way he had treated me and how this guy lying next to me made me feel. I was a princess living in a fairytale.

CHAPTER 22

IN TWO WEEKS, finals and school would be over, Robert would have graduated, and I'd be Mrs. Robert Pennington. So much was happening in such a short time. I was floating on cloud nine, but what would my parents say when I tell them. Would they come to Robert's graduation? Would they let me marry him? If not, what would we do?

My stomach knotted up as I walked to the Cave, lost in my thoughts. Matt ran up beside me just outside of the Student Center and took hold of my arm. "I heard something I want to check out." He reached for my hand and frowned at the ring. "I guess it's true, you're engaged to him. So, you're in love?"

He gripped my hand too tight. I pulled it loose. "Yes, I love him."

The usual sparkle in his eyes faded. "Well…I hope you'll be happy together. But remember." He pointed a finger into his chest. "I was the one who warned you."

Matt's attitude about Robert annoyed me. I hadn't seen anything in Robert that Matt had predicted. I opened my mouth to give him a piece of my mind but Robert walked up and put his arm around my shoulders, giving me a slight tug. "What's going on?"

Matt reached out to shake Robert's hand. "Congratulations, you're a very lucky guy."

Robert hesitated and looked at me. He cocked his head and let out a small huff. Even though Robert didn't like Matt, he was too much of a gentleman to make a scene. He reached out and shook Matt's hand in return. "Thank you."

Matt half-smiled. "I wish you all the happiness in the world." He turned and slowly walked away. That was the first time I realized my relationship with him and Beau had come to an end. Pity. Beau would be the one I missed the most.

"Angel. Come back to me." Robert tugged at me. "Are you okay?"

"I'll never see Beau again." A tear escaped.

Robert wrapped his arms around me. "Would you like me to try to buy him for you as a wedding present?"

"What?" I shook my head. "No, Matt would never sell his horse. Besides, I won't have time to take care of him and we'll have to watch our budget." I put my arms around his neck. "Next to the roses, you loving me, you wanting to marry me, and you being Mr. Wonderful, that was so thoughtful." I brushed my lips against his. "Thank you." My heartstrings vibrated in full force.

"You're welcome. Anything to keep my girl happy. I aim to please."

We started heading to the Cave. "Have you talked to your parents yet about coming to my graduation?"

"No, I need to do it soon. I'll call tonight when we're at home."

"What if they won't come? Will you go through with the plan?" He looked serious. We made ourselves comfortable at one of the Delt tables.

"Yes, absolutely. If they say they can't come, I'll tell them they're going to miss me getting married. That'll make them come, but they'd try to talk me out of it. 'You're too young. It's too soon. You haven't finished school yet.'" I glanced down. "They won't let me go to summer school. They think I need some time away from you." Now, I was more downhearted and my voice reflected that.

"I don't want to cause problems between you and your parents. Maybe this isn't a good idea." He shoved his fingers back through his hair and rubbed the back of his neck before he continued. "Will you miss not having a big wedding?" He shifted in his chair. "We never discussed that. I don't even know if that was something you wanted."

My heart jumped. All I could do was think about how sweet this guy was and how much I loved him. "I wouldn't mind a big wedding, but it isn't something I've dreamed about. Hell, for a long time I wondered if I'd even get married. I'm more concerned about my parents."

I was making myself upset. The notion of our plan backfiring and all the problems that could arise started to fill my head with one thought after another coming so fast. Tears started to well up in my eyes. Ashamed and on the verge of a full-blown meltdown, I hid my face in my hands. "I need to go to class." An overpowering urge to run came over me. I stood and rushed out as "Monster" raised her ugly head, again.

"Belinda." He caught up and grabbed me around the waist from behind. I was weeping, almost sobbing. He tried to console me with a hug as he placed his chin on my shoulder. "Everything will work out. Let's think positive." He gave me a gentle squeeze. "Look, after everything's over, we can plan to renew our vows and have a proper wedding."

His arms around me made everything feel all right and melted away my fears, forcing "Monster" back into her lair. "Okay, I'll see you after class."

Robert wiped my tears away and kissed me on the lips. Immediately, pleasure-filled me and I responded by kissing him back.

I was about to put both my arms around his neck when he broke away and stepped back. "Later."

∞

I stared at my cell phone. Robert sat next to me on the couch with his arm around my shoulders. He encouraged me to confront the situation. My conversation only lasted a few minutes, but Mom agreed she and Dad would attend Robert's graduation and meet his parents since they'd be here to move me home. It surprised me, but Robert was right. Making the call and confronting my fear wasn't as bad as I thought.

"See, that wasn't so hard. We can meet at the apartment after graduation. We'll introduce our parents to each other and tell them we're taking them out to eat, but, instead, we'll head for the Justice of the Peace." He had constructed the perfect plan. "Okay, now let's go celebrate. What are you hungry for?"

"What do you want?"

Robert sat upright and had the strangest expression on his face. "Do you have to ask? What I'm always hungry for." Now he had a full-blown smile, waiting for me to say something.

"Okay, Mexican. You know I'll always choose that." I grinned. He looked at me and said nothing. I obviously missed something. A light bulb went on in my head and I closed my eyes. "Wild, crazy sex." When I opened them, he appeared satisfied that he had made his point. "Later, Cowboy. First, we eat Mexican food."

∞

After our classes on Tuesday, we joined Abby and Garrett in the Cave. "Have you talked your parents into coming to his graduation yet?" I gave Abby a quick explanation of the phone call to my mother and how we would pull off our deception.

Robert interrupted, leaning in close to my ear. "We have something we need to do now."

I looked at him puzzled. "What?" I couldn't think of anything.

"We need to ask Garrett and Abby about standing up for us at the ceremony." I felt stupid. I hadn't asked my best friend to be my maid of honor yet.

"Abby, there's something I need to ask you. You promise not to jump up and down and get all crazy on me?" She gave me a nod yes, but squirmed in her seat. I kept my voice low. "Would you be my maid of honor?"

Abby's eyes misted over. "I'd be honored." I reached for her hands and held on while Robert asked Garrett to be his best man. I could feel Abby's bubble level rise, but my grip on her helped keep it under control.

Robert looked back at me. "There's still one more thing we need to do." He smiled and held up his left hand, inconspicuously rubbing his thumb against his ring finger. "Our wedding rings."

When we arrived at Downtown Jewelers, the salesman greeted us as we entered the store. "Can I help you?"

Robert acknowledged him with a nod. "Yes, sir. We're interested in looking at your wedding bands."

"Right this way." The man led us to a glass display case. "Do you see anything you're interested in?"

"I like that one." I pointed to a plain white-gold band.

The man handed it to Robert and he slid it onto my finger.

My skin prickled as I breathed, "I do." I held my hand out in front of me. The band balanced well with the engagement ring. The diamonds sparkled under the lights. "I love it." I nudged Robert. "See anything you like?"

"One like yours, but a little wider." The salesman showed us some men's bands and handed me one. I slipped it onto Robert's finger. "I do," he reciprocated then half grinned.

Robert handed the rings to the man. "We'll take these two bands."

In the car, I opened my ring box and fingered the thin band. "I promise I'll never take my ring off. 'Til death do us part."

"'Til death do us part." He briefly slid his eyes in my direction then nudged my arm. "Nothing is going to stop us."

"Oh yes there is."

He wrinkled his brow. "What?"

"I don't have a dress to wear. Do you want to go with me?" Oddly, Robert jumped at the chance. Hopefully, him seeing the dress before the wedding wouldn't jinx our marriage. Who believed in those wives' tales anyway? I didn't.

I think.

Inside the boutique, I glanced around at the dresses displayed on racks. Everything looked expensive, but that was okay because this dress had to be special, and, surely, they had what I needed. I grabbed Robert by the hand and led him over to a saleslady who asked, "Can I help you?"

"I'm looking for a nice dress that I can be married in."

"I have a few that would work perfectly." She sized me up. "I'll be right back." She reappeared with three pretty dresses and one suit that were shades of white to cream in my size. Then she led me to a dressing room.

Robert sat right outside and waited for me to model each one. He was adamant about his opinions. He liked the cream-colored, strapless, silk dress with a short straight skirt and matching short-sleeved bolero jacket the best. Robert pulled out his credit card. "We'll take this one."

"No!" I tried to grab the card, but he held it up over his head and well out of my reach. "Robert, you've given me enough."

"What, an heirloom engagement ring?" He looked perplexed.

I placed my hand on his shoulder. "You gave me you. That's enough."

He replied in a loving tone, "Angel, you've given me more—you gave me you, your love, happiness, understanding. I could go on and on. Let me do this for you, please."

I rubbed my hand over his shoulder. "Okay, if it'll make you happy."

The saleslady rang up the sale and handed the card back. "Angel, would you mind staying here while I run a quick errand? You can shop for something else." He slid the card back to the saleslady.

"Robert, n—" He put his finger over my mouth. Not saying a word, he let his eyes speak for him. His message was loud and clear. I gave up my protest as he walked backward out of the store. Just before he closed the door he threw me a kiss.

The saleslady approached me. "Is there anything else you'd like to see?"

I shrugged. "There isn't anything I need."

"Have you thought about what you'll wear on your wedding night?"

I shook my head.

She walked to the back room and returned with a sexy, little, sheer, pale blue teddy. "Wear this for him." She lifted one brow and draped the garment across the counter.

I felt the fabric of the minimal excuse for sleepwear. "This is his favorite color." I held it up against me. Just looking at it made my cheeks burn. It would be fun to watch his face when I walked out in it. "Okay, I'll take it." I handed her my credit card. "This will be my gift to him."

"I think he'll like it." She handed me his card.

As I browsed and flipped through the clothes, a low familiar, sexy voice filled my ear. "Well, did you buy anything?"

"I did." I turned toward him and glanced at the saleslady. "We think you'll like your wedding gift." He had a confused look on his face. I strutted by him and waved his credit card in front of his face. "Just wait until you get the bill."

CHAPTER 23

SCHOOL KEPT US busy with projects, papers and cramming for finals. Robert had the extra chores of preparing for graduation and summer school. We hardly saw each other and were grateful when the school year ended.

For once, I awoke before Robert. I slept very little all night as I went through my mental list of everything that we needed to do to pull off our plan. I turned toward Robert and tried not to disturb him. Unlike me, he was a sound sleeper. His hair was tousled, but, even as he slept, he looked perfect.

My resident butterflies swirled and caused my heart to thump. I'd be married to him today. I tried to slip out of bed, but it didn't work. Mister Wonderful woke up and pulled me to him. "Where are you sneaking off to?"

"It's eight o'clock. I need to shower and dress so I can be at my place when my parents arrive. I'm not sure when they'll get there."

"Can you believe that in a few hours you'll be Mrs. Robert Pennington?" He beamed, and then his expression turned solemn. "I hope your parents will be happy for us. Call'em to see when they'll be here."

I called Mom. They were about an hour-and-a-half away. I only had enough time to get ready and have a quick breakfast. "I hope everything goes as planned."

"Don't worry. If we have to, we'll elope. Nothing is going to keep us apart." His mood was determined, but his touch gentle when he stroked my hair. "I have a surprise for you."

He opened the drawer of the nightstand, pulled out a small, black velvet box, and handed it to me. I fingered the fabric. Slowly, I opened the little box and lifted a double heart necklace. Two diamond-studded hearts linked together. He'd had our initials engraved on the back, his initials on one heart and mine on the other. "Oh, it's beautiful! Thank you." I hugged and kissed him. My senses ignited, so I squirmed away. "Not until after we're married."

He let out a long breath. "So now you go all virginal on me?"

I giggled. "You know what I mean, silly. When you get your wedding gift tonight, we'll see who's going virginal," I teased and headed to the bathroom.

Robert went to the kitchen to fix us something to eat. When I entered the room in my wedding dress, a huge smile flashed across his face. "You look gorgeous."

"Thank you."

"There's your glass of juice."

I leaned up against the counter. "I kinda like that look you've got going on there." He was dressed in baggy shorts that sat low on his hips and didn't leave much to the imagination.

He grabbed a bagel out of the toaster. "Remember. No touching until after the wedding. I'm saving myself."

I had just taken a swig of orange juice and had to fight not to spit it out or get it up my nose. "Robert!" A burst of laughter followed. I gave up on the juice. "Would you put this on me." I handed him my necklace, turned my back to him and lifted my hair away from my neck. He secured it then placed his hands on my shoulders and pivoted me around. With tender lips, he pressed his against mine. I pulled away when I began feeling all zingy inside. "Not until after we're married." He grimaced but complied.

I managed to scarf down some breakfast before heading to my place. Robert came along to pick up the remainder of packed boxes that were going to the apartment and to have his first tour of my soon-to-be-vacated room.

Abby was up and dressed in the light blue polished cotton dress trimmed in white that we had picked out. It was perfect and casual enough for the graduation ceremony and dressy enough for a bridesmaid. Since Garrett, her new favorite man, was a senior in Business Management, he would be graduating alongside Robert. She gushed about how beautiful I looked in my wedding dress, and I returned the compliment before we hugged.

"So Robert, you finally made it up here." Abby snickered. He flashed a grin at her and responded with a snort.

I gave him the nickel tour of my humble dwelling. "See, you haven't missed much."

He quickly scanned the place, appearing satisfied. "Angel, I'm going to head back to get ready and wait for my parents." He kissed me and then picked up the two remaining boxes before he left.

Looking at Abby and around our room, a heaviness filled my chest. This would be the last time she and I would be together as roommates. "Abby, are you staying here this summer or are you going home?"

"I'm moving in with Garrett. We're taking the summer off to enjoy ourselves before he starts grad school in the fall."

My mouth fell open. "I had no idea things were going that well?"

Abby nodded slowly. "Yep. Belinda, I think he's the one."

We hugged and bounced, swinging each other around. "I'm so happy for you!"

"Belinda. We need to stop or we'll wrinkle ourselves. I love you to death, but you're not worth another hour over an ironing board."

I laughed. "Okay, but we really need to keep in touch and talk more." My moment of elation sank. For the first time, I realized my best friend and I were on different paths and would be starting new lives. "Abby, I'm sorry I wasn't around very much. I haven't been the best roommate lately."

"Yes, you have. Remember, I was also out a lot with Brent and Garrett. However, I did miss talking to you…discussing our dates…stuffing his car." We laughed then sat in silence for a few seconds. "Robert sure seems eager to marry you."

"We both are, but everything has happened so fast." This whole affair mystified me. Often I would run the events of the past few weeks through my mind. I would ask myself if I was doing what he wanted so I could keep him or did I really want to get married as well? The only answer I always came up with was yes. I loved him with all my heart.

"I'm glad you changed your mind and decided to get married in a chapel."

"Me too. We lucked out when we applied for our marriage license and Mrs. Matthews suggested her husband could perform the ceremony."

I paused and looked at Abby. "We have to keep in touch more."

"We will. Remember, we're sisters."

∞

My parents and I found seats near the stage. Those dang butterflies of mine just kept swirling around and around, waiting for Robert's name to be announced. As he walked across the stage to accept his diploma I jumped up and screamed, "Robert!" He scanned the crowd and found me. Our eyes locked as he mouthed, "I love you."

The two-hour ceremony ended, and my parents and I headed for our apartment. Robert and his parents were already there when we arrived about three o'clock. He handled the introductions. Sandra jumped right in with her remarks. "We just love your daughter. We can't wait for her to become part of our family. We're so happy Robert found her."

Everyone made themselves comfortable in the living room. The moms sat on the couch and were engaged in planning the wedding. Robert looked at me and then his watch. "Belinda and I are taking you out to eat. We need to go before the graduation crowds arrive. You can continue getting acquainted at the restaurant." We left with Robert driving his parents in their car, and I followed in mine with my parents aboard.

To keep myself calm, I told my mom about the reaction to the dress she altered. I knew if I kept the small talk going, I could contain myself, and maybe my parents wouldn't suspect anything.

When we arrived at the chapel, there were a lot of cars parked around.

"Are we eating at a church?" My mom looked around bewildered.

"No, Robert and I have a surprise for you." We started walking toward Robert and his parents. They were smiling, and I hoped it was because they approved of our plan.

I motioned to Robert to stay put. When I stopped walking, my parents turned toward me with their backs to Robert and his parents. I needed to talk to them with no one else around. "Mom, Dad…Robert and I want to be together this summer and from now on. So we made arrangements to be married today. Reverend Matthews is waiting inside." I tilted my head toward the church.

Dad frowned and stiffened, folding his arms across his chest. "Don't you think you're rushing into this? You're too young."

"She's as old as I was when we were married," Mom reminded him, placing her hand on his arm. She stood behind his shoulder and flashed me a wink. I knew she had my back.

"I love him." I lowered my chin and glanced up through my lashes. "I want to be with him."

Dad relaxed and let out a huff. "Okay, if it makes you happy." He struggled to display a half-smile.

I reached over and hugged him. "Thank you. I love you."

We joined Robert and his parents who had waited patiently. Everyone exchanged handshakes and congratulations. I could tell my father wasn't sure about this wedding, but he managed to act cordial.

As Robert and I walked arm-in-arm toward the chapel, the crowded parking lot made me wonder what was going on. "Why are there so many cars here? I hope something didn't get messed up with the minister's schedule." I squeezed Robert's arm and gasped. "What if he forgot?!"

He attempted to ease my concern. "Maybe there's something else going on."

We walked into the foyer, surprised to see Brian standing with Abby and Garrett, waiting for us. The center doors that led to the chapel were open. Inside, frat brothers and their dates filled the pews. Two white rose floral arrangements on pedestals decorated either side of the open doors. Blue bows and ribbons were tied on each pew. A white runner led to an arch where the minister stood at the front of the chapel. Two more white rose floral arrangements were on either side of the arch. I was astounded at the sight presented before me.

"Robert." I grazed his hand.

"I know. It's perfect."

Robert didn't move. "How did you find out?" he asked Brian.

"Oh, a little bird told us. We all wanted to share this special occasion with you." Brian wasn't going to divulge his source.

I looked at Abby. "Why didn't you say something to me?"

"And spoil the surprise?" She glowed. "I have a bouquet for you. Cheryl made all the floral arrangements, and she and Russell are having a reception for you this evening at eight." She handed me a bouquet of white roses, light blue ribbons, and baby's breath. "I hope you don't mind, but, after all, I'm your maid of honor, and Garrett is your best man. We're supposed to help with the planning." She shrugged her shoulders. "In this case, we did most of it."

My eyes filled with tears. Abby was such a good friend. I was so lucky. She handed me a tissue. Dabbing at my eyes, I turned to my father. "Dad, will you walk me down the aisle?" He smiled and extended his elbow. I linked my arm in his.

Brian escorted our mothers and Robert's father to the front pew. Robert and Garrett walked up the right aisle to stand with the minister. Abby started down the center aisle. My father and I positioned ourselves between the doors. Almost like magic, the minister's wife started to play the wedding march. My heart skipped a beat, and I focused on Robert. His gaze was intense and full of love. At that moment, I stepped onto the white runner and walked toward my love, to become Mrs. Robert Pennington.

The ceremony was perfect. We exchanged our vows and placed our wedding rings on each other's fingers followed by the words, "I do." I could hardly wait for the minister to say, "I now pronounce you husband and wife. You may kiss your bride." The kiss was...well, he had to peel me off of him. It was a kiss he'll never forget.

After the ceremony, everyone congratulated us and said they'd see us at the reception. The chapel quickly cleared and became reverently quiet. A small group of us remained in the foyer.

Robert gathered the parents together. "Can you stay for the reception?" Our parents agreed. Robert called the hotel downtown and made two reservations.

I turned toward Abby and Garrett. "Come eat with us. Our treat." With her usual enthusiasm, Abby latched onto Garrett's arm, nodding her head with a Cheshire grin.

As we exited the chapel, I nearly lost my breath. All the attendees were lined alongside the pathway, armed with bottles of liquid bubbles. Thousands of tiny iridescent globes floated around Robert and me when we walked down the steps and past our guests as Mr. and Mrs. Pennington. Our beautiful BMW Roadster, decorated with white paper carnations, streamers, and cans tied to the rear bumper, had a sign stretched across the trunk announcing Just Married in big bold letters. We wondered how the car found its way to the chapel. No matter who we asked, no one knew or would admit to anything.

∞

The front yard of the Hinds' residence gave off a romantic glow. Candle-lit white paper bags lined both sides of the driveway, marking a path that led all the guests to the back of the house. There were two huge white bows on either side of the six-foot gate. Two of Robert's frat brothers posed as sentries, stopping us from going in. One brother slipped behind the gate as the other stood outside and visited with us. Finally, it opened. Robert linked his arm with mine and we were escorted to the backyard. Robert's elusive frat brother announced, "May I present to you, Mr. and Mrs. Robert Pennington!" All the guests stood up and clapped. The frat brothers made so much noise with their animal sounds and screaming cheers, it was deafening. Robert motioned for everyone to calm down and be seated. This took a few attempts, but finally, he could talk. "Belinda and I would like to thank everyone for this wonderful surprise. We didn't expect any of this. So, from the bottom of our hearts, thank you very much for all you've done."

While Robert talked, I looked around and almost cried. Cheryl had transformed her backyard into a wonderland. Hundreds of twinkle lights hung everywhere. Floating candles and white balloons drifted over the pool surface. The flickering flames between the bobbing balloons gave them an effervescent appearance. The atmosphere had a mystical effect.

White floor-length tablecloths covered with pale blue toppers adorned the tables. On each one set a hurricane-covered candle with white flowers and ribbons encircling the glass shade. The front table held punch, petite sandwiches, and other assorted snacks surrounding the feature piece, an all-white wedding cake scattered with small, pale blue flowers.

People congratulated us as we made our way around the yard greeting and thanking everyone individually. Our host and hostess were last. "Cheryl, I can't believe you did this for us. Thank you so very much. I just love it." As I threw my arms around her neck and gave her a big hug, tears welled up in my eyes.

"Yes, thanks so much," Robert agreed as he shook Russell's hand.

"Your brothers chipped in and helped. They wanted to share in this special moment." Cheryl still had me clinging to her. She returned my affection with an embrace.

The rest of the night we spent socializing and drinking until the time to cut the cake. I got very close to Robert and whispered, "If that cake goes anywhere but my mouth, you're on the couch and you will never lay eyes on your wedding gift." I smiled ever so sweetly. He knew I meant business. With our hands on the knife, we sliced the cake, retrieving the first piece. We fed each other a bite, which met its mark, then drank a sip of wine with our arms linked as Russell made a toast.

The first dance of the night was ours. Robert took me in his arms, and we glided around the pool like we were on air. My body moved with his. I couldn't and didn't want to restrain the shivery feeling inside. When the song ended, he gave me a long savoring kiss and my knees buckled. His tight hold kept me from falling and making a fool of myself.

Robert only let me go because of all the hooting and hollering from the frat brothers. I remember something about us "getting a room" being shouted. I felt embarrassed at our display, especially in front of our parents. Robert didn't seem bothered at all. He just chuckled and went on.

The next song, Robert danced with his mother and I with my father. When he took me in his arms and started dancing, his body stiffened. I realized he was trying to hold back the tears. When the music stopped, I leaned close to him. "I love you." With this simple statement, my father attempted to wipe his eyes as discreetly as he could while we walked hand-in-hand toward Mom.

Robert danced next with my mother and I with his father. I liked Mr. Pennington for what he told Robert the first time I met him. He thought I was a keeper. His opinion meant a lot to me. Since our first meeting, I'd had the opportunity to talk with him a few more times on the phone. He made me feel welcome and part of his family. I felt accepted and that I belonged. It wasn't because of the money or the fact the house was so big. There was something else, but I couldn't quite put my finger on it.

Everyone was enjoying themselves while visiting, eating, and dancing. Around eleven, I prepared to throw the bouquet. Cheryl made the announcement that all the single girls should gather around the patio steps. On the count of three, with my back to the crowd, I threw it in Abby's direction. When I turned back to see if I'd been successful, Abby was jumping up and down with it in her hands.

The reception was winding down as the guests started to dwindle. "Robert. I'm exhausted. I want to go home." *Home.* The word took on a new meaning. Before we left, we told our parents we'd see them in the morning.

Robert whisked me off my feet and carried me across the threshold. "Welcome home, Mrs. Pennington." His eyes sparkled and he smiled more than I had ever noticed before. His pace seemed more confident as he walked straight into our bedroom. Placing me on the bed, he lay on top of me.

"Mr. and Mrs. Robert Pennington." My pulse quickened. I wrapped my arms around his neck and kissed him. Zing! I didn't want to stop, but I stiffened in an attempt to restrain myself. "I'm going to get cleaned up and ready for bed."

He jerked his head up. "Can I join you?"

I smiled and agreed. I didn't want my hair all wet but how could I say no to my husband. I reached for his hand and led him into the bathroom.

Like I expected, the shower took a long time.

I towel dried my hair as much as I could while I waited for him to finish. When I tried to kick him out, he put up a fight as he attempted to persuade me to come to bed.

"I don't care if your hair is wet." He pulled me in the direction of the door. I latched onto the sink and wouldn't let go.

He was ruining everything. The more he pulled, the more I dug in my heels. He started to pick me up.

I screamed, "NO!"

He stopped and let go. He looked shocked.

"Robert, please. You're ruining your surprise."

"Oh." He pointed to the bedroom with me pushing him out of the bathroom. After securing the lock, I blow-dried my hair and parted it on the left side, letting it hang partially over my face. Then I pulled the teddy and three-inch heels out of the cabinet I'd hidden them in last night and slipped them on.

I studied myself in the full-length mirror and felt self-conscious looking through the veil of pale blue fabric that hid nothing. After practicing a few seductive poses, I placed my hand on the doorknob and took a deep breath as my butterflies whirled like a tornado. I opened the door and struck my pose.

Robert was lying in bed with one lamp on. His head swung in my direction. His jaw dropped and his eyes turned a deep ocean blue. "You look so hot!" For a few more seconds, he admired the view. "Thank you, it's the perfect gift." Then he hooked his finger at me. "Come here, my gorgeous wife."

The lustful look in his eyes sent liquid heat coursing through my veins and straight to my core. I moved toward him as he crawled across the bed and sat on the edge. Taking hold of my waist, he tugged me to him. "I love you more than you can imagine." He rubbed his cheek against my belly and then showered it and other areas with kisses, making my skin prickle. I shuddered.

I dove my hands into his hair and over his tense shoulders. He reached up and pulled at the thin straps of the teddy allowing it to slip to the floor. My body hummed beneath his wandering hands. My desire for him grew with every pass.

With lust in his eyes, he looked up at me and extended his hand. "Mrs. Pennington." My heart almost leaped from my chest as he pulled me down to him, and we made love as husband and wife for the first time.

CHAPTER 24

THE NEXT TWO weeks were spent being newlyweds. We stayed home relaxing, watching TV, cooking together, and more bedtime when the notion struck either of us. Of course, it struck Robert the most, but making love to him felt more special now, knowing he would be mine forever. Nothing could have been better than being with him as his wife and lover. We made the most of every minute of each day, knowing that when summer school started, class would take him away from our perfect life.

Summer school began without me. We agreed, if we both took a class, we would be too busy with no time to be newlyweds. So, I took a break from studying to relax.

Unfortunately, our plan didn't work out like we'd expected. We forgot to take into account that his class was on the graduate level and crammed into a shorter-than-usual time span. He spent most of the time studying and working on reports and projects after class. In the evenings and on weekends, he was with his study group. At first, he always managed to arrange his schedule so we could be together, but that changed.

So for now, we treasured our stolen moments. One rare evening, he came home early. We cooked then relaxed in the living room, sipping wine. I lay across his lap and looked up at his perfect profile.

He didn't look at me but fixed his eyes across the room. "Are you happy, Mrs. Pennington? Any regrets?"

"I couldn't be happier. No regrets at all. I got what I wanted…to be with you. Why did you ask me that?"

He looked down at me. "You didn't get to wear a beautiful wedding gown and have a fancy wedding to invite all your friends and relatives. Did I rush you into this marriage?"

I watched him as his face grew more serious. "No, I wanted this as much as you did. And those things don't matter to me, only you do."

He skimmed his fingers up and down my arm. "I'll make this up to you. When we graduate next year, I'll take you on a long babymoon wherever you want to go."

I shot up, shocked. "What babymoon? Are you planning a family without asking me? Don't you think I might have some say in the matter?"

"No! I wouldn't plan something like that without your input, but it is something to think about. And we could have lots of fun trying." His eyes lit up as he stroked my face. "Did you just stand up for yourself and confront me?"

Somewhat taken aback by his question, I gave it some thought then straightened my shoulders. "Yes. I did and I'm damn proud of it."

The July Fourth weekend was quickly approaching. Cheryl and Russell were having another swim party, but this one was also to introduce Russell's nephew, Declan, who belonged to the fraternity where he did his undergrad. In the fall, he'd start his master's here as a fellow Delt. Robert thought he'd be able to take some time off from studying to accompany me. If not, I'd go with Abby and Garrett.

Our best friends had moved into the same house we lived in. Their apartment was located behind ours. Abby and I had access to each other daily, and it was almost like being roommates again. Since neither of us had signed up for a class, we spent almost every day together.

The day of the July Fourth party, Robert informed me he couldn't go. He had to meet with his study group to work on a project due on Tuesday. I'd be going with Abby and Garrett as the third wheel.

With my head nestled against his chest, Robert cupped my chin and lifted my face to his. I gazed into his blue eyes now bloodshot and set off by dark circles. Summer school was taking a toll on him. He needed more rest.

He kissed me softly and then with more intensity, sparking a response. I attempted to wrap myself around him, but he stopped me.

"I wish I could go with you. I don't like you going by yourself."

I raised an eyebrow and smirked. "I'm not going by myself. Remember, I'm going with my chaperones."

He frowned. "Yeah, but you're going to be there without me."

"I'll be okay," I reassured him. "I'm an adult. I can take care of myself."

"Well, I'll try to be home by nine so we can have some time alone." He winked and gave me a half-grin, then picked up his backpack and keys. He nodded his head as a further goodbye and walked out the door.

As Abby, Garrett, and I walked into the Hinds' backyard, I passed a stranger who reminded me a lot of Robert. He wasn't as tall, but very handsome, with dark brown hair, nice build, and captivating green eyes. He caught my glance and winked. I returned the flirt with a half-smile and a nod.

Garrett stopped to talk to some of his brothers, while Abby and I claimed three lounge chairs by the pool. After stripping down to my bathing suit, I strutted to the deep end and dove in. I swam the length of the pool and back.

The new guy now sat on the edge, his legs dangling in the water. "Seems like you're the only girl here who doesn't care if she gets wet. Hey, I'm Declan Hinds." He extended his hand to me. "And you are?"

"Married." A gruff, recognizable voice came toward me.

I glanced up. "Hey, Garrett. This is Declan Hinds, Russell's nephew. This is Garrett Barnett."

"You two are married?" His hand retreated back to the edge of the pool.

"No, she's married to a Delt brother, Robert Pennington." Garrett looked like a pit bull, frowning at me and Declan.

"Okay, she came with you and that other girl." Declan appeared to be trying to figure out the pecking order.

"My husband is studying today. So I'm here with my pit bull." I pointed at Garrett.

"And you are?" Declan asked again. I climbed out of the pool and sat next to him.

"Belinda Pennington." This time I extended my hand. I turned toward Garrett and glared, warning him to keep his distance.

Declan glanced at him before he shook my hand. "Nice to meet you."

Garrett just stood there frowning.

"Chill out, Garrett. He's just being friendly. Can't I be sociable toward a new brother?" I waved him off. "Just go tend to Abby."

I wanted Garrett gone. I wanted to enjoy myself today. He walked far enough away to not be too bothersome, but I noticed him look my way every now and then. I frowned at him each time I saw him keeping tabs on me.

Declan gazed at me with those clear, sea-green eyes. "How long have you been married?

"Oh, uh…a month and a half. We tied the knot after his graduation."

He smiled with his eyes, if that was at all possible. Boy, his eyes could suck a girl in and never let her go. Thank heavens I was taken.

"Have you been dating all through college?"

"No, we just met the first of April." I looked at the water to avoid his gaze. I didn't want to be distracted again.

"Man, that was quick!"

"Yeah, kind of love at first sight." I played in the water, making whirlpools with my feet. "Where are you from?"

"Dallas, and you?"

"Sugar Land. It's southwest of Houston."

We chatted and laughed until Russell announced that the grilled hamburgers and hot dogs were ready.

"Are you hungry?" I nodded. Declan extended a hand and helped me up then placed his hand on the small of my back, escorting me toward the food.

Just then, Robert made an unexpected appearance. As he walked toward me, I could tell by his knitted brow and drawn mouth that he was upset.

Robert wrapped his arm around my waist and tugged me to him. A little too forceful for my taste. I managed to stay upright and hoped no one else noticed.

Declan spun around. "Hey. What the—"

"Declan, it's okay. He's my husband. Go ahead and get your food."

He studied Robert. "Are you sure?"

"Yes. I'll catch up with you later."

Every muscle in my body tensed. Heat rose up my neck. I spoke in a soft, muted voice. "I'm glad you came. Did you finish your project?" I tried not to draw any attention to us. It was very evident to me that Robert was not a happy camper. It was bad enough what Declan witnessed.

"No. Garrett called me." His words were low, deliberate, sharp and direct.

I pulled away. "Why?" I clenched my fist and scanned around for Garrett.

Robert leaned toward me. "He just thought I *needed* to be here."

My heart beat rapidly. I snapped my head toward him whispering in my own stern manner. "So, I'm not allowed to talk to guys?" Geez. I wanted to punch Garrett in the mouth for starting this.

Robert didn't say anything for a few seconds but never took his squinted eyes off me. I felt my skin being cut by his glare. Then his eyes change and softened a bit as he gave a quick glance toward the food station. Declan was walking toward us with his plate of food. Robert reached out to shake his hand, stretching to invite him closer to us. "Hey, I'm Robert Pennington." He now spoke in a friendly voice.

Asshat!

"Declan Hinds." Stepping closer, he reached over to take Robert's hand, never taking his eyes off of Robert's, nor letting go of his hand. "You have a very nice wife. I've been enjoying her company." The two just stood there for a few more seconds not saying anything, still in a handgrip.

"Thanks." He broke the stare-down with Declan and released his hand. "Excuse us for a minute. I need to talk to her." He took hold of my elbow and walked with me to the front yard. Coming to a halt near his car, he turned toward me, a frown marring his face. "What are you doing getting all friendly with him? You're married remember? What are my brothers going to think?"

My breath hitched when my chest tightened. I'd never seen him this way before. I had only seen him for short periods in the past few weeks as he darted off to class. This was the first time I had the chance to really study him. His face looked drawn. The dark circles under his eyes made him look ten years older and he had lost weight. The long hours and lack of sleep were getting to him. No wonder he was on edge.

"What gives you the right to come in here acting like a tool? I haven't done anything except talk to one of your brothers. You talk to their girlfriends." Just as that comment spilled from my mouth, I remembered how I felt at the first swim party when he talked to the two girls at the pool. My monster had reared its jealous head. Was Robert jealous? I was afraid if I asked it might make this situation worse.

"Robert, Baby. I'm in love with you. No one could ever take your place in my heart. Don't you know that?"

He didn't say anything. He just stared at the ground.

"Robert. Look at me." I reached up and lifted his chin. With his brow still furrowed, he stared into my eyes. "I hardly ever see you anymore. I get lonely sitting at home, especially at night all by myself. I can't intrude on Abby and Garrett all the time. I miss you terribly. I realize summer school is harder than we expected and it's taking up all your time. I'm coping with that." I looked down at the ground and muttered, "Sometimes I wonder if I should've just gone home for the summer. Had I know this would happen, I—"

"You regret marrying me and being here?"

Snapping my head up to meet his eyes, I immediately regretted saying that, even though I'd thought it several times. "No. Absolutely not. No regrets at all. Baby, I love you," I laced my fingers through his. "But today gave me a chance to get out. I promise, nothing happened. I was just being friendly." Eyes still locked on each other, I reached up and lovingly stroked his cheek.

His brow relaxed. He looked away, shaking his head. "I just don't want other guys touching you. I guess I'm concerned you'll have a connection with another guy…that you'll react to his touch. Remember you hadn't dated very many guys when we met. There could possibly be others."

"Even if there were, I'm yours. Forever. Am I sensing a little jealousy?"

"I don't know. When Garrett told me you and that guy looked a little too cozy…maybe I was. I just have this gut feeling you're going to leave me."

"I think your lack of sleep is causing you to overreact." I stroked his cheek. "You look like hell. You need to slow down and get some rest."

"Maybe."

"No. You need sleep. We can go home right now."

He shook his head. "I can't."

A huge sigh glided out.

His brow furrowed again. "I'm spoiling today for you. I better leave. I need to get back." He turned to leave but I grabbed his hand.

I tensed. He frowned. "Wait a minute. Can't you stay long enough to grab something to eat? You need to eat."

"No. They're waiting for me." He gave me a peck. "Look. I'll see you later tonight."

As he turned to leave, I reached up and tried to hug him. He scowled and stepped back away from me. "Belinda. You'll get me all wet."

I froze. "Geez! It's just water. You'd be dry before you get back." I didn't want to cause him any more stress, so I dropped the issue. "I'll see you at home." I turned and walked away.

"Belinda…"

"I'll see you later." I twisted at the waist and blew him a kiss. My chest tightened. I continued toward the backyard. Robert had just rejected me for the first time and it hurt. This was a side of him I hoped I'd never see again. I missed the loving, caring person who usually couldn't keep his hands off me, and I prayed I'd find him when I arrived home.

After picking up some food, I sat next to Abby. Garrett was sitting with my best friend. He looked all around. "Where's Robert?"

"He had to go back to his study group. I guess you're still on chaperone duty." I pursed my lips trying very hard not to tell him off.

"Just hang around with us." Abby leaned over and butted heads with me. I couldn't hold my anger any longer, so I leaned around her and punched Garrett in the arm. "Why did you call him? You just created a bigger problem."

"Ouch!" Scowling, he grabbed hold of his arm. "I didn't like the way that guy was looking at you."

"Oh, never mind!" I was so upset, I lost my appetite.

Declan walked over and scanned the group. "Is this seat taken?"

Garrett frowned at me. I scowled back at him and stuck out my tongue. I knew it was a juvenile thing to do, but it felt good. I motioned with my hand to a chair next to me. "No. It's all yours."

"Where's your husband?"

"Study group. He had to go back." I opened the bun and glared at the wiener, wishing I had a fork to stab it.

Several couples started to dance after Cheryl put on some music. Declan reached for my hand. "C'mon, let's dance."

"Wait a minute." I put on my shorts and jacket, trying to look like a respectable married lady. We danced to several slow songs and talked. I also danced with Brian, Paul, and then Garrett.

"Are you going to tell Robert I danced with Declan? Oh, and don't forget Brian, Paul, and you." I said it as sarcastically as I could. I wanted him to get the point. "It really wasn't a big deal, you know. I was having fun and you were ruining it." I quit dancing and strutted away, not giving him a chance to reply.

On my way back to my chair, I overheard Brian say he was leaving. "Hey, can you give me a ride home?"

"Sure, I'll wait for you out front."

"Thanks, I'll be right there." I looked around and found Abby lounging by the pool. "I'm leaving. Brian is taking me home." I gathered my things.

Abby looked at me and sat up. "Why?"

"Do you need to ask?" I jerked my head toward Garrett.

"Oh, sorry. I guess he's being overprotective. Do you want me to talk to him, tell him to back off?"

"No, that's not necessary. Brian said he'd drive me home. See you later." I turned and headed out.

Not far from the front gate, I saw Declan. As luck would have it, he was in clear sight of Garrett. So, I approached Declan, and politely shook his hand. "Thank you. I had a great time."

"Me, too. Hope to see you around." He smiled and cupped my hand.

He didn't have any effect on me. He was just a nice guy.

"Same here."

I could feel Garrett glaring at me. I turned around and glared back. With a bounce, I flipped my hair and headed for Brian, putting my sassy strut in full swing.

∞

I entered our empty apartment feeling relieved. Still upset from the way Robert had treated me, I wasn't ready to face him. A long hot shower relaxed me before I crawled into an empty bed. I just lay there staring at the ceiling, running the disturbing events over and over through my mind. Robert's appearance bothered me the most. At one a.m., according to the clock, I heard the click of the front door closing. I didn't want to talk. He needed sleep, so I rolled onto my side and pretended to be asleep.

Robert quietly crept into the room and began to strip. I peeked over and saw him pull his shirt off over his head, exposing his silhouette. He was thinner. He discarded the shirt on the floor. The sound of the zipper and the rustle of him removing his jeans thrilled me, but I continued pretending.

He slipped into bed and tried to pull me over to his side, but I didn't budge. He rolled over next to me and put his hand on my arm. "Belinda." I didn't answer. "Belinda." I remained still. Before he rolled over away from me, I heard him murmur, "I love you, Angel."

I smiled to myself. I wanted to grab him. Be in his arms. It had been so long, but I was still upset and knew he'd be up early and needed to rest. So I ignored him.

I finally dozed off. That was the first time I wasn't in his arms when we went to sleep. I didn't like it. Sometime during the night, I awoke and scooted over, curling up over his side, laying my head on his shoulder. His arms wrapped around me, and I whispered, "I love you, too."

CHAPTER 25

THE SLIGHT MOVEMENT of Robert creeping out of bed awoke me. "Where are you going?" I reached out for him. "Come back. It's Sunday." I knew I should still be upset, but I just couldn't. So for now, I rationalized that if I tried to keep the peace, all would work out. He wasn't around enough, so what time I did have had to be the best. "What time is it?"

He stood next to the bed, looking down at me. "It's seven o'clock. I have to get ready and meet with the group. Hopefully, we'll finish today."

"Can't you come back to bed?" Giving him a pouty look, I squirmed seductively under the sheet, trying to have my way. That was all it took. Robert flashed that irresistible smile and rolled his eyes, then slid back into bed. He ran his warm lips and exploring hands all over my body, exciting my senses and reminding me of what I'd been missing. I loved every splendid second!

"I'm sorry I upset you. The pressure from my class is really stressing me out. I didn't mean to take it out on you. I'll try to come home early." He sounded very sincere as he rose and headed to the bathroom to shower. I jumped out of bed and made breakfast.

Robert emerged from the bedroom and slung his backpack over his shoulder. "Whatever you're making smells great, but I'm late and have to go."

"I made breakfast burritos. It's kinda grab and eat on the way." I held three bundles, each wrapped in a paper towel. "There's no excuse not to eat breakfast."

"You're watching out for me." He took the food and gave me a sweet kiss.

I also packed some snacks. They're in your backpack."

"I love you." He stroked my cheek.

"I love you too. Now get going."

After he left, I crawled back into bed and slept as long as I could to make the day shorter. When I couldn't sleep any longer, I spent my time cleaning the whole apartment, doing some laundry, watching TV, and making us lasagna for dinner.

Robert's promise was short-lived. I ended up eating by myself and crawling into an empty bed. As usual. About two in the morning, I woke up and found him asleep on the couch with an open book lying across his chest. On the coffee table lay a single rose, but no card. Knowing what it meant, I placed it in the vase, now a permanent fixture on the kitchen table. Fetching a blanket, I covered him the best I could without waking him and kissed his forehead. I went back to bed, feeling a little more loved by his simple gesture of taking the time out of his busy day to pick up a rose.

Morning came and I was alone in the apartment. After eating, I walked to the campus and went straight to the Cave, hoping to see Robert. He wasn't there, but Declan was, so I sat and talked to him for a while.

Again, the rest of the day was spent by myself. I ate some leftover lasagna and later went to bed alone. Once more, I found Robert asleep on the couch. This was becoming our routine, and I didn't like it.

We needed to talk, so I called the next day. At first, he said he was busy and couldn't talk. He'd call me back later, but no call was returned. Over the next several days, I tried calling, but all of them went to voice mail, with no return calls. I even tried texting. His response was either "can't talk now," or no reply. I was confused and felt abandoned.

Thursday after lunch, I was tired of being alone. Normally, Abby would be a good source of companionship, but she had decided to take a trip to see her parents. So I strolled to the Cave on the off chance I might see Robert or anyone else to hang out with.

Declan sat alone at the Delt tables. He smiled and waved me over. We sat and talked like we had almost every day that week. Wanting to do something different, I took a chance. "How would you like a tour of the campus and town?"

His eyes lit up. "Sure, I'm game."

We walked to the student parking lot and looked up and down the rows until I found Robert's car. Declan's eyes grew wide as I opened the door and looked at him. "Get in." I put the top down and drove off. I gave him a quick tour of the campus, before heading out of town. Taking the winding road to the top of the hill, I parked, facing the view of the town below. "This is 'Make Out Ridge.' At night it's so beautiful with all the campus and town lights reaching up to the stars." I glanced over at him. "You need to see it at night sometime."

"You'll have to bring me whenever you can."

I ignored his comment. "We need to head back."

Down Main Street, I gave Declan the nickel tour of the shops that made up the hub of the town, then we stopped for sodas on our way back. Robert's parking spot was taken, so, I parked in the first available space.

Declan began to lift his cup from the holder, but I covered his hand. "Leave it." I hoped seeing the two cups would entice Robert to come home.

"Thanks for the tour. I look forward to seeing the night lights with you." He grinned before he closed the door.

"You're very welcome. See you around." Lowering my head, I slowly shook it as I walked away. There was no way I'd be the one to take him to 'Make Out Ridge' at night. That task would be left to some unmarried co-ed.

The lights flickered on with a flip of the switch. The sinking feeling meant one thing, I was about to spend another night alone.

Again, I ate by myself, and then sat around, staring at the walls. 'Monster' twitched her tail. Exactly what was Robert doing? Could he really be studying this much for one class? 'Monster' opened her eyes. I sat straight up. If I stayed on this path I'd drive myself nuts. So at about nine o'clock, I called Declan. "Hey, this is Belinda. Do you want to see the lights with me *now*?"

"Sure. But what about you-know-who?"

I didn't respond to his question. "Meet me out front of your house. I'll pick you up in ten minutes. Watch for a silver CR-V."

He was waiting by the curb when I arrived. We drove in silence toward 'Make Out Ridge.' Almost there, Declan broke the ice. "Is everything okay? You seem upset."

It was dark. I concentrated on my driving up the winding road. "I'm fine. I wanted to get out of the apartment."

"Where's Robert?" Declan sounded concerned.

I didn't think I should discuss my problems with him, but I decided to open up a little. It would be nice to talk to someone else in Abby's absence. The pitch in my voice dropped. "He's busy with the study group. I hardly see him anymore." I kept my eyes on the road. Declan didn't comment.

We were the only car on top of the hill. We climbed on the hood and leaned back against the windshield. "Isn't it beautiful and so peaceful here? I just love to look at the stars." The coolness of the night air made my skin prickle, but the stillness caused my breath to slow.

"Beautiful, indeed."

"The whole sky looks like twinkling lights." I looked over at him.

His voice was soft, almost a whisper. "I probably shouldn't say this, but I wish you weren't married. I'd like to have had a chance to date you. I really enjoy being with you."

I elbowed him. "I've enjoyed your company, too."

Declan turned onto his side and looked down at me. "You know, no one needs to study all the time, especially when he has a beautiful wife at home waiting for him. Have you seen this study group? Who's in it?"

I stared at the stars for a moment trying to organize my thoughts. A gripping feeling in my chest turned to agony. "Do you think he's cheating on me? Have you heard anything? Tell me!" I begged, holding back my budding tears as 'Monster' stirred.

"No, I haven't heard anything."

Was he telling me the truth or just not outing a fellow frat brother—bro code? At first, I just passed off Robert's mood and absence as being due to the stress and complexity of the class. But Declan planted the cheating seed that now had me wondering if something else was going on.

"I need to trust him. When I don't, I get hurt." A frenzy of emotions gnawed at my insides. Tears leaked from the outer corners of my eyes into my hair. I tried to hold them back, but they just came. I had promised Robert I'd trust him. We made a pact and shook hands on it. I couldn't go back on my promise to him.

"Why are you putting up with this?"

"Because I love him," I sniffled in a pitiful voice.

"Then give him an ultimatum. Let him know you don't like being alone."

I spoke through the sniffles, and tears trickled down my cheeks. "I can't do that. I don't want to add to the pressure he's under."

He locked his eyes on mine. "Belinda, I didn't mean to upset you, but, do you want to be with someone who doesn't want to be with you? You deserve to be happy."

A wave of panic overcame me and I looked away. I'd be hysterical in a minute if I didn't get my mind on something else. "Okay. Let's change the subject. Now, look at the stars."

He heaved a sigh and jumped off the car hood. Great, now I had three guys mad at me—Robert, Garrett, and Declan. I heard the passenger door open then slam shut. He came back and handed me a tissue. "Now dry those eyes. We have some serious stargazing to do." We spent the next hour pointing out constellations and visualizing funny pictures in the stars. I hadn't laughed so much in a long time. My spirits lifted and for a short time, 'Monster' slept and time passed peacefully, for a change.

I nudged him. "Hey, what time is it?"

"It's almost midnight."

"Jeez. I need to go home."

About twenty minutes later, we pulled up in front of Declan's place. "Thanks for coming with me. I had a great time."

He closed the car door. "Thanks for inviting me. I'll see you around."

At the apartment, Robert's car was parked out front. *Oh shit*! My heart sprinted. He would decide to come home early.

He was sitting on the couch watching TV when I walked in. He ignored me.

I took a second to breathe and said in an upbeat tone, "Hey! What are you doing home?"

With emotionless eyes, he looked up. "I thought I'd spend some time with you."

"Oh, I didn't know. You should've called." Now I was being sarcastic as I locked the door.

"I did. We decided to stop around nine." He was upset.

"I didn't hear my cell." I dug around in my purse. "It's not in here. Call my number." He reached for his phone and complied with my request. The music came from the kitchen. "I forgot to put it back in my purse. I left around then."

"Where did you go?" I noticed his brows were drawn together.

"I got bored, so I went to see the lights."

Now he was glaring at me. "By yourself?"

Oooh, I'm in trouble now. I had two choices. Tell the truth or lie. Truth. "No, I told Declan about the lights. I didn't want to go by myself. So I called him to see if he wanted to go. It was such a beautiful night. I wish you could have been there."

"I would have if you'd been home," he spat out. I flinched at his tone. "But, for three hours?"

Was he implying otherwise? I didn't like where this conversation was heading. "No, about two hours." I walked into the kitchen to get my phone. "He's a real nice guy, and he's been a good friend. We talk almost every day in the Cave." At the island, I watched Robert. He sat straight up, almost stiff. "Oh! By the way, I borrowed your car today to give him a tour of the campus and to—"

He cut me off, scowling. "Is there something going on you need to tell me?"

Blood bubbled and heated my neck. "*What*? How *dare* you ask me that? I could ask you the same." I tromped into the bedroom, dug my sleep t-shirt out of the dresser drawer, and went into the bathroom to shower. I slammed the door shut and locked it. The hot water eased the tension in my neck. I hated fighting and just wanted him wrapped around me in bed.

After showering, I put on the t-shirt, the same one I had borrowed the first time I slept in the apartment. I kept it and had cut the neck hole bigger so it wouldn't choke me. It hung off one shoulder, and just barely covered my butt.

Robert sat stewing on the couch as I padded to the kitchen to get my romance novel. To reach the book, I leaned across the table. My shirt crept up, exposing just enough of my bare bottom. In a flash, he was off the couch and was all over me. He held me tight and murmured, "Oh, God. You feel so good." He peppered kisses up my neck. "It's been too long.

I moaned and leaned back into his chest. Wanting my mouth on his, I turned and ran my hands up the back of his neck into his hair to pull his head down to mine. As I planted my lips firmly on his, a deep groan of pleasure resonated up from his throat. He deepened the kiss. His response and the kiss excited me to my depths. He returned the emotion with enthusiasm. His warm hand slid under the bottom of the t-shirt and up my back. It arched as he tugged me closer. Fire ignited my skin from his touch. My breath hitched with every sweep of his hand. He lifted me up, and I locked my legs around his waist. He carried me to the bedroom. Our reactions took over. The results were explosive.

Fulfilled, I slid over his side and held him tight as I started to fall asleep. "I love you…and I miss you."

"It'll be over soon." He nuzzled my hair.

"You promise."

He squeezed me to him and didn't answer.

When morning came, he was gone.

Each day, the pattern continued. I went to the Cave hoping to see Robert. Instead, I talked to Declan until he left for Dallas. The fraternity brothers would ask where Robert was. I didn't know, so I lied. "Studying," became my usual answer. It was becoming embarrassing, so to avoid the awkward questions, I quit going. I spent nearly all of my time in the apartment. For all I knew, I would be the last one to find out Robert was busy with someone else.

I decided not to burden Abby with my problem since I didn't know what my problem was. She and Garrett were busy being a couple and she didn't need me stomping all over her happiness.

One day, I waited outside Robert's building to talk to him, but he never came out. I went to the parking lot. His car wasn't there.

Lonely days and nights turned into weeks. The only time I saw him was at two or three a.m. when he was asleep on the couch. There was always an open book nearby. Was he really studying or just faking? Each night I curled up in a ball and cried myself to sleep. Why was he doing this to me? Why weren't we talking about whatever the problem was? I tried calling and texting, with no response. I even woke him up one night and asked him what was wrong. He just said everything was fine. I asked if he still loved me. He took in a deep breath and exhaled loudly as if he were upset. "Of course."

One other night he came to bed, but he insisted he was exhausted and told me to go to sleep. That upset me and I started crying. He spooned me with his arm over my waist. I laced my fingers through his and hugged his hand over my aching heart as I tried to stop crying. His response was cold. "Belinda, nothing is wrong. Just go to sleep."

Belinda? What happened to Angel? What happened to my warm and loving husband?

In the morning, I tried to talk to him, but, again, I was told there's nothing wrong. "I'm just under a lot of pressure and stressed out. Don't worry. Please don't add to my stress," was his final answer as he walked out, leaving me alone.

I put those thoughts out of my head and just endured the heartache, convincing myself that everything would return to normal when summer school was over. *But what about the fall semester?* The thought that this could continue made me shudder.

The next morning was more of the same—no Robert. I forced myself out of bed and walked to the kitchen for a cup of coffee. There on the counter was a single rose lying in front of my empty vase, but no card.

I studied it, trying to decide what to do. As I saw it, I had two choices. I could pick it up and put it in water then dry it, or I could just leave it there. A single red rose is the symbol of love. I wasn't feeling very loved, so I decided to leave it. That afternoon, I found it in the vase on the table. He evidently stopped by while I was out. "Huh! He cares more about the rose than he does me."

CHAPTER 26

IT HAD BEEN weeks since Robert had kissed me, made love to me, or even had a conversation with me. I felt deserted. It was the last day of summer school—finals. I decided to surprise Robert, hoping I could talk him into having dinner, a kind of finals celebration.

I drove to campus to wait for him by his car. After driving up and down several aisles of the parking lot, I finally spotted the Beamer an aisle over. I headed for it, looking for a close parking place, but none were available. As I approached his car, I slowed down to look through the Beamer's back window to see if he was in it and noticed movement. Squinting my eyes, I froze as my brain tried to make sense out of what I saw. He was in there, but not alone. He and his blonde study partner, Erin, were leaning toward each other, her hand splayed over his cheek, kissing him.

Pain knocked the breath out of me like I'd been stabbed in the heart. Tears flooded my eyes. Unable to stomach the view, I snapped my head forward and stomped on the accelerator. One brief look was enough. I warred with my conscience whether I should go back and confront him or run. *Screw our deal*! *Why confront him*? There wasn't any acceptable explanation for what I saw. My stomach knotted. I gagged and wanted to puke. I sped out of the parking lot toward home with tears of disbelief flowing down my cheeks. This explained his ignoring me and all his late-night excuses. Study group my ass! The bitch! The nerve of him accusing me of being too friendly with Declan when he's messing around with her. Asswipe! Matt and Abby were right about him being a player since he was cheating on Lora. "I'm a one-girl-at-a-time guy," my ass.

I managed to make it into the apartment before completely falling apart. A stabbing pain doubled me over. Wrapping my arms over my belly, I fell back against the door and slid to the floor, tears still streaming down my cheeks. I cried out, "Why? Why? Why did this happen? I trusted you with my heart. Cheater!" My voice cracked with a sob.

I needed to stop and get a grip. Robert could be home any time now and I didn't want to be here when he arrived. I couldn't put up with this any longer. I had promised not to run, but catching him for the third time kissing, his study partner no less, was not acceptable. At all. I needed time away from him to think. After taking a deep breath, I stood up. I yanked my bag off my shoulder and tossed it on the table, then headed into the bedroom to pull out my two suitcases and packed whatever I thought I might need. I left my wedding dress and the pale blue teddy lying on the bedroom floor where I had thrown them. Tears streamed down my face the whole time. He needed to know why I left, so I decided to leave him a letter. Unnerved, I shuffled through the desk drawers for a pen and sheet of paper. Teardrops blurred the words as I wrote…

Robert,
I trusted you.
   You promised you wouldn't do it anymore, but you did. I can understand with Lora. She wanted you and she hated me. But with Erin? Well, I hope she was worth it. I guess that explains all those late nights and ignored phone calls and texts. You abandoned me and now betrayed me.
   From the first day, I saw you, I knew you were the one for me—that we'd be together forever. But I'm questioning that now. It's hard to imagine my life without you, but I don't trust you. So what do I do? I'm in pain with you and without you. I can't keep going through this. It hurts too badly. I gave you my heart and you're ripping it out piece by piece, leaving a painful void that will always ache for you.
   Please, don't look for me. I need time and space to think and hopefully heal.

   B

   When I finished the letter, I placed it on the coffee table and went back to packing. The whole time my life with him was going through my mind. I went back to the letter and wrote…

   PS—Remember what I told you in the beginning? I can do what you do!!! Well I can and will!!!

I let the pen fall next to the paper and took the packed suitcases to the car. Still reliving our short life together, I returned to the paper…

   PPS—Do you recall your gut feeling I was going to leave you? Maybe that was your subconscious warning you that you'd cause me to leave. Something to think about!

I got up to make sure I had everything I needed then decided to write one more thing before leaving…

   PPPS—Keep the engagement ring. It belongs to your family. It wasn't good luck for us. At all.

I left the tear-stained letter on the coffee table with my engagement ring and double-heart necklace lying on top. I kept my wedding ring on. I had never taken it off and promised I never would—*'til death do us part*. It had never entered my mind that our marriage could end in divorce.

Giving the apartment one last check, I saw my treasure box and retrieved it from the end table. With it tucked under my arm, I stood in the middle of the living room looking around. The memories of better times flooded my head. I started to doubt myself. Was I making the right move? I shook the thought off.

Now it was time to say goodbye, but I'd always have the good memories. I'd never forget the times when Robert swept me off my feet and took me to the bedroom. And there were the long night talks lying next to him, wrapped in his arms. I don't think I ever felt so safe and protected. Hearing his voice always drew me into whatever he said.

No, I would always have good memories. Unfortunately, there were also bad ones. Those would be harder for me to recover from. At this point, it didn't matter who was at fault, Robert or me. I still would have the bad ones and all the feelings that went with them, making me a victim of my own shattered fate.

For now, it was time to leave. I reached for my purse on the kitchen table and snatched up the handles, not slowing my pace. With one swift movement, I dragged the purse across the table. The crash of glass shattering caused me to turn. On the floor, my precious vase was smashed with the rose lying on top. The scene before me compounded my already bruised emotions as I stared down at the mess. I bent to pick up the rose and accidentally dropped my treasure box of dried rose petals. My tokens of his love spilled like teardrops over the broken glass. My first instinct was to pick up my memories. I squatted down. A sharp stab in the center of my chest stopped me. They no longer held any meaning, so, I stood and turned for the door.

I hesitated, taking one last look around, then stepped into the entryway, and shut the door on my life with Robert. Opening the outer door of the building, I stepped into the sunlight. My cell rang as I stood on the porch. It was Abby. I was too upset to talk to her, so I ignored it.

I didn't know where to go. My parents' house was out of the question. If Robert looked for me that would be the first place he'd check. I didn't want them having to lie about where I was. It would be best not to tell anyone of my whereabouts. As I drove past the campus toward Houston, I saw, in my rearview mirror, a blue roadster pull out and head in the direction of our apartment. Again, I questioned my decision to leave, but there was *NO* acceptable excuse for what I'd seen today. This was the right decision. I left my love and my life behind.

Though I wasn't in any condition to be driving, I had to leave town. The drive to Houston seemed to take forever. It gave me too much time for my mind to keep playing the car scene over and over again. I felt like hurling, my stomach twisted in knots. I used almost a whole box of tissues to wipe away my tears.

The nearer I drove to the city limits, the heavier the traffic became. So, I pulled into the first decent motel and checked in.

I sat on the bed and studied my phone. The voicemail icon showed four messages and one text.

Abby was the first to call. "Belinda, where are you? Call me." The second call was also from her. "Belinda, are you okay? Why aren't you answering your cell? Call me."

The third call was, again, from her. "Belinda, what happened in your apartment? Answer your cell. I'm worried." The fourth call was from HIM. "Belinda, where are you? Call me." There was one text message. It was from him: Are you OK?

I sent Abby a text instead: Don't worry. I'll text later.

I turned my cell off.

Was leaving the right decision? *Yes.* I gave up and grabbed my wallet to check how much cash I had. Stuck between a five and ten dollar bill, I found Mr. Johnson's business card for his modeling agency, that he had given me at the Mexican restaurant in Sugar Land. I realized it could be the answer to another problem I faced—the need to support myself. Maybe I could model. How hard could it be? Just pose in front of a camera. Surely I could do that as long as I didn't have to walk a runway. In the morning, I'd call and try to make an appointment. At this point, I had nothing to lose.

I tried to watch some TV, but that didn't help, so I picked up my cell and called Abby.

"Oh! Hi Mom!" Abby answered in her normal tone.

"No, it's Belinda."

"Hold on, Mom, I'm having bad reception. Let me go outside." I heard a door slam. "Belinda, sorry about that. I figured you didn't want to talk to Robert. Garrett and I are at your place. Are you all right? Your text worried me."

"I'm fine. I didn't mean to upset you."

"I stopped by your place. The door was open and I saw the mess on the floor. Then I ran to the Cave, to look for you, but found Robert with Garrett. I asked him where you were, and told him what I saw. He tried calling you. When he couldn't reach you his face went white and he said, 'Oh crap,' then jumped up and ran out."

"Guilty conscience. He must've realized I saw him."

"What happened?"

I huffed. "Erin and Robert kissing in his car. That's what happened."

Abby let out a gasp. "Belinda, I'm sorry."

I swiped my eyes to control the tears. "What was he doing when you came over?"

"Sitting on the couch with a letter in his hand. Your engagement ring and necklace were on the coffee table." Her voice wavered, "He said your clothes were gone and then mumbled something about you promising not to run."

"Abby, I can't keep going through this. It hurts too bad. It's like waiting for the other shoe to fall."

"I understand. I probably would have done the same thing." She took a deep, shaky breath. "I'm so mad I could punch Robert right now. That SOB."

"Well, what excuse did he give for what he did?" I was really curious to hear how he planned to explain this time.

"Robert wouldn't talk about it."

"I know now why he was coming in at two or three every morning. He was busy with Erin." I sucked in a sob. "Abby, he hasn't kissed or touched me in weeks. One day everything was perfect, the next I was alone. I was married, but I had no husband." Tears began rolling down my face.

"Why didn't you say anything to me?"

"You and Garrett seemed so happy. I didn't want to drag you into my mess." I started to sob, and my voice cracked. "I've missed him so much, but I guess he's found a replacement. After all, he's a one-girl-at-a-time kind of guy."

"You said he was coming home at two or three in the morning." Her voice conveyed concern about what I'd been going through.

"He'd come home after I'd already gone to sleep. I never saw him and he didn't return my calls." I sniffled and wiped my nose. "I don't understand what happened." My voice quavered through my sobs.

"Where are you? Can I come see you? We can talk." Abby sounded really upset.

"I'm not telling anyone where I am right now. I'll let you know later after I find a job and settle somewhere."

"So, you're not coming back to school?" Her voice broke.

"No, too many bad memories and definitely not with him there." A lump formed in my throat. "I need to go."

"I love you." She added, "Please stay in touch."

"I will. Bye." Looking at my phone, I imagined Abby telling Robert about our phone call and wondered if he would be sadder because he was losing me or because he'd been caught again. I guess none of that mattered at this point. I'd been alone for the past several weeks, and I was alone now, something I was used to. I grew up alone and if I needed to, I could do it again.

I was exhausted mentally and physically from the most horrible day I'd ever had. But I still held a small glimmer of hope that we could work things out in the future. For now, I needed to find out who I was and if I could live without him.

After a quick shower, I crawled into my empty bed. Sleeping was difficult until I curled up around a spare pillow. It wasn't warm like Robert, but it filled the void.

CHAPTER 27

MY FIRST TASK for the day was job hunting.

"Johnson's Modeling Agency, may I help you?" A nice, older-sounding lady answered.

"Yes, please. I'd like to make an appointment with Mr. Johnson. Does he, by any chance, have an opening today?" I was ready to start my new life in some direction.

"Yes, he's available at two. Will that work for you?"

"That'll be fine."

"And your name, please."

"Belinda Pen...ah. I mean Davies. Belinda Davies." *Why use my married name if it might change*?

"Belinda Davies, see you at two."

"Thank you."

No sooner had I ended my call, Robert's ringtone played. There were enough reminders of him in my head, so he was bumped back down to the standard ringtone before I turned it off.

It was nine o'clock and I had a lot to do before my appointment. I studied myself in the mirror and almost fainted at what I saw. My eyes were red and puffy from all the crying yesterday and my hair resembled a rat's nest after my restless night. I took a shower, fixed my hair, and spent about an hour on my eyes.

Dressed in my newly purchased pair of slacks, an aqua blouse, and my espadrilles, I had about two hours to find the Johnson's Modeling Agency. I typed the address into my GPS. The agency was located across town. I decided I'd better be on my way because in Houston, being stuck in traffic was the one thing you could count on.

For once in the past twenty-four hours, luck was on my side. I saw a branch of the bank where Robert and I had our savings account. I stopped and withdrew several thousand dollars. It would be enough for me to live on for a while, and Robert probably wouldn't notice the money missing right away. But as I saw it, he owed me.

I pulled up to the agency early, which was located in Bellaire, and decided to text Abby.

| Me: | Wish me luck. I'm going for a job interview. |
| Abby: | Good luck. Doing what? |

Me: Secret, I'll tell you later if it works out.

In the front office of the remodeled house sat an attractive, middle-aged lady. She looked up from her desk when I entered. "May I help you?"

"I'm Belinda Davies. I have an appointment at two."

"One moment please." She left the room for a few seconds and then returned. "You can go in now." She pointed the way.

"Thank you." I entered the door she directed me to.

Without looking up at me, Mr. Johnson motioned to a chair across from his desk. "Have a seat." Then his eyes met mine and addressed me from behind his big wooden desk. "What can I do for you?"

"My name is Belinda. Do you remember me?" His eyes followed me as I walked over and sat on the edge of the chair. "A few months ago at a Mexican restaurant in Sugar Land, you gave me your business card. You told me if I wanted to make some money to come see you."

He nodded. "Oh yes! You and a young man. I remember now."

"I found your business card in my wallet when I arrived in Houston yesterday and thought I'd give you a call." I tried not to sound desperate, but this was my quickest option for finding a job. I might have been able to make another withdrawal from the joint account, but it was logical that at some point the well would go dry.

"When you arrived in Houston? Where are you from?" He looked puzzled as he stroked his chin.

"I'm from Sugar Land, but I've been away at college."

Mr. Johnson's eyes wandered over me. "So, are you only looking for summer work?"

"No. I'm looking for something full time because I'm planning to stay in Houston."

Over the next two hours, Mr. Johnson asked me all kinds of questions which led to a two-way conversation. As I talked with him my concerns about the past few days dwindled. The tension in my shoulders released. He made me feel so comfortable, I even told him about Robert and my need for permanent housing.

"Are you interested in renting a room or an apartment?"

"I don't know. I haven't thought that far ahead."

"I know of a nice place. It's run by a woman who's an ex-model. Now she rents out rooms to ladies." He pushed back in his chair. 'It's very reputable." He leaned forward. "I'll give you the address and if you like it, you can make the arrangements with Mrs. Foster."

What did I have to lose? I nodded in approval.

He picked up his phone. "Adele, it's Frank Johnson. How are you doing?" He grinned. "Oh, good to hear that." He toyed with a pen. "I'm doing fine, thank you. Say, do you have a room available? You do? Great." He gave me a thumbs-up. "I have someone in my office who might be interested. Can I send her over?" He nodded. "Okay. Thanks." He hung up. "It's all set." He scribbled the address on a sheet of paper and handed it to me. "The next thing we need is to put a portfolio together." He laced his fingers in front of him on the desk.

"You're giving me a job?"

"Well, not really. Think of it as getting you ready for me to launch your modeling career." He came around and sat on the edge of his desk. "The way it works is I have to sell your abilities as a model to a client. Once that's done, we both get paid."

"Oh." I wrung my hands. I needed an income, *now*. "How long could that take?"

"That all depends. It could take weeks to months."

I lowered my head to hide the blood draining from my face. My shoulders tensed. I wanted to cry. He didn't say anything and I didn't look up, afraid tears would stream down my cheeks.

"Belinda, if your pictures turn out the way I think they will, I'll start making phone calls immediately.

I kept my head down. That wouldn't help. *Weeks to months*. I could be on the street by then or back living at my parents. I didn't want Robert to find me.

"Can you answer phones and take messages?"

My eyes met his and I tilted my head. "What?"

In two day my secretary leaves on vacation. Do you think you can fill in?"

"Yes. Definitely."

He slapped his hands on the top of his desk. "Great. I want you here at nine tomorrow. Joan will show you around."

I sucked in a lung full of air.

"I'll pay you the same I pay Joan and so far, she hasn't complained."

Now, I really wanted to cry. But how did he know I needed money? I didn't care. "Thank you very much."

"Go see Mrs. Foster and I'll see you in the morning."

Mrs. Foster's house was just around the corner. She met me at the front door. She was an attractive sixtyish, white-haired lady who had retained a shapely figure.

"Belinda? Hi. I'm Adele Foster." She reached her hand out.

I shook her hand. "Belinda Davies."

"So, you ready to see the room?"

Nothing about this woman put me on edge. "Sure."

The house was a white two-story—very similar in layout to the house I had lived in with Abby at college. She led me upstairs to a good-sized room. It was furnished with antique cherry furniture, lace curtains, and a chenille bedspread. It was dated, but very warm and inviting. "Rent is six hundred a month and that includes breakfast and dinner. My only rules are no loud music and male guests stay downstairs." She stood quietly as I roamed around, occasionally touching the furnishings. "Will this do?" I scanned the room quickly, once again, and gave her a nod, sealing my status as her tenant.

I unloaded my car and was unpacking when Mrs. Foster knocked.

"I brought you some towels." She placed them on the bed and was about to close the door. "I'll have dinner ready by six." She winked. "Just relax until then."

The mattress felt like a cloud. The lavender scent of the silky sheets waft upward and encircled my nose. I settled in expecting to doze off. Instead, my mind decided to run on a treadmill. I wondered why Abby had to ask him where I was. Wasn't he concerned about me? Maybe I should have confronted him and asked why he was treating me this way. But that kiss! There was no excuse for that. I guess he'd grown tired of me. *Oh, stop thinking about him or you're going to drive yourself crazy!* This went on for an eternity until I drifted off.

"Belinda. Belinda. Dinner's ready." Mrs. Foster shouted from the bottom of the stairs.

I opened my eyes and yawned. "Okay. Thanks, I'll be down shortly."

I took my cell phone out of my purse and turned it on. It started ringing. Robert's number appeared. I wasn't ready to talk to him, so I let the call go to voice mail. I checked my text messages. There was one from him: I'm sorry, please call.

I glared at the phone. "Yeah. In your dreams."

I listened to his voice mail. "Angel, Abby told me you talked. That kiss you saw, it's not what you think. We need to talk. Please call me." Hearing Robert's distressed voice made me want to cry. *Get a grip. No crying.* I had made the right decision to leave. I turned my cell off and headed downstairs.

We finished eating, and I helped her clean up the kitchen. With the last plate put away and the counters wiped down, Mrs. Foster turned to me. "Now, go relax." She motioned with a wave for me to leave the kitchen.

Alone in my room, I needed to talk to someone I knew, so I called Abby.

"Belinda, I'm so glad you called. Are you all right?"

"Yes, just lonely. Although I should be used to that feeling. Where are you? I hear a lot of voices in the background?"

"I'm with Garrett at the frat house."

Out of curiosity, I asked, "Is Robert there?"

"Yes, they're outside, and Garrett's reading him the riot act. Do you want to talk to him?"

I spat out, "No, definitely not." I heard Robert's voice in the background.

"Is that Belinda? Let me talk to her!"

Abby snapped at him. "She doesn't want to talk to you."

The phone went dead. A few seconds later my cell rang. My heart skipped a beat. It was Robert. I didn't answer and waited a few seconds to check my voice mail. There were two new messages. The last one was from Abby saying he's gone and to call back. The first one was from Robert. "I miss you. I love YOU, please call."

I texted: You didn't miss me before. You love me? You sure have a strange way of showing it.

I didn't wait for a response and called Abby.

"Belinda, sorry about the hang-up."

"That's okay. Is he still there?"

"No. I'm hiding outside. What are you going to do?"

"I'm not sure." My throat closed as I tried to speak.

"Maybe you should talk to him."

"Why? He's the one who needs to take responsibility for his actions. I wasn't the one kissing someone in my car. If he still wants to play around, then I want a divorce. I can't live this way. It hurts too much." My tears threatened. *Get a grip. Don't cry! Don't cry!*

"Do you still have your wedding ring? Robert wasn't holding it."

"I still have it on. I promised to never take it off, and I won't until a divorce is finalized, if that happens. I don't want a divorce. I love him so much, but he needs to change, and I don't know if he can." *Don't cry! Don't cry!* "Abby, I can't talk anymore. Good night."

The next morning, I jumped out of bed and headed for the agency. Joan wasted no time showing me the ins and outs of the office.

Just before lunch, Mr. Johnson emerged. "How's everything out here?"

"She's a quick learner and she'll do fine." Joan stacked some folders before pulling her purse from a desk drawer. "Belinda, would you like to join me for lunch?"

"I'd like that."

Mr. Johnson spoke up. "Before you two leave, Belinda, tomorrow we'll be getting your portfolio pictures taken."

A flutter filled my chest. "You got me an appointment already?"

"There was a one o'clock cancellation. We'll leave about twelve-fifteen. Now, go enjoy lunch."

At the end of the day, I started my short walk to the boarding house. I was floating on the high of excitement when my cell rang. "Hello."

"Belinda, please don't hang up. I need to talk to you."

My chest tightened. My mouth dried. I couldn't breathe. I disconnected the call. I wasn't ready to talk or try to deal with Robert's explanation. His voice made me tremble. If I talked with him now, I'd be lost forever. I needed to be strong and stand my ground. He had no right to do what he did, but hearing his voice made me realize I still loved him.

∞

"Belinda." Joan poked my arm.

"Yeah." My heart hammered and wouldn't stop. I looked at the clock. It read five minutes 'til the time to leave. "I can't concentrate. I'm nervous about the photoshoot."

Joan sighed. "Okay. We've covered everything you need to know to run the office and I think you'll do fine."

"Thanks."

Joan's face lit up. "You're a fast learner."

I smiled, but I couldn't get my thoughts off the photoshoot. I knew nothing about what was expected. My summer modeling class wasn't meant to prepare me for anything on a professional level. What if I made a fool out of myself? I did that once before when I landed on my butt on a practice runway.

Mr. Johnson strolled out of his office. "Belinda, it's time to leave."

Joan gave one last reassurance, "You'll do fine."

The studio wasn't far from the agency. On our way, I asked, "Who's the photographer you're using?"

"Kyer Saunders."

I sucked in a deep breath and exhaled. "Oh good! Mrs. Foster said he's the best."

We pulled up in front of another old remodeled home in the area. "Kyer's expecting you. Just let them know who you are."

"You're not coming in?" My hammering heart sped up a few paces.

"Kyer knows what he's doing. You'll be fine. Just listen to what he tells you."

I inhaled. "Okay."

"Call me when you're finished and I'll pick you up."

I stepped out of the car and walked toward the studio, all the way repeating, "You've got this."

A young lady looked up from the front desk. "Can I help you?"

"Yes, I'm Belinda Davies. I have an appointment with Mr. Saunders. Mr. Johnson sent me."

"Have a seat, please. I'll let him know you're here." She left the room and returned shortly. "He'll be right with you."

I thanked her and waited. Looking around the room at the framed photos of beautiful models, I wondered if I really looked like them.

"Belinda?" A short gentleman with ash blonde hair entered the room. "I'm Kyer." He reached out and shook my hand. "Come with me." I followed him into his studio. "Turn around slowly. Let me look at you." My nerves were doing a number on me, but I did as he requested while he propped his chin in his hand and studied me. "Okay. I understand this is your first time to pose."

"Yes, sir."

"Don't worry. We'll get some great shots."

We spent two hours taking pictures in a variety of poses. It was exhausting but fun. Mr. Saunders was very patient and I learned a lot. When he finished, he pulled the photos up on his computer, and we analyzed each one. It helped me see what I should and shouldn't do. He put my ten best shots on a flash drive for Mr. Johnson to view.

"I think you have some good shots here. Tell Mr. Johnson I'll make prints for him. He can pick them up tomorrow."

When we returned to the office, Mr. Johnson put the flash drive in his laptop. I stood beside him at his desk to view the photos.

"These are terrific. For a first-timer, you did great," he said in a voice full of enthusiasm. "There's a new jeans manufacturing company looking for a model for their ads and commercials. I don't know if they've picked someone yet, but I'm going to email these to them first thing in the morning." A huge smile spread across his face. "You look terrific in jeans."

"What's the company's name?"

"Every Body Jeans Manufacturing Company."

"Interesting name." The clock on his desk flashed six o'clock. "Are we finished?"

His eyes never left the computer. "Yeah, go home. I'll see you tomorrow."

The next morning, I arrived at nine sharp and made coffee then set out the donuts.

Minutes later, Mr. Johnson stomped in. He poured himself a cup of black jo and took a bite of a donut. With a full mouth, he managed to say, "email," as he pointed to his office and walked in, closing the door behind him.

All I could do was wait.

For the next hour, I tried to focus, but I kept wondering about the blasted email and if it got sent. It was time for action. I rapped on Mr. Johnson's door.

"Come in."

"Mr. Johnson, do you need a refill on your coffee?"

He was tapping the keys on his computer. The corners of his mouth lifted. "I sent the email and pictures." He stopped. "All we can do is wait."

"Oh."

He must've heard the disappointment in my voice because he continued, "If we're lucky, maybe by Wednesday or Thursday next week we'll hear something."

"Okay. But, do you need a refill?"

"No. I'm fine."

I returned to my desk to start the longest wait of my life.

∞

Mid-Saturday morning, I decided I needed to visit my parents. It didn't take long to drive from Bellaire to their house, but I should've called because no one was home. I drove around and soon I found myself in very familiar surroundings. I was in the Penningtons' neighborhood. I'd only been to their house one time, so I wasn't sure where it was. Whatever possessed me to start looking for my in-laws' house, I'll never know. I drove all around, finally seeing a house that looked like theirs.

I was about to turn into the cul-de-sac when I saw Robert getting into his roadster parked in the circular drive. *Oh shit*! He saw me. I zoomed by. My hands trembled when I looked in my rearview mirror and saw him closing in. My breath accelerated. I still wasn't ready to face him. Speeding up, I made several turns and zipped through a yellow light. He was stopped by a car that pulled in front of him when the light turned red. With some other fancy maneuvering through adjacent neighborhoods, I was sure I had lost him and headed straight for the safety of Mrs. Foster's.

Having been so close to Robert, even just for a minute, made the emotional part of me wish he'd caught up. The practical, more logical side told me to stay away. I was so conflicted, but I knew logic would win because it had to for me to pull through this.

In my new sanctuary, I figured he'd called, so I checked my voice mail. He had. "Why didn't you stop? Please call. We need to talk. I love you." Hearing his voice sent a pang that jabbed at my heart. I knew there was no way I could talk to him and think straight, so I texted instead.

I texted:	I went to see my parents but they weren't home. I'm not ready to face you. No will power.
Robert:	Please come back and let me explain. It's not what you think.

Me:				I can't. I need time to heal & forgive. No excuse for what I saw. Why are you at your parents?

Robert:			I'm moving back. I can't stand being at school w/o you. Give me another chance.

My judgment was being tested. I felt bad that he quit school because of me. Now I wasn't sure if leaving was right. One thing I did know—I needed time to think without being influenced by our physical connection. I looked back at my phone and turned it off.

The smells from the kitchen made my mouth water and I realized I hadn't eaten all day. So, I headed downstairs. Mrs. Foster set pot roast on the table as I slid into my chair. "It smells delicious. I'm starving."

We ate and chatted about the day.

"I went for a drive and found myself in my in-laws' neighborhood. Just my luck, my husband was there and saw me. He tried to follow me, but I lost him."

Mrs. Foster's head tipped to the side. "Why did you go there?" She took a bite of meat.

I shrugged. "I don't know. I was going to visit my parents, but they weren't home. Before I knew it, I was near Robert's parents' house." I shook my head. "I feel close to my mother and father-in-law. Maybe I was looking for some help figuring all this out."

"Do you think, maybe, subconsciously you were hoping to see him?"

"You think so? But I didn't know he was in Sugar Land." I sunk back into my chair. "Maybe so. I feel like a part of me is missing." Looking down, I played with my food.

"If you feel this bad, you should go see him or at least call him. Try to work out your problems."

"I can't. If I do, I'll just forgive him and nothing would've changed. Then, I'll feel worse if it happens again. He needs to realize I'm not going to put up with his behavior. He needs to change, but I don't know if he can or will. He said he's a one-girl-at-a-time guy, but he acts like a player. Can a player change his ways?" Tears threatened to well up.

She placed her hand over mine and looked me in the eyes. "If he truly loves you, he can do anything." Her hand was the first human contact I'd had since I'd left school. It felt good. I was glad I decided to take refuge with Mrs. Foster.

Sunday was a do-nothing day. I slept late and just relaxed around the house. After a while, boredom allowed my mind to start thinking about Robert. So, to keep myself busy, I volunteered to help Mrs. Foster clean the house. About halfway through, I decided I should try to contact my parents and let them know what was going on. I didn't want to talk to my father. It would be hard to admit defeat to him. Besides, I'd have to break the news about leaving school and was confident that would send him over the edge. Hopefully, Mom would answer. I knew I could get more sympathy from her. "I'll be back shortly. I'm going upstairs to make a call."

She stopped dusting an end table. "Are you calling your husband?"

"No, I need to let my parents know what's going on. This will be almost as hard as talking to him." I was very conflicted about this. I ran upstairs and retrieved my cell from the nightstand. After taking a deep breath, I called my parents' house.

"Hello." Thank goodness Mom answered.

"Hi, Mom. How are you and Dad doing?" I plopped on the edge of my bed.

"We're fine. How are you and Robert?"

"Um…well, that's what I'm calling about. We've separated." I waited for her reaction to this startling development. There was only stunned silence on the other end. I stood and paced around my room.

"*What*?" Dead air came over the phone. "You two were so much in love. What happened?"

"We had a big argument and I left." I didn't want to give her all the details and have them hate Robert.

"Moved out? Where are you?" Mom sounded concerned and upset.

"I left school. I'm living in Houston at a boarding house with a nice elderly lady. She's like a grandmother to me. So, Mom, I'll be fine."

"Come home until you go back to school."

"I can't. He'll find me there. I'm not going back to school, at least not now. Maybe next year."

"He doesn't know where you are?"

"No. And I don't want him to. That's why I'm not telling you where I am. Then you won't have to lie if he calls. I have enough money to live on and I'm waiting to hear about a job."

"Doing what?" Her voice went up a notch.

"I'll tell you later if I get it."

Mom remained quiet for a few seconds. "Is it serious enough that you'll be getting a divorce?"

"I don't know what's going to happen. I just need some time away from him so I can think." Tears filled my eyes. My voice became shaky. "Mom, I still love him."

"Have you talked to him?"

"Texted."

"Belinda, Sweetie, come home."

Tears rolled down my cheeks. "Not yet." I swiped at the tears and sniffled. "Don't worry about me. I'll be all right. I'll see you soon."

"Okay, keep in touch." Mom sighed. "If you need anything, just call us. You know we'll help anyway we can."

"Love you, Mom. Will you tell Dad about this for me? I don't think I can face him." I hated the thought of letting him down.

"Don't worry about him. You just get your life straightened out. Sweetie, I'm here for you."

"I know. You always are. Love you. Bye." That went better than expected. I was so lucky I had my parents and a good friend like Abby. With their support I'd be fine someday, but would I ever really be happy without Robert?

One last wipe took care of the remaining tears. I ran back downstairs to continue helping Mrs. Foster.

CD

Work was a piece of cake on Monday. Plenty of calls came in to keep me busy and my mind occupied. Before I knew it, it was almost five, time to leave, when I took the last call for the day. "Johnson's Modeling Agency."

"Mr. Johnson, please. This is Jayne Carter with Every Body Jeans Manufacturing Company."

My heart sputtered. "One moment, please." I almost dropped the phone, but managed to place the call on hold then sprinted into his office. "It's them. Ms. Carter wants to talk to you."

Mr. Johnson gave me a knowing wink that seemed to say "you're in," and invited me to eavesdrop. "It's narrowed down to one, but not announced yet." He scanned some papers on his desk. "Okay." He picked up his pen, rolling it between his fingers. "You liked her photos. Great. Thanks for giving her a chance." He jotted down something on a notepad. "Okay, Wednesday at three. See you then." He had a big grin on his face as he ended the call and then gave me a thumbs-up. "We've got our foot in the door. They want to meet you this Wednesday in Atlanta."

"Really? The day after tomorrow?" I couldn't believe how quickly everything was moving along. I had just left school and now I was going for my first modeling job interview. All of a sudden, I shook all over.

Mr. Johnson cocked his head. "Are you all right?"

"I don't know what to do!"

"Don't worry. I'll be with you. They'll ask some questions and probably have you do some poses. Just remember—it's all about the jeans. They'll also want you to demonstrate your runway walk."

"Runway? You mean I might have to walk down runways?" I had assumed this job would only involve photography. How naïve of me. Bile rose in my throat as my nerves jumped into overdrive.

"You can do this. Now, let's see your walk."

"Okay, I have two." Remembering my modeling class fiasco, I dug deep to concentrate. I showed him my straight walk—one foot crossed over in front of my other foot, and then my sassy strut—same walk, but more hip emphasis.

"They both look good, but I like the second one best. Show them both." He winked. "Okay, go home and tell Mrs. Foster. Ask her for some pointers. She's been through this many times. Stay home tomorrow and sleep and relax because Wednesday will be hectic. I want you looking your best, and no worrying." He wagged his finger. "Now, go. I have airline reservations to make. I'll call you tomorrow."

When I reached my room, I turned my cell on to check my messages. There was one voice mail from Abby asking me to call. One text from Robert: Do you live in Sugar Land?

I sat on my bed and texted: No.

I called Abby. I had to tell her what was going on.

"Belinda, I'm so glad you called back. I have some good news. Robert quit school and is moving to Sugar Land. So now you can come back. We can be roommates again. I miss you." Her words came out in a high-pitch rush.

"Abby, I don't think Garrett would like me taking his place, but thanks for thinking of me. I called to tell you I'm flying out of state to my first job interview on Wednesday."

"Out of state! Doing what?" Abby suddenly sounded sad.

"You have to promise not to tell anyone, not even Garrett. If I get the job, everyone will find out soon enough."

"I promise, not a word."

"A modeling job with a new jeans manufacturing company. They liked my photos and want to meet me."

"How did this happen?"

I lay back on my bed, knowing this conversation could last awhile. I filled her in on the Mr. Johnson story.

"Wow! That was quick."

"Yeah. Now, remember, not a word. And I know Robert is moving home. I saw him in Sugar Land."

"You saw him? Did you talk to him?"

"No," I told her what happened.

"What are you going to do?"

"I don't know. He needs to see what it feels like to be left hanging." My chest tightened. "And that car scene." I heaved a sigh. "That was no misunderstanding." A lump formed in my throat and I swallowed hard. "Abby, I miss him now, but he didn't miss me then. He was too preoccupied with his new friend. Anyway, if I land the job I won't have time for him right now."

"Garrett's talked to him. He says Robert is really hurt and worried that he's lost you."

"Yeah. Well, his actions made that happen. Now he wants to explain, but I told him in the letter there's no reason that can justify what I saw. I gave him my heart, and he just stomped it into the ground." I buried my face in a pillow. If I kept talking about him I'd start crying. "Abby, lets change the subject."

"You're still in love with him, aren't you?"

Her question made me pause and tears welled. "Yes." I could feel a wave of despair creeping over me when I snapped at Abby. "Let's change the subject or I'm going to hang up. How are you and Garrett doing?"

"Do you really want to know?"

"Yeah, I do." I wanted to talk about anything that didn't involve Robert.

"It's great. He's so nice and loving. He'd do anything for me." She paused. "You know he still cares and worries about you."

"As a friend. He's great, and I know he'll never hurt you. Well, I need to let you go. I hear my landlady coming. She's bringing me some chamomile tea to help me sleep. I'll keep you informed. Miss you."

"Miss you, too," Abby said as Mrs. Foster set the cup of steaming tea on the nightstand. I nodded. She smiled and left.

My cell chirped and indicated I had a new text.

Robert:	Do you live in Houston?
Me:	Yes
Robert replied immediately:	Where? I need to see you.
Me:	NO
Robert:	Please, I'm begging you.
Me:	No, I'm going out of state tomorrow.
Robert:	Why?
Me:	Job interview.
Robert:	What?
Me:	I'm not telling.
Robert:	Are you moving out of state?
Me:	I hope not.
Robert:	Please don't.
Me:	I've got to go. Good night.
Robert:	I truly do love you. I miss you.

I stared at my phone. My chest rose and fell. My hands trembled so badly I couldn't even text back. I turned off my cell and squeezed my eyes shut.

The whiff of chamomile hit me. I scooted back and propped myself against the headboard and slowly sipped the tea. It worked its magic until I couldn't keep my eyes open. I fell fast asleep, letting my thoughts of Robert drift away.

Mr. Johnson called in the morning to tell me our flight would leave at 9:30 a.m. the next day and he'd pick me up at seven. He instructed me to pack for several days and be prepared for any scenario. At the end of the call, my butterflies fluttered. Crap, I had so much to do.

After breakfast and a short nap, I scanned the room, trying to decide what to do first. Denim jeans were a staple, so I pulled out my two best pairs. Next, I tackled the closet and shuffled through my knit tees and blouses, pulling out the ones I thought best complimented my complexion and shape. Doubting my selections, I paced around. The slight queasy feeling that lingered in the pit of my stomach began to erupt into a gut-wrenching panic. This interview was a chance of a lifetime. I knew I needed to be perfect, but I wasn't sure I could pull it off.

Before going to bed, I had packed and repacked enough clothes for a week. My suitcase was so crammed full I had to sit on it to zip it closed.

Mrs. Foster's warm chamomile tea relaxed me. Her simple remedy worked like a charm. I slept well.

CHAPTER 28

THE NEXT MORNING, my butterflies bashed against my stomach walls. The three-hour flight seemed to take only an hour and the entire time those damn butterflies never quit. After we checked into our hotel suites, there were only a few minutes for me to unpack before meeting Mr. Johnson. We were to have lunch in the hotel restaurant, then I'd come back to my room to prepare for my interview. I was excited about this opportunity, but, at the same time, I looked forward to this ordeal being over.

There was a knock at my door. "Are you ready for lunch?"

"Be right there."

Striking gray eyes of a handsome young guy, scanned down my body as Mr. Johnson and I entered the elevator. He stood there with his hands crossed in front of him. His chest seemed to puff out more after his brief inspection, as if he were attempting to look more attractive than he already was. I flashed him a smile in acknowledgment. Again, he gave me the once-over while I turned to face forward. His reflection in the elevator doors gave him away as he paid more attention to my backside before he positioned himself closer to me, smiling. "Ay," he uttered, full of confidence.

I continued to watch his reflection and returned the greeting. "Hey."

We exited on the main floor and headed for the restaurant. The man from the elevator followed behind, but he was met by the hostess and seated first. He said something to her as he glanced in our direction. That piqued my curiosity, but my questions were answered when the hostess led us to our table. I was about to sit down when a waiter pulled a chair out for me in the direct line of sight of MR. ELEVATOR.

Every time I looked up, the guy smiled at me. Then he winked. Oh my God! He was flirting. My face heated and I'm sure my cheeks glowed red. To hide, I gave my head the customary jerk to flip my hair in front of the side of my face.

"What's wrong? You're turning red." Mr. Johnson appeared bewildered.

"The guy from the elevator just winked. He's flirting." I cupped my hand over my forehead to shield my face as much as possible.

"Well, if I was his age and single, I'd be flirting with you, too. You're the prettiest young lady in here." A big grin formed on his face that made me smile.

When we finished eating, Mr. Johnson went to the bar and I headed for my room. The elevator arrived and I walked in. The doors started to close when a hand slid in between and forced them open. It was MR. ELEVATOR. He entered with a swagger and then resumed his military-like pose.

"You here for business or pleasure?" He gave me the once-over again.

"Business. Job interview. And you?" It seemed as if I was being stalked, but I felt free to scrutinize him as well, starting at his feet and ending with his head. He seemed to enjoy the returned attention and gave me a wide grin when my inspection reached his face.

"Both. Meeting some people for business and pleasure." He pointed at his ring finger. "Married?"

"Aren't you getting a little personal for a stranger?"

The elevator stopped on my floor and he held the door open. "Oh…uh. Sorry. I'm Jonathan Morse. I wanted to ask you out for a drink this evening, if you were available."

"Ummm…I'm Belinda Davies. And if you must know, I'm married, but separated." I stepped out of the elevator.

He jumped at the door and held it open. "Sooo…would you join me this evening?"

I twisted at the waist to face him.

A huge grin of perfect, pearly white teeth appeared while the pressure of Jonathan's hand prevented the repeated attempts of the elevator doors to close.

"I guess so, but only here in the hotel." *Why not? Robert was seeing Erin.*

"That's fine." With brows drawn together, he gave me yet another once-over. "So, who's the old guy?"

"My agent."

"Let me guess." He winked and pointed. "Model or actress?" He gave me the once over. "My guess. Model."

"Aspiring model. This is my first job interview."

"Well, good luck! Then, I'll see you at seven. What's your room number?"

"I'll meet you in the bar. Bye." I walked down the hall in the direction of my room and glanced back to see him still watching me.

"I'm just making sure you get to your room all right. I'm a gentleman." He grinned ear to ear, still fighting the elevator doors, now with his back against it and the buzzer blaring.

I looked him squarely in the face, and with an air of authority. "How do you know this is my room?" I waved him on to let the elevator doors close. His expression was priceless as his image disappeared. Once I was sure Mr. Morse had left, I stepped across the hall and opened my door. Great! I wouldn't be alone this evening.

Now my focus shifted as I hurried to prepare for my interview. One last glance in the mirror, I realized I needed Mr. Johnson's opinion. I dashed down the hall toward his room. As I passed the elevator, the doors opened and there he stood.

"Oh, thank heaven." I pivoted around. "Do I look all right?"

He chuckled. "Perfect. They'd be crazy not to pick you. I'll meet you here in fifteen minutes."

Even with me pacing in my room, the butterflies refused to cooperate until my cell rang. I'd forgotten I changed Robert's ringtone and answered without checking the display.

"Belinda, don't hang up."

My heart skipped a beat, and the butterflies took a nosedive at the sound of his voice.

"I just wanted to tell you good luck with your interview."

I hesitated. I was already on edge and didn't need to become more upset by getting involved in a long conversation.

"Hello? Belinda, are you there?"

His voice snapped me out of my thoughts. "Yeah, I'm here. Thanks. I'm so nervous, I feel like I'm going to faint. I have to go. Call me later. Bye." As I pulled the phone from my ear I could still hear his voice.

"Angel, no! Wait! Don't hang up!"

I took a moment then realized I'd only start crying. My heart was broken with or without him. It was a no-win situation. My finger hovered over the end call icon. I could still hear him pleading for me to talk with him, then I lowered my finger and closed my eyes, fighting back the tears.

As I headed out the door to meet Mr. Johnson, my cell rang again. Instinctively, I answered it.

"Angel, it's me again. Just checking to make sure you're not passed out on the floor."

I chuckled at his statement, but it still wasn't a good idea to talk to him right now. "Thanks for checking. I'm fine, but I still can't talk, really." My next response came as a surprise to me. Impulsively, I blurted out, "I'll call after the interview. Love you." When I heard the words, my heart stopped. There was no response from the other end. "I gotta go."

Mr. Johnson was waiting at the elevator. "You ready to get this over with?"

"Definitely." My mind was still on the conversation with Robert. I had encouraged him with my response, giving him hope and myself as well. But was it false hope?

Mr. Johnson and I walked to the building next door. He announced to the receptionist that we had an appointment with Ms. Carter. She sent us up to the ninth floor. There, a lady asked us to be seated. "Ms. Carter will see you in a few minutes."

My knuckles blanched white from knotting my hands together in an attempt to stay still. The gentle touch from a warm hand covered mine. It was unexpected and so comforting, my fidgeting stopped. I looked over at Mr. Johnson. His slight, warm smile and the subtle glint in his eyes washed most of my fears away. I hadn't realized how much I missed the ability to touch another person almost at will. Since I'd left school, Mr. Johnson's touch was the second human contact I'd had.

He must have felt my muscles relaxing. "You'll do fine. I'm here for you." He patted my hand. "Now take a few deep breaths. Okay, straighten your back, look straight forward, and when we go in, walk with all the confidence you can muster." I followed his instructions and he never removed his hand from mine the whole time we were in the waiting room. His simple gesture helped me stay relaxed. Finally, Ms.

Carter's secretary asked us to come in. I strutted in with self-confidence—head held high.

A well-dressed executive type woman rose from behind her desk to greet us. She was wearing a tailored crisp, white blouse and a black pencil skirt. Her dark hair was meticulously styled in a short bob with bangs. She was definitely a power dresser. "Thank you for coming." She pointed at a handsome, middle-aged man seated in a wingback chair near the window. "This is Steven Burton, the owner and founder of Every Body Jeans Manufacturing Company, and I'm Jayne Carter, head of advertising."

"Thank you for inviting us. This is Belinda Davies, and I'm her agent, Frank Johnson."

Ms. Carter motioned for Mr. Johnson to sit in the other wingback before she turned her attention to me. She circled, checking me out. "First, we need to see you in our jeans. What size do you wear? A six, I'm guessing?"

"Yes, ma'am." This lady made me feel uneasy by the way she scrutinized me.

She pulled a pair of jeans out of a pile on her credenza and handed them to me. Then she pointed to a door. "You can change in there."

They were stretch jeans and felt great on, but they needed to pass a certain test, my pet peeve. I stooped down and checked out my backside in the mirror. Great. Nothing revolting showed. After a few practice poses that accentuated my ass, I felt confident that the jeans and I were a good match. I strutted back into the room.

Ms. Carter approached me. "Rotate around so we can see how they fit."

I pivoted slowly. She reached over and pulled my sweater up to see the waist. "She wears them well. Perfect. How do they feel?" Ms. Carter tugged at the jeans.

The way I was being groped by this strange woman came as a surprise to me, but everyone else acted as if this was a normal procedure. So I played along. "They're very comfortable. They fit well, not too tight, and just right through the crotch. They're long enough and best of all, they're not *butt crack jeans*." Everyone smiled and chuckled. "I think you have a winner. I'd buy a pair. I live in jeans."

"Let's see your walk." Ms. Carter waved her hand. "Walk away from us and back."

I took a deep breath and prayed I wouldn't fall down. "I have two. This is my straight walk." I demonstrated it. "This is my sassy strut." Again I showed them.

Ms. Carter and Mr. Burton raised their eyebrows at each other. She walked over to Mr. Burton's chair and stood next to it, facing me. "What do you think, Steven?"

Mr. Burton leaned forward with his head cocked. "Do the sassy again."

This time I emphasized the hip action.

Mr. Burton nodded. "I really like that sassy strut. It draws attention to the jeans. That's what we want the public to see."

"Can I make a suggestion?" I walked over to Mr. Burton and turned around, then twisted at the waist to point at the right hip pocket. "Stitch 'Sassy' across the top of this pocket on some of the jeans in the style I'd be wearing." I straightened and faced him. "Then some girls can be sassy gals, too." I flushed at my faux pas and glanced at the floor. "Ahhh, I meant the style the model you pick would be wearing." I watched Mr. Burton's smile slip away and his brow crease.

"I like it, but why the right pocket?"

"Um." I shrugged. "Right pocket. Right jeans. I'm not sure. Right sounds 'right.'"

Mr. Burton grinned and gave a big nod. "Okay, I like the idea. Have you ever thought about going into advertising, young lady? Jayne," he addressed Ms. Carter by her first name, "you should think about hiring her."

She smirked and crossed her arms over her chest. "Have you modeled before?"

I hesitated and looked at Mr. Johnson. When he nodded, I took it as a sign to tell the truth. "No, but my photographer said I'm a quick learner."

"Do some poses for us." I did several that Mr. Saunders had recommended and a few I had practiced on my own.

Mr. Burton turned toward Ms. Carter. "I like her. I think her style will sell a lot of jeans for us."

"I agree."

YES! A rush of adrenaline coursed through my veins. I couldn't fist-pump, so, I did the next best thing. I sassy strutted toward them, stopped, and posed with one hand on my hip. "Be a Sassy Gal." I spun around and strutted away.

"I think we just saw our first commercial. I liked that. Belinda, you have the job, if you want it." Mr. Burton's confirmation was music to my ears.

"Thank you, sir!" My excitement of employment was overridden by a concern. "Excuse me. I want the job, but do I have to move to Atlanta?"

Ms. Carter's brows pinched. "Would that be a problem?"

"I'd like to keep my home in Houston."

Ms. Carter peered over her glasses to Mr. Burton.

He answered, "We won't need you every day, so I don't see that being an issue."

Ms. Carter nodded and addressed Mr. Johnson, "Have the details delivered to my legal department ASAP. I want this project started right away."

Mr. Burton walked over to shake my hand. "Welcome to our family."

I gripped it with confidence. "I'm looking forward to it."

Ms. Carter chimed in, standing behind her desk, "We need to start preparing ads and commercials, and prepping you for the fashion show. My department can start working on those layouts. As soon as all the legal paperwork is in place, we'll be good to go."

My shoulders tightened. The words almost stuck in my dry throat. "What's this about a fashion show?"

"We're doing a fashion show in New York City with Mr. Burton's designer friend, Jessica Loren Deats of Fashion Designs by JLDeats. It will be good exposure for the jeans. We have two-and-a-half weeks to prepare you for the catwalk. Can you stay here 'til after the show?"

"Yes, but I didn't bring enough clothes to stay that long."

"Don't worry about that. I'll give you a company credit card so you can buy what you need. I'll also give you some more of our jeans. It'll be good advertising, you walking around in the stores showing them off."

"That'll work."

"Well then, be in my office about nine tomorrow morning." Ms. Carter made herself comfortable in her large, leather desk chair. "Mr. Johnson, I'll have the papers for the salary advance ready in the morning, so get me a signed contract as soon as possible."

"I'll start on that right away. It was nice meeting both of you." Mr. Johnson and Ms. Carter shook hands. Facing Mr. Burton, he repeated the gesture. "I'm looking forward to doing business with you."

"No…thank *you*, Mr. Johnson. I think we have a winner here." Mr. Burton looked at me, nodding his head in my direction.

Mr. Johnson acknowledged his gesture, then turned and walked toward me where I stood by the door of the office. I leaned closer to him. "Do you need me anymore? Remember the guy that was flirting with me? His name is Jonathan Morse, and he invited me for drinks tonight."

"Belinda." Ms. Carter interrupted our conversation. "I'm sorry. Did you say you're meeting Jonathan Morse?"

I turned toward her. "Yes, why?"

Her face changed when she cocked her head. "Do you know who he is?"

"What do you mean?"

Ms. Carter smiled, shaking her head. "So…you don't know? Well, I'll let him tell you. Have fun, but be careful."

"Tell me. Be careful of *what*?" Now she had me curious. What was I getting myself into?

"No, you'll find out soon enough." She smiled, raising an eyebrow. "Go have fun."

I returned to my hotel with the feeling I was in for a big, big surprise.

Jeez, Is this elevator ever going to get here? When the doors finally opened, there stood Jonathan. "Oh! Hey."

"Well, how did your interview go?" He flashed his pearly whites.

"I got it. I can't believe it. I'm on my way to my room to make a call."

"Congratulations! I had a feeling you would." He raised an eyebrow. "Do you want to start celebrating early? Join me for dinner?" Jonathan extended his hand to me.

"Sure, I'd like that. I'll make my call later." I hesitated for a moment, remembering Robert's worried comment about me reacting to someone else's touch. I surveyed his hand and then took hold of it. Luckily, no zing.

Our waiter took our orders which included a very expensive bottle of wine. I'm sure it was an attempt on Jonathan's part to impress me. We engaged in small talk until the wine was poured.

Haunted by Ms. Carter's last comment, I decided to dive in. "What line of work are you in?"

He leaned forward, crossing his arms on the table. He looked befuddled, almost hurt, as he studied me. "You've never seen or heard of me before?"

"No, should I?" He didn't look familiar. I was being honest. He looked at me like I'd been living in a cave all my life.

He cocked his head. "Do you watch movies?"

"Not much." I was confused by his question. What difference did it make if I watched movies?

"Oookay." He pursed his lips before continuing. "I'm an actor. We're getting ready to start filming a movie here next week. I have the lead part."

"Oh." Leaning forward, I rested my crossed arms on the table. "You're a movie star? Sorry, I didn't know."

"That's all right. In fact, it's kind of nice meeting someone who doesn't know. Less baggage. Why did you pick modeling?" He leaned in closer, giving me the impression he was interested in what I had to say.

I sat back in my chair and explained how I met Mr. Johnson and started working for him. "He heard that a new jeans company was looking for a model. So, he emailed some of my portfolio photographs to them." I shook my head in disbelief. "Everything is happening so fast."

His eyes widened as he cocked his head. "That's really quick to land a major modeling job. Your agent must be good."

I leaned forward. "Where are you from? You have a slight accent."

"Canada. I take it you're from Texas. I like that cute drawl."

"Oh. You're good. I'm from Sugar Land. It's southwest of Houston." I took a sip of my wine. "How did you become an actor?"

"I took drama in high school and joined the drama club. I was in a few school plays." He leaned back against the chair. "After graduation, I landed a few parts in some local plays, then moved to LA and the rest is history. Right now, I'm in demand." He fiddled with the base of his wine glass. "Can I ask you a personal question?"

"I guess, but I won't guarantee I'll answer it."

"What happened? Why did you leave him?"

His question took me aback because it was so personal, yet I needed to talk to somebody who had nothing to do with the whole mess. Abby was great, but she was biased. Jonathan had no vested interest in the outcome of my drama at this point, so I took a chance. "I really don't know what happened. We met in April and were married after his graduation in May. Up until the Fourth of July weekend, everything was wonderful. Then about a week later, he just kinda' left me." Jonathan's face told me he didn't understand my last statement, so I gave him a bit more information. "He was busy with school and almost stopped coming home, except to sleep. Then on the day of finals, I saw him making out with a girl in his car." I had to look away to fight back the tears and gain some composure. "I packed and left."

He frowned, shaking his head. "He's crazy."

I shrugged, not knowing what to say.

"Are you going to divorce him?" He took a drink of his wine.

"I don't know. I still love him and miss him very much. He's called and texted. He keeps apologizing and says he wants to explain what happened. But one look, one touch, one kiss, and I'd forgive him for anything and that wouldn't solve the problem." I stared at my wine glass as I fingered the rim then looked back at Jonathan. "He says he doesn't want to lose me and misses me." I shook my head. "I just can't face him yet.

He needs to realize that I'm not going to keep putting up with this. He'll just have to live without my reactions for a while."

A quizzical expression appeared on his face. "What do you mean 'one-touch' and 'reactions'?"

I stared at him. *Oh, great. I shouldn't have mentioned that.* Another personal question I decided to answer. "We have this physical connection. When he touches me, it's beyond exciting. It ignites all my senses, and when he kisses me...." I closed my eyes briefly, remembering. "There are no words to describe how wonderful it is when we're together." I couldn't believe I told all this to a stranger.

He frowned, shaking his head in disbelief. "He's crazy, no *stupid,* to have it all and throw it away."

"I don't see a ring on *your* hand. Sooo, why aren't you married? You seem like you'd be a good catch for some lucky lady."

"I just haven't met the right one...until now...and she would be married." He smiled and winked.

I let out a loud breath. "Yeah, right. I have too much baggage. I don't know what I want to do with my big mess of a life."

"We can at least be friends, can't we?" He reached over and placed his hand on mine.

I looked at it but made no attempt to pull mine away. If this were Robert, I would have experienced a reaction, but he was Jonathan and offering something I needed—friendship. "I could use a friend right now."

A grin spread across his face. "Vincent Morrison, the producer of the film I'm starring in, is having a party tomorrow evening. It's in this hotel by the pool. Would you like to go?"

Needing something to keep my mind off Robert and figuring a party would be a nice diversion, I accepted.

"I need to turn in early. I have to be at work by nine. Thank you very much for dinner and listening to me. Talking about it helped. You're a good shrink." I winked at him.

"Thank you." He walked me to the elevator. "I really enjoyed your company." We stepped in. "Now, will you give me your room number?"

"603."

The doors slid open and he escorted me to my room. At my door, I turned to face him. He pointed to the lock. "Now swipe it so I know this is your room." I clutched the card in my hand and shook my head. Then he did something that was totally unexpected. He took me in his arms and kissed me. Great kiss, so I went along with it, but it was nowhere in the same league as Robert's. I justified my action because I could do what Robert did. Although, now my conscience was starting to bother me.

He frowned. "No reaction?"

I pulled away. "Sorry. But I enjoyed it." I didn't lie. I did enjoy it, but not as much as with Robert. It only made me miss my husband, but I was still mad at him. Now, I felt guilty. Was I cheating? I needed to keep this a friendship only. Without saying another word, I reached behind me, swiped my card, and opened the door. I waved goodbye and went inside.

As I started to close the door, he put his hand up to stop it. "He is *definitely* crazy." He took me in with his gray eyes and nodded then left.

CHAPTER 29

WITH CONTRACTS SIGNED, the following days brought new experiences. They photographed me in a number of different poses and then with a so-so looking male model. Jonathan and Robert were a lot more handsome in my opinion. However, the male model did fill out his jeans nicely. I found the experience fun until Ms. Carter ruined my mood by informing me that tomorrow I'd be practicing on a freaking runway. Great!

The day flew by faster than I'd realized. During my afternoon break, I remembered I hadn't called Abby and Robert back. Before leaving the studio, I told the aide I'd be in my dressing room. To my surprise, I was assigned a plushy furnished room. It was my own little oasis away from the hustle of the studio.

I tried to contact Abby, but she didn't answer, so I left a message that I got the job and I'd call back later. My cell indicated a voice mail from Robert. I listened to it. "Did you get the job? Call me, Angel."

Hearing him call me Angel caused my lungs to constrict, making it difficult to breathe. I paced around the room. Should I return the call or should I ignore it? I did say I'd call him and I hadn't. I nervously studied my cell phone then hit number two.

"Angel." He answered after the first ring in a soothing voice that made my spine react.

"Hey. I'm sorry I didn't call sooner."

"Well...did you get the job?"

"I signed the final contract this morning. Today was my first day."

Silence followed. Neither one of us said anything until he broke the void. "What kind of job, if you don't mind me asking?" He was being extremely polite and not pushing for answers.

"Something you told me I could do very easily."

"Well...are you going to tell me?" A somber tone filled his voice.

"I'm modeling. I signed a contract with a jeans company." I waited for his response, letting him lead the conversation.

There was a long, awkward pause. "Will you be moving out of state?" Robert's hushed voice had a distinct quaver.

"No, but I'll have to travel."

More silence.

"When…when can I see you?" His pleading voice tore at my heart.

Not knowing what to say, I spouted off, "You'll see me in commercials and ads in a few weeks."

He took a deep breath. "You know that's not what I mean."

"I have a very busy schedule for the next few weeks, and I'll be gone a lot."

"I could fly to meet you anywhere."

His idea made my stomach flip. Hesitating, I thought about his proposal. I'd love to be in his arms again, to feel the warmth of his body next to mine, to make love to him, but I had to be strong. If I gave in, I was afraid I wouldn't learn how to set limits. Keeping a distance between us prevented him from physically touching me so I could maintain some semblance of control. I needed this time to learn who I was, and to heal my heart. I finally answered. "No, that wouldn't be a good idea. I still need time."

The next question caught me off guard. "Do you still love me?"

Without hesitation, my answer flowed out. "Yes."

"So, I still have a chance?" He sounded uncertain.

"I have to go now." By this time I was fighting back the tears. I didn't want to cry, but it was so hard not to.

"Belinda?"

"What?"

"You know you're breaking my heart."

My breath stopped as pain so strong hit me just below my breast bone. "You *did* break mine." I ended the call and dropped my cell to the floor. Collapsing into a chair, I cradled my head as I wept.

Someone knocked on my dressing room door. "I'll be right out. I just need a few more minutes." I went to the dressing table and looked at my reflection. I was so torn. Closing my eyes, I cleared my mind, pushing Robert back as far as I could. I had a job to do. I dried my eyes and started repairing my makeup. After one last glance, I went back to work.

We finished early, so, I headed back to the hotel to take a nap. I was on the verge of falling asleep when my cell rang. "Hey, Abby," I yawned.

"Congratulations, I bet you're thrilled. I wish I were there so we could celebrate." Her high pitched, bubbly voice pierced my ear.

"Me, too, but I did celebrate and you'll never guess with who."

"Robert?" She trailed the last part of his name in a higher pitch.

"No, silly. Jonathan Morse."

Abby went silent, which was unusual. Her tone changed. It became more cautious. "*The* Jonathan Morse? The movie star?"

Her comment surprised me. "So you know who he is?" Like me, she hadn't been to very many movies in the past few years. "I didn't."

"Of course, I do! How did you meet him?" From Abby's response to Jonathan's name, she sounded impressed.

"He's staying in this hotel." I gave her the rundown on how we met and the dinner that followed. "He's a really nice guy. He invited me to a party tonight."

"OMG! Are you going?"

"Sure. I need some fun."

"Well, be careful. He's really hot, but the tabloids say he's a player."

"Oh, great, that's just what I need, another player. Is there a sign on my back saying, 'Wanted! All Players'? What is it about me?" I couldn't decide if Robert was one or not, but he seemed to be, considering his actions with Erin.

"Look in the mirror. You could have any guy you wanted if you were that sort of girl. You don't use your looks like other pretty girls, because you don't see yourself that way. But, Belinda, you could if you chose to."

I was speechless. Abby was right. I could use my looks to get what I wanted, but that's not who I was nor did I want to be. "I have to let you go now. I need to take a nap. I worked most of the day. I'm a little tired."

"Oh! You started working today?"

"Yeah, they want ads and commercials out to the public as soon as possible. It was fun but tiring. Oh! I found out that I'm going to be in a fashion show in New York in two-and-a-half weeks. I'm nervous about that. With my luck, I'll probably fall and embarrass myself. Well, I gotta go." I was about ready to say goodbye when Robert popped into my head. "Oh, one more thing, Abby. You have to promise me you won't say anything to Garrett about Jonathan. I don't want him mentioning him to Robert. He might take it the wrong way."

"Okay, I'll keep my mouth shut."

"You swear, Abby?"

"I swear."

"Thanks, I have to go. I'll call you later." I wrapped myself around a pillow and imagined it was Robert as sleep fell upon me.

∞

The party was a good filler for the night, and I enjoyed Jonathan's company when he was around. I danced with Mr. Morrison, Jonathan's producer, and several cast members as Jonathan schmoozed his way around the room.

With the busy day catching up with me, I hunted down Jonathan and told him I needed to leave because I had an early morning planned at the studio. He insisted on walking me to my room.

I leaned against my suite door with my key card in my hand. "Thanks for another nice evening."

"I'm glad you enjoyed it. By the way, I have an extra ticket for a charity benefit I have to attend tomorrow night. Would you come as my guest? Mr. Morrison's wife can't attend and he didn't want to waste the ticket. He asked if I knew someone who would like to go." He placed his hand against the door above my head as he leaned in closer. "I think he had you in mind." His pearly whites flashed into a full-blown smile.

I giggled. "Is it formal?"

"Black tie all the way, Baby."

"I would love to go. Thanks." With one swipe of my keycard, my door opened. "Good night." If he had other ideas for the evening, I couldn't do that to Robert. Even though I'd told him in my letter that I could do what he did and will, I just couldn't. I felt bad enough after Jonathan kissed me the first time. I wasn't a cheater.

"Okay." He seemed to understand and backed away. "I have to be in LA, Monday. But, I'll be back Wednesday. How about giving me your cell phone number so I can keep in touch?"

I ignored his request, but a small wave of sadness came over me. Jonathan was the only person I knew in Atlanta. "I'll still be here. They want me to stay until after the fashion show in New York. It's in two-and-a-half weeks. Then I guess it's back to Houston. How long will you be filming here?"

"I'm not sure. It depends if we have any delays." He glanced down. "Well, I guess I'd better go. I'll come to your room around 6:30 tomorrow to pick you up."

"If you don't mind, let's meet in the lobby." He didn't question my decision but nodded in approval. Before leaving, he gave me a sweet kiss on the cheek, sighed, and left.

I slipped on my favorite t-shirt I'd confiscated from Robert. It brought back memories of how he used to hold me at night. Heading to the cold, empty bed, I imagined his arm's wrapped around me to get me through the night. My cell rang. "Hey, Abby."

"Belinda, can you talk?"

"Sure, Jonathan left a little while ago. I'm just about to crawl into bed."

"Well, how was the party?" From the pitch of her voice, I pictured Abby sitting on the edge of her bed waiting for any details I was willing to offer.

The next thirty minutes were spent going over the events of the evening. Abby, as usual, wanted to hear everything. "We've been spending time together, and I'll probably see him some more."

Abby's voice became very low. "What about Robert?"

"Jonathan is just a friend. Robert, well, I've talked to him." Blood drained from my limbs as I thought about Robert. "I do miss him, but I'm still hurting. Abby, if I go anywhere near him, I'll give in. I need to learn to be stronger, to stand up for myself." I let out a deep breath. "I have to be sure I can trust him. Without that, nothing will change."

"Are you going to give him another chance?"

"Probably, but later. Don't tell him."

"Garrett has talked to him several times. He says Robert's lonely and misses you terribly." Abby became quiet and I didn't say anything. Suddenly she changed the subject. "I almost forgot! You're invited to the Delt homecoming party. It's the third weekend in September. All the brothers want to see you."

"Is he going to be there?"

"I don't know. Would that be a problem?"

"Could be if I'm not ready to see him. Besides, I don't know if I'll be free that weekend. I'll have to let you know closer to that time. I have to go, it's late. I have an early meeting tomorrow morning and then I need to get to the studio. I'll try to call you later."

So much had happened, keeping me busy. As glad as I was to have things to keep my mind off Robert, now I was alone and he was back in my thoughts.

Ms. Carter had invited me to take a look at my new layout for one of the magazines. When I entered, she was sitting at her large, modern wood-and-glass desk, looking at several photos spread out across the top. Ms. Carter looked up over her black-rimmed glasses. "Hi, Belinda. Your photos for the magazine ads are really good. Come look."

I stood next to her as she, in a methodical way, handed me photos, one by one. She paused in between to allow me enough time to study each picture. I had never thought of myself as pretty, but the female I analyzed in these pictures was me, and I was beautiful.

After I saw the ad layout, my newly found awareness made the mid-morning shoot more fun. Mr. Burton requested I show off the jeans the same way I did at my interview. I strutted toward the camera, posed, and said in a sexy voice, "Be a Sassy Gal." I winked "And wear jeans by Every Body Jeans Manufacturing Company." Then I turned and strutted away. We shot several takes consuming most of the day. I asked when the first commercial would be on TV and was told they would start airing in about a week. The jeans would be in the stores around the same time. Soon everybody would know—my secret would be out.

When we wrapped up the commercial, Ms. Carter took me to a large room with a stage that T'ed out into a runway. The time had come to face my fears. She directed and observed my movements with every pass I made. She gave me little hints. The one that would help the most was to not look down during the show but to keep my eyes above the heads of the people in the audience and look to the back of the room. Then she left for her office, and I continued to practice.

The more I walked, pivoted, and turned, I realized I needed Abby in the audience. She always helped me when I needed a self-confidence boost. So, I called her.

"Hey, What's going on?"

"I have something I'd like to ask you."

"What?"

"Would you like to go with me to New York to that fashion show I told you about? I could use your support. It's the first weekend of September."

Abby didn't respond at first. Then in a loud, almost deafening shriek, she cried out, "AAAH! SHUT THE FRONT DOOR! Yes! Yes! I'd love to go!"

I held the phone about six inches away from my ear until I was sure it was safe to resume our conversation. "I'm really nervous about walking down that runway. I keep visualizing myself falling on my butt."

"Don't worry, you'll do fine. But, how would I get to New York? How can I even get to an airport?"

"I was thinking maybe Garrett could take you to Houston. I'll fly both of you to New York. Do you think he'd mind doing that?"

"He better not! I'm sure he wouldn't want to pass up a chance to see you. And all those models."

"I'll try to reserve a room for you two in the hotel."

"No, no. I want to stay with you so we can visit. We can have a girls' night in. Oh, but where would Garrett sleep?"

"I'll have a suite, so he could sleep on the couch. On second thought, I'll try to reserve you a room. He doesn't need to be uncomfortable."

"No, don't bother. The two airline tickets will cost you enough. You don't need to pay for a room too. He won't mind sleeping on the couch."

"Don't worry about the cost. I'm being paid very well. Talk to Garrett and let me know ASAP, so I can make the airline reservations."

"I'll call you tomorrow. I can't believe I'm going to New York! I won't be able to sleep from now until then."

I chuckled at her. "Okay. Bye." My fear of embarrassing myself on the runway calmed, knowing I'd have my best friend in the audience.

CHAPTER 30

AS SOON AS we finished the day's shoots, I rushed back to my hotel room to dress for the benefit. I didn't have a lot of time. I put on my little bit of make-up, curled my hair, and dressed in the same gown I had worn to the Delt formal. At 6:30, I stepped from the elevator into the hotel lobby. Mr. Morrison saw me first. His eyes widened and his lips parted. Jonathan must have seen his reaction because he turned and looked. The same expression soon covered his face as I walked over to them and said, "Gentlemen."

Mr. Morrison stuttered, "You look absolutely ravishing."

Jonathan didn't respond for some time. He just stood there. His eyes slowly softened, becoming seductive as they roamed over me. "You are the most beautiful woman I've ever seen. I love that dress on you." With a slight shake of his head, a smile spread across his face before he winked.

The corners of my mouth slowly turned upward.

"Shall we go?" Jonathan extended his elbow, so I linked my arm in his. Mr. Morrison did the same. I was escorted out to our limo by two very handsome men. When we walked out the door, camera flashes began bursting everywhere.

"I can't see. What's going on?" I lowered my head to shield my eyes.

"It's the paparazzi." Jonathan was right behind me guiding me through the open car door before he did an about-face and posed for the cameras.

In the safety of the shiny black limo, I had a chance to recover from the barrage of lights. "So some of these pictures could be in newspapers and magazines?"

"Probably in tomorrow's tabloids and maybe on TV," Mr. Morrison explained as he took a seat across from me in the limo. "Paparazzi follow Jonathan everywhere."

Oh no! What was Robert going to think? What would the tabloids say? And I certainly would need to call my parents in the morning.

When we arrived, I walked arm-in-arm between the two of them up the steps of the massive Gothic stone structure. Cameras flashed everywhere, blinding me. As soon as we walked through the doors, the sporadic lights stopped. It was a relief to be able to see normally again. "Why aren't they following us?"

"Oh, they're not allowed," Jonathan said as he looked around, scoping out the crowd in the foyer. "This is a safe zone, so to speak. Only authorized pictures are allowed beyond this point."

We entered a huge grand ballroom that had the most enormous crystal chandelier

I'd ever seen. Large round tables with floor-length black linen tablecloths surrounded a spacious dance area. A huge floral arrangement and candles decorated each table. There were crystal goblets, silver plate chargers, white linen napkins, and fancy silverware at each place setting. In the dim light, the room looked elegant.

Our names were on place cards perched in silver holders sitting on the chargers. I was Mrs. Morrison for the evening, so I was seated next to him. Jonathan found his place next to me. We hadn't been seated very long when the ballroom came alive with waiters dressed in white jackets dashing from one table to the next. They started off the meal by pouring ladles of cream soup into china bowls for the first course. Four more courses followed with the last being a luscious rich dessert. The wine flowed freely at the hint of a half-full glass.

Shortly after indulging ourselves, Mr. Morrison excused himself and disappeared. Jonathan extended his hand to me. "Come on. I'm going to show you how to schmooze." Jonathan flashed that bright smile as he looked over the attendees and focused on his target. "Let's go." He led me to a group of young people gathered across the dance floor. We managed to cover the entire room, meeting and greeting all of Jonathan's associates. Mr. Morrison was now sitting alone at the table. I excused myself and went over to join him.

The orchestra started playing my favorite song and people began filling the dance floor. I looked across the room and saw a band of white teeth rushing toward me. "May I have this dance?" Before I could say anything, Jonathan twirled me onto the floor. Listening to the rhythm of the song, I laid my head against the hollow of his shoulder, closed my eyes, and began singing softly. He bent his head down closer, resting his cheek on my head.

When the song was over, I opened my eyes and saw a lot of people with smiling faces staring at us.

"That was beautiful." He hugged me.

I looked up through my lashes at him. *Oh, no, not again.* "I hope I didn't embarrass you." Feeling my cheeks getting warm, I knew I was blushing.

"No, not at all." He was studying my face, but I tried to avoid his gaze. "Are you blushing?" My hands went to my cheeks to hide the increased redness. He wasn't making this any better. He gave me a huge grin and remarked, "You're so adorable."

We resumed dancing to a few more songs. As the music faded, the crackle of a microphone turned the audience's attention to the stage. Sporting a wide smile, a man holding a mike made an announcement. "An anonymous donor has offered to contribute ten thousand dollars to our cause." The crowd started clapping. "Only if…" The crowd started clapping louder. The announcer raised his hands to quiet the audience. "Only if the young lady who was singing would share her song on stage with everyone. So Miss, if you're still out there, we could use the money." He started scanning the room for anyone coming forward.

I froze. The sound of my pounding heart rushed to my ears. "Is he talking about me? I can't get up in front of all these people and sing. My mind will go blank." I trembled from head to toe.

"You can do it," Jonathan encouraged. "Just take some deep breaths and close your eyes. Imagine you're singing for just me. It's for ten thousand dollars. Charity!"

I clung to his arm. "You have to come with me." No way was I going up on that stage by myself. I tugged on his arm. As we made our way there, people noticed our movement. The applause started slowly and increased in intensity as Jonathan led me up the stairs to the stage. As he wrapped his arms around my waist, I took the microphone and made an announcement in a quavering voice. "I've never sung on a stage before, but I'll try."

The orchestra played, but I missed my cue. Closing my eyes, I took a deep breath and exhaled. They started again, and I began to sing, softly at first. I was surprised the spotlight on me blacked out the audience. I couldn't see anything past the end of the stage. Becoming more relaxed, I put my soul into my performance with, *"Dear love, my only sweet true love. You've captured my lonely heart."* About the second verse, Jonathan released me and stepped away. With more confidence, I gave it my all until I finished with, *"As our world is in perfect rhyme. You're forever in my mind."* The spotlight dimmed. I saw everyone stand and applaud. It was an amazing feeling. I graciously bowed my head.

Jonathan suddenly rushed in, taking me in his arms, and planted a heated kiss on my lips that lasted a bit too long. From the corner of my eye, I saw flashes everywhere. He had put me in a compromising position. What if these were in the tabloids and Robert saw them? I pressed my hands against his chest. "Jonathan, please." With enough distance between us, I rushed off the stage.

Jonathan found his way to my side after my speedy departure. A crush of people complimented me as we made our way back. They even came to our table. The attention started to get to me.

"You look like you need a break." Jonathan took me by the hand. "Let's dance."

On the dance floor, I found peace. I only danced with Jonathan the rest of the night. Others tried, but he refused to let them cut in. He shielded me.

I had a great time, but as with all fairytales, they must come to an end.

Lights flashed as soon as we exited the building. Again my eyes needed to adjust to the darkness in the limo. "How do you get use to that?"

Jonathan laughed. "It takes practice."

Thankfully, our arrival at the hotel was far less dramatic as we walked to the elevator. No paparazzi.

"Thank you. This is an evening I'll never forget." I extended my hand to Mr. Morrison, expecting a handshake.

"I also had a great time. Thank you." He took my hand in his and kissed it.

When we arrived at my floor, Jonathan and I exited the elevator. He turned back and addressed Mr. Morrison. "Good night, Vincent. See you tomorrow."

Jonathan walked me to my room. "Thank you for a wonderful evening." After unlocking my door, I held it open a few inches. He evidently didn't want the evening to end, because he took the liberty of pushing it open as he escorted me in.

He clutched my face between his hands and started to kiss me, but I pulled away.

"Jonathan, stop. I'm sorry, but I can't do this. I can't cheat on my husband, no matter how upset I am at him. That's just not me. It doesn't feel right."

He looked upset. "Okay. But I really like you."

"I like you too…as a friend. If the roles were reversed, how would you feel if I kissed him?"

He frowned. "I wouldn't like it, but I'd never leave you. So this situation wouldn't have happened."

"That's what you think now, but you're a player and apparently so is Robert. Life was wonderful one day, and the next. Nothing." I could feel my eyes begin to moisten.

"Did you ask him why he was treating you that way?" Jonathan wiped away an escaping tear.

"I tried, but after that kiss I saw in his car…I left. I couldn't bear any more pain." Tears began to trickle down my cheeks.

Jonathan and I sat on the couch. "He wants to talk to you, so talk. Get him to answer your questions."

"I'm not ready. I need some time away from him." I laid my head on his shoulder. "He could have any girl he wants, so why me?" Tears seeped out.

Jonathan hugged me tightly. "He saw how special you are, just like I have. You're beautiful inside and out."

"Thank you, but I'm not special. I'm just an ordinary girl from Texas."

"Belinda. You could have anything you want." He squeezed a little tighter. "Look, you captured the heart of a campus player and married him."

But, is Robert really a player? He said he isn't. So confused.

"He still wants you. Hell, I want you, and I don't say that to just any girl."

I could tell he was trying to cheer me up. "But he was never around. It felt like he abandoned me. And let's not forget I caught him cheating."

"That wasn't your fault. It was his. Something must have freaked him out—maybe that everything happened so fast. I don't know, but I'm sure you didn't do anything to cause that. Look, he misses you and wants another chance. Let him explain." He kissed my forehead. "I can't believe I'm not looking out for my own best interest, and I'm telling you to talk to him. I'm an idiot." He shook his head. "It's getting late, but first we need to exchange phone numbers."

We entered each other's number into our cell phones. "I'll try to come see you in the morning before I leave. Do you want me to get you anything?"

I shook my head. "There is something I've been meaning to ask you."

"What?"

"Would you consider going to the fashion show? I could use all the support I can get. My best friends, Abby and Garrett, are coming. Abby would love to meet you."

"I'd love to be there. I'll check my filming schedule and let you know."

"Thanks." I walked him to the door.

"Good night." He placed his hands on either side of my head and kissed my forehead. "You'll get through this. You're stronger than you think. You'll make the right decision, and everything will fall into place." He gave me a wink and left.

After I got ready for bed, I turned my cell on to check my messages. Abby left a voice mail to call, then I listened to Robert's. "Angel, please come back. I miss you terribly." Before responding to him, I had to think if our relationship would even work. I had a decision to make.

I now had a job that required traveling to who knew where, and Robert would have to stay in Sugar Land to work for his father. No matter how I looked at my possible chaotic schedule, there would be little time for Robert and me to be a couple, let alone see each other right now. Maybe it would be better to just let things be, to let him go. It wouldn't be fair for him to expect me to give up my plans for him, just as I shouldn't expect him to do the same for me.

There was still the issue of Erin and the kiss. Was he ready to change like he said? He'd told me that before, but he'd strayed. If I ended our relationship, it would end the pain I've endured as a result of his cheating, but I'd be giving up the strong connection I had with him. Was I willing to let him go and take the chance I'd be able to find another man I'd be as close to? I could sense a void in my heart when we were apart. Leaving after witnessing the kiss was the hardest decision I'd ever made, but I hoped we'd eventually work things out. I knew I still loved him, but could I actually leave him for good? It wouldn't be fair to continue to lead him on, to give him false hope. I knew I was making the right decision as I picked up the phone to send him a text.

Me:	I need to tell you something. I don't see how we can be together w/me out of state & traveling, & you in Sugar Land. I don't want to keep you hanging on. Get on w/your life & be happy.

A response came back immediately.

Robert:	NO Angel. I can't be happy w/o you. It's not just your decision. Mine too. I will never leave. I will follow u anywhere. We can find a way to make this work. No more texts. ☹☹☹ Talk only. ☺☺☺ I won't let go. I'm your pitbull now!
Me:	How? It's so complicated. Confused. Frustrated.
Robert:	It doesn't matter. We love each other. We belong together.
Me:	My heart hurts. My mind hurts. I still need time.
Robert:	Talk ONLY!!! Please.
Me:	Ok. Tomorrow.

I lay back on the bed, staring at the ceiling for a while. My heart was more settled. I now had some hope Robert and I would find our way to happier times. Sleep came quicker than it had for days. I wasn't crying.

CHAPTER 31

SATURDAY MORNING CAME with a knock on my door. It was only eight o'clock. Whoever was there couldn't read the "Do Not Disturb" sign. I covered my head with a pillow. Knock knock knock! The force vibrated the door. I threw my pillow across the room.

I gave in and found my robe then staggered to the door. I was about to twist the doorknob when I remembered the paparazzi from the night before. What if one of them found out what room I was in and was waiting to snap a picture of me? I scrutinized my reflection in the mirror. I was a mess. I looked through the peephole. Jonathan had his fist raised. Timing it perfectly, I opened the door just before he made contact. He almost fell into the room. I giggled.

Jonathan regained his footing and produced a smile wider than the Pacific Ocean. "Good morning gor…geous." He hesitated, looking me over. "You're a mess! Like the robe though." He reached out into the hall and pulled in a cart. "Ready for breakfast?" He was just too energetic for this early in the morning. He reminded me of Abby. I followed him into the living room and sat on the couch. "I have to leave for the airport soon."

Reaching under the tablecloth covering the cart, he pulled out a stack of tabloids. "Have you seen any of these yet?" He was too excited. "And look at this!" He reached for the TV remote and turned it on, flipping through the channels until he found what he was looking for. Right in front of me was a clip of Jonathan kissing me, and I was being referred to as "Jonathan Morse's new mystery girlfriend."

I scooted to the edge of the couch. Jonathan handed me tabloids. He had all the pages turned and folded back. I glanced over the pictures. My mouth popped open. "How could this happen?!" I shouted in total shock. "I thought no one was supposed to take any pictures."

"Isn't it great? We're going to get so much mileage from this!" Jonathan was too full of exuberance.

"Are you happy about these?" I stood up, crushing and shaking the papers in my hand.

He threw his hands up. "Whoa! Whoa! Hang on, princess. Of course, I am. We made the news. Any time you can be in the public eye, it's a good day."

"Jonathan, my parents don't know anything about this. What about Robert? How do you think he'll react?" Robert was all I could think about. I had such hopes that we had a chance, and, now, that could be ruined. I sank back on the couch trying to make sense of everything and figure out how I was going to explain away this new drama in my life.

Jonathan came down from his tabloid high long enough to see my reaction was the total opposite of his. "You don't understand what's going on, do you?" He was more solemn as he sat next to me. "Okay, last night was a real advantage for both of us. I thought you understood that."

I glared at him. I couldn't believe what he was saying. "Are you telling me, you were just using me to get publicity?"

Now Jonathan was very serious and concerned. "Well, yeah. Whenever I'm out I look for every opportunity to get into the papers. Last night was no exception." He was so matter-of-fact about the whole incident. "Why are you so upset?"

I looked at him dumbfounded. "You used me?" I was hurt and still confused by all of this.

"I did. That's just part of this whole lifestyle."

"How could you? And what about all this?" I motioned with my hands to encompass our situation. "Are you going to tell the tabloids about everything we've talked about as well?" I crossed my arms and huffed.

"Hell no! What we have here is private. What we say to each other is for us only, but when you go past that door, all bets are off. That's the way it works, and you better start learning that really fast." He was direct and to the point. "So you better get on that phone when I leave and tell everyone who means anything to you that what they see is not necessarily true. Once your butt gets plastered all over the place, you'll be fair game for anyone with a camera." He stopped and just stared at me with warm, gentle eyes and took my hand. "Look, let's keep it simple. Once you become a celebrity, you have to be very protective of your privacy. You have to make very sure, *very sure* you can trust the person you tell anything to."

I jerked my hand from his and looked him straight in the eye. "Can I trust you?"

He readjusted his position. "Whatever we talk about in private is between us. Whatever we do or say out there is an open book."

I thought about what he said for a few seconds. "How will I be able to learn all this?" I knew he was right. Once the ad campaign went public, so would my life. I didn't need this right now. There were other problems I needed to deal with. I just never gave this any thought. It all had sounded so simple—get a job, make some money, and live my life. I felt like I had been kicked in the stomach. It would take hours on the phone trying to talk my way out of this mess. I was glad I didn't have a lot of people in my life that I was very close to.

Jonathan placed his arm around my shoulders. "I'm sorry. I've been doing this for so long I just take it for granted. Call your family and tell them we're just friends and nothing more. Call Robert and tell him I would be glad to talk with him if he wants."

He was trying to soften the mood, and I appreciated his effort, but it didn't help much.

"Look, I have to leave in about thirty minutes. Do you want to eat?" He pointed to the cart of food.

My appetite wasn't that great after this morning's events, but I figured I'd better eat something since he'd gone to all this trouble.

After Jonathan left, I went to the bedroom and picked up my cell phone. I sat on the side of the bed just staring at the little device like it was alien to me. Considering who to call first, I made a mental list of whose would take the longest. Mom and Dad first, then Abby, and then Robert. Robert's call would be the hardest one of all to make. I pressed number four to speed dial my parents, praying that my mother would answer.

"Hello."

"Hi, Mom."

"Belinda, how nice to hear from you. Are you all right? Did you get the job?"

It was twenty questions time. I had to slow her down so I could go through everything about the job, Robert, and the tabloids. Our conversation lasted over an hour. Robert hadn't contacted them about our separation and she hadn't seen or heard anything about Jonathan and me, so it made the situations easier to discuss.

In fact, talking to her helped me put some things into perspective. Mom pointed out that I had blown some of the recent events out of proportion. She helped me to look at the reality of the situation and not what could happen.

"Honey, I know you are mad at him, but too much is happening to you with this job. You have to talk to him every day to let him know what you've been doing. Let him hear it from you first. Then when you're ready to see him, it'll be easy."

We said our goodbyes, and then I was on to my next call, Abby. This one would be easier now. I was glad I'd called Mom first. I felt more grounded. Abby would want every sordid detail like she always did, but I'd be able to put her off with a shorter call if she knew I needed to call Robert.

"Belinda, what do you think you're doing?" she spat out.

I knew exactly what she meant. "You saw the pictures?"

"They're spreading like wildfire around here. Everyone is talking about you. After all, you just left a few weeks ago."

We continued our conversation and covered most of the bases. She had no idea if Robert had seen or heard anything about the pictures. I was hoping to get more information from her, anticipating Garrett had talked with him. Abby also told me that they could meet me in New York. I told her we'd work out the details later. My next call wasn't going to be as easy as I had wished.

Taking a deep breath, I pressed the number two on my phone. It rang and went right to voice mail. *Oh shit*! He saw the tabloids. He always answered immediately. My pulse spiked and my stomach knotted. "Robert, call me." All I could do now was wait.

I lay back on the bed, holding my cell phone and wishing it would ring. Fifteen minutes went by, and then thirty minutes. No call. This wasn't like Robert. I called again and left another message. "Please," I emphasized. "Call me." What if he never took another one of my calls? He was probably paying me back for the times I ignored his calls.

I decided to text: I left a voice message. No return call☹.

Now all I could do was wait again.

After an hour passed by, I was getting panicky. I decided to call Abby back to see if they could reach him.

"Hi. Did you talk to him?" I could tell from Abby's voice she was worried.

"No. He's not taking my calls or replying to my texts. Usually, I receive an immediate answer. Do you think he saw those pictures and he's mad at me?"

"I don't know. Could be."

"Would you ask Garrett to call him to see if he answers?" If Robert took his call, that meant he was pissed.

"Okay, I'll see." I heard Abby say, "Sweetie, would you give Robert a ring to see if he'll answer? He's not taking Belinda's calls."

"Okay, give me a minute," I heard Garrett say in a muffled tone.

"He's calling now." She paused. "Is he answering?" she asked Garrett. The conversation turned back to me. "He's shaking his head no. I'd take that as a good sign. Just keep trying."

"Okay. Tell Garrett thanks for me. I'll call you later."

While I waited, I got ready to go out for a late lunch. I wasn't very hungry. My resident butterflies swirled. Still, no call from Robert.

The day was overcast and as dreary as my mood when I left the hotel. I found a small bakery a short distance down the street. They had just what I wanted—blueberry bagels with cream cheese and coffee. I hadn't eaten much of the breakfast that Jonathan had served me. I was too upset from the thought of Robert's reaction to the tabloids. Hanging around with Jonathan wasn't a good idea, but he was my friend, and being in the news would continue to happen once my ads and commercials became public. Robert would just have to understand that. I had decided, from now on, there would be no more physical contact in public with anyone, except Robert.

As I made my way back to the hotel, I was lost in my thoughts of him, wishing he'd return my calls. The sound of my cell phone caused me to frantically dig in my purse. I pulled it out. But no such luck. It was Jonathan.

"Hey, Jonathan. Have you left yet?"

"Nope, I'm waiting to board but it looks like I'll be back late Tuesday." A garbled overhead announcement blocked out his voice. "How you doing?"

"I'm okay." I faked trying to sound in a good mood.

"Have you talked to everyone yet?"

"No, Robert's the only one left. He's not responding to my messages and I hope it's not because he saw the photos."

"Belinda, I'm sorry. I shouldn't have kissed you like that in front of everyone. I hope I didn't hurt your chances with your husband. Again, I'd be glad to explain to him."

"Thanks, but I'll tell him we're just friends. I'm going to let you go and try texting him again."

"Okay, call if you need to talk."

Back in my suite, I decided I'd waited long enough to hear from Robert, so I sent another text.

Me: Why aren't you responding to my calls? Are you okay?
             Is there something wrong?
He texted immediately: Is there?
Me: I dont know.
Robert: So what I'm looking at is ok?

Oh shit! He was looking at the pictures now. I needed to call.

He answered on the first ring.

"Robert, please let me explain." My voice cracked. I was scared stiff this wouldn't go well.

"I'm listening." His tone came across cold.

I was taken aback for a second by his voice, then attempted to recover with my next words. "We're just friends, that's all."

"Looks pretty intimate for a friend," he snapped back.

Tension crept in and my face flushed. "Hey, bud, what I saw was pretty intimate-looking! *Payback*, remember. Except you weren't here watching my kiss like I was there seeing you kiss Erin." I paused to let what I'd said sink in. "So, what about Erin?"

"What about her?"

"Your fling with her? Is it over?" I used a sharp tone to make my point.

"What? I wasn't having a fling."

"What about all those days and late nights?"

"I was with the study group. We were working on class assignments. I'll give you their names and numbers. You can call them."

"Then what about that kiss in your car?" I demanded incredulously.

"Belinda, calm down and let me explain. Okay?" When I remained quiet, he began.

"With all the working together, she developed a crush on me. I told her I was happily married, but she wouldn't listen. She just kept pushing. The day of the kiss, she surprised me in my car. She jumped into the passenger seat and professed her love for me. Next thing I knew, she lunged at me and kissed me. I pulled away and told her to get the hell out of my car. God, I was so pissed. I went to the Cave." He hesitated for a few seconds. "I should have headed home. If I had, we could have avoided all this. I'm so sorry."

"You left me. You didn't answer my texts or calls. What was I supposed to think?"

"I know. There was no excuse for that."

"So, why?" I felt he owed me an explanation.

He didn't say anything at first. "This might sound like an excuse, but I had so much happening. The class was stressing me out, I had you to think about, and Erin wouldn't leave me alone."

"Are you trying to tell me stress caused you to have no time to invite me for coffee or join you for lunch? You couldn't pick up the phone to tell me you'd be home late or just say hi." I waited for an answer. My gut twisted and then the tears followed. "Do you know how much that hurt?"

"Yeah. As much as seeing pictures of you kissing this Jonathan guy." He paused, "I'm sorry about everything."

"Sorry? Sorry is easy to say. Now prove it."

"How?"

"I can't tell you how. That's something you'll have to figure out for yourself."

Several seconds passed before he spoke. "I guess I ran away by isolating myself like you promised you wouldn't do."

A lump formed in my throat. I knew he was right. "So, we have the same problem, but deal with it in different ways."

"Yep. Seems so."

After a pause, I asked, "So, where do we go from here?"

"I don't know. What's going on with the guy in the papers?"

"His name is Jonathan Morse." I filled Robert in on my relationship with the movie star and how he sucked me into his twisted need for publicity. "Despite his faults, he's really a nice guy. He even offered to talk to you, thinking it might help."

"Tell him thanks, but I'm good."

"So, now what?"

"Let me come to Atlanta."

"No, I need to concentrate on my job. You know as well as I do, if we touch, we'll never leave the hotel room. Then there goes my career."

He sighed. "I'm sorry. I can't change the past, but you're making some good points. God, I miss you."

"I miss you too, but I can't change what happened, either." I paused, proud of myself that I told him how I felt. "So what next?"

A puff of air came over the phone. "How about we talk frequently." He paused. "Would that work for you?"

"It's a start."

"If that works would you be willing to meet me at the Delt homecoming party?"

My pulse raced. "I'd be willing to consider it." Hell, I'd jump at the chance. At least now I had hope. "I'll see what I can do about the time off."

"I'd like that."

"There will be all kinds of changes in the next few weeks, and I want you to know about them before they happen, whenever possible." I paced the suite. "A friend of mine, who knows a lot about the paparazzi, told me I need to tell you everything, to explain what's going on, and to keep our lives private."

"Sounds like a good friend. Tell *him* thank you, and that I look forward to meeting him in the near future."

I was relieved he understood, or at least was trying to. Our conversation continued for several hours. We made a commitment to talk every evening after we were both finished with work. I fell asleep with Robert still on the phone. The last words I remember hearing were, "Angel, I love you."

Sunday, Robert had a golf date scheduled with his dad, so I had to wait to talk to him. Time was creeping by, and, with every minute, the butterflies in the pit of my stomach increased as my anticipation grew. To pass the time, I took a walk. On my way back to the hotel, my cell chirped that I had a text message.

Robert: Golf boring. Like being w/dad. Love you. Talk tonight. ☺☺☺
Me: ☺☺☺

Before I could return to the home page, my phone chirped that I had a response.

Robert: Glad to hear from you. Miss you.
Me: You're not playing golf?
Robert: Not my turn. Playing with 3 others. In cart thinking about you.
Me: Same here. Teach me to play golf.
Robert: You have to be in the same city.
Me: SMARTASS. Be patient!
Robert: I'm too good to you. My turn. Love you.
Me: Love you too!

I lavished in the thought of seeing Robert and being with him. I missed his irresistible touch and my insatiable response to it.

Robert was on my mind as I opened the door to my room. I couldn't open it fast enough, fumbling in my purse for my phone to call him. The conversation was short. He was just finishing up with golf and would be heading home. He'd call in about an hour. With my phone in my hand, I made myself comfortable on the bed and tried to relax. My fluttering butterflies were telling me it was close to the time Robert assured he'd call. I couldn't wait any longer, so I called him.

We spent the rest of the evening chatting. I told him about my decision to have limited contact with any male counterparts at any time. He seemed to appreciate that decision more than anything else we talked about.

Robert's mood shifted, becoming more playful. "What are you wearing?"

I played along and answered in a soft, sexy voice. "Nothing, I'm naked."

There was dead silence.

"Robert?"

"One second, I'm picturing that."

I jumped in. "I suppose you just got out of the shower and only have a towel wrapped around you."

A moment of silence elapsed. "As a matter of fact, I did just get out of the shower when you called and I've been naked this whole time."

My heart jumped at the memory of his well-formed body and how much I missed being touched by him. The memories were overwhelming, and I started thinking that maybe he could get his father's corporate jet and be here in a few hours. He could leave in the morning and be back to work a little late. Lost in my fantasy, I heard, "Belinda?"

"I'm here."

"I could switch to facetime to show you."

"No. No. Let's save that for later."

"You know I could be there in a few hours and back by morning."

Did he just read my mind? I couldn't answer immediately. I had to get a grip. "Very tempting, but I don't think that would be a good idea. I have to be up early and look like I slept. You know we'd get very little of that." I was biting my tongue because I wanted him here so badly. "We have to change the subject."

"Why?"

"Robert, change the subject or I'll hang up!" My voice was firm so he'd get the point. After a short pause, he complied with my wishes. We started talking about his work and the things that were different from what he'd learned in school. He liked what he was doing but was very busy. He felt confident that once he learned the ropes and the menial details of the office routine, he'd be in more control. For now, the job seemed to be controlling him.

When the call ended, the image of Robert's body haunted my mind. It kept me up most of the night. To feel his warm body next to mine was what I needed to sleep. It may have been easier having him fly here or use facetime.

CHAPTER 32

OVER THE NEXT two weeks, there were more photoshoots and we taped another commercial. Every day I practiced on the runway, my poses, and walking in the stiletto pumps. My confidence level rose and I began to believe I could do this. The ads and commercials hit the media around the same time. My face and butt were now plastered everywhere.

Jonathan checked his schedule and found out he'd be filming the weekend of the fashion show. At least Abby and Garrett would be there. I wanted to ask Robert but I knew when we did get together, we'd end up locking ourselves away for days. With the tight show schedule, there wouldn't be time.

Having Robert more involved in my life made me realize how important he was to me. As promised, no matter what was going on, we talked every night. That was our time to be together. We'd go over our day and were always there for each other. We talked about our careers and started making work decisions based on how it would affect our lives as a couple.

One evening, he seemed distracted and his tone was off. "What's bothering you? You sound upset."

There was a brief silence before he began explaining, "I made a very bad business decision for one of my clients. It's nothing that can't be repaired, but Dad and the client aren't too happy. Dad had to step in to fix the mess. So you can imagine I'm not feeling real proud of myself at this point." There was another pause. "I'll be all right. To tell the truth, I'm feeling a bit stupid right now."

"You're far from stupid. Everyone makes mistakes." He didn't respond. "Baby, you're still learning."

"Yeah. I know. I'll get over it, but believe me, it will never happen again."

I giggled. "See you're learning."

"Okay. Enough about me. What's new with you?"

I decided to bring up the fashion show. It didn't feel right keeping it from him. I wanted him there to share the experience with me. "The first weekend of September I'll be flying to New York to be in a fashion sho..."

Immediately, he cut in. "Can I come watch you?"

"Of course you can. I'd love for you to be there."

"How much time would we have together?"

"I'm not sure. I know I'll be busy." I sighed. "I'll talk to Ms. Carter and let you know." I wanted my first time back with him to be special and was afraid we would only have a few stolen moments. I tried to lift the downtrodden mood by giving Robert what I thought would be good news. "Abby and Garrett will be coming to the show. You could hang with them. They're flying in at noon on Saturday."

"You invited them before me?" He sounded wounded.

"Sorry, but we weren't talking when I asked them to come." Instantly, I knew I had put my foot in my mouth. Again.

"Correction, I was trying to talk to you. You weren't talking to me," he quickly reminded me.

"I stand corrected. Surely, we'll be hanging around there for a little while after the show. Then all four of us can visit some. I really miss y'all."

"Angel, I can fly you back to Atlanta. Remember, corporate jet. Talk to Ms. Carter and see what you can work out. Ask her if you can have the week off after the show. You know we'd need at least that to catch up."

A tingle hit me down south. "I like the way that sounds. Baby, I'll see what I can do from this end."

"I'll be waiting for that call. Hope it works out."

All the flight arrangements for Abby and Garrett were finalized. I managed to reserve a room in the same hotel I was in, and arranged for limo service to take care of all their transportation needs.

Robert's and my plan to take time after the show fell through. After talking with Ms. Carter, she informed me I would be needed back in Atlanta on Monday. The preliminary market testing and sales of the jeans were showing strong numbers and another magazine had a photoshoot scheduled.

"I have some good news and some bad news. Which do you want first?" This was my greeting to my husband during our nightly call, a week before our planned rendezvous at the fashion show.

He was quiet, but I gave him time to decide what he wanted to hear first. "Okay, hit me with the bad news first." It tore my heart apart to tell Robert we only had one day to be together. "Okay, I'll take whatever I can have right now. I'll use the jet and fly in on Saturday. Right after dinner with Abby and Garrett, we can fly back to Atlanta." He chuckled. "Let's see. It's maybe a three-hour flight. That should be enough time."

"Time for what?"

"The mile high club in the back bedroom of the jet."

My cheeks went hot. My mind went straight into the gutter. The heat sensation rushed down to my toes as I imagined his naked body.

"You still there?"

"Can we change the subject?"

This time he laughed. "Now what's the good news?"

"Are you sitting down?"

"Uh, yeah. What else would I be doing?"

"Come on, Robert, play along."

"Okay. I'm sitting down."

"I have the whole week off after the Delt homecoming party. I told Mr. Johnson to make the arrangements with Ms. Carter so that I wouldn't be available for the week. Mr. Johnson told me today everything was set. Do you think you can arrange for some time off that week? If you can't, I can stay with your parents, and, at least, we could have the nights together."

I would have kept talking if Robert's laughter hadn't interrupted me. "Whoa, Angel. Come up for air. I'm sure I can take the week off."

The remainder of our conversation concentrated on our plans to meet in Texas.

∞

The Thursday night before the fashion show, Robert called.

"Hey Baby. How was your day?" We would be seeing each other in two days and I couldn't wait for Saturday to arrive.

"Angel, I have some bad news." A gush of air-filled the phone. "I'm not going to be able to come to New York."

Budding tears filled my eyes. "Why?"

"Remember the bad business decision I made?"

"Yeah."

"Well, Dad thinks I need to be the one to rebuild the rapport with the client before he leaves the country. So, I and the corporate jet will be leaving on Saturday morning for Chicago and I don't know how long the meeting will take. I'm so sorry." He cleared his throat. "I was really looking forward to this weekend."

"Me, too." I wiped an escaping tear "Robert, promise me nothing will interfere with our plans to meet at the Delt homecoming party."

"I'll do everything I can to not let you down again."

∞

Friday morning, Ms. Carter and I were off to New York in the company jet. That afternoon we met with Ms. Deats, the designer of the blouses I was to model in the fashion show. I'd be third in the line-up of ten models. She told me that I'd have a lady to dress me. She explained the changes would be easy since I'd be wearing the same black stilettos, black SASSY jeans, and three of her blouses. Her fashions were contemporary, so she also wanted her models to match. Hired cosmeticians and beauticians would be applying our make-up and styling our hair. She wanted my hair pulled up in a knotted ponytail on top and offset to one side of my head. Ms. Deats didn't want anything covering up the clothes.

After our meeting, Ms. Carter took me to the room where the show would be held. She wanted me to practice walking down that catwalk. The room was spacious with a countless number of chairs. When I walked up on the stage, my stomach kinked as I peered down what seemed an endless strip. I took some deep breaths then proceeded to rehearse my walk and poses several times until Ms. Carter seemed satisfied. "We should head to the hotel to eat dinner and get you to bed early. Tomorrow is going to be an extremely busy day, and you need lots of rest. You have to look perfect."

The first thing I did when I arrived in my room was check my cell phone for missed messages. Robert had called.

"Hi, Angel. Have a good day?"

"It was okay, but it would've been better if you were here."

"You don't know how much I wish I were, holding you, kissing you." He heaved a loud sigh. "I miss you so much." His voice cracked before he changed the subject. "So, you were telling me about your day."

I filled him in with all the details. "My stomach is doing flip-flops right now. I keep seeing myself falling on my butt and everyone laughing at me." My lack of self-confidence was coming out in force.

"Don't worry. Angel, you'll do fine. If you can get up in front of the people at the benefit and sing, you can do this."

"But I wasn't up on the stage by myself. Jonathan was my support."

"Then pretend. Visualize me standing at the end of the runway, waiting with open arms."

"If I do that, I'd be running to you and would probably fall off the end." I giggled.

He chuckled at my comment. "Angel, I know you can do this. I have faith in you."

"Thanks. When are you leaving for Chicago?"

"Tomorrow morning about eight. I have a lunch meeting scheduled at a restaurant near the airport."

"I hope everything works out okay for you. Show him your charismatic personality. You can talk anyone into anything."

He snorted. I could imagine him rolling his eyes and shaking his head. "Now, who's encouraging who? Thanks. I think everything will work out just fine."

"Well, I hate to do this, but I need to go to sleep. I can't look tired tomorrow. I wish you could be here."

"Me too, Angel."

"I'm going to curl up around the spare pillow and pretend it's you, so I can sleep. Good night. Love you."

"Good night. Love you, too." His voice resonated pure affection.

Saturday morning was hectic. Upon arriving at the convention center, I was met by Ms. Deats' assistant and taken to a large open area sectioned off by racks of clothes. It bustled with activity. The assistant introduced me to Lorraine, my dresser, and left.

Lorraine took me to a beautician. He already knew how my hair was supposed to be styled. It didn't take him long to do my knotted ponytail.

While I was with the hairstylist, I received a text from Abby telling me that they were at the hotel. I texted back that I'd see them after the show.

Next, I was off to the cosmetician. She applied all kinds of stuff to my face. I had never worn so much makeup in my life, especially eye makeup. I almost didn't recognize myself and had trouble seeing from under the fake lashes. Finally, I was sent back to my dresser to relax until it was time to get dressed and in line.

That morning, I had awakened with some knots in my stomach, but now it was worse. I was becoming a nervous wreck. Butterflies were bombarding my stomach walls. With me wringing my hands and fidgeting, I guess Lorraine could tell I was uptight. She massaged my neck and shoulders and told me to take some deep breaths and try to clear my mind. She said to think of something pleasant. I thought of Robert and how he used to gently rock me in his arms. I started to sway ever so slightly, side to side to calm down.

The time to start dressing finally arrived, kicking up the calm butterflies. Lorraine helped me put on the jeans and my favorite blouse of the three. It was a brightly-colored, abstract-print, with butterfly sleeves, and a hem that ended at my waistline. I slipped on the heels, stood in line, and then waited to complete my first walk.

Ms. Deats' part of the show began with her introduction and then the peppy music started. The first model began her walk down the catwalk When halfway back, the next model started. During her walk, she tripped but managed to stay upright. I heard a mixture of gasps and laughter. My agitated butterflies were now frantic. A shudder raced through me. *Oh, please, don't let that happen to me.*

When she was halfway back, I took a deep breath and strutted out. I posed and then sassy strutted down the catwalk with my arms held out from my sides so that the butterfly sleeves fluttered behind me. I kept my eyes above the heads in the audience, looking to the back of the room.

When I reached the end, I did another pose and then turned, whipping my ponytail around, looked back over my shoulder and forward again, and then repeated my strut back to the stage. I turned and posed and then walked off behind the curtain. On my way back, I saw Abby, Garrett, and Jonathan sitting in the front row of seats. As I passed by, I half grinned to acknowledge them.

Rushing back to Lorraine, I started removing my blouse. She met me with my next one and tried to get this oddly shaped wraparound top on quickly. She tugged and straightened the hem as I began to get back in line for my second walk. Everything moved so fast, I forgot about my heightened nerves.

This time as I headed down the catwalk, I saw what appeared to be a tall male figure, enter the back of the room. The bright lights of the runway hampered my view. It was too dark and he was too far away to see any features. I thought of Robert, but it couldn't be him. He was in Chicago. I concentrated on the figure as he moved to the center of the room—facing the end toward me. Watching him took my mind off the walk and helped keep me calm. During my pose, I strained to see him, but couldn't. I spun around and headed back up the catwalk, completing my routine.

On my third run, I wore a dressier accordion-pleated royal-blue blouse. I concentrated at the tall, dark figure. It made my walk easier. I didn't feel uptight. *Thank you, whoever you are.* My part was over. The only thing left was the grand finale parade of models. I waited in my area until that time came then got in line. As the parade made its way around the catwalk, I nodded at the dark figure of a man, and it appeared that he nodded back.

Ms. Carter met me in the back behind the curtain. She smiled a mile wide. "You looked *great* out there. Our jeans and your sassy walk are going to bring us a lot of customers. Cha-ching! We had several buyers already contact us about orders right after your first walk." She glowed with excitement. "Go enjoy yourself with your friends. We won't be leaving until tomorrow around noon. Have fun. You've earned it."

"Thanks. It was more fun and easier than I thought. See you tomorrow." I headed for my dressing area and Lorraine helped me change. I thanked her for her help then rushed out to where my friends were waiting. I hoped the mysterious man was still there, so I could thank him, but I got sidetracked.

Jonathan grabbed my waist, swung me around, and then planted a kiss on my cheek.

Garrett, my pitbull, scowled.

I pulled away. "Um. Have you met my friends, Abby and Garrett?"

"Yes, this one." He pointed at Abby. "She recognized me and introduced herself. She said you two are best friends."

I hugged Abby and Garrett. "I've missed you two."

"We've missed you." Abby flashed her engagement ring in my face. She looked so happy, and so did Garrett.

I took her hand. "Abby, it's beautiful."

She hugged Garrett. "I couldn't be happier." She looked around. "Is Robert here?"

"No, that fell through. He had a last-minute meeting with a client."

Jonathan reached down to his chair, picked up a bouquet of long-stemmed red roses, and handed them to me.

"Thank you! They're beautiful. I thought you said you couldn't come. What happened?" I had this strange feeling like someone was watching me. As Jonathan replied, I looked to the back of the room just as the tall, dark figure turned and walked out the door. I had to find out who this mysterious person was.

"Excuse me for a minute." I shoved the roses back at Jonathan and took off running. When I reached the lobby, it was still fairly crowded. On my tiptoes, I craned my neck to look above people's heads to see where he'd gone. I managed to spot the back of a man's head with dark hair, leaving the building. I rushed to catch up, but, by the time I arrived outside, I'd lost him. Scanning around, I even checked inside taxis, but he was nowhere in sight. I would've liked to thank him for being my rock.

I walked back through the lobby. As I passed the last row of chairs in the show's ballroom, I noticed a single red rose lying across one of the seats. I picked it up. My heart sank to my stomach. Was my mystery man, Robert? That didn't make sense. He would've made sure I knew he was here. So, I left the rose on a chair and went back to my friends.

"Sorry about that. I thought I saw someone I knew, but I guess not." I reached for the roses. "You were explaining how you got to come."

"Are you okay?" Jonathan looked concerned.

I nodded. "I'm fine."

Jonathan proceeded to explain. "Mr. Morrison asked where you were. I told him you were in New York for your first fashion show. To give you the direct version, he ordered me to get my butt on the next plane to New York." Jonathan raised his brows." "Ta-da, here I am." He half bowed.

He made me laugh. "Thank you and remind me to thank Mr. Morrison later."

We all decided to go out and celebrate. The exit doors were surrounded by paparazzi wanting pictures of Jonathan. Every time a door opened, all that could be seen were camera flashes. I turned to Garrett and Abby and warned them of what was about to happen. "Head straight for the limo. Don't stop. It's going to be a zoo out there." We all exited together and aimed for Jonathan's limo. Paparazzi were everywhere, but we managed to make it unscathed.

"Holy smokes! Does that happen all the time?" Abby's head was bobbing around, looking at the rapid explosions of light from the cameras.

Jonathan closed his eyes and shook his head, letting out a long deep breath. "Yeah, all the time. These pictures will be in the gossip rags tomorrow."

Abby's eyes got big. "Belinda, I want one of those, especially if I'm in one of the pictures with him." She pointed at Jonathan and smiled.

Garrett's look soured. She glared back. "What? It's not every day you meet a popular movie star and I'm in a picture with him." She snapped her head toward Jonathan. "Would you sign it for me?"

"I'd be glad to. But I think Ms. SASSY over here may have something to do with this as well. You need to get her autograph, too."

I looked at Jonathan. "Why me? I'm nobody."

He hung his head and laughed in a low snicker. "Who's butt and face is everywhere, Missy? Don't you think we'd be newsworthy for the paid-for-hire photographers?" He gestured with his thumb connecting us as a couple.

I scowled, popping him on the arm. "It's not true!"

"Go with it. Remember, we talked about this. Play it up and have fun. Otherwise, you'll go nuts."

I needed lots of practice when it came to the tabloids, but for now, I was going to enjoy my friends.

♡

Back in Atlanta, Sunday evening, dusk was approaching, and I was anxious to talk with Robert. I wondered if he had a hard time winning the client back into his confidence. I decided to send him a text.

Me:	Can you talk? I miss you.
Robert:	At SL airport. I'll call when I get home. I miss you. Love you.
Me:	Love you too. I can't wait to talk to you.

I put on my favorite t-shirt and crawled into bed with my cell and answered on the first ring and connected to facetime. "Hi, I missed you." I gave him a kiss. He returned it. Chills ran up my spine as I imagined the soft connection of our lips.

"Belinda?"

"Sorry, I was just imagining that kiss and how it would feel. I miss them and my reaction."

"Me too, Angel."

"How was your meeting? Was it successful?"

He chuckled. "Slow down. You sure are wound up. Is this twenty questions?"

"I'm just excited to see you. Continue." I loved listening to him talk.

"I think the meeting was sort of successful. He's an older client, and I sensed he'd prefer Dad to handle his account. I assured him he had nothing to worry about." A moment passed. "So, tell me about the fashion show."

"I was a nervous wreck at first. But after I completed the first walk, I took your advice. There was a man, about your height standing in the back. I focused on him and pretended he was you. You'll have to be there next time, okay?"

"I'll try." He furrowed his brow. "So, who was that tall, dark figure?"

"I don't know."

Robert lowered his head before asking the next question. "What happened after the show?"

"Jonathan showed up, so we all went out to eat and visit. Abby and Garrett got to experience the chaos of the paparazzi." I chuckled. "She didn't care. She was thrilled to meet Jonathan. I think Garrett was a little jealous the way she was flirting with him." I gave a brief description of the impromptu sleeping arrangements. "Did you know Garrett popped the question?"

"No. Man, he's in trouble now."

"Robert. They're really happy."

He barked out a laugh. His wide, sexy smile flashed across my screen. "I'm sure they are. Otherwise, it sounds like you had a great time without me."

"It was nice, but *nothing* could replace you being there."

After talking for a couple of hours, Robert suggested we plug in our cells before we both fell asleep. It was one of our phone sleepovers and the closest thing I had to being with him all night.

In the morning, I woke up to the sound of his voice. "Belinda, are you still there. Angel, it's time to wake up." My eyes fluttered open and rested on his face, while he lay in his bed miles away.

After breakfast, we'd got ready for work, and hung up when it was time to leave. Such would be our lives until we could meet in Texas in two, long weeks.

∞

The fashion show had been a huge success. I became the signature model for Every Body Jeans Manufacturing Company with an exclusive side contract with Fashion Designs by JLDeats. My life would become extremely busy in a short time.

As promised, Robert and I talked every night and, sometimes, slept together on facetime. Our relationship was more solid than it had ever been. My self-confidence was stronger. I no longer felt pressured about our relationship but saw myself on a more equal basis with him. He was still *My Mister Wonderful*, but his responses to me were different. He was more open about how he felt about decisions, and, surprisingly, I opened up to him. This was a new approach. It was working and it was marvelous.

CHAPTER 33

ROBERT HAD PLANNED to pick me up at the airport and drive us to the fraternity homecoming party. But, a last-minute business meeting changed our plans. He didn't know how long it would last, so he suggested I should go without him. I made him promise to meet me there.

Saturday morning, I flew into Hobby Airport, then caught a taxi to Mrs. Foster's boarding house to get my car, and headed for the college. After checking into our room about two hours before the party, I began preparing—wanting to look sexy and perfect for Robert. I wore a pair of my SASSY jeans and a pale blue, deep V-neck sweater. I left my hair down, parted on the side, the way he liked it.

I was ready, but it was too soon to leave. Wanting to hear his voice, I lay on the bed and thought about calling him, but I knew it might interrupt his meeting and cause a delay in his arrival. My stomach roiled. It seemed like years since I was able to feel Robert against me. I closed my eyes and imagined his strong protective arms around me. My heart accelerated. The thoughts caused my lady parts to tingle. This was a place I didn't need to be going right now. I rolled off the bed, picked up my bag, and headed for the car. The drive around campus relaxed my hyperactive libido.

The frat house held so many good memories and I wished Robert would be standing with open arms in the doorway waiting to greet me. I missed him so much, but I only had to wait a little longer.

On the front porch, I took a deep breath and knocked before entering. Immediately, several of the brothers yelled, "Belinda, the *SASSY GAL* is here!" They rushed over to hug me. I was surrounded by people all talking at once. It was a regular mob scene, but I was getting used to this and learning to handle it.

I was managing the group when Abby and Garrett arrived. "Guys, I'll catch up with you later. Abby just came in." I thumbed toward her. "Have to say hi."

I hurried over to fling my arms around my best friend. "It's so good to see you." I swayed back and forth, keeping Abby in a bear hug. I flipped Garrett a wave then whispered in Abby's ear. "Things still good between you two?"

"Never better. We're doing great." Abby whipped her head around. "Where's Robert?"

I loosened my grip and stepped back. "Another last-minute business meeting. He said he'd be here as soon as he can. I can't wait to see him."

Garrett placed his arm around his soon-to-be wife. "Why are you always with that Moose guy?"

I glared at Garrett. Abby poked him in the ribs. "You know perfectly well his name is Morse."

He rubbed his side. "Who cares what I call him."

Abby pursed her lips and raised a brow.

"I just want to know why everywhere I look, I see Belinda and him." He grimaced for my benefit but gave Abby a scowl of disgust, attempting to make his point.

"Like I explained at the fashion show, we're just friends. Don't believe those tabloids. They're just assumptions, not true. Besides, Robert knows all about my relationship with Jonathan and understands." I poked Garrett on his chest with my finger. "So butt out, buddy." I smirked at him.

"Belinda, look at that." Abby pointed to the other side of the room.

My mouth dropped open and I grabbed the first brother who walked by and I pointed at a large poster of one of my SASSY advertisements. "Where did you get that?"

"Brian liked that ad and had it enlarged. He wrote DELT above SASSY." Paul handed me a black marker. "Would you sign it?"

"Sure." I walked over and wrote, *Love you all, Belinda.*

Music started playing. Paul grasped my hand and led me into the gyrating crowd. We were on our third dance when I saw Declan walk in alone and survey the room. The second he saw me he rushed right over and politely asked to cut in. Paul stepped back.

With a gigantic smile on his face, he pulled me close and gave me a big hug. "I was disappointed when I got back and found out that you'd left." He took a step back, just far enough to look me over. "Sooo, now you're a model and dating movie stars. I like those commercials. You're perfect for that jeans company." He gave me a nod of approval. He took my hand, and, with a snap, I was back against him dancing.

"Thanks, I've enjoyed my new occupation so far. But I miss everyone here. It's lonely in Atlanta, and Jonathan Morse is only a good friend who has helped me through it."

"Sooo. What about your husband? Are you getting a divorce?"

"No divorce. We're getting back together. He'll be here soon." I noticed a hint of disappointment on his face before he responded.

"That's good." He hugged me.

When the song ended, Garrett walked over and asked if we'd be interested in a game of pool. He winked at me, and I knew exactly what he was thinking. So I played along. I impishly smiled at Declan. "Do you play pool?"

"Yes, once or twice a week."

I turned toward Garrett, making sure my hair shielded my face from Declan before I winked. "You're on."

Garrett racked up the balls, handed Declan a cue stick, and told him to break. He sank three balls. Garrett sank three. Now it was my turn. Taking small deliberate steps around the table, I contemplated my best shot. I sank one, then six more, and had two balls left. I was setting up my next strike when I heard, "You better watch out. She's a pool shark."

I froze. My heart thundered. I shot up on my tiptoes to look around and caught a glimpse of Robert moving across the back of the room. I dropped my cue stick and pushed my way through the crowd, rushing toward him. When I broke through, I was being pummeled from the inside. My butterflies crashed against every inch of my belly.

I leaped into his outstretched arms, wrapping my arms around his neck and my legs around his waist, almost knocking us both over. I planted a kiss on his waiting lips. I didn't just quiver. I trembled all over as I tightened my wrap around him. I was lost in him and the moment.

Robert squeezed me tight to him. His hand knotted in my hair, holding me close. We kissed each other fast, with short and long kisses. We might never have stopped if it wasn't for the chanting of the other partygoers. It started out in a low whisper then rose to an ear-splitting shout, over and over again. "Get a room!" Get a room! Get a room!

We both looked around and laughed. Robert may have been more cavalier about what had just happened, but we hadn't seen each other in months. We were on the verge of losing control.

"Damn, you feel good! I've missed you so much." Tightening his grip, he carried me to the back porch and set me down. With my hand in his, he led me out into the starlit night. "It will be quieter, more private out here." We walked across the yard to a wooden bench situated beneath a large oak tree. There on the bench was my treasure box with a single red rose lying across the top. Attached to the rose was a note with little hand-drawn hearts that read, *To Our New Beginning*!

I brushed my fingers across the letters and then gazed at his face. He just shrugged his shoulders and smiled. I sat on the bench clutching my gifts as tears flowed. He gently wiped away the droplets. "Why are you crying?" His brows drew together over his caring eyes as he sat next to me.

"I'm just so glad to see you. I've missed you so much." I pulled myself across his lap, wrapped an arm around the back of his neck, and laid my head against his shoulder. He slipped his arms around me. I was home. "This is where I want to be. Where I'm supposed to be. With you." I looked up into his eyes. "And I've realized I don't want to be without you. I gave you my heart and you still have it. A little trampled on, but I still love you. I don't want to live without you in my life."

He hugged me tight to him and kissed my forehead as I experienced a faint shiver. "Me either. I'm so sorry I made you feel unwanted. It was my fault. Can you ever forgive me?" He paused and stared into my eyes before he continued talking. "I've loved you from the first moment I saw you. It took me by surprise. I liked the way my life was, carefree. But I couldn't stop thinking about you. Wanting you." He brushed a stray hair from my face.

With both arms wrapped around his neck, I pulled my body close to his. "I only wanted to be with you and still do. I'm in love with you." I closed my eyes.

He lifted my chin so I'd look him in the eyes. "And I love you and always will." He kissed me long and deep. When I quivered, he pulled away and grinned. "I missed that." He leaned his head against mine. "I'm so glad to be away from here." He sounded relieved.

"Why?"

"Because of all the problems it caused us." He hugged me tight and buried his face in my hair. He raised his head. "I've worked out a solution so we can be together."

I turned and stared at him. "How?"

Gazing into my eyes, he explained his plan. "Dad is hiring Garrett when he graduates to help run the business when I'm out of town with you. I can work with Garrett online."

"I don't want to take you from your obligations. Your parents are counting on you."

"This will work. They would do anything to help us get back together. Angel, every time I saw your picture in the tabloids, the magazines, even your commercials, I looked for your wedding band. Seeing it still on your finger gave me hope." He held up his left hand to show me his ring. "My wedding band has never left my finger, either. And neither has this." He pulled on a chain around his neck, lifting out my engagement ring. "It has been hanging close to my heart ever since you left. Angel, I will always want you. Never doubt my love for you."

"I will always want you, too."

He adjusted me on his lap. "I now know how you felt seeing her kissing me. I swear these lips will never again touch anyone's but yours." He gave me a sincere look.

"What?" My eyes blinked wide.

"I saw Jonathan kiss you at the fashion show. I...I didn't like it."

I sat up. "How?"

Before he continued his explanation, he tried to pull me close but I held my hand to his chest. "Start talkin'."

"I was there. I came to the fashion show. I was your man in the back of the room."

"So that was you? Why didn't you tell me?"

"I wanted to surprise you. After the show, I noticed Abby and Garrett and was headed their way, when I saw your tabloid friend next to them. When he handed you the roses, I stopped. I wasn't supposed to be there, so I left." He shrugged his shoulders. "But seeing how you looked with him, it tore me up."

"Robert, I asked him a while back but he told me he couldn't come. I didn't know he was going to show up. He surprised me. That seat next to Abby and Garrett was yours. I wanted you there, not him. Look who misunderstood and left this time." I ran my fingers down his cheek. "I sensed the guy in the back of the room was watching me. I saw him leave and chased after him to see who he was, but I lost him. I wanted to thank him for helping me make it through the fashion show." I combed my fingers through his hair as my eyes roamed his face, settling on his eyes. I smiled. "I should've known it was you, but I couldn't see any features because of the lighting and distance."

"When you nodded, I wondered if you recognized me. But you made no attempt to head my way. Instead, you headed for Abby, Garrett, and him.

"You left the rose I found?"

"I saw the bouquet he gave you, so I just dropped it on the chair." He sounded jealous and hurt."

I gazed at him. "I gave *you* my heart and I'd rather have one single rose from you than a field of roses from someone else." I kissed Robert on the cheek.

The corners of his mouth turned up.

I rested my head against his chest to listen to the beat of his heart. I missed hearing it as much as I missed him. He began to sway ever so slightly and I was lost in his arms.

I pulled him close to my lips and longed for his kiss. Knowing what it would do to both of us, I couldn't wait any longer. I crushed my lips to his and we both shuddered.

He gently placed his hands on my shoulders and pulled me from his lips. Our breathing was heavy. He gazed into my eyes. "Let's go. We can continue this at the hotel. I've missed holding you at night...and loving you."

"Okay. But wouldn't it be rude if we left now?"

He was pulling me behind him as he walked across the yard when he stopped dead in his tracks. "Who cares!"

I looked at him, surprised. I only had a brief moment before he picked me up in his arms. He continued his pace, like a man driven, bypassing the house as he headed for the cars. "You can call Abby later to fill her in. For the next few days, you'll have other things to keep you busy."

In the hotel elevator, he crushed his lips to mine in a slow-burning, toe-curling kiss that made me trembled and my legs give out from under me. Thank goodness he was holding me tight as I went limp in his arms. When we reached our floor, he picked me up and carried me to our room. I somehow managed to unlock and open the door. We almost didn't make it to the bed. Clothes miraculously disappeared within seconds as our hands explored each other's body. Our kisses were wild as we fulfilled our desires. The night was spectacular, making up for lost time.

Six-thirty Sunday morning, I awoke before Robert. I decided to go for our favorite coffee and bagels from the bakery. I thought I'd be able to make it back before he woke up but to be safe, I left a note. *Back soon, Love Belinda.*

I drove straight to the bakery and bought two coffees and four blueberry bagels, his favorites.

At the intersection, the traffic light glowed red and seemed to take forever to change. I was sure Robert would be up by now. When the light turned green, I pulled forward. My head snapped in the direction of the squealing tires, a blaring horn, and the grinding of gears. My head snapped in the direction of the sound. Everything seemed to be moving in slow motion as I watched the grill of a semi come closer to my car, just before it collided with me. Like a ragdoll, I felt my body being whipped about before it slammed into the driver's side door. A searing pain shot through my body as my head smashed the glass and my arm melded into the door. There was a sharp pain on the side of my head followed by something warm running down my face. The horrifying sound of crushing metal and shattering glass filled the air as everything around me went black.

CHAPTER 34

I KNEW MY eyes were open, but the light was so bright I couldn't see anything. The light hurt. So, I closed them again. I tried to lift my arms to rub my eyes, but they wouldn't move.

I heard a faint voice in the distance. "She's waking up!" Moments later, a different voice, much louder than the first, kept repeating my name. "Belinda! Belinda! Belinda!" I heard the louder voice again. "Go get the doctor." This is when I realized I was in a hospital.

I must've blacked out. This time, when I opened my eyes, the light was much dimmer. I looked around, observing more of my surroundings. I saw a clock on the wall across from my bed. It read four o'clock, but was that morning or afternoon? I couldn't see any windows. I tried to move my head, but I couldn't. Why couldn't I move? I tried to call out for help but nothing came out of my mouth.

I heard a voice, a familiar one. It was my mother. She leaned into my field of vision and told me not to try to move, the doctor was on his way. I could feel her lift my hand and hold it. With all the strength I could gather, I managed to stroke her hand with one finger. Tears began to run down her face. I wanted to tell her I was okay and everything would be fine, but I couldn't. I wanted to ask her where Robert was. I needed to know he understood I was alive. Surely, someone called him to let him know I was in the hospital. I, again, drifted out of consciousness.

I opened my eyes to the same dim light. This time the clock said six. There was no way of knowing if it was morning, evening, or what day it was. Hearing whispering nearby, I tried to turn my head and I did. So I turned it in the other direction, just to see if I could. I did! I tried to lift my arms. This time I could move my hands a little bit. They felt heavy as if they weren't part of my body.

Two men approached my bed, each standing on either side of me. The one with the white coat introduced himself.

"Hi, Belinda, I'm Dr. Shane Covington, your neurologist. This is Dr. Martin Rosen, your psychologist."

Psychologist? Why did I need a psychologist? I understood a neurologist but…this didn't make sense.

Dr. Covington continued. "We have you under sedation. That's why you're having difficulty moving or talking right now. As we wake you up, you'll have many questions. Things may be confusing at first, so that's why Dr. Rosen is here. He'll help answer all your questions and readjust."

Readjust to what? I wanted answers now, not a few days from now. I somehow managed to grab the wrist of the doctor in the white coat. His eyes widened as he looked down at my grip. I could feel his hand cover mine. His eyes softened.

"Okay, this is enough for now. The nurse is going to give you something to put you back to sleep. The next time you wake up, we should be able to talk."

Wanting him to understand I needed to stay awake, I moved my head side to side. I tightened my grip on his wrist. From the far reaches of some unknown place, I heard a sound resonate in an almost animalistic tone. It was guttural, a growl. I realized the sound was my voice, screaming, "No!" I wanted to see Robert.

The sedative Dr. Covington gave me did the trick. I slept. The next time I opened my eyes, the clock read ten. No electric lights on, yet the left side of the room was illuminated. Turning my head toward it, I could see a window. It was sunlight. Okay, it was ten o'clock in the morning. I didn't know how long I'd been asleep.

I faintly remembered my mother and, I think, Dr. Covington talking about me during one of the times I was supposed to be sleeping. He was explaining something to her. I didn't understand what he was saying.

I tried to move my arms, but all I could move was my hands. So, I tried my toes and was able to wiggle them. Then I fell back asleep.

Now, the clock said seven. Light streamed in the window, so I knew it was daylight but not what day or how long I had been out this time. I tried to lift my arms. I raised them off the bed, but not enough to see them. They felt like lead.

A nurse approached my bed. "Relax. Things will start coming back. Please, look straight ahead for me. I need to check your pupils." She waved a small flashlight from one eye to the next. The brightness hurt. When she finished, she told me the date, month, and year. I tried to talk to her. The only thing that came out was mumbled syllables. What was going on? I should be waking up. Why was I being drugged? Sleep overcame me again.

The next time I awoke, my mind was foggy. This time the light was bright from the ceiling fixture. I closed my eyes and did a mental check of what I knew. I was in the hospital. I couldn't talk. I was having trouble moving.

I opened my eyes. The bright light hurt. I lifted my hands to shield my face. To my surprise, I could move. It felt good, but when I took my hands away, I caught a glimpse of my arms. These *couldn't* be my arms. They were pale and horribly thin, with very little muscle mass. My arms were well-shaped and had more color than these. Yet these foreign arms were attached to my shoulders. I could move them at will.

The door opened and the two men came in, followed by a nurse. The one who called himself Dr. Covington had a concerned look on his face. I guess he could see the horror on mine. He rushed over to the bed and took hold of my hands, cradling them. Something was terribly wrong. My eyes started to fill with tears.

"Okay, we're going to start from the beginning." He sat on the side of the bed. "Can you talk?"

I opened my mouth, and, to my surprise, words came out. "Yes...yes, I can." I looked over at Dr. Rosen. He was writing in a notebook.

"Dr. Rosen is just taking notes for this session. He'll be doing that frequently. Now, what is the last thing you remember?"

Struggling to form the words, I answered. "I...got...up...left a note...for Robert." It was all I could get out because I fell back asleep again.

The next time I awoke, my mother was standing beside my bed. "What happened to me? Where's Robert?" That was all I could say before drifting away.

"Belinda, wake up." I heard a male voice that kinda sounded like Robert. Something wasn't right. It wasn't his voice. I opened my eyes, and there stood two white-coated men.

"Belinda, we need to talk."

I fought to focus as I woke up.

"Okay, I need you to tell me the last thing you remember."

Struggling, I answered. "I was with Robert. I left him a note that I was running an errand and would be right back. I was driving to our favorite bakery to pick up breakfast. Blueberry bagels are Robert's favorite." The memory of Robert sleeping came back and made me smile. I was getting lost in my thoughts of him.

Dr. Covington interrupted. "What happened next?"

I snapped my gaze back to his face and became more serious. "I left the bakery and headed back, but when I drove into the intersection, a big truck seemed to come out of nowhere." I gasped. "It hit me."

"Where were you?"

"At college." I looked over at Dr. Rosen who was writing everything that was being said. He made me uncomfortable, so I looked back at Dr. Covington. "Does Robert know I'm all right? Why isn't he here with me?" My mind started jumping to conclusions.

Dr. Covington's gaze intensified. "Belinda, who is Robert?"

Dr. Rosen stopped writing in his notebook. He didn't look at me. He simply lifted the pen from the pad.

"Robert's my husband." With my answer, Dr. Rosen again began to write. What did I say that had him so interested?

"Can we talk about something else right now?"

"No!" I scowled at him. "What is more important than my husband knowing I'm okay?"

Dr. Covington didn't respond. He simply changed the subject. "What year did you graduate from college?"

His question baffled me. "I didn't finish. I became a model." Dr. Covington straightened. One of his brows shot up.

My horrible thin arm came into view. I reached out with my other arm, in the same condition, to touch the first. I looked at the doctor. "What happened to my arms?" I stretched them out in front of me as far as my strength would allow. "This doesn't happen in a week." I looked at him, the salt from welling tears stung.

He glanced at Dr. Rosen who had stopped writing. Turning his attention back to me, he took a deep breath before starting. "You had a car accident. You were hit by a semi, but it didn't happen last week. It happened six months ago. Belinda, you've been in a coma for six months. That's why you're so thin. You haven't been using your muscles. They atrophy without use."

There was silence. I didn't know what to say as I studied my arms. Running my fingers over my face, I could feel my cheekbones were more pronounced. I reached for my hair, which was wadded up in a makeshift bun on top of my head. It felt dirty and gnarled.

"Your hair had to be cut. The nurses did the best they could to take care of it. Look, Dr. Rosen and I will be back later this evening. For now, I'm going to put you back to sleep."

Panicked, I looked at him. "No, you can't. I have a million questions I need to sort out."

He picked up my hand ever so gently. I was beginning to like Dr. Covington. He seemed so understanding and had a sense of when I needed to be consoled. He patted my hand.

"I promise you, we'll give you all the time you need to find the answers you're looking for. Right now, your mind needs to rest. You need time to process this new information. Your brain needs time to wake up as well."

I was starting to trust this man in the white coat. "Okay, only if you promise." He motioned to the nurse who had been standing behind him to give me the medication. As I drifted off, the words spilled out. "What about Robert?"

Dr. Covington stood at the side of my bed. "I promised I'd be back."

I smiled and pointed to the other doctor, the psychologist. "When does this one stop writing and start talking?"

Dr. Covington grinned. Dr. Rosen steps in when I'm done. I guarantee you two will become well acquainted."

Dr. Shane Covington flashed me a huge captivating smile. In the dim lamplight, he looked to be about thirty-five years old. His sandy-colored hair was tousled about the top of his head but styled that way. He was neatly dressed in a starched, collared shirt and tie covered by the white lab coat that proudly displayed his name and title in blue thread embroidered across the breast pocket. I could tell he kept himself in good shape. His lab coat fit him like a well-tailored suit. On his left ring finger was a plain gold band.

Dr. Rosen looked the opposite. He was casually dressed, had beard stubble, and his hair was an unkempt mess. It looked like he hadn't combed it in a week. There wasn't a wedding band and I could understand why. I imagined his house being as untidy as he was. Most likely, his life was the same.

"Belinda, let's get started." Dr. Covington pulled up a chair. "Do you remember anything before the accident?"

"I think so."

"Can you tell us?" He encouraged.

I smiled as my thoughts rushed back to Robert and our many intimate encounters. I was embarrassed and could feel myself blushing. "I met the most wonderful guy. His name is Robert Pennington." I stopped for a moment. "I can truly and with all honesty say, he is my...my soul mate." I reached over and fingered the gold band on the doctor's hand. "Do you love your wife?"

"We're trying to find out about you, Belinda. How I feel about my wife is not important." He was more reserved as if his privacy was being invaded.

"No, it is important. If you truly love your wife, then you will understand how I feel about my husband." I paused while I tried to think of the words to explain my relationship with Robert. "My husband is the most important person in my life. He is my other half. It's like we reached beyond our own limited existence and found each other. We have this irresistible connection between us that is so strong. I'd gladly give my life for him."

Dr. Covington didn't respond. His dark brown eyes met mine. They made him look intense as he just stared and studied me.

From the opposite side of the bed, I heard a soft, mousy voice. "Shane...Shane, we need to keep going."

I turned my head in shock. "It speaks!" My tone was sharp because my exchange with Dr. Covington had been interrupted. I didn't want anything to do with "The Other Doctor." I was not impressed by him.

"Belinda."

I turned back to Dr. Covington.

"When did you meet Robert?" He furrowed his brow.

"In the spring semester, last April. Why?"

"Belinda." He picked up my hand as he looked at me with intense eyes. "It's now the end of September. How long have you been in a coma?"

At first, his question confused me. I'd been in a coma for the past six months. He knew the answer to his question better than I did.

Then I stopped and froze. It hit me.

I squeezed his hand as tight as I could. My breathing faltered as an ache hit where my heart dwelt. The pain of my revelation was so intense, I almost stopped breathing. Tears filled my eyes as they locked onto his. I shut them and squeezed the doctor's hands harder.

Memories rushed into my head like waves crashing against a rocky shore. I was an art teacher. I had dated Matt all through college. After we graduated, he left to take a job in California. He gave me Beau. Abby and Garrett were my best friends and should be married now.

I had a car accident leaving Abby's bridal shower.

Taking short shallow breaths, I felt the pain over my heart grow in intensity.

"Robert doesn't exist!" I shouted out between the sobs. "He's only in my head and in my heart."

I wished I had never awakened. If I'd stayed in the coma, Robert would still be real. I couldn't talk because I cried so hard. My shoulders heaved as I sobbed. Dr. Covington never let go. He sat holding my hands, offering what support he could, while I experienced the most terrifying moments of my life.

I realized that I'd just lost my beloved Robert.

I sobbed for what seemed like an eternity. The psychologist handed me some tissue, and I dabbed my eyes. I felt dead as I stared into space.

"Belinda, we're going to put you back to sleep. Tomorrow is going to be a busy day. Your work with Dr. Rosen is going to start. It won't be easy. You've had multiple losses. It'll take time, but I'm sure you'll overcome this. In the morning, my job will be to put you in touch with a physical therapist. We have to start working on those muscles to get you back into shape. A nutritionist will also come to see you, and we'll need to do a swallow test. If you pass that, we'll start to feed you real food. Since the accident, we've been feeding you through that tube that goes into your stomach."

He paused from his clinical explanation. "I'm sorry about Robert."

I looked at him wide-eyed. I could swear I saw light tears well in his eyes. He was softer, less reserved.

"If I lost my wife, my life would end." He stiffened to regain his composure. "We'll see you in the morning. I'm going to call your parents. I'd like someone you're close to, to stay with you twenty-four hours a day. It will help you reconnect with your *new reality.*"

I nodded to let him know I understood his instructions and concern.

Heather came in and asked if there was anything I needed. What I needed no one would ever be able to provide. Robert was gone in my "New Reality," as Dr. Covington coined it, but I hoped I could find him in my dreams. Welcoming the sedative this time, I wanted to stop the pain. If Robert was a dream, maybe I could find him again in sleep.

My mother and Abby were the first things I saw when I woke up. Both had grins from ear to ear, looking like Cheshire cats. "Hi, guys. Long time no see," I whispered in my sleepy state.

"Oh, sweetie," Mom said. "I missed you so much. Welcome back." She started to cry and turned away to find a tissue.

"How much do you remember?" Abby took a seat on the bed next to me.

"Enough to know I missed your wedding. Never a bride. Never a maid of honor."

Her face lit up, and her smile became more exaggerated as she realized I was back. Well, at least, part of me was. Due to my debilitated physical state, the simplest task was difficult. I couldn't even sit up without support.

Also, there was my mental state. There were things that happened before the real accident that I had trouble remembering. I guess the psychologist was going to be needed after all. Every time, I let my mind wander back to Robert, a heaviness came over me.

I was glad Abby was here. I could always talk to her. She might know if Robert was a real person I had met that I didn't remember right now. Maybe he was someone I had a crush on in college. I had so many questions that needed to be answered, and I prayed Abby could help.

"Belinda, what are you thinking about?"

"I'm still feeling the effects of the sedation. I'll be more awake soon." I didn't want to say anything about Robert in front of my mom. I'd have time to talk to Abby later.

"Your mom and I will be taking turns staying with you for a while," Abby said in her usual upbeat voice.

"Don't you have to work? You graduated with me and have a job...right?"

She laughed. "Yeah, I have a job. I'm Mrs. Garrett Barnett. Okay, I'm, also, an art teacher. I'm taking a leave of absence until you don't need me anymore. I'll be on the night shift. I figured that way it would be like old times. Kinda like a girls' night in but without the booze for now. We might be able to get some singing in. That is if the nurses don't quiet us down."

"Sounds good to me! Anything would be a diversion. Maybe you can help me do something with my hair. Wait a minute, do you have a mirror? I want to see what I look like."

My mother and Abby exchanged a concerned look. "Um, Belinda, Dr. Rosen asked us not to let you look at yourself yet. He wants to be here." My mother said it softly as if her tone of voice would make me less worried.

"Did my face get scarred in the accident? Was I burned or disfigured?" My fingers frantically traced over my face.

Both of them reached for my hands saying in unison, "No! No! Nothing like that."

"Then what?" I darted my eyes back and forth to each of their faces.

"Sweetie, you're just thin. You've lost a lot of weight. The way Dr. Rosen explained it was...your brain needs time to register these changes. He wanted to be here so you could talk with him. He saw how upset you were last night."

I looked at my mother. "He asked you about Robert, didn't he?"

Now, mom was sitting on the bed. "Yes, he did." She was very serious. I could see her concern.

I saw this as an opportunity to have some questions answered. I looked at both of them. "Well, do either of you know him or do you have any idea how I could know him?"

Putting their heads down, they wouldn't answer me.

I picked up Abby's hand. Tears flowed down my face. "If either of you can help me, if either of you want to help me, I need to know. This guy was so real. I can remember how he felt. How I felt when he touched me. I was so connected to him. I'm still connected to him. I'm not crazy."

They didn't have the opportunity to answer. The psychologist walked in. "Good morning, Ms. Davies. How are you feeling?"

"How do you think I'm feeling?" I was being as sarcastic as I could. I didn't like this shrink. He was always such a mess.

"She asked us to give her a mirror," Mom said. "She wanted to take a look."

"Okay, I'll go get one." He left the room and returned in a very short time. He placed the mirror face down on the bedside table so I couldn't see the reflective side.

"Before I let you take a look, we need to talk. You've changed in the past six months, but it's nothing that can't be reversed. When you start eating, you'll start gaining weight. With exercise, your muscle mass will return. That, along with the other therapies you'll receive, should help greatly. Now, it's going to be your job to recuperate back to the Belinda you knew."

He put his hand on my shoulder. "Belinda, no one ever expected you to wake up. We all believed you'd be in a vegetative state for the rest of your short life. You need to know you have a second chance here. From now on, the time after you woke up will be referred to as your *new reality*."

My mind wandered back to my life with Robert. I had my second chance when we decided to make our marriage work. No, *Dr. Psychologist*, I would have gladly stayed asleep for however long my life was, as long as I could be with Robert. He was my second chance and now I'd lost him.

"Okay. Now, can I have a look?"

He turned the mirror over and handed it to me. It was small enough for my weak hands to hold and, yet, big enough for me to see the severity of my affliction.

I stared at my reflection. The person staring back looked like me in some ways. I still had striking blue eyes, but now they were sunken. My cheeks were hollowed. My skin color was paler. My long flowing hair was matted and piled on my head with a rubber band. There was a scar at the small hollow place in my throat, I assumed from a tracheotomy. I rubbed my fingers over it, almost in disbelief. I couldn't stop staring. I looked like a concentration camp survivor.

"Belinda, do you have anything to say. Do you want to talk about how you look?" Dr. Rosen waited patiently for my response.

My practical side kicked in. I looked at him. "Yeah, when can I wash my hair and start my physical therapy." I was determined to keep Dr. Rosen from knowing my motivation, but, in my heart, I had decided Robert was real and he wasn't going to see me like this.

∞

My determination to get stronger paid off. After two months of therapy and the right foods, my treatment team was talking about discharge. I had put on at least ten pounds and was walking by myself. I could shower and dress myself.

Abby kept her word and stayed with me every night. She even helped me do something with the gnarled mess on the top of my head. My hair had lost its body due to nutritional deficiencies, but still, it came below my shoulders. I was grateful no one had decided to chop it all off. I later learned my mother had insisted it be trimmed, not cut. She wanted me to wake up with long hair. She'd never given up hope.

During one of our talks, my mother told me how hard it was for my father and her to take me off the respirator. My parents agreed I'd either breathe on my own or I'd die. They risked the chance of losing their only child. Then again, it wasn't like I was alive to them.

She told me when the time came to turn off the ventilator, I started breathing on my own. My mom took this as a sign that I'd be back. She has always been in my corner, even on the brink of death.

So here I was, breezing through physical therapy. I was told if I continued at this rate, I'd find myself almost back to where I was before the first accident, the real accident. I'd never recover one hundred percent, but it would be very close, and the loss would be negligible. In short, I could live a long healthy life.

Not only could it be a good life, but it would also be a rich one. My parents received a huge settlement from the trucking firm. No one knew if I'd ever awaken, so a large sum was set aside in a trust to take care of me for the rest of my life, however long that might be. Since I awoke and seemed to be on the road to recovery, the remaining funds were mine, and they were substantial.

It was discovered that the driver who hit me at the intersection of Highway 6 and the Southwest Freeway was smoking weed. The trucking firm knew about their driver's recreational diversion, but they'd needed someone to deliver a load that fateful Sunday evening, the night of Abby's wedding shower.

I just happened to be in the wrong place at the wrong time. If I'd entered the intersection two seconds earlier, I would've never met Robert and my life would've never changed.

With a few more pounds, I'd look as good as my pre-accident self. My body was shapelier and toned from all the exercising and proper eating. In my *old reality* and *dream state*, the ways I now referred to my past lives, I never worried about exercising or what I ate. In my *dream state*, people told me I was attractive. My *new reality*, my life right now, was much different. I had to work hard to get back to my goal image. When I did find Robert, he was going to see me as a knockout.

Dr. Rosen and I met three times a week. I'd started out on the wrong foot with him. He had helped me more than I could've ever imagined. I was working through the insecurities I'd experienced during my high school years. It seems everything I knew in my *old reality*, before the real accident, never changed. It seemed I'd managed to intertwine that reality with how I fantasized I would've liked my life to be in the *dream state.*

I figured out from my sessions with Dr. Rosen that my love for Robert was perfect and the problems we had were created from my real lack of confidence. It seemed I couldn't convince myself that someone like Robert could be in love with me. So, I kept sabotaging our relationship.

In my *new reality*, I was more settled with who I was and was becoming. My inner self and my "Monster" were at peace. I felt, with the continued help of Dr. Rosen, I'd be saying goodbye to my "Monster" forever.

However, despite all his attempts to "cure" my delusion about Robert, I wouldn't let it go. He knew I was determined to keep Robert as a real person and that I believed I'd find him again. So, in our last session before my discharge, he'd finally had it with me.

"Belinda, you know as long as you hang on to this delusion, I can't say you're all right." Shaking his head, he crossed his arms over his chest.

By now, I was very comfortable with this man and felt I could discuss anything with him. "I'll never understand. A man can have all the fantasies he wants about women. Yet, when a woman has a fantasy, it's called a delusion, making it seem that there's something wrong with her."

"Belinda, you know that's not what I mean." He shook his head. "We've spent all this time analyzing your life with Robert. You thought you were dying, and, before that happened, you wanted to experience love, and you did with him." He shifted in his seat. "You made up Robert and this whole life around him so you could have those experiences. Since you couldn't be an active participant in the real world, your mind created one. This is what kept you going."

"Robert is what kept me going. I owe my life to him, and, no matter what you say, I will always feel he is out there somewhere."

Dr. Rosen shook his head and responded, "We still have a lot of work ahead of us."

∞

My discharge day arrived. I couldn't wait to leave. I was packed and ready to go when Mom and Dad came to pick me up. All the staff had been wonderful. This was the biggest bunch of caring people I'd ever met. I loved every one of them right down to Mrs. Franks, who cleaned my room every day. I don't think I could ever repay all of them for the encouragement and support they'd given me. I'm sure it wasn't every day that they had a patient leaving in better condition than when they arrived. I was the walking, breathing result of all their good work, one of the limited success stories of a long-term care facility.

After the many goodbyes and tears, I sat in the ritualistic wheelchair, my chariot to my parents' car parked under the portico. As the orderly wheeled me down a corridor, I imagined how it would feel to be free again, out of the confines of the hospital, when I heard a rhythmic beating sound. It was familiar. One I'd heard many times before, but not in this reality. I listened closely to what sounded like Robert's heartbeat. I tensed up and looked around. The orderly asked me if I was all right. Wondering if he heard the sound as well, I took a chance and asked if he could hear the rhythmic thumping noise. He stopped pushing me to listen. "Yeah, I hear it."

I wasn't losing my mind. "What is that?"

"I'll show you. We'll be passing it on the way out."

We came to an open patient room. I saw an unresponsive man on a bed. It was tilting from one side to the other in a methodic, rhythmic motion. With every shift of movement, there was a soft thumping sound. I asked the orderly if I'd ever been on a bed like that. "All our head trauma patients are on one. The movement helps with circulation."

I froze as I watched it simulate what my mind had turned into a gentle rocking motion Robert had used when he cradled my head close to his beating heart. This was the first sign Robert was only a figment of my imagination. It terrified the hell out of me.

CHAPTER 35

IT FELT GREAT to be home. Mom did the best she could to make my old room comfortable for me. Before the accident, I'd been living in an apartment close to the school where I taught. After the wreck, Mom and Dad cleaned out the place, sold all the furniture, and selectively kept only a few of my possessions. What was left was moved to my old room.

I was discharged from the hospital on Saturday. Sunday, we made the drive to Brookshire, Texas, a small town west of Houston, to see an old friend. I missed him and was excited to see Beau, my horse.

On some sick level in Matt's mind, Beau was my compensation for him not inviting me to join his new life. After three years of dating, I thought we were in love. He had a different view of our relationship and never gave me a second thought when he accepted his new job. I was never a factor in his plans, and that crushed me.

Dr. Rosen and I concluded Matt dumping me the way he did, the car accident, and my perception that I was dying all contributed to my life with Robert. Dr. Rosen always maintained Robert was just a character of my dream, but I could never convince myself of that.

For now, I was glad to have Beau. My relationship with him started in my sophomore year of college. From the first day, I saw him and took my first ride, I was in love.

Dad told me he couldn't stand to sell Beau because of my affection for him. A close family friend agreed to board him on his ranch for free after the accident. He wanted to help my father by taking care of Beau until I woke up. I'm sure, at some point, my dad would've found Beau a permanent home if my coma carried on too long.

I planned on moving him closer to Sugar Land as soon as I could find a suitable stable. For now, riding would take place in Brookshire. It would be a great exercise to increase my stamina and coordination. I'd have to start out slowly and under supervision, but I suspected Beau and I would be on our own in no time.

In my dream, Beau was the reason I attracted the attention of Robert. He was a connection to Robert, and I hoped Beau would remember me.

It was the perfect day. Soft fluffy white clouds were scattered in the big, brilliant blue Texas sky. The air felt crisp and fresh. The wind occasionally gusted into a stiff breeze that made the leaves rustle as the sunlight darted through tree limbs.

We arrived about one o'clock at the house of Paul and Sarah Jensen. Paul had worked with my dad for years and had retired early on a one-hundred-acre ranch near Brookshire. I'd never been there, but my parents assured me it was the perfect place for Beau. The Jensen's had other horses, so he had company.

"Howdy, young lady!" The burly, king-sized man put an arm around my shoulders and nearly squeezed the life out of me. "We're so glad you came out of that ordeal. Your mom and dad sure were worried about you. This is my wife, Sarah. She's the horse person around here."

He let go of me and walked over to his wife, replicating his hold on her. "She does the ridin' and I do the laborin'." He let out a hearty laugh and almost lifted his wife by the shoulders as he gave her a squeeze.

She wiggled free and approached me with a warm smile and took my hand in hers. "I'll bet you're anxious to see that big boy of yours. He's such a good-natured animal. Come on, I'll take you to him."

On our way, she explained how well he fit in with her other horses. She told me she rode him at least twice a week to keep him ready for me. As we approached a grassy paddock, she placed her hand on my shoulder and pointed to just beyond the fence surrounding the enclosure. "There he is. He's alone. I figured you didn't need the other two botherin' you on your first reunion."

My eyes drifted from Sarah's face and followed her hand in the direction she was pointing until I saw the figure of a chestnut horse, glistening as he grazed in the sun.

"There's a lead rope on the fence. I thought you'd like to spend some time groomin' him. I'm sure he'd enjoy a good bath. After you say your hellos, take him into the barn. You'll find everything you'll need in there. Go on. Go say howdy." She gently nudged my shoulder.

"Thank you. He looks as magnificent as I remember. You took good care of him."

I grabbed the lead and climbed over the paddock fence. The gentle breeze touched the top of the tall grass causing it to sway from side to side. Beau got a whiff of my scent. He lifted his head and stood erect with his ears straight up. He snorted at the air then pawed at the ground. I approached, taking small, cautious steps. When I was within ten feet of him, I took the baby carrots I had brought for him out of my pocket and extended my hand.

"Hey, Beau, carrots?" He studied me. To my surprise and joy, he slowly relaxed his head and walked toward me, then placed his nose in my hand and took the carrots. Beau took a few more steps that placed his head at my side and I rubbed him behind the ears.

Thoughts of Robert flooded my memory. Tears escaped.

∞

The next several weeks were spent in physical therapy, Dr. Rosen's office, and at the Jensen's with Beau. Sarah was my designated riding supervisor. She knew enough about horses and riding to make sure it was safe for me to be on my own. We quickly became friends, and, on weekends, Mom or Dad would drive me out on a Friday then pick me up on Sunday evening. I'd help around the place with chores. The exercise was good for me and gave me something to do. I owed a lot to the Jensen's and didn't mind pitching in.

∞

My first few weeks home were busy with my parents driving me to and from all my treatments. I wasn't allowed to drive. I had to be out of the hospital for a month, and then more tests needed to be run before I was certified safe to be behind the wheel of a car. As I improved, all the therapy and psychology sessions would decrease.

I was still having trouble with Dr. Rosen. He was convinced Robert was a manifestation of my mind that helped me make sense of my life I lived in my coma.

"You have to move on. You can't linger on someone who isn't real," he harped on a regular basis. "How do you expect to move forward with your life if you hang on to his memory? I know it's only been a short time since you woke up, so you need time to mourn his loss. I understand that." His tone was more sympathetic. "We'll be cutting back on our sessions in a few weeks, down to one day a week. Your physical therapy sessions will, also, be decreasing to two days a week about the same time, and soon you'll be driving again." He was calm and reserved, like he always was, as he described my treatment plan. I just listened.

"When the time comes, I want you to go back to school to see if you can find any indication that Robert is real."

Air refused to exit my lungs. My mouth dropped open. "Are you telling me I should try to find him?"

"That's *exactly* what I'm telling you. I know you look for him everywhere you go, always scanning crowds at the mall or looking at the people in the grocery store. You'll continue to do this until you're convinced he was a dream. Once your mind is at peace with that, you'll mourn him and move on." He was leaning forward in his chair, trying to make a point. "Do you understand what I'm saying?"

At that moment, I didn't care. He was giving me permission to search for my beloved Robert. My heart somersaulted. If I could prove Robert was a real person, I might have a chance to be with him.

"I understand. Do I have to wait until I start to drive?" I hoped to hear the answer I wanted.

"No. I don't think so. You told me he was from Sugar Land. See what you can find on the Internet. You're jogging in the evenings, so see what you can find. Just be safe and don't do anything foolish."

I started making a mental list of all the things I could do to look for Robert. Did Dr. Rosen think I was an idiot? I had already utilized my computer, to exhaustion, trying to find any link to a Robert Pennington of Sugar Land. All my efforts only led to dead ends, saddening my heart.

"If this man exists out there, I want proof. Go back to your college and see if he was real. I know you won't be reconciled with this until you're convinced he was only in your head. You'll always be looking for your 'Milk Carton Lover.'" He huffed and wagged a finger. "But I want reports and you have to balance your search with other activities. I don't want to hear all you're doing is looking at milk cartons."

I couldn't believe my ears. For the past month, I'd been told I was delusional. Now he wanted proof. The more I thought about it, the better I liked his idea. I looked over at Dr. Rosen. "Thank you," was all I could say.

I was dismissed from the session with a new hope. My search would start this evening with jogging. Under the ruse that I needed a change of scenery, I'd ask Mom to drive me to the neighborhood where I remembered my in-laws lived. When I was finished, I'd call her to pick me up. She'd never know what I was up to.

As planned, Mom dropped me off at a running trail near the subdivision I planned to scope out. Once Mom was out of sight, I changed direction and headed to the route I had driven with Robert.

With every step I took, my heart raced. Knots of anticipation twisted my stomach. I was a block away from the last turn. If I was right, the entrance to the neighborhood would be right around the next bend. I took a deep breath and rounded the corner, then stopped dead in my tracks. There was no entrance. Just the continuation of another subdivision like the one I was in. Taking heavy breaths, I bent over and planted my hands on my knees. Tears clouded my eyes. This was another dead end.

Feeling more defeated than ever, I called Mom and she met me close to where she'd dropped me off.

"Are you okay? You look sad." She could always read me like a book.

"I'm just tired. My session with Dr. Rosen was draining and now with all the running...." I trailed off my sentence as I turned toward the passenger-side window. The explanation was enough to satisfy her. I didn't want her to know what really bothered me. We drove the rest of the way home in silence. I started to doubt myself and Robert's existence.

After we arrived at the house, and I told my parents I was tired. I didn't want my parents questioning my mood, so the sanctum of my bedroom was the safest place for me to be alone and sulk.

∞

"Belinda, are you okay?" I opened my eyes and gazed into Robert's glacier blue eyes. He had tears running down his face. "Angel." He felt so good, cradling me in his arms.

"Robert?" I was sore with pain all over. "What happened?"

"You've been in an accident. A truck hit you. Be quiet until EMS has a chance to look at you. You'll need to go to the hospital." He was comforting me. "I was so scared I'd lose you."

"You're crying." I reached up to wipe his tears. "How did you find me?"

"I read your note so I figured I'd come get some bagels. I drove to the bakery and saw you pulling away." He swayed, ever so slightly, as he cradled me in his arms. "I got a chuckle out of us having the same thought." He swallowed hard. "You entered the intersection, and I saw the truck run the light and hit you. I was never so scared in all my life." His eyes became more penetrating as they reached deep into my very being. "Please don't leave me." He gently tightened his hold on me.

I wanted to tell him I loved him and would never leave him. Suddenly, I heard a knocking, followed by, "Belinda, wake up. It's time for breakfast." It was my mother.

I shot up in bed—my respirations heavy, my heart racing and my hair wet from perspiration. *Did I just dream about Robert? Was I in his arms?* I embraced my pillow, holding it tight in front of me. I rocked back and forth with my eyes shut tight and sobbed. "He is real," I repeated over and over again. The soreness in my legs overrode my thoughts of him. I'd overworked them the evening before, and they were stiff. The dream was so real and so short. I heard my mother call me again. "I'm up. I'll be right down," I shouted from my bed.

∞

As soon as I was cleared to drive, I made plans to leave for my college on Thursday and return no later than Saturday. This would be my only chance to prove Robert did exist.

The Registrar's Office was my first stop. "Excuse me. I'm looking for someone who may have attended this school. Is there any way you could give me that information?"

"Are you related to this person?" A well-dressed woman rose from her desk and walked over to the counter.

I didn't feel the need to go through my state of affairs with her and thought, if a small lie helped me, then so be it. "Yes, I'm his wife."

She looked at me with a smile that was both puzzled and amused. "You're his wife, but you don't know if he attended school here?"

Having nothing to lose, I gave her a brief description of my recent love-at-first-sight romance and fast wedding. Then I dropped the bomb. I told her my husband was killed in a car accident, and I was trying to find out more about him. Our life together was so short. Parts of the story were true. I just changed things around a bit. It worked, and she asked me to fill out a form giving her enough information so she could look for him.

She left with the paper and returned in about ten minutes. "Are you sure you have all the information correct. I cross-referenced his name, date of birth, and years. I can't find a thing. Sorry." She handed me the paper. Staring at it and afraid to take it from her, I was brokenhearted but not finished.

Next, I went to the library to pore over yearbooks, searching for someone who looked like Robert. I went back five years, still nothing, and, to my dismay, there was no mention or pictures of the Delta Lambda Nu brothers in the fraternities sections. With my curiosity piqued, I decided to drive by the Delt fraternity house.

I had turned off the main street toward the frat house when I noticed an old Victorian mansion. It was the one Robert and I had lived in. I swerved into the first parking place I could find. As I approached the house, I saw a "For Rent" sign in our old apartment window. I dug my cell out of my bag and called. A woman answered, and I explained that I'd be attending grad school and wanted to see the apartment. She said she'd meet me in ten minutes.

Memory upon memory of Robert and our relationship began to overwhelm me while I paced back and forth in front of the house. Just when I thought I couldn't stand the deluge of thoughts, a woman approached me. "Are you the lady interested in the apartment?"

"Yes, ma'am. I need something close to campus." I lied again.

We walked up the steps. I knew the house could be a memory from my college days. Although I didn't remember having ever been inside this building, my memories of pre-accident events were fuzzy at times. The porch was just as I remembered from my dream. The doors were a little different, more worn but still beautiful. When the realtor opened the door, my mouth dropped as I scanned the interior of the foyer. Everything looked just as I had remembered. Not one thing about it was different.

My heart started to pound. My stomach flip-flopped as I heard the key turn, and I entered Robert's and my apartment. My knees started to buckle, but I braced myself against the doorjamb. I could've been back in my make-believe life. I now stood in the apartment I had shared with Robert. I asked the woman if I could look around, explore by myself. She agreed and walked out.

My eyes filmed over with tears as my life with Robert became something I could touch. Again, as with the foyer, nothing, not one thing, was different. It was like the first time I'd walked in. I had time to take in the beauty of this small abode and half-expected him to come walking through the door any minute, carrying a box of his packed belongings, like he had the morning he moved in. The memories showered my brain and so did the pain. I walked into the bedroom where I first made love to him. I relived the feel of his touch as I sat on the bed, taking in everything I could remember. I missed him terribly. I loved him so much and I cried as I remembered.

I stepped out onto the porch, thanked the woman for letting me look at the apartment, and walked slowly to my car, realizing this proved nothing. Had I been to a party there and plugged it into my dream as our first home? I almost started crying again because I hit yet another brick wall, but I still wasn't ready to throw in the towel.

The next morning, I drove straight to where I remembered the Delt house was located. As I walked to the house, it struck me how quiet it was. There were no parked cars or frat brothers bustling around. To my shock, a little silver-haired lady answered the door. I asked if this was or had ever been the Delt house. She told me no, that it was her residence, and she had lived there some thirty years. Her words hit me like a fist in my gut. I realized the fraternity was also just a figment of my imagination. This was the last disheartening dead end.

I walked back to the car, fighting back the tears, and wondered why my mind had created this imaginary life. Why hadn't I dreamed that Matt and I lived happily ever after? That would've been easier to deal with. As I left town in a cloud of tears, reality hit that my beloved Robert didn't exist in this world. Somehow, I'd have to move on with my life alone and dreaded having to explain my failure to Dr. Rosen.

∞

"I'm sorry, Belinda, that your trip didn't uncover more information about Robert. Are you willing to start to let go now?" Dr. Rosen leaned back in his chair, waiting for my response.

I didn't want to answer. "It doesn't look like I have any choice." I felt as if I'd had my heart ripped out of my chest. I had never experienced emotional pain like that before. Robert was truly gone to me.

He nodded his head in approval. "If you forget about Robert, then you'll be able to move on, make plans for the future, and have a life. You need friends and you need to socialize. I'll help you through this."

All I could do was stare back blankly because I knew he was right.

It was close to the end of the year. The holidays were approaching.

I found a good stable for Beau next to a gated subdivision that consisted of acreage estates so the owners could keep horses on their property or in the stable next door. Trails surrounding it were shared with the stable. The plan was to move Beau just before New Year's Eve.

I'd, also, been thinking about buying a place of my own. There were some patio homes in the same planned community, close to the stables, but since I hadn't discussed moving with my parents and didn't want to interfere with Mom's holiday plans, this decision would have to wait until after the first of the year.

There was, also, the matter of a job. I thought about going back to teaching high school art. I could start out as a substitute then go full-time when something became available. After the first of the year, I would start looking. I would need something to fill my days and make the trust fund last longer.

By now, I'd been released from physical therapy. They could no longer help me. I was fine and progressing very well on my own. As long as I kept up my current physical routine, I'd only improve with time.

CHAPTER 36

I AWOKE DREADING the arrival of the party. It was, December 31st, and I wasn't quite ready yet to be around a group of strangers. Staying home alone sounded more appealing. I would've loved to call Abby and tell her I'm not going to Garrett's company's New Year's Eve party, but she'd be upset with me, and I needed to start socializing again as part of my recovery plan.

I arose, ready for some breakfast, trying to stop thinking about the party. Mom and Dad were finishing their breakfast, and reading the newspaper at the table.

Dad peeped over the top of the Business section. "Good morning, Sleepyhead."

"Good morning," I mumbled on my way to the kitchen. I gathered up my bowl of cereal and glass of orange juice, then went back to the table and sat next to Mom.

"I'm so glad you're going out tonight." She patted my hand. "You never know, you might meet 'Mister Right.'" She rolled her eyes. "Or at least someone to date."

Mom was in her usual form and on a roll. Listening to her, I could understand where I got my ability to ramble. "I know. I'll go and try to have some fun." But, how much fun could I possibly have at a formal party?

"What did you decide to wear tonight?" Mom looked up at me over the rim of her mug filled with steaming hot coffee.

"That long, pale blue, chiffon dress that I wore to the formal with Matt. It should be perfectly fine for this occasion." After I placed my dishes in the dishwasher, I told my parents Beau was arriving today, and I had to go to the stables to meet Mr. Jensen.

Paul Jensen was due to arrive with Beau around 2 p.m. This was the first step in my plan to change my life in the New Year. Beau's relocation should've taken place days ago, but Paul couldn't make the trip until today. The box stall was ready and I'd planned on just grooming Beau on his first day. I wouldn't have much time to settle him in before the party.

♡♡

I paced around the interior of the stables as I waited for Paul, who was running a little late, pressing me for time. If he were much later, I wouldn't have time to clean up and be ready to leave when my "dates" arrived.

Impatiently, I stepped outside. The crisp air smacked me in the face and for the first time, I enjoyed this winter day. In Texas, December can be tricky. There are days when full winter garb is appropriate and others when shorts are the style. Today, however, was perfect. It was overcast, low humidity, with a nice gentle breeze swirling through the now-partially bare trees. I took a deep breath and filled my lungs with fresh air. As I exhaled, I saw the F150 and horse trailer.

The truck stopped and Paul hopped out. I was always amazed at the amount of energy he had, given his age.

"Howdy, there!" he shouted as he strode to the back of the trailer to release the hatch. He backed Beau out and handed me the lead. "Here's your big boy, as promised." The smile across his face could fill Texas.

"Hey, Beau, carrots?" I held the horse's usual treat out for him then stroked his neck as he ate.

After saying our goodbyes, I led Beau into the barn. I tied him just outside his stall then pulled two brushes from the tack box. With a systematic motion, I began to brush the horse's sleek coat, first with one hand brush, then the other, repeating the motion.

I was working on the left side of my horse when a brisk gust of wind swept into the barn. The breeze lifted my hair, and it felt as if someone had caressed the back of my head. I stood erect, not moving. In a gentle, barely audible voice, I could swear I heard, "Angel."

The usual steady beat in my chest zoomed into overdrive and my breaths matched the speed. I turned around, looking over the interior of the barn, but I was alone. Walking outside past the protective covering of the entrance, I stood in the yard and looked toward the woods to the right. The most overwhelming compulsion to walk into them came over me. I took a step in that direction, but, before taking the next step, I stopped. This was nuts. I didn't have time for this foolishness. I had better things to do, so I turned and proceeded back to the barn, stopping to give the trees one last look. But the feeling continued to linger, invading my thoughts.

The strange feeling I had experienced haunted me during my drive home. For a fleeting moment, I wondered what lay beyond the wooded area. I put the incident out of my mind as I made the five-minute drive back to my parents' home. Having Beau this close would be easier and fun. I looked forward to our first ride, but now, it was time to rid myself of the horse smell. I had a party to attend.

It's amazing how fast time flies when you're not looking forward to doing something. It was 6:15, so I decided to start prepping since Abby said they'd pick me up around 7:45. The party was supposed to start at eight p.m., and it wasn't far from my parents' home.

I took my time putting on a little makeup. I decided to wear my hair straight and sleek with the ends curled under. That took more time than I had allowed. It was now 7:20. I needed to hurry up if I was going to be ready.

I went to my closet and dug through it, looking for the long, blue dress. No dress. I searched again, then yelled, "Mom, where's my blue dress? It's not in my closet."

"I sent it to the cleaners," she shouted back from the den. "Go look in my closet. I probably put it in there by accident."

I rushed to her room and rummaged through her closet. To my relief, it was there. The plastic dry-cleaning bag rustled when I snapped the hanger off the rod. I held it up to inspect the dress. Yep, it would do fine. I started to turn to leave when my eyes drifted to the shoulder of another dress encased in plastic. The cream fabric caused my heart to stop. I stared and the formal puddled around my feet. I snatched the bag and ran to the stairway. "Mom, Mom! Where did this dress come from?"

"What dress?"

"This cream-colored silk dress with the bolero jacket," I rattled off, holding the dress out in front of me.

Mom walked to the stairway and looked up at me. "Oh, I forgot about that one. I was on my way to the hospital to see you when I noticed a dress shop with a 'SALE' sign in the window. You know how I am when I see those signs. I stopped and found that dress. I thought you would look so pretty in it. So I bought it for you."

I creased my brow. "Was I still in a coma when you bought it?"

Mom looked at the floor then back at me. "I always felt that you'd come back to us, even though the doctors kept telling us you probably wouldn't wake up. And if by chance, you didn't, I wanted you to sleep forever looking beautiful." A few tears escaped and ran down her cheeks. She quickly wiped them away with the back of her hand. "Why are you so concerned about that dress?"

I held it up in front of me. "You won't believe me. This is the exact same dress that Robert picked out and bought for me to wear when we married in my dream."

Mom's eyes became big and her mouth gaped open. "How can that be? I brought it to the hospital and showed it to you. But you couldn't have seen it. You were unconscious. I did try to describe it to you. I told you that you needed to wake up so you could wear it, and how pretty you'd look in it." There was a brief silence. "You better forget about it right now and finish dressing, or you won't be ready when Abby and Garrett arrive."

I carried my dream wedding dress into my room and laid it out on my bed then rushed back to Mom's closet to pick up the pale blue formal. I decided to put the dress on in front of her big, full-length mirror that hung on her closet door. I couldn't quite reach the back zipper, so I called Mom for her help. She zipped the dress. Her eyes opened wide and her hand flew up briefly covering her mouth. "Oh, my! You can't wear this dress. The top is too small. You're flowing out of it." She sighed "You wore *this* dress to that frat formal last year?"

"Yeah, and I got a lot of compliments. Everyone said I looked gorgeous, and a lot of girls asked where I bought it. I told them you made it."

"You didn't! I'm so embarrassed. I'll bet Matt enjoyed that date, looking down at you all evening." She smiled, shaking her head, and snickered. "I didn't realize you had developed so much. I should have insisted you try it on a week ago to see if it needed any altering." She yanked at the sides trying to pull the bodice up.

"Why? I think it looks fine." My voice trailed off and my mind wandered to a different time when I was totally in love. I remembered Robert's face when he saw me and the great time I had that night.

"Belinda, come back down to earth." Mom snapped her fingers in front of my face, breaking my trance.

"Sorry."

My mother gave the bodice another tug.

"Mom. Stop. It's fine." I looked at myself in the mirror and fingered my neck. "I need some kind of necklace. Do you have one I can wear?"

Expelling a long, deep breath, I remembered the nonexistent diamond, double-heart necklace that Robert had given me as a wedding gift.

I had to stop myself or I'd ruin what little chance I had at having a good time tonight.

Mom returned with a beautiful, sparkling, wreath necklace and placed it where his had once hung. She pulled some of my hair forward, over in front of my shoulders to cover the exposed part of my breasts. She was shaking her head, but she made me smile. The necklace hit my neck low enough to cover the trach scar.

Mom headed into her closet and returned with a long, black cloak. "You'll definitely attract the attention of all the men tonight. You look beautiful, but you better not let your father see you. You know how protective he is of you. Here, put the cloak on before you come down."

"Thanks, Mom."

I went back to my closet to slip on my silver heels and grab my small, silver clutch purse. With my cloak on, I headed downstairs to wait for Abby and Garrett.

As I reached the last step, the doorbell rang. It was my "dates" for the evening. Abby wore a beautiful, long, black-velvet, fitted gown, and Garrett had on a tuxedo. They looked very elegant.

"Ready to go?" Garrett asked with a huge smile across his face.

"As ready as I'll ever be." I called out to my parents and told them I was leaving. Mom said to have fun. Luckily, Dad didn't see me.

I was on my way to the dreaded New Year's party. Garrett said the neighborhood wasn't very far. The GPS directed us right past the stables, Beau's new home, and along the gigantic stone fence of the gated community next door. We turned between the large stone columns of the entrance and down a winding road where enormous two-story homes appeared. The GPS guided us to a huge two-story, Tuscan-style home, set back from the street on a large lot with big oak trees all around.

As I gazed wide-eyed at the house, my mouth fell open, my heart sputtered, then started thumping. It looked just like Robert's parents' house, except it wasn't sitting angled on a corner lot.

It couldn't be the same house. I didn't say anything about it as I tried to make sense of what I was seeing.

Garrett pulled into the circular drive. Men dressed in tuxedos opened our doors and helped us out, then valet-parked the car. As we approached the front door, another man in a tux opened it for us. "Welcome, I hope you enjoy yourselves."

Who in the world were these people?

My heart sputtered again as we walked into the entry. I gasped as I looked around. The inside looked just like the house in my dream, right down to the two cobalt-blue vases sitting on the two matching Bombay chests. My heart started pounding in anticipation of what else or who I was going to see. My legs started shaking. I gripped Abby's hand to calm my panicky feeling.

She gave me a surprised look. "Are you okay? You look like you've seen a ghost."

"I'm all right. This house is...fabulous." I was afraid to tell her my *dream reality* was crashing in on my *new reality*.

In the foyer, the stairs and balcony formed a horseshoe shape. At the top, overlooking the living room, a quartet was playing. I took off my cloak. A lady took our coats and purses, placing them in the study to the left of the double staircase.

Garrett's eyes popped. "Damn! You look gorgeous in that dress." Abby elbowed him in the side.

He laughed then sniffed the air and scanned the area, pointing to the dining room, which was to the right of the staircase. "I'm going over there." He glanced at Abby and me. "Ladies. Care to join me?" He held his elbows out to his sides. We latched on and he walked us toward the elaborate food display.

"Now I need something to wash all this food down with." Garrett scanned the room. "I don't see any waiters with trays of drinks."

I figured the drinks would be set up in the kitchen. I led the way for Abby and Garrett. After all, I knew more about this house than they did. I walked through the butler's pantry and into the vast, open kitchen area. There was a large island in the middle of the room covered with all types of liquor bottles. Garrett asked what we wanted and then started to pour out three glasses of white zinfandel. The bottle went dry after the second glass. He picked up a new bottle and looked around for a corkscrew.

I turned and walked to a lower cabinet drawer, opened it, and pulled out a corkscrew. Walking back to Garrett, I extended it to him. Our eyes met. He looked puzzled, staring at me with it in my hand. He reached out to grab it from me, but, before releasing it, I said, "This is Robert's house. I've been here before."

Abby stood frozen in disbelief.

"There's only one way to settle this. This place belongs to my boss. I want you to meet him." He took me by the hand and we were off. Abby followed. Garrett suddenly stopped and surveyed the great room. When he found his mark, we were off again, squeezing through the crowd until we stood behind his boss and his wife. Garrett reached for Abby and placed her on his other side. He cleared his throat and tapped the gentleman on the shoulder. "Excuse me, Sir. I'd like to introduce you to my wife and her friend."

The man turned around and before me stood Robert Pennington, Sr. When his wife turned around, it was Sandra. These were my Robert's parents! I took a few deep breaths to calm my rattled nerves.

"Mr. and Mrs. Pendleton, I'd like you to meet my wife, Abby, and our friend, Belinda. I hope you don't mind that we brought her along."

"No, we don't mind at all." They looked at me. "We're glad you came. Enjoy yourself." When Mr. Pendleton smiled, his resemblance to my dream Robert was uncanny. "And I must say, you look very beautiful."

"Thank you."

Pennington??? *Pendleton*??? I had to ask. "Would your first name happen to be Robert?" My mouth went dry anticipating his answer for a nerve-racking moment.

"Yes." Mr. Pendleton studied my face. "Have we met before?"

I swung my eyes to Mrs. Pendleton. "And you're Sandra?"

They looked at each other and then at me. Mr. Pendleton, again, asked, "Have we met before?"

I didn't know what to say. I couldn't tell them yes, in my dreams. "I don't think so. I'm not sure how I know," I lied. "Do you by any chance have a son named Robert?" I held my breath.

Mrs. Pendleton tilted her head. "Yes, we do. Do you know him?"

I inhaled a soft breath at her response. With butterflies taking flight in my belly, the room started to spin. I reached out for Garrett's arm to steady myself. "I met a Robert once who looked a lot like you." I nodded to Mr. Pendleton.

"Robert does look like his father, just a lot younger." Mrs. Pendleton raised an eyebrow and smiled.

"Is he here?" I scanned the room.

"No, he was here earlier this afternoon. He left for another party, but said he might be back."

I nodded. My knees wobbled, but I managed to steady myself.

"If he does, I'll tell him you were asking about him. It's Belinda, right?"

"Yes, ma'am. Thank you." Now a full-blown beehive churned where my stomach should be.

Garrett led Abby and me away. They stopped and stared at me. Abby placed her hand on mine. "Belinda, what's going on? This is really getting a bit strange, even for me."

"I knew he was real. I could feel it. This is the exact same house, and they're Robert's parents." A numbing sensation started coming over me. "I'm getting light-headed. I need to sit down before I faint." I took hold of Garrett's arm, and he led me over to a wingback chair. I supported my forehead against my hand until the feeling passed. "I think I need to eat something."

"I'll get you some food." Abby hurried to the dining room.

"How can all this be happening?" Garrett had a deep look of concern.

"I don't know. It's freaky. Have you met their son?"

"No, but I've heard that he's a nice guy."

"In my dreams, you were best friends and fraternity brothers."

Abby returned with my food. "You two go mingle. I'll be fine. I don't want to spoil the party for you. Go!" I waved them away with my hand.

They walked a little ways off to talk to a group of people. Abby kept looking back at me. I shook my head.

I finished eating and then wandered through the sea of guests that occupied more public areas of the house. Everything was familiar. It was like I was back in my dream.

I meandered to the large, two-story windows in the great room. As I looked out over the patio, my eyes wandered past the pool to the manicured lawn beyond and stopped at the tree line. I realized that stand of trees also flanked the stable yard of Beau's quarters. These were the same woods I had the urge to enter this afternoon. If I'd followed that whim, the path would've ended right in the back yard of this magnificent home, just about the same time Robert would've been here.

A waiter disturbed my thoughts. "Miss, *hors d'oeuvre*?" I never took my eyes off the trees and shook my head to signal him to leave.

I broke my self-imposed trance by turning toward the party participants. People started to dance to the slow music. Soft chatter with the occasional burst of loud laughter came from different areas. Glasses being raised and clinked together all added to the ambiance of the party. I felt my surroundings weren't real. It made me wish I were with Robert. It was difficult to believe that the man of my dreams was so close yet still miles away. What if this Robert Pendleton wasn't my Robert Pennington? If he were the Robert I remembered, he wouldn't know who I was. I had to be prepared for that.

During my coma, I had placed the people I knew before the accident in the life I had lived with Robert. But, when I woke up, they knew nothing about what I had experienced. They were there, but only in my head. So, if this was my Robert, he wouldn't be the Robert in my dream.

I began searching around for Abby and Garrett. They were across the room, so I strolled over to them. Garrett introduced me to everyone standing in the group.

Garrett turned to Abby. "Sweetheart, would you mind if I ask Belinda to dance first?"

"No, I don't mind. Just keep your eyes straight ahead, not *down.*" Abby kidded, making a reference to my bust line.

"Yes, ma'am." He grinned as he flashed a quick glance in my direction.

Abby scowled at him then laughed. "Behave, you bad boy."

Garrett made a face back and then turned to me. "Belinda, would you like to dance?"

"Sure." He took my hand and led me over to the other dancing couples.

Garrett whispered in my ear, "What are you going to do if it is your dream Robert? He's not going to know who you are."

I whispered back to him, "I know. I can only hope he'll feel the connection we had."

When the music ended, we walked back to Abby. Several other guys asked me to dance. Thanks to the wine, I began to relax and have fun mingling. My hopes of meeting Robert Pendleton tonight had dwindled away. I met several nice, single, young men who I'd consider going out with if they ever asked. After dancing with a guy named Colin for the third time, I decided to join Abby and Garrett. I wanted to celebrate the coming of the New Year with them, so I excused myself.

As I made my way through the crowd a clock started to chime. The guests amplified their shouts as the last few seconds of the old year came to an end. I'd spotted Abby and Garrett across the room when I felt a hand gently rest on my bare shoulder.

I froze. The pounding of my pulse accelerated as a familiar, arousing feeling stirred within me. It was Robert.

A male voice whispered close to my ear, "Belinda?"

Robert's voice.

My breathing faltered. My heart sprinted. My head fogged. I turned toward the man with his hand still on my shoulder. That familiar sensation didn't fail me. I found myself looking into the soft, glacier blue eyes of a real version of Robert. The man I had loved in a different realm.

I didn't know how or why, but every cell in my body told me that this Robert would remember. He would be the man who would love me and I would love him right back, in my *new reality*. As his touch surged through me, his pulse kept time with mine, and I knew we would have a long life together.

I opened my mouth to speak but my head began to spin. I wobbled and started to fall. Robert reached out as my knees buckled just before everything faded to black.

Coming 2020

ABOUT THE AUTHORS

Linda Fagala, retired co-writer of PF Karlin, was born and raised in Texas, and currently resides there with her husband. She graduated from Stephen F. Austin State University as an art teacher. She took a leave from her retirement to help with the rewrite of this second edition.

Karen Pugh, writing as PF Karlin, was born in Chicago, Illinois and graduated from Amundsen-Mayfair City College with an ADN in Nursing. She has had a long interest in writing, practicing the craft with contributions to local newsletters. She is a member of RWA. Currently she lives in Texas with her husband.

Shattered Fate is a fictional love story. The Belinda and Robert saga came to Linda after reminiscing about some of the fun experiences that occurred during her college years and is loosely based on those events. She approached Karen about turning the idea into a romance novel. Karen's experiences in nursing and varied life interests contributed to the theme of the plot. Combining their talents and ideas, they embarked on their first novel.

Destiny Reborn is the sequel of Belinda and Robert's life, as the two discover the reasons for their attraction.

For more Information Visit:

www.pfkarlin.com

www.ingramcontent.com/pod-product-compliance
Lightning Source LLC
Chambersburg PA
CBHW050413260626
47156CB00003B/989